D0897194

MELT DOWN

"What makes you think the terrorists had access to design plans?" O'Brien asked.

"The accident sequences," the scientist answered. "No amateurs could have hit upon those specific systems. They have threatened to cut the primary sodium loop lines serving all pumps. They know enough about the system to go a step beyond the failure we deemed to be *worst case*."

"Jesus Christ," O'Brien said softly. "So we're dealing with an assured melt down!"

"Without a doubt."

THE JUDAS SQUAD
A Novel of Nuclear Terror
James N. Rowe

THE JUDAS SQUAD

JAMES N. ROWE

A BERKLEY BOOK
published by
BERKLEY PUBLISHING CORPORATION

This Berkley book contains the complete
text of the original hardcover edition.
It has been completely reset in a type face
designed for easy reading, and was printed
from new film.

THE JUDAS SQUAD

A Berkley Book / published by arrangement with
Little, Brown & Company

PRINTING HISTORY
Little, Brown edition published September 1977
Berkley edition / July 1979

ISBN: 0-425-03937-4

A BERKLEY BOOK ® TM 757,375
Berkley Books are published by Berkley Publishing Corporation,
200 Madison Avenue, New York, New York 10016.
PRINTED IN THE UNITED STATES OF AMERICA

To Breezy, Missy, and Gunner

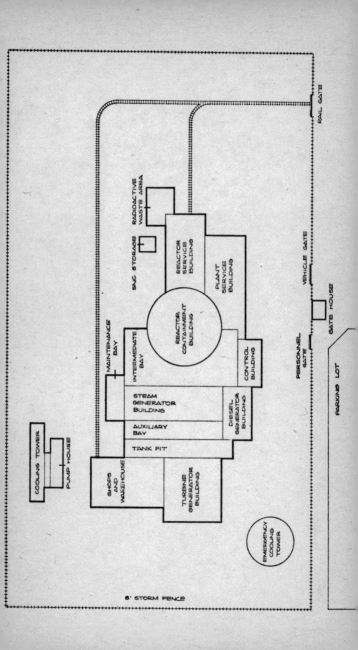

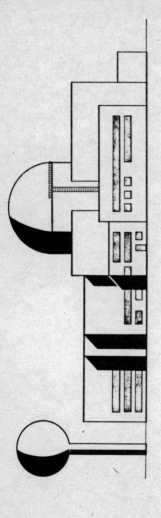

Bartonsville Fast Breeder Reactor

Monday, August 15, 1977

"Good Afternoon. This is WGU twenty, the Defense Civil Preparedness Agency Station, serving the East-central states with emergency information. Eastern Standard Time, two hours thirty-six minutes, twelve seconds."

He fumbled for the volume knob on the Panasonic shortwave radio. Their small TV set carried minicam coverage of what looked like Labor Day traffic jams on the freeway. Nothing was moving and there were so many cars, it could have been a parking lot.

"Turn down the TV some, Ann," he said to his wife who was standing uncomfortably beside the set, her approaching motherhood obvious under an ill-fitting maternity dress. "I want to catch this."

"Emergency conditions exist in the Pennsylvania and Eastern Ohio region," the sonorous voice went on. "The threat of a nuclear accident continues at the Bartonsville Breeder Reactor Plant, thirty-two miles northwest of Pittsburgh. All possible measures are being taken by federal and state authorities to restore the plant to normal operation and citizens are requested to remain calm.

There are precautions being taken to avoid inadvertent harm to persons and property in the affected area. Martial law has been declared in Beaver County, Pennsylvania; Hancock County, West Virginia; and portions of adjoining Jefferson and Columbiana Counties in Ohio. All persons in those areas are instructed to comply with regulations which have been posted by authorities. They are for your safety and protection.

"All vehicular routes in the area are extremely congested and citizens are cautioned to avoid the following major routes: the Pennsylvania Turnpike from points south of Youngstown, Ohio, to Somerset, Pennsylvania; Interstate seventy-nine, Routes nineteen, twenty-two, twenty-eight, thirty, fifty-one, sixty-five, and two-seventy-nine within a radius of forty miles of Pittsburgh. I repeat, motorists are cautioned to avoid the following major routes: the Pennsyl..."

"For God's sake, Tommy, copy the routes down. You've got to get us out of here and we can't get caught in a traffic jam." The young woman's voice crept toward a panic pitch as she stalked in front of her husband, nervously pulling on a cigarette.

"Take it easy, hon. I'm trying to hear what he's saying." Tommy Elder wrote quickly as the report continued, glancing at the road atlas on the Formica-topped kitchen table. There weren't many major roads left open from the couple's small, sparsely furnished apartment in the Pittsburgh suburb of Millvale.

"Tommee," her voice rose, "let's just go. Please, let's get out of here."

"Ann, damn it, give me a chance. It's gonna be hard enough as it is, so please don't you get on my back. I'm doing the best I can."

He was fast losing the bit of confidence he had felt earlier in the day. There was no way he could take a chance going out on jammed roads with only enough cash for a couple of tanks of gas, no money for motels and barely enough for food. Their nearest kin were her folks in Tallahassee, almost a thousand miles from Pittsburgh, and that hog of a Trans Am wouldn't get more than eleven miles to a gallon. They wouldn't make it anywhere. Maybe her folks could wire some money to the Western Union office in Charleston. Shit, this would be the time to have a VW or anything that would get thirty-five miles to a gallon. With traffic though, if they got stuck now, they'd burn a tank off just sitting and idling. Jesus Christ, what a mess.

The TV suddenly blared, making his head jerk up. His wife had turned up the volume and stood transfixed by a scene of smoke and wreckage. Cars were burning on one of the freeways and a jackknifed semi-trailer perched over one of them, like a giant insect devouring its prey. Other vehicles to the front and rear of the flames were pulling onto the shoulders or attempting to cross the median to escape.

From a helicopter overhead, a reporter described the scene, "the semi-trailer, apparently trying to push a disabled vehicle out of active traffic lanes, rode over the vehicle's trunk and ruptured the gas tank. Somehow, we can't tell just how, the gas spill ignited and flames spread across the roadway, enveloping other cars. There are men down there with fire extinguishers. Yes, I can see at least five or six of them trying to smother the flames before other gas tanks go. My God, this is terrible! The cars on all sides are trying to get off the roadway, to get away from the flames. Tires are burning now on some of the cars. A police helicopter just landed on the other side of the freeway and more extinguishers are being brought into play. People are abandoning their cars, running to safety. This is Route twenty-eight, near New Kensington, and it is a trouble spot."

The helicopter camera panned along the obstructed highway past the tall concrete faces of industrial buildings and the winding Allegheny River back toward Pittsburgh. The lines of cars were packed bumper to bumper as the rolling clouds of thick black smoke climbed skyward. "The traffic on this route was barely moving because of construction work when this accident occurred, and it is at a dead standstill now. If you are on the roads and can get to an exit, avoid Route twenty-eight north of the city. I see another helicopter landing now. It's a larger National Guard HU-one. Men are piling out of the chopper and running to the scene." The set dimmed to blackness.

"I can't watch anymore." Ann's fists jammed against the sides of her mouth after she had slapped at the switch. Her shoulders began to shake and she collapsed into a chair. "Oh God, this is a nightmare. I can't, I can't, I can't. Tommy," she was sobbing now. "Tommy, please get us out of here. Please." The sound quavered as if it were being dragged from her.

He was kneeling beside her, pulling her close to him, trying to give her reassurance that he didn't feel. Tommy had been laid off his job four months ago and they had barely been able to make it on his unemployment checks and what little he could pick up moonlighting on odd jobs that wouldn't show up as employment and take away his $288 a month from the state. With Ann six months pregnant, the pressure had been building. Rent, utilities, food, doctor bills and medicine, the car payments already two months behind had pushed him to the wall. Now this thing at Bartonsville. A fucking nuclear reactor ready to blow up and kill us all if we don't get out of here. He kissed her gently on the cheek, smoothing strands of her auburn hair away from the tear-streaked face.

The transistor maintained its impersonal flow of news. "Motorists already on these routes are instructed to follow these directions: Should you have a mechanical problem with your vehicle, pull to the shoulder of the road, out of the flow of traffic, and raise the hood. Help will reach you as soon as possible. Should you require medical or emergency aid pull to the shoulder of the road and place a suitcase, large bag or article of clothing on your hood. Do not raise the hood. Military or police helicopters will reach you in a short time."

The repeated instructions for people to remain in their homes had gone unheeded since the panic began Sunday night and Pittsburgh was voiding itself of inhabitants. Television and radio had carried early reports of the potential fallout of radioactive wastes over the Pittsburgh area and now the emergency networks were broadcasting news and instructions just as if it were a nuclear attack. No matter what reassurances were given that the situation was being brought under control, the first reaction, the instinct, was to get far away from the threat. Now the people were finding themselves trapped, either unable to leave the city or caught in the gigantic traffic snarl that blocked all roads leading away from Bartonsville.

December 11, 1976

Spirals of smoke rose from the chimney and dispersed moments later, swirled away by the gentle but persistent afternoon breeze that swept across the slopes. The chalet, perched above the Beatenberg ski station, could have been a picture from a Swiss travel poster with its gaily painted balconies and shutters in sharp contrast to the backdrop of deep powdery snow that had fallen the night before.

Inside, two men sat hunched over one of the high carved oak tables in the sunlight-splashed room, oblivious to everything but their work. Through the broad front window, the towering fourteen-thousand-foot Jungfrau massif soared above the glacial blue waters of Lake Thun. Nearby, brightly garbed skiers crisscrossed their tracks, some schussing down the steep expert slope toward the lodge with its fireplaces and waiting brandies. December was a month of magical beauty in the Bernese Alps, which had little to do with these individuals' presence here.

Alec Bakary, the weasel-faced Tunisian, was a buyer

for several clients who dealt with the international arms black market. He had finally removed a sealed manila envelope from his briefcase and placed it in front of Henri Raboud. "This is the special order which I was instructed to present to you, Monsieur Raboud," he said in a rasping voice. "My client is anxious to know if you can obtain these items."

Raboud pushed aside the stack of order forms that already represented nearly three million dollars worth of weapons newly purchased by the agent on behalf of countries and groups that dealt through the black market to equip clandestine armies. In the transactions just completed, Henri was providing an arsenal ranging from 2,000 U.S. M-16 rifles with ammunition and some 750 Soviet RPG-7 antitank rockets to 25 Redeye surface-to-air missiles. These were normal items that he had contracted for numerous times in the past in varied quantities. He was mildly curious as he opened the new envelope that his companion seemed nervously eager to discuss. Bakary's dark, close-set eyes continued to search the other's face for some indication of response as Raboud read through the documents.

"Mon Dieu," was a low exclamation of surprise and concern. "Nuclear weapons, Bakary? Surely you must be jesting." Raboud sat back in his chair, fingering his neat mustache. "I am not a moralist as you well know, but some of your children are doing substantial damage with the toys you already supply to them. Now they want more advanced and dangerous playthings." He shook his head slowly as he tossed the papers back onto the desk. "I'm afraid our stocks do not include weapons of this type." He pointed to the papers. "Atomic Demolition Munitions, half- and two-kiloton warheads for the one-hundred-fifty-five-millimeter Howitzers and eight-inch guns, and even ten-kiloton aerial bombs. Merde, even if they would be obtained from our stocks, the cost would be prohibitive."

Bakary leaned across the table, palms flat on either side of the envelope. His face, a cruel joke of genetics, was a composite of the unrefined peasant background that had spawned him, and the ruthless society which nurtured him. It was as repulsive to Raboud as the odor that permeated the man's clothing. Gaudy and cheaply tailored synthetics were a gesture to the European mode of dress, but Henri could still imagine the stench of goats clinging to a native kaftan. Bakary smiled and gold-capped teeth glistened among lumps of tobacco-stained enamel, "I assure you, Monsieur Raboud, my client has authorized me to pay quite reasonably for delivery of the special weaponry. There is, of course, a bonus for you to indicate the great pleasure we have in doing business with you." The ingratiating smile reminded Raboud of a man pimping for his wife or sister. Anything to get his hands on the nuclear weapons.

Henri concealed the feeling of uneasiness that came over him after reading the special order. Not that it was unusual to receive an order for nuclear weapons; there had been several such requests in the last few months, but to have one come from this "belette," Bakary. Everyone from the PLO, FRELIMO, and the Tupamaros, through the lowest band of scabby cutthroats in Algiers must be shopping for them.

"I can't promise anything, Bakary, but I will forward your order. There is nothing else I can do on that score."

"You will please keep the special order in strictest confidence when relaying it to your organization. My client does not desire for his needs to become public knowledge. I'm sure you understand."

"Perfectly. Be assured that this will be treated with utmost discretion."

The Tunisian shrugged and sat back in his chair, gathering his papers together. "I can ask no more than that, my friend. Should you need to reach me, I will be spending a number of days at the Arca Hotel in Bern. The basic order will be handled as usual, no?"

"Payment made half when the shipment is put together and half when it arrives, just as in the past. I assume you will attend to the financial matters as you did in our last transaction."

"Most certainly. I am the single agent in my client's

business arrangements. It makes for an uncluttered organization." Bakary had finished placing his papers back in the briefcase as he spoke, struggling into his overcoat, which had been thrown across a nearby couch. "When does the last cable car run down to the lake? I left my auto in the parking area rather than riding that bus from Bern."

Raboud glanced at his watch and realized how anxious he was to terminate this meeting now that the negotiations were completed. "You have eighteen minutes to reach the station. It's only a ten minute walk from here unless the drifts block the lower pathways. Here, let me show you to the door."

He and Bakary walked down the flight of stairs, past ornately carved panels depicting boar and stag hunting scenes, chatting inconsequentially about the advantages of leasing from Hertz at fifty-eight francs a day rather than paying the outrageous taxi fares in Bern.

After bidding good-bye to the agent, Henri closed the massive door and turned back to the wide fireplace with its broad mantel and overhanging antlers. It was perfect here, he thought. The comfortable old world setting, the fireplaces, the charm of the wood carvings and painted scenes, the feather-down comforters on the beds, and the location; only twenty-nine miles from Bern, yet remote enough for his business. The atmosphere made it so much easier to deal objectively, to forget that the products he sold carried the promise of death.

Several weeks later and an ocean away, the equatorial sun scorched São Paulo on an unusually steamy afternoon that drove native Paulistas to the beaches. High above the blistering pavement, a group of businessmen lounged in air-conditioned comfort on the thirtieth floor of the São Paulo Crown Hotel, a towering, glass-walled cylinder near the city's central business district. Twelve top dealers in the arms black market had interrupted other business in various parts of the world to fly into Brazil. Recent orders placed by clients for nuclear weapons were the topic of discussion, and among the sets of orders on the polished jacaranda wood table were the cryptic notes written by Henri Raboud. All of these indicated the growing determination among third-world nations, and the laundry list of political factions, to secure nuclear weapons for their own uses.

The multinational operations of the arms black market had the scope and flexibility that permitted its members to service every order, from a band of terrorists in the Caribbean to the rightist faction in Lebanon or Libyan requirements for weaponry to support other terrorist groups in the Mideast. Several months before, anti-Duvalier exiles contracted for a small shipment of Soviet AK-47 assault rifles, ammunition, several 60-millimeter mortars and fragmentation hand grenades. In a matter of days after the order was received, the shipment was put together in one of the organization's Venezuelan warehouses in Maracaibo and placed aboard a fishing boat. The boat belonged to an independent gun runner who made the delivery off the coast of the Dominican Republic. In a larger transaction, the organization obtained nearly the entire stockpile of U.S. materiel abandoned in Laos after the fall of Indochina. In delicate negotiations, the Pathet Lao agreed to sell the weapons and equipment, which were loaded aboard freighters and shipped to the Latin American storage facilities. Within months, the weapons were appearing in Angola, Mozambique, Algeria, Libya, and Lebanon.

The diverse backgrounds of these businessmen gave the organization its necessary talent and resources. The acting chairman of the de facto board was Bernard Albritton, born Alberto Castelloni, the fifth of eight children in a Bronx cold-water flat. Tough, street-wise, shrewd; by eighteen, he was being groomed for the Syndicate's gambling enterprises and moved rapidly through the New York–Chicago circuit in his rise to mob power. At fifty-eight, Albritton had mastered conceal-ment of his past. Urbane, slightly graying at the temples, a nose job that straightened the twisted lump of cartilage left by a pair of brass knuckles, he was smooth and polished from his carefully tailored Feruch suit to the handmade alligator shoes. Albritton was the Syndicate's coordinator for international pari-mutuel betting operations and was designated its man on the board of the arms black market. Albritton in his world travels had been in contact with all the members of this loose confederation and acted as the single point of contact on large operations such as this one today.

To his right, in the white, raw silk suit, the shorter, stockily built Prussian, was Franz Heitzman, a former Nazi munitions maker who had fled to Argentina just before the fall of the Third Reich. Franz was only twenty-three when he assumed control of his ailing father's firm and had managed to bring the company to rank behind only the Krupp Works in Hitler's wartime production of armaments. In January 1945, he escaped along with several of his top executives and nearly six million dollars in gold bullion with which to reestablish himself in South America. Within four years, he succeeded in building a successful import-export business and managed to dissociate himself from his wartime activities. In an ironic twist, Franz's aged father and older brother sat accused in the docks at Nuremburg while Franz built a new empire in virtual anonymity. During the rise of terrorist activities in the 1960s, Franz recognized the lucrative market for contraband armaments and shifted his attention back to that familiar field. His import-export trade was a perfect cover for the covert operations.

Tran Van Hung was the innocuous appearing Asian who stood slightly away from the others, near the heavily draped, curving windows, talking with Ernesto Vargas. Tran's bland moon face and perpetual smile gave the impression of a benevolent Buddha, but the numbers of Tran's former competitors and enemies whose bodies were fertilizing rice paddies on the outskirts of Cholon or staring upward through sightless eyes from the mucky bottom of the Saigon River bespoke the calm ruthlessness with which he did business. He had run a profitable black market operation in Vietnam during the conflict and moved his business to Bangkok shortly before the North Vietnamese entered Saigon. Because of his extensive contacts in Laos and Cambodia, he was selected to act as the chief negotiator when the arms black market cartel arranged to purchase the abandoned U.S. materiel. It was a major coup for Tran, which vaulted him from the ranks of pushers of contraband PX and quartermaster goods to the league of international black marketeering.

Sipping a daiquiri at Tran's side was a Brazilian double for Anthony Quinn. Ernesto Vargas was a wealthy man in the ranks of multimillionaires. His investments, which included coalfields in the Tierra del Fuego territory of Argentina, telecommunications in Bolivia and a chain of warehouses that stretched from the ports of Central America to Buenos Aires, enabled him to bankroll key political figures in successive regimes of the South American countries that were vital to his business interests. The black market was unnecessary as a source of income, yet it provided both an element of excitement in Ernesto's otherwise carefully controlled enterprises and a vital tool in his manipulation of power. He was keenly aware that his association with the suppliers of arms to the terrorist groups in Latin America guaranteed his protection from extortion and attack. In an extension of this protection, authored by himself, Ernesto had ensured that government officials who threatened his empire or who failed to respond to gentle bribery generally were found dead, victims of terrorist ambushes.

Reciprocally, Ernesto was the key to black market logistics in the Western Hemisphere. His warehouses held weapons and equipment destined for client countries. All of the buildings were exempt from government search and seizure. His agents and contacts guaranteed the passage of clandestine cargo through port authorities and customs inspections. His bribes effectively provided cases of temporary blindness among officials as crates of unmarked cargo were off-loaded from specified freighters. It was a neat package of mutual benefits that this intensely ambitious man found helpful in his quest for power.

Equally important in the organization was the swarthy Sicilian sitting on the long couch in the center of the room and gesturing expansively to his amused audience.

Giancarlo Luccavita came from the quaint town of Taormina on the eastern coast of Sicily. Although his business interests forced him to live away most of the year, he maintained an opulent villa in the shadow of Mount Etna, near where he had been born. Like the smoldering volcano, often glowing red in the evening and rumbling deep inside itself, Luccavita was a man of potentially explosive passion, anger, or mirth. His shipping firm carried cargo around the globe, servicing ports on all continents and usually delivering loads of strangely unmarked crates that disappeared rapidly from the docks. Four freighters belonging to his firm, sailing under the Norwegian flag, had docked in the port of Sihanoukville six months after Communist control was imposed on Laos. An entire week was required to load the cargo of weapons and ammunition, equipment and vehicles for which Tran had successfully negotiated. Within a month, the shipments were secure in Vargas' warehouses.

Conversation in the room died away as Albritton walked to the conference table and tapped the striker against a small silver bell beside his leatherbound folder. In twos and threes, the men joined him around the oval table, leisurely seating themselves and examining the briefing packets that had been placed before them. Albritton took his seat and waited until all were settled before he began. "Welcome to São Paulo, gentlemen. I'm pleased that all of you could arrange to be here with only short notice given you. I apologize for the inconvenience; however, I believe you'll find this meeting well worth it."

"As long as we were being inconvenienced, Bernie, couldn't we have suffered in a more appropriate location?" asked René St. Jacques, the effeminate head of a Gallic chemical manufacturing firm. René had arrived from his Cannes villa only moments before the meeting began and was already commenting about the accommodations. "I would have thought you could have chosen a more intimate and tasteful atmosphere. You know how commercialism infects its patrons with its own sterility. Mon Dieu, a chain hotel, enfin."

"My apologies, René. Circumstances dictated that we gather as inconspicuously as possible and, at the height of the tourist season, what could be more so than this?" Albritton smiled, "If you noticed, even the names under which you are registered have a proletarian ring to them. Again, I assure you that the substance of our agenda will offset the discomfort any of you might feel. So, with that, I'll spare you any preliminaries and address the purpose of the meeting."

The pleasant smile remained fixed on Albritton's lips as he paused to pick up a sheaf of papers from his folder. "Gentlemen, in the past months we have received a large number of specific requests for weapons which bear either nuclear warheads or fall in the category of nuclear munitions. For the first time we have had sufficient and continuing requests to make it operationally rewarding should we decide to honor them. I don't suppose it's necessary to tell you that the effort and risk involved in acquiring these weapons will exceed that which we normally accept; however, the benefits far surpass those we normally demand."

He dropped the order forms back onto his folder and waited for reactions or comments from the group. At the first mention of nuclear weapons, mild interest and studied boredom had vanished, to be replaced with the keen attention of hunters stalking prey. As he had expected, there was no conversation among them. They were too self-contained to show visible surprise.

Albritton selected a five-by-eight card from a stack on his folder and referred to it as he continued. "At the outset we have a two-fold consideration. First, can the weapons systems be obtained and how? Second, can they be transferred to the client's possession without intercept? In the latter case, none of us, I'm sure, would agree to endanger our established supply channels by attempting to run a load of extremely hot cargo through without safeguards."

"Bernard," Vargas broke in, "safeguards might be quite difficult to provide with a shipment of this nature. Our friends in the federal services sometimes develop nervous bowels when they have to ignore large standard shipments. Think of what would occur when the offended nation exerted maximum efforts to recover the weapons. If anything were to go wrong, the officials could be executed as easily by their own government as an example...as by our insurgent friends. A man in that situation is highly unreliable."

"Another consideration is the tremendous pressure that could be brought to bear in the international community if it were learned that we were responsible for the theft of nuclear weapons. The major countries turn their heads from our present trafficking in armaments unless we step too hard on their interests," Luccavita added, "but if they found us making off with their precious nuclear trump cards, they would spare no effort to squash us."

Albritton agreed. "This is why we are about to be briefed on the critical aspects of deployment, storage, security, and transportability of the weapons systems in question. We will be better equipped to discuss the merits of this project after becoming acquainted with the strengths and weaknesses of the targets."

Franz Heitzman stared idly at a series of Picasso reprints on the far wall as he fitted this project into a matrix he had established years before in his discussions of world power. Here was the final piece, waiting to be introduced. He drew slowly on his cigar, savoring its flavor before releasing a puff of blue smoke toward the ceiling. A shift of the nuclear sword outside the control of the superpowers could bring the new dawning of the anti-Marxist crusade. It would take more than a few tactical nuclear weapons, but this was a beginning.

The heavy curtains had been drawn to black out the sunlight, and a projection screen slid downward from its ceiling recess with an indistinct whirring sound. Lights in the room dimmed. "In the presentation, we will consider only the U.S. weapons systems because they are the most accessible and the best available types." Albritton turned to the crew-cut European who stood beside him. The man's handsome features were marred by an irregular scar that ran from below his left temple, across his cheek, to the point of his jaw. "Ernst, you can begin now. Oh yes," Albritton caught himself and turned back to the group. "Should you have any questions or comments during the briefing, please offer them."

Ernst Mueller, former mercenary, veteran of Stanleyville, wore the scar as his only decoration from years of combat. The brutal slash of a Congolese rebel's panga nearly split his skull before Mueller's Schmeisser submachine gun cut the man down. After acting as a military advisor to FRELIMO forces against the Portuguese in Mozambique, Ernst became Albritton's bodyguard and companion. It was a contrast in physical characteristics, Albritton's refinement and the rough masculinity Mueller exuded.

Mueller began in a firm, guttural voice, "The weapons systems we consider are found in the inventory of the U.S. Army and Air Force in both Europe and the continental United States. For your purposes, only the storage sites in West Germany will be discussed. The other locations have security measures or removal problems which exceed the organization's capabilities to deal with them."

"Amazingly articulate for one so crude," René commented in a conversational tone to no one in particular. Ernst gave no indication of having heard as several men turned to look at the smirking Frenchman.

The screen flashed with the picture of a squat, cylindrical object that appeared to be a truncated garbage can with two narrow bands around it and a control or timer on one side. "The Atomic Demolition Munition is used for cratering and destruction of roadways, airfields and dams as well as denying access to an area due to radioactive contamination. It is configured in two basic yields: the half-kiloton 'sadam' or SADM and the one-and-a-half kiloton 'madam' or MADM. Special engineering units in West Germany possess these devices, particularly five units located along the border of Warsaw Pact nations where it would be employed to hinder the advance of Communist forces."

Ernst took a flashlight pointer from his pocket as a

detailed map of West Germany replaced the first slide. "The special units are stationed as indicated by the arrow on this slide, here at Kassel...at Minden, at... Bad Hersfeld, here...Würzburg, here...and at Bamberg, here. The weapons are stored in what we found to be a standard secure area as shown on this slide."

On the screen was a concrete cube set into the ground with dirt mounded to roof level on three sides. A narrow entranceway on the fourth side was flanked by sandbags and a guard bunker. There were a number of similar structures in a rectangular compound surrounded by parallel barbed-wire fences.

"Because of NATO regulations and the proximity of U.S. nuclear devices to a Communist bloc nation, security is stringent, but not insurmountable. The normal laxity found in routine protective details is absent at all locations. Punishment for infractions of guard regulations is harsh and the caliber of personnel performing security details is unusually high. In this respect, there has been no success in cultivating relationships with personnel assigned to the detail or the unit; therefore, we cannot anticipate aid from anyone with access to the storage site."

The chairman acknowledged a question from the far end of the table, motioning Ernst to hold his briefing.

Sven Langaard sat rubbing his pipe alongside his nose, then pointed its stem toward the briefer. "Is there any information on attempted exploitation of security personnel? They must have weaknesses like any other men. What about gambling, sex, drinking problems, bribery? In an isolated duty post they should have the same failings as any of their compatriots."

Ernst flipped quickly through several folders while listening to the question, and he scanned the documents one of them contained. "Herr Langaard, our contacts with East German and Czech Military Intelligence sources indicate numerous attempts to compromise members of the security details, all of them unsuccessful. Entries in their records date back to a period only weeks after the first unit moved to Kassel.

"In one instance I have here, an army captain commanding the security company was led into a sexual encounter with a young local girl in the employ of East German Intelligence. His wife and children were still in the United States awaiting passage to Germany and, later, when they arrived, he attempted to break off the liaison.

"He was threatened with exposure, the girl claiming pregnancy, and was placed in contact with known E.G.I.S. agents who attempted to exploit him. Unfortunately for them, he reported everything to his own counterintelligence personnel, resulting in the apprehension of the Communist agents. The captain and his family were returned to the United States and, although he will never again hold a top security clearance, he is continuing a career in the military.

"This operation and similar ones failed because the weak men are given the option to aid in breaking up enemy intelligence networks. In another instance, a sergeant who had been compromised by the East Germans was revealed to be an undercover operative. It is dangerous business for those who attempt to subvert these units."

"Does that answer your question, Sven?" the chairman asked. "It would seem that the professionals in the penetration game have found this quarry too tough." Langaard waved his pipe indicating he had nothing further.

For the next forty minutes, Ernst covered the number and disposition of security forces that would oppose a raid on the sites, the early warning devices that would be encountered, routes into and away from the sites and means of transporting the devices out of the country. By 5:30, the presentations were complete and a weary group of men pondered the mass of information they had received on ADMs, warheads for artillery shells, surface-to-air missiles, and city-leveling, air-dropped bombs. The sumptuous luncheon had been very enjoyable and the only break in the schedule. Detail had piled upon detail until it became impossible to remember which security system protected what weapon. There was, however, a clear picture in every man's mind of the vast amount of planning and preparation that had gone into establishing security for the nuclear weapons. It would require a total commitment of the organization's various assets to raid even one site and successfully transfer the weapons to the clients. Surprise would be their greatest ally; their only ally.

Chilled magnums of Dom Perignon were passed by two of Vargas's house boys who attended to the needs of the group. The champagne was an elixir that lifted them from the tedium of the afternoon to a tingling anticipation of the evening ahead.

Ernesto took responsibility for their entertainment during the visit and, although somewhat miffed by the restrictions imposed by the need to avoid undue attention, he was confident of meeting the exacting tastes of his compatriots.

Luccavita had hosted their last gathering in his own Sicilian villa. The bacchanalia left them satiated, fortunately with an extra day for full recovery from the exhausting effects of the full-bodied young nymphs and liberal amounts of fine wine. For men who were accustomed to satisfying their physical and psychological needs in unlimited manner, it became a matter of selecting that which gave them the greatest pleasure.

Aside from Albritton, who still insisted on establishing his prowess through numerical conquests, each of the men had a particular fetish with which Vargas was familiar. The young women from his "executive escort service," a subsidiary business in his empire, would enfold each man like a warm, moist vacuum, pulling his very essence from him before the night was over.

Luccavita finished his second glass of Perignon and excused himself. He was exhausted by the long hours of technical information and details of military installations. It was all necessary to making the decision, but even so, a grueling day. Outside the suite, his mind focused on a relaxing sauna and rubdown before supper; the perfect remedy for depleted energy. With typical thoroughness, Vargas had reserved the hotel's spa for them during the next hour and a half. Most accommodating, Luccavita mused.

Later, refreshed and invigorated, Luccavita stood in front of the dressing room mirror in his suite, humming bits of *Rigoletto* as he finished knotting his bow tie. His secretary had seen to laying out his dinner clothes earlier and prepared a shaker of martinis to sustain him before supper.

"Ah, Carlo," he said aloud to himself, "you have the charm of a thousand years of lovers in your face, and if that doesn't work, there's always enough money to make an actress out of any woman." He brushed his thinning hair straight back from his forehead, smoothing it with his other hand as he counted the brush strokes. His profile pleased him. The moderately high forehead was accentuated by his receding hairline, but combined with his aquiline nose and dark eyes and strong jawline, there was a classic look of power.

Once again satisfied with his appearance, he walked into the bedroom and slipped into the brocade dinner jacket, pulling the lace cuffs of his shirt out slightly from the sleeves. Good, very good, he thought as he turned in front of the full-length mirror, inspecting himself. "You are a tribute to your parents, Carlo," he said to the image in the mirror. "Some lovely lady will discover this fact later in the evening. After all, they had what, fourteen of us children? To have that many, you have to perform."

In the penthouse, Ernesto surveyed the final preparations being made for the supper. A twenty-eight-foot table had been set within the sweeping arc of the terrace, offering a spectacular view of the city lights spread below and on all sides. Overhead, the night sky of the Southern Hemisphere was alight with a thousand brilliant pinpoints. Dorado, the swordfish; Equuleus, the colt; Mensa, the table; all the works of the heavenly artisan were scattered across the black velvet canvas. The night air was cool and soothing after the heat of the afternoon.

Ernesto's staff worked quietly and efficiently as they added minor touches to the flower arrangements and table settings. There was a spaciousness in the suite that had been enhanced by opening the sliding glass doors leading to the terrace, blending the rooms with the night outside. The rugged natural stone walls and geometric symmetry of the wood and leather furniture were softened by lavish arrangements of native flowers and plants, turning the atmosphere to one of primitive splendor. Soft, indirect lighting gave the room a glow.

"José," Vargas motioned to his wizened major domo, "have the ladies arrived?"

"Si, Senhor Vargas. They are in the side rooms freshening their makeup."

"Amazing, these women, José," Vargas smiled, "no matter how beautiful nature made them, no matter that they just finished putting on their makeup in their rooms, four floors below, they must always take time to try to improve on both."

"Senhor, if you will allow me, these ladies are of a beauty upon which cosmetics have no effect." The older mestizo smiled gently. "I worry that the flowers will bow their heads in comparison."

José excused himself as two waiters walked up to the buffet table carrying a three-pound lobster in garnished glory. The centerpiece in the array of appetizers was a trio of Lobster en Bellevue Parisienne, a particular favorite of Ernesto's and a colorful focal point for the table. Each of the crimson lobsters, after being prepared, was posed on the platter in a walking position with claws at the front edges of the plate. Around the circumference of the bed of lettuce were alternating artichoke hearts and stuffed hard-cooked eggs. Down the lobsters' backs were plump mounds of aspic, topped with truffles. As a final touch, a silver skewer with artistically cut tomato, artichoke heart, and radishes, pierced the lobsters' heads like the prow of a ship.

José had chosen the appetizers and Ernesto indicated approval as each was brought to him for inspection. A cut-crystal container of Beluga caviar rested in a bowl of ice. Lemon slices radiated around the crystal—like petals on a flower; and on the silver tray beneath, triangles of fresh toast completed the serving. There were separate bowls of finely chopped egg yolks and egg whites as well as thinly sliced onion rings, though the purists would disdain all but the toast and perhaps a spread of butter.

The sommelier presented a chilled magnum of Heidsieck '59 for Ernesto's consideration. He nodded approval and waved the man on. There would be chilled vodka and the Heidsieck Brut to go with the caviar.

Next came slices of foie gras in aspic followed by a chilled platter of wafer-thin sections of pinkish smoked salmon surrounded by lemon wedges, capers, and lightly buttered toast. José added the pepper mill and cruet of olive oil for those who desired to embellish the flavor. Finally, the long serving dish with fresh oysters on the half shell resting on their bed of cracked ice. There was a properly chilled Johannesberg to complement the oysters, and Ernesto was again pleased with José's choice.

He checked his watch as the last dish was placed on the table and turned to greet his guests at the door. The timing was perfect as Tran had just entered, thoroughly punctual and looking somewhat ill at ease in dinner clothes.

José raised his hand as a signal and the string quartet on the terrace began a medley of classics. It would be an evening worthy of the patron, he thought, as he made a last-minute check around the room to see that all was perfect. The staff of waiters had vanished as the first guest arrived and they would appear unobtrusively during the course of the evening as needed. Once assured that the preparations were satisfactory, José stepped to the corner of the room where Vargas could signal him if he were needed; otherwise, no one would know he was there.

Albritton and Langaard arrived together, both elegantly dressed and in a festive mood. They joined Tran at the bar as Ernesto greeted the others.

"Lovely setting," Langaard remarked, glancing around the suite. "Our host has created a masterpiece this evening."

"You expected less of him?" Albritton asked. "I hope we shall have guests equal to the setting."

"Bernard, knowing Ernesto as we do, there should be no disappointments." Langaard smiled.

Tran stood quietly by, sipping anisette over ice as he

listened to the conversation. His indelible smile gave no indication of his impression of the other men or the occasion. Tran found that silence was his best weapon in meeting the unknown rather than speaking unwisely and losing status in the eyes of those around him. Before long, his position within this group would be as secure as it had been in his own enterprises; but until then he would accept their methods with discretion. All of this was interesting, however, and would be of value to him in the future.

Luccavita, Oldham, St. Jacques, and Parker, one of the others, joined them for drinks as Ernesto led another group onto the terrace. The Sicilian was in high humor and set the mood for the group. Even Tran began to relax under the influence of Luccavita's spell and his second glass of anisette.

After a period of male conversation and drinking, Ernesto nodded to José and joined the men around the dining room bar. "My friends, enough of this stag affair. Your ladies have arrived and await you." He swept his arm toward the inside door, which opened to reveal the first of Ernesto's Latin courtesans.

"Carlo, may I present Elena." The men unconsciously placed their glasses on the bar as the slender, high-breasted beauty stepped into the room. Her glistening black hair was coiffed gently back into a chignon, accentuating her high cheekbones and full, luscious lips. Luccavita, for all his experience, was momentarily stunned, something Vargas noted with a touch of satisfaction.

Luccavita's eyes swept down the girl's body to the flash of thigh that slid temptingly from the deep slit side of her peach silk gown. The fabric seemed to cling and caress her legs and breasts as she walked toward him.

He moved to meet her, extending his hand in which she lightly placed hers.

Carlo bent and touched his lips to the warm flesh, conscious of the pounding veins in his temples as her sensuous fragrance wrapped around him. His senses tingled with the headiness of jasmine, the hint of sandalwood. The delicate woman scent entrapped him before he could look up into the dancing lights of her hazel-brown eyes.

"Senhor Carlo, you excite me and we have just met." The clear contralto voice was low enough that he knew the remark was meant only for his ears. He offered his arm and drew her close by his side as they walked down the steps to a couch.

"Signorina, my words fail me. Were I an artist, I would not dare attempt to portray your beauty on canvas, or as a poet, to compose verse extolling what my eyes see."

"Senhor, you are more likely to captivate a woman with what you don't say than other men with what they do say." She smiled warmly as she sat, drawing him down beside her. "If you will call me Elena, may I call you Carlos?"

"I was about to ask you the same thing... Elena."

A white-jacketed waiter appeared beside them with a tulip-shaped glass of champagne and a martini on a small silver tray. Luccavita handed her the champagne, then took his martini.

"To amore... that nourishes the human soul... as the sweetest water brings life to a parched and dying flower." He touched her glass with his and returned her gaze as they sipped their drinks.

The other girls had entered the room in swirls of flowing chiffon, crepe, and silk; a fashion parade of Diors, Givenchys, and de la Rentas that was heightened by the loveliness of each of Ernesto's women. The men found themselves engaged in delightfully stimulating conversation that touched on topics ranging from the intimate flirtations to art, world travel, and sports. The girls were easily able to slip from conversations about polo to St. Jacques's discourse on Degas's spontaneity, to gossip about the film festival at Cannes.

On the terrace, Albritton stood close behind the tall, full-breasted Peruvian girl, pressing himself gently against the firm swelling of her buttocks. His hand raised from the railing in front of her to cup her breast.

"There must be a thousand lights out there, just for us," he murmured into the musky fragrance of her hair. She was nearly as tall as he and their bodies meshed perfectly.

"And a sky full of stars," she responded, leaning her head back for him to nuzzle her neck. "Could there be a more beautiful night?" She parted her legs slightly, allowing his leg to slip between them. The filmy chiffon of her gown did nothing to hide the promise of what lay beneath. Albritton felt his breathing become ragged. She had clasped his leg with hers, almost imperceptibly, but with calculated sensuality.

To hell with supper, he thought. I want this broad in bed. He felt a flush of delight as she moaned softly and leaned forward against his hand. He felt her braless nipple harden. Oh God, this is going to be something. And another one just like her waiting in the room for them after supper.

Ernesto glanced over Heitzman's shoulder, noting Albritton's less than discreet activities. Concha was handling him well. The man shows an uncorrectable flaw with his lack of restraint, Vargas observed.

He turned toward José, who stood watching in the corner of the room, and nodded toward the table. The major domo acknowledged the signal and spoke to one of the waiters, who moved quickly to the terrace and lighted the candelabra arranged down the center of the table. As José finished, Ernesto took his lady's arm in his and walked slowly toward the terrace followed by Heitzman and fair-skinned Alicia. Around the room, couples began walking to the table.

On the buffet, one lobster remained. The caviar, replenished twice, was reduced to a thin layer of glistening black on the bottom of the crystal bowl.

The menu, José's masterpiece, was combined with a selection of wines from Vargas's personal cellars. At each place setting was a Carte de Menu in flowing script.

St. Jacques leaned forward to study the menu as they were being seated. There was a great deal of money in this business. His eyebrow lifted slightly as he read the accompanying wines. Once comfortable in the velvet-cushioned oak chair, he looked approvingly toward Vargas at the table's head. "You do us an honor with your selection of wines, Ernesto."

Vargas smiled, "For my good friends, what I have is

MENU

Piper Heidsieck	*Homard en Bellevue Parisienne*
magnum	*Caviar Aspic de Foie Gras Sousceyrac*
1959	*Saumon Fumé Huîtres Impériales*
Royal Amontillado	*Consommé Brunoise*
Sherry	
Les Clos Chablis	*Filet de Sole Laguipière*
1972	
Château Cheval Blanc	*Chateaubriand Prince Orloff*
1955	*Chou-fleur Polonaise*
	Petit Pois Florentine
	Asperge de Alexis sauce Hollandaise
Château Carbonnieux	*Caneton Rouennaise*
1974	
	Artichaut Vinaigrette
Château d'Yquem	*Coupe Glacée Mirabelle*
1969	
Château de la Grange	*Café*
Jonzac Charante	
Cognac	
1893	

yours." He tilted his head slightly and raised his hand, palm up, with a tiny shrug. "But, I'm afraid I can claim credit only for my choice of major domos, René."

As the meal progressed, superlatives were uttered after each course. José had supervised the preparation of each dish and it pleased him to see the obvious appreciation of his efforts. Only the American, Albritton, appeared indifferent. He eats as if he were in a third-rate restaurant, the old man observed. There is no savoring of the food, no sipping of the wines. He makes the motions of good etiquette, but there is no real love for the food or drink. Look at St. Jacques and Heitzman. They know how good wine should be treated. The Frenchman, ah, he tilts his glass to enjoy the beauty of the wine's color, then inhales its bouquet. Only then does he sip the wine, taking fullest pleasure in the exultation it carries to his palate. But Albritton, *cabron;* he is more interested in playing with the woman's underthings.

At 11:30, somewhat over two hours since they sat down to dinner, the final empty brandy snifter was placed on the table and the party retired to the living room. The table was removed and a dance group replaced the strings, as the terrace was readied for those who could muster the energy to maneuver through a samba.

"Ernesto, a magnificent meal," Franz complimented the host. He accepted a cigar from one of the footmen, allowed the man to clip the end with a pair of tiny gold snips and puffed heartily as it was lighted for him. "You've made this visit most memorable."

"A meager effort, Franz, but I am pleased that it has been satisfactory."

"I look forward to the opportunity to return your hospitality when you honor me with a visit," Heitzman answered.

"We live so near one another, it's a pity that we don't do this more often, you know." Vargas took him gently by the elbow and moved him slightly away from the other men. "Before the ladies return from powdering their noses, I want to ask one thing of you."

Franz leaned closer, "Certainly, anything I am able to do for you."

Vargas dropped his voice, "I would like to talk with you before the meeting tomorrow. I've uncovered a few items which caused me to reconsider today's conclusions and have a viable alternative. I'm asking you, Carlo, and Sven to join me."

"If you wish. Say for luncheon at about one. I doubt that we'd be able to rouse either of the other two before then."

"Excellent. Here then, at one." He placed his hand on Heitzman's broad shoulder as they turned back to the others.

The men were rejoined by their partners and while several couples walked toward the terrace for dancing, others prepared to leave. Vargas reached St. Jacques, who was finishing a glass of champagne, and took him aside. He nodded toward René's approaching date. "She'll leave with you when you're ready to go and you can bid her farewell at the elevator. I have a surprise waiting for you in your room."

René's brow raised quizzically. "Surprise? In my room?"

"I believe you'll find him a most satisfactory substitute for the lady."

St. Jacques colored slightly, but maintained his composure. "Then you know."

"What is there to know, my friend? We take pleasure where we find it. I only wish for your evening to be as perfect as possible. I hope I haven't offended you."

René looked at Vargas with a mixture of understanding and appreciation. Replacing his glass on the table, he touched the man's arm, "Thank you, mon ami, for a truly grand evening. I think I will go now and ... ah ... see to my surprise." He smiled broadly at the young lady as he offered her his arm.

Luccavita and Elena were among the first to leave. Vargas said goodnight to them at the door and observed the authentic signs of desire in Elena's eyes as she held Luccavita's arm. No need for her to act tonight, Vargas thought as the couple walked down the hall. Carlo is in for a workout.

Elena did her best to match Carlo's outward calm even though she was quivering inside with the need for him. It had been so long since a man had been able to arouse her this way.

He seemed so calm and reserved, it both heightened her feeling of urgency and frightened her. What if he were impotent or if he didn't really want her? She was unaccustomed to the fear of inadequacy; yet this man had touched something in her that she couldn't control. She would make him love her; she'd love him as he'd never experienced love before. But he had been with so many women before. Would she be able to be special, so he would remember her?

Carlo opened the door to his suite, allowing Elena to precede him. His eyes traveled down her back to the rounded buttocks, enticingly outlined by the close-fitting silk. Her skin must be as smooth to the touch as the gown, he thought, closing the door behind him. He barely noticed that only the softest lights were glowing in the room and that the gently pulsating sound of Ravel's Bolero enfolded them. Candles lit the low table in front of the couch where Elena stood, waiting for him. The flickering candlelight brought moving reflections in her gown and caught highlights in her hair as if she were gently swaying with the rhythm of the music. Her eyes, soft, luminous, held him... then drew him to her.

From the first touch of flesh on flesh, sensations dominated thought and time. The slow, sensuous pleasure of her lips and tongue carried him to a pounding need for her body. Elena yielded to the strong, yet gentle, stroking of her body, releasing herself to him totally. There were no barriers, no restraint. Finally, she took him by the hand and pulled him onto the deep, soft carpeting.

Lying on his back, he watched as she knelt over him, her long black hair spilling almost to her waist, each of her breasts cupped in one of his hands, swelling under his caress. Their eyes locked and held in a separate world. There was the tense excitement as her fingertips found him and guided his hardness into her, then the sweet rush of moist heat that gripped him as she sank down. Neither of them was conscious of the softly driving rhythm of the Bolero that matched the thrust of their bodies.

The next morning, the persistent jangling of the phone woke Franz Heitzman. He rolled over, throwing off the covers, and stretched before picking up the receiver. "Good morning. It is ten A.M. and the weather for today will be sunny and twenty-nine degrees Centigrade. Have a pleasant day, senhor."

"Um, thank you," he grunted, shaking off the sleepiness. He hung up and walked slowly to the bathroom for a shower. Franz felt rested after the party and reminded himself to include Vargas in one of his next big suppers. It would have to be a major affair to match last night.

Studying his gray-stubbled face in the mirror, he felt a twinge of annoyance with himself for sending Alicia home after they left the party. She was a beautiful girl and probably would have been quite satisfying in bed, but there was always that chance. No matter how clean she appeared, one never knew. Too bad there were no truly Nordic types available for these dalliances; some good Aryan stock to fill a man's needs.

He finished his shower, shaved, and dressed in a comfortable white, tropical weave linen suit. After a light breakfast alone on his terrace, he went out for his daily walk, negotiating the crowded streets as he briskly stepped out the half-mile distance that was part of his regimen. By noon, he was back in his room and placed a call to his office to check on arriving shipments before going to meet with Vargas.

In the penthouse, Ernesto had been at work since early morning, reviewing reports and articles that had been brought to the hotel from his São Paolo office. A conservatively dressed Brazilian executive, one of Ernesto's industrial research branch chiefs, was explaining a series of excerpts from the U. S. *Congressional Record*.

"These are the essential passages from the hearings that were conducted, Senhor Vargas. The underlined elements provide the findings with regard to nuclear power plant safety and security." He pointed to one of the red-lined paragraphs. "This confirms your recollection of the weakness of security measures in the existing power plants in the United States."

Vargas scanned the document quickly. "Do you have clippings to substantiate this?" he asked, still reading.

"Yes, senhor." He picked up an acetate-covered page of newspaper articles and placed it beside the *Congressional Record.* "These relate to specific instances at various installations and can be expanded to cover industrial practices as a whole."

"This is good, Fernando. Just what I needed," Vargas said as he read through the page of clippings. "Where is the statement you wrote for me to cover all of this?"

"Here. It is conclusive and all points are substantiated by the supporting documents you have before you and in this file." He handed Vargas a looseleaf folder, thick with acetate sheets.

Ernesto took the folder and placed it on the table, leaning back in his chair after gesturing toward the bar. "Get a drink for yourself, if you'd like one before lunch, and relax until the others arrive. I'll want you to give them the same explanation of the situation you've given me."

This was a far more logical solution to the problem than had been presented yesterday, Vargas thought. With this information, it merely became a matter of choosing the correct plant to satisfy the demand; somewhat like shopping in a nuclear supermarket.

Shortly after one o'clock, the three men arrived and spent less than an hour listening to the argument Vargas had prepared. They left for the board meeting excited and in total agreement with the new concept. Vargas was satisfied that with their support, this plan would be accepted.

Gathered in Albritton's suite for the meeting, the group exchanged quips about the previous evening's affair before settling down to the business at hand. Albritton again chaired the meeting when they were all seated. He was unusually subdued and stared tiredly at the group through bloodshot, baggy eyes, something that didn't go unnoticed and unappreciated by his companions. The discussion began with Albritton's summation of the preceding afternoon's presentation and when opened to comment was seized by Vargas.

He stood before the group, carefully phrasing his counter-proposal to play on the business sensibilities of his contemporaries. "We consider the commitment of our organization's full capabilities against a military base of the United States. We are attacking strength instead of weakness and, in doing so, guarantee that there will be relentless pursuit and pressure from a superpower to recapture what we have taken." He shrugged expressively. "And what will we have taken? Nuclear weapons, yes; but enough to make the venture worth the long-range price? I think not."

He took a sheet of paper from the table and referred to it as he continued, "Eight ADMs, perhaps twenty artillery shell warheads, a few bombs of minimum yield . . . enough to fill one or two rounds of orders and then what? We not only guarantee continuous pressure on the organization, but we eliminate the opportunity to repeat the raid. I do not doubt that if we were successful, there would be such an increase in security that no further ventures could be considered." Looking around the table at the silent and contemplative men, he pointed to his chest, "I, for one, am unwilling to accept that prospect." A slight smile altered the stern expression. "The securing of nuclear material for our clients can be reasonable and will be profitable, but there is a better way." He picked up the statement and before beginning it noted, "Some year and a half ago, I became involved in negotiations for the introduction of nuclear power plants into Brazil as a part of my involvement in development of energy resources. During that time, my staff did a great deal of research into the problems of nuclear power as experienced by countries already utilizing it. Today, that research may provide us with the answer to our problem."

In the next fifteen minutes, Vargas revealed the weakness of security against terrorist attack in U. S.

nuclear plants. Citing the *Congressional Record,* General Accounting Office reports on the need for improvement of in-plant protection of strategic materials, Nader studies of safety and security weaknesses and a variety of newspaper articles, he outlined the vulnerability of the plants.

"This is the weakness we should attack, not a military stronghold. Consider that it took only a melon-sized lump of Plutonium to level the city of Nagasaki and think of the amounts that are stored in many of those plants." He looked at Heitzman and Luccavita, then to Langaard. "Gentlemen, I submit that we need only to select the single plant which will meet all of our clients' needs and use this information to prepare a reasonable plan to secure it. Once we have the plant, we have the Plutonium." He replaced his papers on the table and sat down.

Heitzman motioned for recognition. "I am in accord with Ernesto. He has stated a clear case which will allow us to proceed with less risk while at the same time allowing us to operate on a broader scale than if we were dealing in completed weapons systems. Those systems could be marketed only to countries possessing the capability of deploying them ... one could not expect a rebel band to carry a sophisticated weapon across country and hand deliver it. What I have in mind, I suspect lies in the back of all our minds. A more significant element which has not yet been voiced."

Luccavita leaned forward in his chair, "Prometheus, Franz?"

"In a sense," Franz answered. "The gift of fire to the mortals. What we are considering is not limited to acquisition and sale of a unique type of weapon to our clients, but a reordering of the political balance of power in the world." He paused to light his amber meerschaum and puffed it into life.

"I have contended for some time that the threat to stability in the world lies not with disruptive revolutionary factions who create limited spheres of conflict, but with the superpower domination which insures their meddling in the internal affairs of smaller nations to settle disputes. These settlements are generally based on the perceived best interests of the superpower, not the smaller country."

"Indochina," St. Jacques interjected.

"A most recent example," Franz agreed. "The Mideast, a continuing case in point; the African nations; I could go on, but it delays my point. One equalizing factor which has been unobtainable by these developing or metamorphosing nations is the nuclear sword or even a nuclear dagger. They are dependent on the superpowers for economic and military aid, which effectively commits them to the ideological camp of whatever power feeds and arms them. Nationalism is a rallying point which is prostituted in the course of events as the piper demands his wages for the tune he played. The ideal drama for the world stage would be played if nationalism could be elevated to a state of purity and each small crisis be resolved in the confines of its own borders."

"You propose using nuclear weapons, marketed by us, to circumvent the major power control?" Oldham asked.

"It would be a beginning," Franz answered. "There would be two results. First, the countries or groups to whom we sold the nuclear material would have advantage over their immediate adversaries and would, no doubt, use it to hasten the evolutionary survival of the stronger. Second, we would be the new power broker in the immediate changed environment since we were the Prometheus who passed nuclear fire to the mortals."

"Tenuous, Franz. Tenuous. We might suffer the same fate as the original Prometheus and have an American or Soviet Zeus chain us to a cliff for a liver plucking," St. Jacques countered.

"But the advantages of securing that type of influence in developing nations for our personal interests are substantial. We depend on power to develop and advance...some corporations use bribery to gain financial advantage...here we have a unique means."

"You've opened a broad topic for consideration, indeed, Franz," Vargas interrupted. "It will require consideration on the same plane as the careful selection of clients to receive the material we provide. A moderating factor in this discussion is the level of technology we provided the recipient to build a weapon or weapons with the Plutonium or Uranium. There are balances we can apply to keep the client under control. All of this will have to be worked out, but do I hear a consensus on my proposal?"

The brief discussion around the table was skillfully turned to acceptance of a general outline of the proposal. Ernesto's forethought in bringing the three men into his confidence before the meeting paid off. With only Albritton and Tran dissenting, the decision was made to proceed with development of an operational concept.

"I nominate Franz to head the planning group," Vargas offered after the vote. "With his grasp of the scope of this undertaking, he should ensure our success."

"I second," Langaard added.

The vote was unanimous and Franz Heitzman took charge of what the board chose to call "Operation Prometheus." In the weeks ahead, he would be responsible for selection of the target plant, recruitment and training of a select team of men for the operation, and development of a master plan.

Cleave Jones grunted as he heaved his bulk up against the high vertical wall, grasping the top plank and hauling his chest over the edge. Even in the cool, still afternoon air, perspiration streamed over his ebony body. There were two obstacles remaining before him in this seemingly endless infiltration course that had been hacked out of the forest.

"Gawddamn you, bastid," he cursed as he dropped free on the other side, scraping a wallet-sized chunk of skin from his rib cage against the crudely hewn logs. He paused momentarily to catch his breath before attempting the water barrier to his front and stood with legs spread, chest heaving as he rubbed a sweaty forearm over the bleeding patch of flesh.

Ed Moran, up ahead of him, had finished traversing the precarious forty-five-foot handwalk dangling under the overhead rope. Had he dropped off, it would have been a forty-foot fall into the water below. Behind him, Cleave could hear Pete Alexander straining to top the wall. He sucked a final deep chestful of air and forced his burning legs to propel him toward the pit.

"Come on, legs...come on, lungs...come on, Jones! Just a little longer." Cleave was reaching the same point of near exhaustion experienced by the men who had preceded him through the course today. This physical toughening of the team was a crucial part of the training program they had found here at base camp upon their arrival one week before.

The narrow trail, cut years before, had been converted into the team's commando-style obstacle course in the highlands northeast of Brasilia. Dense upland forest with trees shooting a hundred feet into the air blocked out the sky. The heavy layers of foliage screening out the sunlight left the men in constant, monotonous gloom under a leafy, green overcast. Tangled vines laced and draped throughout the overhead branches while thick ferns and saplings crowded underneath. Nearby, an abandoned mining camp had been reconditioned to serve as the training site for what was known as "Task Force Prometheus."

The camp was deserted in the early '60s and the vegetation had crept back over the long, low wooden buildings. Of eight original buildings, arranged in a rough rectangle around a partially cleared central area, only four were in use. The interiors of these four had been rebuilt to make them comfortable and functional, yet the camp retained its overgrown, decaying appearance. To a casual aerial observer, flying over this remote region, inspection would reveal only the forest reclaiming abandoned structures.

It had taken Franz Heitzman five months to put together the necessary elements for the operation. This camp and the training of the team would be the last phase prior to execution of the plan. He had worked closely with Ernesto as he selected a target plant and prepared a means of attacking it, and, with those elements under consideration, established criteria for the team of men he would need to carry out the operation.

Immediately after the São Paulo conference, he had spent three weeks poring over the documentation that Vargas's staff had gathered. The two men spent long evenings at the sprawling mansion Vargas maintained on the outskirts of São Paulo, seeking the key to the storehouse of Plutonium. One afternoon in February, Franz was working at a table on the colonnaded inner patio when he began to put the concept into a workable form.

"Ernesto," he called, "here it is, right before us, and I didn't see it before." Vargas arose from the lounge chair where he had been reading an involved Nuclear Regulatory Commission report on safety violations at various plants and leaned over the other's shoulder.

"Look." Franz pointed to his page of handwritten notes. "The elements are basically quite simple. First, the weakness that is stressed in all of the reports is an inability to defend against terrorist attack. They fear the terrorists, so we give them terrorists."

"You mean recruit some of our clients to do the job?"

"No. That would be too risky. We could not trust them. We will only give the impression of being terrorists. We have to put it in a context the government understands; and with their fears, they have already done the job for us."

"Good, that is reasonable."

"The reason they fear the terrorists is the radical's willingness to die in pursuit of a politically motivated goal and of the damage that could be done by the terrorists if they were to destroy a nuclear power plant or to steal nuclear material. Therefore, they would assume theft to be the immediate motive, if the raid were a quick one, and the only mission to seize fissionable material to be used in building a bomb." He shuffled through a file of clippings. "Here, look at these articles and editorials. They all mention the ease with which a terrorist group could build a relatively simple but very destructive nuclear device."

Vargas glanced through the clippings as Heitzman continued. "Since theft is our mission, we will not arouse their fear of possible seizure of the material, but will publicly stress the destruction of the plant."

"Destroy the plant?"

"Only threaten to destroy it. The NRC fears the release of radioactive materials into the atmosphere and the tremendous damage it would do to the surrounding area, particularly if it were an important metropolitan sector of the country—industrial population center, you know."

Vargas straightened up, replacing the clippings on the table. "So we are a band of terrorists who seize a nuclear power plant and threaten to destroy it. What is our reason for doing this and how does it help us to secure the Plutonium?"

Heitzman thought for a moment and swiveled in his chair to face Vargas. "It has to be a good cover for the real intent. Something that will keep the authorities off balance and busy while we loot the storage facility."

"You're not talking about a quick raid then, are you?"

"Not necessarily. If we could seize control of a plant, we could bargain with them, just as kidnappers bargain for the return of a hostage. As long as we threatened to destroy it, they wouldn't dare challenge us."

"Well, what about a ransom?" Vargas suggested. "We would have a hostage worth more than a mere human life. Look at some of the ransoms that the Tupamaros have pulled in with their kidnappings of executives. What was it, fourteen million dollars for Samuelson, the Exxon executive, in Argentina?"

"I believe so," Heitzman answered. "This will have to be a steep one. An amount worthy of the prize."

"And one that would make the government uncomfortable," Vargas added.

Franz wrote quickly on his notepad as Vargas talked, then nodded agreement. "That may be the answer. We can work on the amount later, but I think we have hit on an idea." He leaned back in his chair and closed his eyes, "The power plant is seized by a group of terrorists who threaten to destroy it and create a nuclear disaster if their ransom demand is not met. How does that sound, Mr. President of the United States?"

Vargas grinned broadly and answered in a deep, affected voice, "Senhor terrorist, I would be most willing to deal with you; but in light of your act, which I fear very much, I have arranged to have myself overthrown and placed in immediate exile so I won't have to face this crisis or the impending disaster. My successor will deal with you while I view the catastrophe from another country." He roared with laughter and slapped Heitzman on the shoulder. "Not only will we have the Plutonium, my friend, but a tidy profit as well."

"He might wish to run, Ernesto, but he, the President, was just elected and has four years to wait before he can escape the responsibility of decision. We might just make him wish he had been defeated." Heitzman looked around the patio, "Where is Juanito? I could use a beer."

Vargas clapped his hands and a servant in white jacket and black trousers appeared from the arched entrance to the main house. "Beers and a plate of spareribs."

"Look at this map of the existing plants which use or store weapons quality material," Franz said. "There are only four plants which are near enough to a major metropolitan area to fit our criteria and just one fast breeder variety that qualifies."

Vargas walked over to the table and studied the map of the United States, with the clear plastic overlay indicating locations of nuclear power plants. "Where is the breeder site?"

Heitzman pointed to a red reactor symbol near the border of Pennsylvania and Ohio. "Here at a small town called Bartonsville. It is only thirty-two miles west of Pittsburgh. What could be better with the industrial concentration in that city?"

"Hmm-m-m, it is a relatively new plant."

Heitzman flipped through the pages of his Nuclear Regulatory Commission index of operational plants until he found the Bartonsville entry. "Here it is." He read through the notation, "It was one of the first operational reactors in the United States. Began in 1961, then in 1973, it was converted by the corporation to a pilot fast breeder reactor, came under power in late 1975, and has been in use since that time." He skipped down the entry then stopped. "This should also interest you. It is used as a storage site for Special Nuclear Material: bomb quality Plutonium." He paused. "I wonder if this is one of the sites which was written up in that General Accounting Office report on lack of security for special material?"

"Could be. I can have my people research it. We still have some good contacts in the regulatory commission who could be tapped for the information."

"Excellent. I'll write down the information we need and you can have it padded with some innocuous queries."

Juanito reappeared with a tray bearing two Pilsners and a platter of lean ribs, dripping with barbecue sauce.

"So, we proceed," Vargas said, taking a rib. "I had a question about the terrorist concept."

"What about it?" Franz asked.

"Do you propose to create the impression of a national terrorist organization or an international one? For example, the . . . what do they call themselves . . . Weathermen? Weather Underground? Or perhaps, the black militant groups? Those organizations as opposed to the Black September or Japanese Red Army? You remember the Red Army group at Lod Airport? What a slaughter that was."

Franz took a sip of the beer that Juanito placed in front of him. "I think an international group would have the greater effect since they frequently have established their willingness to die for a political goal. How many of their people have died while killing hostages or bystanders? Lod, you mentioned; München and the Israeli athletes. It would clearly establish a threat to do the same in this case."

Vargas nodded. "In addition, they have capabilities beyond those of the locals. For the sake of creating a realistic threat, it will have to be an internationally based terrorist operation: a group of trained, ruthless, and fanatically dedicated revolutionists who are willing to die for their cause." He repeated the last phrase to himself. "It has a nice ring to it. Trained, ruthless, fanatically dedicated—it would frighten even me."

"A logical extension, Ernesto. We will exploit every

fear and weakness we can find to make this operation successful—use every contradiction in their system against them. Each gap we find in their defenses gives us that much more of an advantage."

Four months later, on a cloudy June seventeenth, five French-model Alouette helicopters changed pitch on their props and flared for a landing, settling one after another into the rectangular clearing that now served as a chopper pad for the base camp. Singularly and in pairs, sixteen men swung out of the nylon passenger seats and dropped lightly to the ground. Their sport trousers, long-sleeved shirts, and pullover sweaters marked them as civilians, but the conditioned manner in which they moved swiftly away from the craft, eyes scanning the surrounding vegetation, betrayed their profession.

Lee Zimmerman, whipcord tough six-footer, and Vince DeAngelo, lean, olive skinned, and menacing, were the first off. They walked in a crouch outside the radius of the still turning rotor blades. Both men carried their small duffel bags as easily as they would M-16 rifles.

"I thought we were in Brazil," DeAngelo said as his sharp gaze swept around the clearing. "Damn if this doesn't look like the Central Highlands."

"Could be, Vince," Zimmerman agreed. "Makes you feel right at home doesn't it?" They stopped at the edge of the cleared area and dropped their bags, waiting for the remainder of the team to join them. Lee pointed to the delapidated and overgrown structures around them. "Doesn't look like anyone has pulled ash and trash detail around here for quite awhile. Damn barracks are pretty sad—can't be more than the vines holdin' them up."

The two buildings immediately to their front were standing only because of their sturdiness in original construction. The single pane windows on either side of the doorless entrance were covered with slashed and hanging wire screen that had, at one time, blocked out insects. The single wooden shutter, hinged at the top of the window, was propped open with a stick jutting outward from the lower sill. On the nearer building, both shutters lay rotting in tall grass.

The stoops just in front of the doorways were decayed

and broken, with creepers pushing their way through the molding boards. From the few curling remnants and cracked patches under the overhanging roof, you could see that the low, wide buildings had been painted at one time. Rain gutters, which had guided fresh water into cement crocks at the front of the buildings, lay twisted and rusting alongside them. The tin roof on the far building had entire sections peeled away from peak to edge, revealing the rotting beams inside. The gaping darkness of the side windows was laced with a vibrant green of vines and creepers roaming along the length of the building.

"And I used to bitch about the enlisted barracks at Bragg," Zimmerman muttered, surveying the disintegration. He felt a hand on his shoulder and turned to see a head of straight black hair and beneath it, the grinning, darkly tanned face.

"Rey Sanchez!" He grabbed the outstretched hand. "You wetback son of a bitch, I haven't seen you since we split at Tan Son Nhut. How in the hell are you?"

The shorter man shrugged his muscular shoulders, continuing to pump Zimmerman's hand. "Hangin' in, man. I thought I saw you boarding the lead chopper, but I wasn't sure. You lookin' good."

Zimmerman returned the grin, delighted to see a fellow NCO from his old unit. They dropped the handshake and Zimmerman punched Rey playfully on the shoulder. "Hey, I thought you were putting in twenty. What're you doing here?"

"Aw, it wasn't the same after we got back to Bragg. Bunch of us from Fifth Group got shipped over to the Eighty-Deuce to fill out their quota of NCOs. I couldn't handle all the Mickey Mouse bullshit and couldn't get back to Forces on a bet. It was nothin' but a hassle and I got into a couple of scrapes. Got hit with a Summary and lost a stripe, so I decided to hang it up while I had some ass left."

Zimmerman shook his head gravely, "Yeah, I heard they were splitting up the NCOs and farming them out to other units. What a bunch of shit."

While they were talking, the other men had gathered in

a loose group around them. At the helicopters, behind them, John LeCourt checked to ensure all equipment had been off-loaded and waved to the pilot, crouching as the rotors increased speed and bits of grass and debris flew around him. The choppers were lifting off for the return trip to Rio as LeCourt strode to the front of the gathered team.

His near six foot height was accentuated by tightly corded muscles, yet his movements were smooth and fluid, those of a natural athlete. His sandy-brown hair was cut neatly short without being a crew cut and his slightly angular face with its regular features would have been considered average until you saw his eyes and the set of his jawline. LeCourt's eyes were an unfathomable gray-green color that could glint with a chill or soften to reflect a usually hidden reservoir of warmth. His strong jaw gave indication of the sense of command and leadership he had displayed throughout his career. There was a weathered parchment texture to his finely lined skin that came from too many days and nights exposed to the elements on forgotten outposts.

He squared away in front of the men and had their immediate attention. "I'm John LeCourt, team leader of this operation." His voice was pitched low but carried over the sound of the disappearing helicopters. "Most of you don't know me yet, but I know all of you, at least on paper. We're going to spend the next six weeks together preparing for an operation which all of us volunteered for. It's going to be a hard six weeks and a tricky operation, but all of you have been there before. That's why you were selected." He paused, looking at the intent faces in the group. It was a familiar feeling for him, a good feeling.

"This camp was prepared for us and all that we need in the way of equipment and supplies has been provided. We'll run our own training program; there's no need for anyone to hold your hands on something like this. I have the master training schedule which we will implement and I will judge how much effort has to be put in to fulfill its requirements. On that point, let me assure you that whatever level of effort is necessary, we will be ready to go in six weeks."

He looked at his clipboard before proceeding, "All right, as far as organization, we'll break into two seven-man squads. We'll all train and pull details based on that breakdown. DeAngelo." He looked directly at Vince.

"Yes, sir," DeAngelo stepped forward automatically.

"Sergeant Major, you'll be my field first-soldier."

"Yes, sir," DeAngelo responded, immediately accepting his normal role as senior NCO. Just like putting on an old, comfortable pair of shoes.

"Miller and Moran will be squad leaders. The rest of the breakdown is on this roster." He handed the list to DeAngelo. "When you get the assignments, get your gear and move into that far building." He pointed to one of the reconditioned structures across the clearing. "The outside appearance is intentionally deceiving, but you'll find the interiors quite adequate. Once you're squared away, I want to see you, DeAngelo, and the squad leaders in my alcove." He looked over the faces once again. "Any questions?" There were none. "Okay, Sergeant Major, take over."

LeCourt bent quickly and picked up his duffel bag, walking off toward the designated building. DeAngelo caught himself starting to salute and then realized it wasn't necessary.

The four buildings that Franz had readied for them were on three sides of the chopper pad. The team hut in front of LeCourt was paired with one of the run-down shacks. To his left was the administration building and classroom combination, again alongside one of the overgrown shells. To his rear, directly across the clearing and under heavy overhanging tree cover, the supply hut and mess hall occupied both of the buildings. Obviously Franz felt the camouflage was adequate to use the two, side by side. To the right were the final two abandoned shacks. LeCourt paused to admire the job that had been done to provide secrecy for their training.

The only people in this remote area were Indian tribesmen who rarely came this far into the mountains,

and an infrequent overflight by an aircraft would disturb
nothing. The main entrance and exit from the huts would
be through the rear doors from now on, allowing them to
use freely the pathways that had been cut between the huts
under the thick foliage. All of their movements and
training would be invisible to an observer. The only time
the camp would be pinpointed would be during the arrival
and departure of the helicopters. Franz had assured him
that unless an emergency arose, the choppers would serve
to bring him in for the technical briefings and, at the end
of the six weeks, to lift them all out. Two more trips and
the last didn't matter. They'd be finished by then.

He reached the team hut and stepped onto the rotting
porch. It was surprisingly firm under his light tread; then
he noticed the new planks braced underneath the rotted
exterior. They even thought to darken the new boards so
they wouldn't reflect in the sunlight that penetrated the
clearing, he noted to himself.

He pushed through a new screen door that had been
cleverly hung inside the old door frame, and stepped into
the building. The long, open-ceilinged room smelled of
freshly sawed wood and citronella. Dark wire mesh had
been nailed over all the windows and swinging wooden
shutters installed on the inside to be closed when
necessary to protect against a rainstorm.

As he walked down the middle aisle, he glanced at each
of the partitioned alcoves with its wooden bunk bed,
footlocker, small wooden table, clothes rack, and chair.
There were eight alcoves along each side, with the last two
slightly larger than the others. LeCourt and Vince
DeAngelo would take the end alcoves since the burden of
administering the camp would fall to them. Each of their
alcoves had a larger table with three chairs and a narrow,
upright bookcase.

Once in front of his bunk, he dropped his duffel bag
and placed the clipboard on his table, then he sat in one of
the straight-backed chairs, leaning back to test its
balance. He rocked forward and lifted the lid of the
footlocker, checking its contents. In the tray were toilet
articles, safety razor, blades, shaving cream, toothpaste,

toothbrush, everything. Several bottles of insect repellant lay in the middle section, and a stack of olive drab handkerchiefs in the far section.

He lifted the tray out and saw the neat pile of O.D. towels in one corner. The rest would be filled with the clothing and equipment they would draw from the supply room later. He closed the lid and turned to his canvas bag, unzipping it and lifting out the few personal items they had been allowed to bring with them.

Franz had specified that there was to be nothing that would link them to their country of origin and no memorabilia, since they would be taking nothing out with them. LeCourt pulled out sets of underwear and placed them carefully on the bunk, to be stored later. His Randall knife, handmade for him almost fifteen years before, went on the table, and under a layer of paperback volumes of classics, his hand hit a piece of wood. He fumbled until it pulled free. The dark mahogany tone of the desk plaque was interrupted by the carved block letters of his name in its center, JOHN M. LeCOURT. To the left, the silver lieutenant colonel's leaf was set into a square recess. At the other end, the proud crossed rifles of Infantry Branch were in a similar notch.

LeCourt turned the wedge-shaped block in his fingers, studying the insignia and allowing himself a moment of retrospection. The years this name plaque had seen . . . the rank . . . changing it on the plaque each time he had been promoted. The battles it had seen him go out to fight . . . Korea . . . Laos . . . Vietnam . . . and had been there watching when he came back whole . . . or bloodied. The men . . . Harry Adams, his Exec in '68 when Tet hit . . . never even got to bring his body out after they finally fought their way clear of the NVA in that damn valley north of Plei Mrong. Damn, Harry, I'm sorry, we should have brought you with us . . . knew there wouldn't be anything left when we went back through. The "Yards" they'd trained . . . stocky little bastards . . . Jarai, Banakei, Sedang . . . they'd fight their way barehanded through a corral of tigers for us . . . and we left them there. These were his ghosts that wouldn't rest . . . the men he'd lost,

even though he'd kept more of them alive ... the promises
he'd broken to a simple and trusting Montagnard
ally ... not of his own volition, but because he had no
control over the outcome. Earlier ones from Korea ... the
long retreat, the fight back to the 38th and, then, the
Chinese. The bargaining at a conference table while his
men bled and died over hills that would be given away
with a signature on a piece of paper. Always that
omnipotent voice of higher command ... "in taking your
objective you can expect to suffer twenty percent
casualties ..." bring them in afterward, some on litters,
some wrapped in ponchos ... statistics for a briefing. And
then the higher voice that says "The situation dictates
withdrawal from our present positions and relocation of
our main effort to the west ..." Pull off the ridge, kick
some dirt over the bloody splotches on the ground where
one of your buddies was two nights ago and hit another
hill mass ... follow me, men ... I only know what I'm
doing from day to day.

He focused on the worn metal emblems embedded
over his name. The Trojan Horse of the Tenth Special
Forces Group, his first assignment with S.F. in the '50s.
Bad Tölz ... the Hofbräu in München ... the Zugspitz
and those first ski lessons. His facial muscles relaxed
slightly as he pictured the white peaks and the laughing
camaraderie between the officers and NCOs as they tried
to master the awkward cross-country skis.

Next to the silver horse was the dagger and crossed
arrow crest of Special Forces with its bold motto,
"De Oppresso Liber." We tried, damnit, he thought
bitterly; you couldn't have asked more from a group of
men. If only someone had understood what they were
sending us to do and had found the guts to back us up
when we tried to do it.

Enough of this. He'd brought it with him and this is
where he'd leave it. This would be the last chapter in a
career that this worn piece of wood symbolized. Looking
back on it ... this, retirement pay, and a thousand nights
of memories were about all that was left of all those years.

John was placing the name plaque on his bookcase

when the men entered the building. DeAngelo designated a side for each squad and waited to ensure that all were settled before walking to his alcove.

He dropped his bag on the footlocker and stood, facing LeCourt. "Squads are set, Colonel. They shouldn't take too long to put away what little they've got with them."

"That's good. I want first squad to pull mess detail and second to take care of supply issue. Make sure everyone gets two blankets. It gets cold up here at night. You can set up a rotating duty roster to handle the necessary details for the training period and post it in the morning." He checked his watch. "It's 1438 now. We should have equipment and clothing issued by 1530. That will leave first squad until 1830 to prepare the mess hall and kitchen for the meal."

"Do you have the training schedule worked out yet, Sir, or should I get to work on it?" DeAngelo asked.

"I've got the master, to include our menus for the next six weeks. All we have to do is break it down into daily schedules. When Miller and Moran get here, I'll go over all of it with you."

"Roger that." DeAngelo grinned. "Makes it a lot easier."

"We're going to need all the breaks we can get, Sergeant Major. You'll understand what I mean when you get a look at our training. Go ahead and get your things put away. We'll talk later."

DeAngelo quickly stored his personal items and made a brief inspection of the quarters. He found a crate of cardboard encased Coleman-type lanterns that would provide the necessary light in the absence of electricity. He distributed one lantern to each two alcoves and brought one each for himself and LeCourt. Blackout curtains were provided and could be drawn to ensure that no light would be visible outside the shuttered windows at night.

Meanwhile, Tony Miller and Ed Moran had joined the team leader in his wood frame alcove. Miller, a brawny, easy-going ex-Air Commando, had eased his heavy frame onto one of the wooden chairs near the aisle and hunched forward with elbows resting on his knees. He had a layer of almost bleached blond hair that hung over his forehead and a boyish grin that flashed a perfect set of teeth across his wide face. He had a disarmingly casual air, but the former UCLA lineman had established himself early as a tough performer who took great pleasure in knocking down opponents. This aggressiveness carried into the air force where it was tempered with a coolness under stress and tested by his penchant for finding tight situations. In the elite Air Commandos, flying everything from converted World War II B-26s on paddy-level strafing runs to overloaded C-123s on supply runs to beleaguered outposts, he found challenge, excitement, and satisfaction.

Beside him, Ed Moran looked smaller than his compact five-foot, ten-inch height. His hawkish face and severe crewcut were set on an unusually broad pair of shoulders that tapered down to a narrow waist. He was nearly LeCourt's age, but had begun as a Private First Class, a rifleman in Korea. Serving with the 187th Regimental Combat Team, he had been promoted to Sergeant E-6, when a heavy engagement in the summer of 1951, just south of the "Punchbowl," resulted in the loss or wounding of his company's officers. Those NCOs who were able, took command and Ed found himself leading his platoon. He was awarded the Silver Star for gallantry, and upon return to the United States, found that he was recommended for Officer Candidate School. He came out of it a second lieutenant, still relatively new to the army, but already a combat leader. He'd made captain when he took the first tour in Vietnam. In his first weeks in the field, he proved that Korea wasn't a one-time flash as the company of Vietnamese Rangers he advised found the tiger-suited American tough and imperturbable in combat. He came out of Vietnam after two tours with decorations for gallantry and meritorious service; a Purple Heart with two clusters was small compensation for the fourteen pints of blood and 188 stitches that went into putting back together what three separate wounds had done to him; he came back with commendations for his leadership, ability, maturity, and professional excellence...but he came back a captain. Ed Moran hadn't met the educational requirements for field grade promotion and when they started cutting through the overage of captains after Vietnam wore down, Ed Moran was riffed. There was little humor left in him, and he seemed to take on each task in his life as if he were trying to prove he was as good or better than the next man.... he usually was.

LeCourt could see the end product of Franz's talent hunt to assemble a team capable of executing his plan, but had no idea of the factors that had brought them together. The human element had been of greater concern to Franz than any other. The mechanics of selecting a target and devising a suitable method of attacking it were mere analytical exercises. With proper intelligence gathering and some technical advice, that was accomplished. Nevertheless, all would be wasted if there were a mistake in the selection and recruitment of the men who would be entrusted to carry the plan to its conclusion. Even the most routine surgical procedure, if carried out by an incompetent, Franz had reasoned, could prove fatal.

Once he and Vargas had established that the Bartonsville plant was to be the target, Franz instructed two of his assistants to leave for Washington, D.C., and complete the required intelligence gathering on the plant and the Bartonsville area.

In addition, Ernesto had assigned a top aide to research the state and federal machinery that could be employed to thwart Prometheus. Within the tangled maze of the American government, he knew there existed agencies and organizations whose resources would be brought to bear against them. He and Franz first had to know their enemy and to understand his weaknesses before they could attack him.

By mid-March, the reports were arriving at the villa. Franz had spent the interim period reading all documents, reports, minutes of hearings, and newspaper and magazine articles pertaining to nuclear power in the United States. His looseleaf notebook was swollen with pages of his precise script, some lines printed in heavy block lettering when he found an item of particular significance. This background material was of tremendous import in his planning, even though it was from open sources, available to anyone.

He and Ernesto were seated in the paneled library examining the Xerox copies of Bartonsville's reactor cooling system. The table at which they were working was one of the pieces of eighteenth-century baroque colonial artistry that Ernesto favored. Its elaborate inlay of woods, ivory, and mother-of-pearl expressed the exuberance of the period in which it was crafted, a time of elegance that Vargas had recreated in the furnishing of his private rooms.

Heitzman had been comparing the designs of the plant's cooling system with similar ones from his notebook. He pushed the open folder across the table to Vargas, pointing at pages taken from an International Atomic Energy Agency information booklet.

"Look at that schematic," he indicated a diagram of a typical liquid-metal cooled fast breeder reactor. "Exactly what we have at Bartonsville. The discussion here on the danger of contamination from the activated sodium coolant is most revealing."

Vargas compared the papers and looked up, "You have already formulated a plan for inclusion of this cooling system into the destruction threat?" He slid the notebook back across the table.

"A crucial part of the sequence." Heitzman flipped forward in the folder to a red tab and read from his notes. "The core disruptive accident consists of several separate and distinct system failures. First, failure of the control rods to adequately regulate the rate of fission. Second, failure of the primary cooling system to maintain safe operating temperatures in the core. Third, failure of the emergency backup systems to correct the conditions created by the first two failures. Finally, failure of the containment vessels to suppress expulsion of the radionuclides, fission products, and aerosols into the atmosphere." Franz glanced up. "There are additional gaseous isotopes which would be released, creating further contamination."

"This 'maximum credible accident,' this is what we are threatening to create?" Vargas asked.

"Precisely. In the extended discussions and verbal battles over these plants, the Nuclear Regulatory Commission has not only told us what elements constitute the greatest threat to plant safety; they have carefully explained, in numerous documents and in great detail, exactly what measures the industry has instituted to prevent such an occurrence." Franz smiled, leaning back in his chair and spreading his arms expansively. "All we must do is take the thread where they have dropped it and unravel their work. We neutralize their emergency systems and initiate the required failures to produce the dreaded 'maximum credible accident.' Neat, achievable, and terrifying."

He sat forward again, gesturing with a finger toward Vargas. "There is another benefit to be derived from all of this paper that has come out about nuclear safety, the editorials, the hearings and reports; all have kept the threat before the eyes of the American people. They are the spectators in the drama we will unfold before them, as well as potential victims. Marighella taught that terrorism preys on the psychology of the spectator. The taint of fear is already spreading under the surface and we will use that preparation to our advantage."

"How far do you intend to go in creating this accident? We need the Plutonium, not the responsibility for destroying the plant." Vargas had felt growing concern over the amount of time Heitzman had devoted to meticulously structuring a sequence of actions that would cause the actual destruction of the plant and subsequent release of radiation. With all the intelligence gathered by the staff, Franz now needed to apply his theory to the actual site.

"Aha! You show a degree of uncertainty regarding my intentions." Franz laughed. "Perfect, Ernesto. If you, knowing what I intend, find it disconcerting, then God help the Americans!" He was instantly serious. "Don't you see? The credibility of the entire threat hinges on the degree to which they believe we are actually willing to carry it out. It follows, then, that what we threaten to do must be feasible in a technical sense." Heitzman shrugged. "For example, I am willing to blow up the plant and myself with it, but I intend to do it by flushing dynamite down the toilet while I am aboard. The threat is there, but it is improperly executed. All I would do is wreck a toilet and my own posterior."

Vargas understood. "So you have created a plan which could truly result in the destruction of the facility and the team we send in will perform all the preparatory maneuvers, short of setting it off."

"And those in authority on the outside," Franz broke in, "would incorrectly evaluate our motivation and assume that the men are, in fact, willing to die for their cause. This will be strengthened by their assessment of our plan for accomplishing the deed... when their experts find that the preparations are adequate to do exactly what we threaten. You see how the parts fit together?"

"You are certain that the government won't call the bluff? What happens if they tell us to go ahead with it?"

"Never fear, Ernesto. The stakes are too high for them to take that chance. I've built the scenario to bring maximum pressure to bear on whoever is unfortunate enough to make the decision; probably the President himself. You'll see, as this comes clear, what a mousetrap I've built."

"I congratulate you, my friend. It appears as if you need only introduce the date and shake it about with your theories to give us our operation." Vargas poured sherry for both of them from a cut crystal decanter.

Franz accepted the glass and touched it to Vargas's. "Salud." "Prosit." The two men relaxed in the velvet curves of their chairs, sipping the fine golden palo Cortado.

"As I bring the elements of this operation together," Franz said, almost too softly for Vargas to hear, "I have yet the most difficult task facing me."

"Still the most difficult?" Vargas leaned forward slightly to hear. "What is that?"

"The men, Ernesto. The team that will carry out the orders we will give."

"What is so difficult about picking a team? We have ample talent within the organization to choose from," Vargas suggested.

"No, I disagree. Our men have talents which are valuable in the armament business. Some are quite capable men, but I envision something different." Franz folded his hands in front of his chest and stared across the room at one of the massive marble busts that occupied niches along the wall of books. "First and most radical of my proposals is that they be Americans."

"Americans!" Vargas blurted. "We do not have that many who could be used."

"They won't be our men until the operation. I plan to recruit them specifically for it."

"But why pick men we don't already know?" Vargas asked.

"I want them to know nothing more about us than I choose to tell them. Should something unforeseeable happen and any of them be captured, I want no direct links to the organization."

"Wise."

"Second, they will be dealing with American authorities and, as Americans, would be better able to judge the psychological state of the authorities. Should any decisions have to be made on the spot, a capable American could evaluate the reaction required better than we."

"Valid also, Franz, but where will you find them? Or to go to the beginning, what type of men are you seeking?"

Franz pondered for a moment. "I wrote down the characteristics I wanted. Not many, you understand, just the principal ones—a skeleton on which I could hang critical attributes and technical skills until I had fleshed him out."

"Well, what did you decide?"

"Discipline. A sense of personal control and response to command. Maturity. That inner maturity that comes from experiencing and surviving hardship. Loyalty. Not the broad nationalistic loyalty with its anthems and waving flags, but the gut loyalty of one man for another, of a man for his leader. Finally, the ability to function well and effectively under extreme stress. This can only come from experience, from the test of fire that either tempers a man to steel or reduces him to brittle fragments. These are the essential foundation blocks."

"When you talk of discipline and command, it could mean only one thing. I hope I am mistaken," Ernesto said.

"The men I am after are not presently in the military. They are the discards, the disillusioned, the men who have all the qualities and talents without the obligation to serve. These are the men that will make up Prometheus."

"You'll use Bernie's contacts to obtain whatever files are necessary to make the choice, I suppose," Vargas said. "There were thousands of men released from the service in the troop reductions after the withdrawal from Indochina, and certainly a good number of them have been unable to make a satisfactory transition to the role of civilian."

"Not only those who have had difficulty adjusting, Ernesto. I will seek out those who were thrust into the civilian community before they chose to go, those who left the military dissatisfied and angry, those who were forced out for various reasons. Their skills are intact, but their sense of dedication to cause has been erased. I will provide them with both a cause, self-enrichment and self-gain, and the opportunity to once again operate in a familiar capacity, that of a commando."

Within three days, Franz had completed his overall plan presentation and by April third, it had been approved by the board. As soon as he received confirmation that the organization had agreed to his concept of the operation, Franz alerted Alec Rettler, a trusted man who was already in the United States at work on the selection process.

Franz had decided to limit his search to former

members of the special counter-insurgency forces. By doing so, he reduced the number of men considered, while virtually guaranteeing that each man considered would have the desirable characteristics. In addition, their training and experience in Indochina would assure military skills and discipline beyond those of the average soldier.

After locating six men on the continent who had been either in Special Forces, Navy Seal Teams, or Air Commandos, Rettler's associates interrupted the men's modest "Military Advisor for Hire" operation long enough to pay them a week's salary for producing the names of seventy-four former teammates. Rettler had carefully specified that the men were to be between the grades of E-6 and E-9, in order to obtain a high level of experience.

Albritton's contacts in the government paid off as they were able to obtain computer records from personnel offices of the army, navy, and air force relating to the seventy-four men. Alec immediately sent copies of the personnel files to Heitzman. When word of the board's approval reached Franz, he had narrowed the list to thirty-seven prospective members of Prometheus. His signal to Rettler initiated the first actual meetings with the men.

Aside from the NCOs on the team, Franz had outlined duties for four officers, one of whom would act as team leader. Albritton had again been of assistance in securing contacts among active duty personnel at Fort Bragg, Eglin Air Force Base, and Little Creek, Virginia, where the chosen units trained. By simple elicitation of information over drinks at the various officers' clubs, screening bits of information about individuals from the war stories that were being traded, names of fifteen officers were gathered and their files secured. Franz had only to review the material and send a list of ten men to Rettler.

On April thirtieth, John LeCourt sat in a corner booth of the dimly lit Down Under Tavern, a roadhouse on the outskirts of Raleigh, North Carolina. Travel posters on the Masonite paneled walls advertised the koala bear, wallaby, white sand beaches, and Sydney skyline of Quantas Airlines' vacation land. The owner and barkeep was, as everything about the tavern indicated, a transplant from his native Australia.

LeCourt had barely gotten his first beer when Alec walked up to the table and introduced himself. The man was well dressed, but so average in appearance that he would have been difficult to describe had he left immediately. Alec was of medium height and build with a pleasant, oval face and absolutely no distinguishing features. John immediately pictured him as one of the intentionally featureless special agents that the CIA and FBI seem to recruit by the hundreds. Alec ordered a Schlitz and chatted for a few minutes about Fort Bragg, Special Forces, and a number of men with whom LeCourt had served. He sensed the suspicion behind LeCourt's replies, but had expected it and continued to touch on topics familiar to the man.

John knew that the meeting hadn't been arranged to trade gossip about mutual acquaintances; nevertheless, he was willing to let Alec take the lead in conversation until he discovered the real purpose, at least for the present.

As they talked, Alec made rapid mental notes. LeCourt seemed completely at ease, sipping his beer and adding enough to the conversation to keep it going without really saying anything. He was waiting, Alec realized, without impatience, for the preliminaries to end. He knew LeCourt was sizing him up and was surprised that he felt uncomfortable under the man's penetrating gaze. It was the obvious calm assurance that surrounded the man; his confidence that whatever this situation was, he would control it.

Franz had chosen three possible leaders for the operation and reduced the three to John LeCourt after Alec had observed them. There was no doubt that LeCourt could handle the job. It was Alec's task to recruit him.

"Colonel LeCourt, you're aware that I asked to meet you here for more than drinking beer and B.S."

"I suspected there was more. I've got enough insurance and I don't want to sell it, if that helps," LeCourt said.

"No insurance. I do have an offer for you, though."

"Fire away." LeCourt shifted his weight on the vinyl-covered seat, sinking down to a more comfortable position.

"I've had access to your military records, so understand that a good deal of research went into your selection." Alec noted a brief flicker of interest that LeCourt quickly masked. "When I say selection, I mean selection to be approached. Nothing happens unless you agree."

"One question, then I'll listen," LeCourt interrupted.

"What's that?"

"Are you government?"

"No. Not U.S. or any other," Rettler replied.

"Okay. Go ahead."

"What I'm authorized to tell you now is bare minimum, but will give you enough to know whether or not you're interested. If it appeals to you, we'll meet again and I'll provide more information." LeCourt sat listening. He gave no response other than to drain his glass of beer.

Alec continued, "There's a relatively involved operation being undertaken and individuals with specific background qualifications are being recruited for it. You're one of the men who was found to be acceptable."

"Hold it a second, will you?" LeCourt broke in. He held up the empty glass. "Another Michelob," he said loudly enough for the barkeep to hear. "How about another for you?"

"Thanks, no. I'm still working on this one."

They waited until John had gotten a fresh beer and poured a glassful. Settling back again, he indicated for Alec to continue.

"This operation will consume no more than one year of your time from beginning to completion. It will require that you leave North Carolina and undergo a training period not unlike some of your Special Forces training. You'll apply the things learned in training during the operation; and afterwards, you'll be free to do as you choose. In return for your participation, there will be a monetary reward which will easily exceed the total salary you made in your entire army career."

There was a look of disbelief on LeCourt's face as he made a rough calculation. "Are you trying to con me? I'd have to be Chairman of the Board of General Motors to make that kind of cash. It's that, or what you want me to do is a lot hairier than you're going to say. Right?"

Alec smiled. "I believe I can safely agree with your assessment. It's a great deal more involved than I can say now, but consider that you'll be financially set for life. When I mentioned that the reward would exceed the sum of your career military pay, I didn't state by how large an amount. When it comes to monetary gain, you'll never have an opportunity like this again."

The two men sat quietly as LeCourt studied the columns of tiny bubbles rising from the sides of his glass and disappearing into the foam. Finally he looked up. "What's your part in this, Rettler; because if you're one of the honchos in it, I'm going to say no."

"Don't do that," Alec replied quickly. "I'm merely a contact man. I told you I was here to provide a basic outline and determine whether or not you were interested. I assure you the offer is valid and your selection was not haphazard."

"Is what you want me to do illegal?" LeCourt asked quietly.

"Yes." Rettler braced for the reaction.

LeCourt eyed the man over the rim of his glass as he rolled it between his fingertips. "I didn't think I'd be making that kind of money doing something honest—spent twenty-two years proving you couldn't make a lot of money. All right, Rettler. What happens if I get caught doing whatever this is? All the money in the world isn't going to do me any good if I'm stored away for the duration."

"The organization doesn't fail when it undertakes a project. You needn't worry about going to jail or even concern yourself with the possibility of being apprehended. I told you before, it's a once in a lifetime shot at everything you've wanted."

LeCourt pondered momentarily. His whole life had been the military and if nothing else, he was a damn good soldier. That was about all though. He had lived to lead men, to charge into combat like some tiger-suited knight, living a quixotic inner role that no one else ever saw, trying to infuse meaning and purpose into the useless slaughter around him.

Vietnam had been the best period of his career and the worst of his life. It had been the culmination of his search for leadership in combat. To compete in an ultimate contest where the prize was life itself. To feel the utter joy of living after seeing death all around him and realizing that time after bloody time, he was still there to see the sun rise, to drink a warm beer, to stand under a jerry-rigged fifty-five gallon drum and take a cold shower . . . finally to go home.

Yeah, finally to go home and find that Karen had been living with an insurance salesman . . . and she was going to marry him. The divorce had been quick and brutal. It still hurt. She had threatened divorce if there was a third tour in 'Nam, but there was no other way. Promotions came easier if you had the credentials and three tours with a good command record should have gotten all the tickets punched.

Karen and the kids gone . . . the loneliness of a second bachelorhood . . . frozen dinners . . . nights in front of the TV set . . . the one-nighters with women whose names and faces he couldn't recall. Then the Pentagon assignment with a thousand other lieutenant colonels, a thousand other green uniforms with the same ribbons, the same goal, the same long corridors to walk with the same staff papers. They'd done a better job of it than he had. His efficiency reports had plummeted and the chance for eagles went down with them.

Then we pulled out of 'Nam and the whole thing fell apart. Passed over for colonel . . . another year pushing papers . . . reviewed and passed over again. Up or out...that's the way it had to be...make room for the hard chargers coming up through the ranks.

His deep-set eyes reflected none of the emotion he felt. He had been marking time, looking for something he couldn't even define. Maybe this was it. He looked squarely at Rettler. "Alec, tell your people that I'm interested. I've got some questions I want answered before I make a final decision, but I'm willing to talk. Is that satisfactory?"

Rettler relaxed noticeably. "I'll relay what you've said and be back in touch with you within two days." He smiled. "I think I'll have that other beer now."

That evening, Alec placed a call to Franz Heitzman in São Paulo, giving him the details of LeCourt's reaction to the proposal. He included LeCourt's remark about declining if Alec were one of the heads of the organization. Franz thought momentarily about the comment and decided to risk a meeting with the potential team leader. LeCourt had to accept and if it required personal contact, Franz was willing to undertake the next meeting.

"Alec, you will book a flight for Colonel LeCourt. Have him schedule a six-day period when his absence will attract minimal attention and get him to Trinidad. We'll see that he gets the rest of the way."

"Should I register him in a hotel?"

"No. Put him in a beach cottage and rent the ones on either side of his. We'll put people in them and cover for his absence. Let me know as soon as arrangements are made."

After he hung up, Franz took out the folders that had been compiled on each man as he accepted the offer to join Prometheus. Miller, the air commando, who would pilot the aircraft during the escape phase; Zimmerman, the demolitions expert; Overmeyer...should be Obermeyer...good Aryan name...the captain with an advanced degree in nuclear physics; Kreutz...another good man...still speaks with a heavy German accent...perfect for communicating with the authorities; Tomlinson and Cooper, the weapons experts...both Special Forces men. Sixteen in all, if LeCourt accepted. He would accept, and Prometheus would have its leader, a man these others would follow.

He glanced at the original list with the men who had been eliminated. Elliot, married; Robinson, disabled...too bad, he was a good man; Lieberman...knew data processing...would have been good to have, but he turned out to be ein Jude...a Jew...he would have been intolerable; Peterson, married; but no matter. The men who had agreed were all superb specimens for the roles they would play. It was only a matter of training them to deal with the specific situation before them.

He carefully tamped tobacco into his aged meerschaum pipe and sat puffing for a moment as he lit it. With LeCourt, the team would consist of professionals, men who had distinguished themselves under the stress of combat, each a craftsman in the art of war. He picked up another folder that had been forwarded by one of Ernesto's men in Pittsburgh. A series of dossiers, each marked "A&T Security Service, Confidential," provided essential background material on the guards assigned to the Bartonsville plant. Franz smiled as he leafed through the papers. The guardians of the plant—mein Gott in Himmel—that they would trust the plant to these men. Most of them should be at home with their grandchildren, not carrying weapons.

The Route 68 exit sign flashed in Sam Waylor's headlights. He glanced down at the dashboard clock, noting that it was nearly 11:45 P.M. Goin' to have to really push to make it tonight, he thought. Shouldn't have stopped for coffee, but seeing Rita was enough to get me through another of these graveyard shifts at the plant. He had left his modest frame house in McKees Rocks, a suburb of Pittsburgh, in plenty of time to make work at the Bartonsville Plant, but the coffee break at the Green Arrow Truck Stop had cost him an extra twenty-five minutes.

As he swung onto the exit road, he was picturing her in his mind. The brunet hair, tied up in a loose bun at the back of her neck, sort of a cruel mouth, like she could take a bite out of you, and that dark red lipstick, like blood. Her boobs pressed out against that white uniform like a couple of grapefruits and she didn't try to keep the cheeks of her ass from jiggling when she walked. Man, that is a chunk of womanhood built for comfort. He felt a tingling in his scrotum as he imagined her hair spread out over a pillow and let his thoughts wander up and down her long, smooth legs, nuzzling the soft inside of her thighs. He reached down, rubbing himself through the crotch of his trousers. Wrap those legs around you and turn you every way but loose.

He was grinning, loose lipped, as familiar countryside sped past in the glare of his lights. There wasn't much traffic as he neared Bartonsville, a small, rural community lying inconspicuously near the tri-border region of Ohio, West Virginia, and Pennsylvania. There were few lights in the town other than street lights and the big overheads around the plant. Things closed down at about nine each night except when there was bingo at the Fire House.

Sam slowed and turned onto Main Street, spotting the town's one police cruiser parked in the Washateria lot. "Must be Benny sittin' there. Probably sound asleep. A traffic cop around here is like fishin' in a mud puddle." He chuckled to himself.

Turn of the century frame houses with their shuttered windows perched comfortably on neatly groomed yards and the street, with its ancient oak and elm guardians, marked the placid age of this community. For years, this little village had blended picturesquely with the hilly, wooded countryside above the Ohio River, like a Grandma Moses painting. Then in 1961, the concrete and steel bulk of a nuclear power plant rose from bulldozer-scarred landscape. With it came contemporary homes in a company development to house plant employees, followed by a shopping center for their convenience. Since that time, Bartonsville had moved, grudgingly, into the nuclear age while keeping one foot anchored firmly in the past.

Sam pulled into the plant parking lot beside the cars of the other security force members. He automatically checked the clock. "Damnit, damnit!" he exclaimed aloud, "Twelve-twenty and me bein' late twice already this week." He climbed out of the car and walked rapidly toward the main gate, checking the other cars as he went. Bennett's green '74 Impala, Joe Zuno's jazzy little red

Fiat, Marascoli's cheap-ass, third-hand Volks and Potter's old Buick were all there.

"Oh Christ," he blurted as he saw Don Ellington's Nova, still parked in its space. "Don's gonna be pissed at me bein' twenty-five minutes late to relieve him. I wish he'd gone on home and let the others cover till I got here. No reason to have five of us on duty at one time at this damn plant except to have someone to talk to."

He reached the main gate and walked under the brightly spotlit arc in front of the gate house. "Evenin', Art," he greeted Arthur Potter. "Things as dull as usual?" The glum-faced gate guard put down the copy of *Field and Stream* he had been reading and stood slowly from his chair in the small guard hut. "Your watch busted, boy?" he muttered as he walked around the side of the hut, searching on a ring of keys. Art Potter was pushing time for a second retirement, having left the Pittsburgh Police Department after thirty years of patrol and desk work. He had taken this job at A&T Security to make enough extra cash to buy a home in Florida. He and his wife, Dolly, had been saving for their retirement, but couldn't make it on his pension, particularly with the way inflation was hitting them. With this job, he was able to put enough away in savings to look forward to getting that home in another year or two. He was getting old and felt it, but the dream kept him going.

Art fitted the key in the lock and opened the gate, sliding it back only wide enough for Sam to squeeze through. "Had to make a stop on the way out here, Art," Sam explained apologetically; "took longer than I thought it would."

"Yep, she did, didn't she," Art grumbled as he relocked the gate and turned to go back inside to his magazine.

At the entrance to the main building, Sam stopped in front of a narrow, bullet-proof window, located to the right of the door. Inside, Cal Bennett recognized him and turned to a stocky young man seated at a control console across the room. "He's here, Al. Go get Don in the snack bar and tell him he's relieved." Al Marascoli looked up from his psychology text and nodded acknowledgment.

He stood, moving his chair back and walked across the room with a peculiar cat-like stride.

Cal pushed the switch to disarm the main door alarm and then opened it. Sam entered, looking sheepishly at his supervisor. "Sorry, Cal. Didn't mean to be late again, but I got tied up on the way out from home."

Bennett closed the door. "You're beginning to make a habit of this, Sam. Better set your watch ahead and build that coffee stop into your travel time. Socializing with waitresses is on your time, not the company's." He tapped him gently on the shoulder, nudging Sam toward the time clock. "Go ahead and punch in. Don't make yourself any later by standing and explaining."

As Sam was placing his time card in the clock, Al Marascoli and Don Ellington entered the room. "Hey, Sam, nice of you to make it tonight." There was an edge to Ellington's voice. "I'm going to apply for pay on both shifts if this keeps up."

Sam reddened with embarrassment. "Damn, I'm sorry, Don. This week's been a bad one. You don't worry though, I'll be here in plenty of time tomorrow night."

"Yeah, yeah. I hear you, man. I'll see about that when the time comes." Ellington punched his time card as the door was opened for him. "See you all tomorrow night. Have a quiet morning." Ellington walked out into the still night air. Marascoli was already seated at the desk, his attention focused on the text.

With no one paying attention to him, Sam walked to the coffee bar set against the wall behind Cal Bennett's desk. The pot was perking amid cups, wooden spoons, and packets of sugar and Preem. A carton of doughnuts was open on the table with several of them already missing. Above the table was one of the reproductions of pastoral scenes that were scattered around the walls of this large, blandly decorated room. This served as both a guard room and reception area, necessitating the mixture of couches, vinyl lounge chairs, a two-tiered Plexiglas coffee table, receptionist's desk and plastic potted plants with the functional pieces of guard furniture.

After filling his cup with steaming coffee, Sam poured

in two packets of sugar and a packet of Preem, glancing around the room as he stirred the sweet mixture. There was the same preoccupation with time-killing routines that existed every night. Marascoli with his head buried in that psych textbook, Cal Bennett working a crossword puzzle, and Joe Zuno, sprawled on the red couch, his huge feet resting on the coffee table, flipping through *Road and Track* magazine. You spent an hour out of eight on this shift actually doing something. The rest of the time, you might as well be somewhere else, anywhere else. He took a sip of the coffee and walked past Cal toward the empty couch.

Bennett's balding head came up as he watched the taller, heavyset man for a moment. "How's your love life, Romeo?" he queried with a smirk. "Have you scored yet or you still running the bases?"

Sam's face brightened even as he sipped his coffee and winced when it seared his tongue. "Ow, shit that's hot," he exclaimed, rubbing the back of his hand against his lips. He smiled conspiratorily. "She's beginning to come around since I've been in there a couple of nights runnin'. She knows I'm interested and I'm playin' it cool, just talkin' with her when she comes over. Not pressin', ya know, just bein' nice and cool."

Cal snorted, "Cool! How's a horny old bastard like you going to be cool? Particularly around a nice young piece like that." He shook his head. "Sam, you'll bust your bladder with all the coffee you'll have to drink before she notices you're there."

"I'm not that much older than her," Sam replied defensively. "Hell, I'm only fifty-two. That's the prime of life for a man like me."

"I don't know, Sam. Seems your old lady would be a better judge of that than either you or me."

Sam hesitated, uncertain how it was meant, then smiled, taking it in the joking vein. "Cal, ol' buddy, after five kids, Martha isn't about to have anything more to do with me like we used to. I love her, but a man's gotta get some excitement to keep the pencil lead sharp. Besides, she won't know anything about it, so it's like nothin's goin' on."

Joe Zuno looked up from the magazine. "Sounds like that's a pretty accurate summary of the action whether she knows about it or not. Nothin's goin' on."

"Come on, Joe," Bennett chided, "let the man enjoy the chase." Zuno grunted and returned to his reading.

Sam ignored the exchange. He was inwardly pleased with his analysis of the situation. He was getting older, but the old stud horse was still able to attract the women. Martha was a good wife, but the kids had caused her to put on weight and she didn't look anywhere as good as she used to. She was happy with the kids and those damn soap operas she watched all day so there wasn't anything wrong with trying for a little action on the side.

"Ya know, Cal, that girl has the finest cheeks on her ass. I'd sure like to . . ."

Cal interrupted, shaking his head in mock disgust. "I take back what I said about you being just a horny old bastard. You're a filthy, horny old bastard. Now cut the dreaming and go make your rounds. Take 'B' route and don't forget to check the generator building and warehouse."

Sam drained his coffee cup and replaced it on the table. "You got the call-box keys?" He readjusted his cartridge belt, trying to pull in the growing paunch so his uniform shirt wouldn't fit so sloppily around his waist. His pistol was a familiar weight on his right hip. Sam liked the way it looked; sort of a symbol of the authority he carried when he was on duty.

He unfastened the holster flap, pulled the Smith and Wesson .38 and spun the cylinder, checking to see that it was fully loaded. Damn thing's cruddy, he realized as he looked at the weapon. Have to clean it one of these days. It had been over a year since he'd fired the pistol; about the same time he cleaned it last. Still, it shouldn't have gotten that dirty.

Cal handed him the key ring that would allow him to call in from specific locations, indicating that all was well on his rounds. Failure to report from any one of the locations would result in an internal alarm to alert the security force to a potential problem. Should they discover a major discrepancy, the outside alarm would be triggered from the control desk.

"See you in about a half hour," Sam said as he walked toward the rear door into the reactor building. Cal half waved good-bye and swiveled around in his chair, returning to the crossword puzzle. A four-letter word meaning very light brown in color. It was 1:15 in the morning; another forty-five minutes before Joe had to relieve Art on the gate.

In Rio de Janeiro, the clock beside John LeCourt's bed showed 3:15 A.M. He hadn't slept since his meeting with Franz Heitzman earlier in the evening. Things had moved too rapidly for John LeCourt since Alec had called him back and put in motion the sequence of events that brought him to the regal Monte Verde Hotel along Rio's Avenida Atlantica. He had made arrangements to take a week away from the car dealership where he had been working for the last year, giving illness as a reason. Sales were slow so there was no problem getting the time off; it was his money he was losing not theirs.

Alec had provided a round-trip ticket to Trinidad, but on arrival at the Port-of-Spain Airport, he had been met with further tickets, sending him into Rio's Galeao Airport. After an overnight delay, he took the required flight and landed at the busy airport in late afternoon. He had no sooner reached the baggage claim area when he heard himself being paged and discovered that a car and driver were waiting.

The dark blue Mercedes 450 SEL was more than he had expected. The driver, who was neatly dressed in a white coat-shirt, white linen slacks, and white, woven-leather loafers, directed the porter in securing John's bags and placing them in the trunk after he had seen to seating the American. John relaxed on the leather seat and quickly glanced around the interior of the car. A telephone was recessed into the rear of the front passenger seat for use by those in the back. To the right of the console in front, he saw another phone and what appeared to be a radio, like a C.B. set. That would explain the dual antennas on the back bumper. The air conditioning was pleasantly cool and a relief after the muggy, crowded terminal building. Not even the air conditioners in the building could eliminate the humidity that penetrated from Rio's streets. A stereo tape was playing Wagner's *Meistersinger* score. Alec obviously hadn't understated the wealth that was behind this deal if this introduction was any indication, LeCourt thought.

When the bags were secured, the mulatto driver slid under the wheel and pulled the car smoothly away from the curb into traffic. John sat back, enjoying the ride, but uncertain about what was happening. The driver hadn't spoken a word to him since he had presented the note in the baggage claim area. It was a handwritten message stating that this man was to meet him and deliver him to his hotel. John had surmised that the man spoke no English and contented himself with observing the scenery along their route.

He immediately recognized Sugarloaf Mountain on its peninsula dominating the sweeping blue of the bay. The rugged terrain was a riot of color with the natural green of the vegetation dotted with whites and pastels of the thousands of homes and buildings. The boulevard along which they were traveling was crowded with vehicles, many of them Volkswagens. Ahead, the tall, modern structures of central Rio clustered in an arc around the bay. The mountains in the background were a contrast in green and the gray of broad expanses of rock. He caught glimpses of the glistening white sand beach that enfolded the deep blue to aquamarine of the sea. It was one of the most strikingly beautiful cities he had seen.

As he sat, captured by the view, the driver had picked up his telephone and spoke in rapid Portuguese. Moments later, he turned slightly and indicated for John to take his phone.

"Hello, LeCourt here."

"Welcome to Rio, Colonel LeCourt. I hope the extension of your trip wasn't too tiring." The deep voice carried a hint of a European accent.

"Not at all. I believe I'd trade Trinidad for Rio anytime."

There was a chuckle at the other end of the line. "We have a saying here, which literally translated into English says, 'God made the world in six days; the seventh he devoted to Rio.' I'm certain that you'll agree after your visit with us here."

"I've barely arrived and, aside from the humidity, it's beautiful."

"Good. I'm pleased that you approve of our choice of meeting places. Now, as to arrangements. The driver will bring you to the Monte Verde Hotel and see you to your rooms. Please take this evening to relax and recover from the long trip. I will stop by after supper so that we may meet and chat briefly, but nothing to tire you further."

John considered asking the voice who it belonged to, but decided against it. He'd meet the man after supper. "You're very kind to make all these preparations." He almost said that he'd never had it this good. Fortunately, he caught himself. "I don't think I'll feel much like going out. Is there a restaurant in the hotel?"

"Most certainly. I recommend the Monte Verde's dining room for excellent food. Their service and cuisine are among Rio's best. If you would like to dine in your room, you may be more comfortable."

"Fine. I think I may do that."

"Very good, Colonel LeCourt. Please enjoy the remainder of your ride and I look forward to meeting you this evening."

"Thank you. I look forward to meeting you also."

The voice bid him good-bye and the buzzing of an open line was in his ear. Well, welcome to Rio, John old man, he thought. Looks like you tied in with a bunch of real operators this time. Must be nice to set something like this up and not have to worry about travel vouchers and per diem, and having a Mercedes pick you up instead of fighting with a dispatcher at a motor pool to try to get a military sedan. He leaned his head back against the cushioned rest, watching idly as the driver wound his way through the busy city streets.

The Mercedes turned onto the Avenida Atlantica, running along the beachfront. To John's right were the lavish hotels and rows of shops that occupied this prime location along Copacabana Beach as far as he could see. To his left, strong surf was breaking white foam over even whiter sand.

There were still crowds of people lying or playing on the sand. Two youngsters were tugging at a kite soaring overhead in the stiff ocean breeze. Peddlers were spaced throughout the crowd, selling soft drinks, coconuts, and pineapples. Farther down the road, John could see the graceful arching Royal Palms lining the roadway.

The car slowed and pulled sharply out of the lane of traffic, stopping in front of an ornate facade in the middle of the block. The awning, which extended across the sidewalk to curbside, proclaimed that this was the Hotel Monte Verde. Before John had finished reading the name, a uniformed doorman opened his door and waited for him to step out. His driver was already opening the trunk, giving instructions to a bellboy who then took John's three bags and disappeared inside.

"Welcome to the Monte Verde, Sir." The doorman greeted him. "It is our pleasure to have you visit us."

He was ushered through the elegantly decorated lobby to the elevator and taken to the third floor. The driver led as they left the elevator, walking a short distance to a pair of carved wooden doors. He pushed one of them open and stood aside as LeCourt entered.

The large room, with its high ceilings, was a rich blend of white, gold, and pale blue. A sparkling crystal chandelier reflected brilliance from the diamond-clear lights at its center. A heavy oriental rug covered the center portion of the floor and under it, a pale blue carpet extended from wall to wall. Armchairs were covered with a gold and blue striped silk, and pieces of furniture that John couldn't identify were obviously valuable antiques.

One of the bellboys walked to the far wall and opened

the champagne silk curtains. Behind them, tall French doors led to a balcony. John crossed the room and looked out over the beach and shimmering blue water beyond.

Hearing a muted pop, he turned to see another bellboy remove the cork from a bottle of Blanc de Blanc and place it in a silver cooler. A basket of fruit and cheese had appeared on one of the tables.

The young man turned to John. "Sir, I hope you will be comfortable during your stay with us. If you should wish anything, my name is Fernando. Please call on me at any time." He gave a slight bow and followed the others out of the room, closing the door quietly behind them.

John stepped over to the table and picked a banana from the fruit basket. As he stood peeling it, he looked around the room. Nice oil paintings; some of them must be originals. Bet they're worth a bundle. Damn furniture is sure nice.

He walked to the French doors and pushed them open, stepping onto the balcony where he stood, leaning against the wrought iron railing and eating the banana. The beach was clearing now as evening began to settle over the ocean. There were still a few cars zipping along the avenue below, hardly noticing the scattered traffic lights along its length. Must be death for a pedestrian trying to cross against those boulevard Fangios, LeCourt thought. He noticed eight or nine women walking unescorted along the sidewalk below. Good-looking heads; nice builds and they sure don't hide it in those dresses, he observed as he peered down at an attractive cleavage passing beneath his balcony. Could be hookers, he decided as one of them approached a single man who had just left the hotel. The man shook his head negatively as he walked past the woman. She shrugged and continued her leisurely stroll.

John dropped the peel into a rubber tree planter and folded his arms across his chest. There was a disquieting sensation as he let his gaze wander from the natural beauty of the mountains and ocean to the splendor of Rio in her electric-sequined evening gown. A man could really get to enjoy this.

He looked back into the room. To have a home

furnished like this; a pool, some acreage, a staff to take care of things while he traveled. Rio, the Bahamas, maybe a condominium on the islands... or a villa, Europe, the Mediterranean. All it took was money.

Money; he chuckled softly; he'd never really had that much. He pulled out the folder of traveler's checks he'd brought with him. Five hundred dollars' worth of checks; showed how well he was acquainted with this life-style. It probably would cover the meals on this trip and the tips. He'd never really had that much money in his life, so it didn't bother him. There was always enough to get by; never any hope of making more than he did as a lieutenant colonel, except if he'd gotten that promotion. He would mail in the forms for all the big giveaways, buy lottery tickets, hoping that he'd hit one of them. Never did, though.

He recalled how jump pay and combat pay were big extras in their monthly budget in those days; a chance to buy something they normally couldn't afford, maybe put some away in savings. Neither he nor Karen were very good at saving until they began the account for the kids' college money. Christ, a year of jump pay wouldn't cover the cost of this trip. This was the league where you spent a thousand dollars as quickly as John LeCourt would spend ten.

There was a hell of a temptation. He'd spent twenty-two years fighting and preparing to fight wars. He'd jumped out of aircraft for $110 a month; put his life on the line for $65 a month combat pay; started a career, with a wife to support, on about $200 a month. They'd lived in cracker-box, off-post housing because there weren't quarters on post for second lieutenants. It had gotten better over the years, but there had always been the comparisons. Classmates of his from college who'd gone into law or medicine; they had their nice homes, big, new cars and everything their wives wanted. Karen had put up with a lot; given up a lot to stay with him. It was tough for her with the separations, hardship tours, the moves. He remembered the second tour in 'Nam. They'd just gotten to Benning when branch called him and said there was an

opening for Command and General Staff College, so they
packed up and moved to Fort Leavenworth for a year.
Then the orders to Fort Bragg and his promotion to
major. A year there and he was off to Vietnam. Karen had
to give up the nice quarters they'd finally gotten on post
and move back with her folks for a year. She moved again
when he came back to Fort Carson. She wanted to stay in
one place at least long enough to get unpacked; not much,
just a stable three-year tour for once.

He shook his head; that was all behind him now. A lot
of his contemporaries had managed to live comfortably,
had managed their money better than he did and were
ready to retire and coast into a second career. He hadn't
been that lucky.

John pushed away from the railing and walked inside.
They'd taken away his career, told him he wasn't good
enough to compete. Well, this might be the answer.
Somebody sure thought he was good enough to handle an
operation that was backed by really big money . . . and
they were willing to put out a bundle of it to get him.

He picked up a slab of cheese and nibbled an edge, then
replaced it and tried a mild Edam. He poured a glass of
champagne and with it in one hand and the Edam in the
other strolled through the other rooms in the suite. If they
were trying to impress him, they were off to a hell of a
start.

Later, refreshed by a bath and a huge steak, he stood
on the balcony, sipping champagne and beginning to feel
as if this were his natural environment. It was strange how
easily one adapted to luxury. He smiled; wouldn't it be
something if all of this didn't turn into a pumpkin at
midnight? If there were really some way to get enough
money to break out of the mold, he'd be willing to try it

He was startled by the chimes behind him. He thought
at first that it was the door until it sounded again. The
telephone. He picked it up, "LeCourt speaking."

"Good evening, Colonel LeCourt. You enjoyed your
meal, I hope." It was the same European voice that had
spoken with him on the way from the airport.

"Yes, very much, thank you."

"Very good. If you aren't engaged at the moment, I would like to introduce myself and visit with you for a few minutes."

"Please do. I'm just standing here admiring the scenery."

"Fine. I will be up momentarily."

John hung up. Now the players were coming onto the field. He set the unfinished glass of champagne on the table. He was feeling a little light headed already and needed his head straight when he met this fellow. This is no time to blow the deal by coming across as a lush. He was standing in front of the etched glass mirror, checking his tie and hair, when he caught himself. Wait a second! This guy is coming to sell me on the idea of joining them and here I am acting like some fresh college grad going on the first job interview. They want me and they went through all of this to see me. Their minds are made up; it's mine that is still open.

There was a knock at the door and John walked over, pausing several seconds before opening it. The man in front of him was wearing a white sharkskin suit and holding a narrow brim Panama hat. His head looked like it had been fashioned from a cube, everything squared off, including the crew-cut graying hair.

"Colonel LeCourt, I am Franz Heitzman, your host."

John took the outstretched hand, feeling the strength in Heitzman's grip. The handshake fit the man's face. His mouth was smiling, but there was nothing even approaching warmth in his eyes.

"Good to finally meet you, Mr. Heitzman. Please come in." John stepped back, allowing Franz to enter the room. "I want to thank you for these accommodations. They're extremely nice."

Franz held up a hand. "Please Colonel, no thanks are necessary. It was my privilege." He quickly glanced around the room. "It seems to be in order. You have everything you need?"

LeCourt nodded, "I certainly do. Won't you sit down?" He motioned toward one of the chairs.

Franz sat comfortably in the chair, placing his hat on

the table beside him. John took a seat on the couch across from him. He was aware of subtle scrutiny in the short silence that followed.

John's self-confidence had returned after he realized that the group this man represented had already selected him for this venture, the same confidence he'd felt when he had been a leader. His was born of proven ability and pride in his accomplishments, but Heitzman exuded a confidence that came from power, from money; one that didn't depend on situations favoring him. He could create his own situations.

"Would you care for a brandy, Colonel, before we become serious for a short while?"

"Thank you, no," John declined. "Could I order one for you?"

"No need to order." Heitzman stood and walked briskly to a cabinet near the bedroom door. "There should be a supply in here," he said, opening the doors. John felt a twinge of embarrassment. Inside the cabinet was a full stock of booze, brandy, and liqueurs, glasses and a small refrigerator. He hadn't even thought to look. Imagine stocking all that in a hotel room.

"I apologize for the staff not showing you the comforts of the suite," Franz said as he poured a snifter of cognac. "It is reasonably well filled, but should you desire a special brand, just notify the bell captain." He walked back to his chair and sat down. "Prosit." He held up the glass.

"Cheers."

Franz swirled the brandy in the bottom of the snifter, savoring the bouquet, before beginning. "Colonel LeCourt, you know why I asked you to make this trip, so I won't waste our time reiterating. You were selected from a number of highly rated men as being best qualified to lead a team in accomplishing a particular venture."

John was suddenly alert. Leading a team. Alec hadn't mentioned him leading the thing.

"Later, we will discuss the details of the project. Tonight, I merely want you to understand the reward you will receive for undertaking this task." Franz took a sip of his cognac. "I am prepared to offer you one million dollars negotiable cash."

John fought to control the sudden pulse-pounding excitement that surged through him. He couldn't believe that he had heard accurately. He managed to keep his voice calm as he asked, "You did say one million dollars, American dollars?"

Heitzman nodded. "Yes, I felt that was reasonable for your level of expertise and the probability of success that your participation will give us. There will, of course, be a bonus for you as team leader." Franz sipped his brandy, cupping the glass in both hands. "Say, an additional five hundred thousand dollars."

John rubbed his forehead with his fingertips, stunned by Heitzman's offer. There was a churning sensation in his stomach just like he got before he dropped clear of an aircraft on a free-fall and despite his efforts at control he could feel his hand trembling. A million five hundred thousand dollars! Christ, that was more money than he'd dreamed of seeing in a lifetime.

"I expected that you might be somewhat surprised at the offer, Colonel, but you must realize that I have selected only the best men for this operation, and I am willing to pay what I feel your services are worth. Of course, if you feel that it is inadequate after I've explained what I want in return, I might be moved to negotiate. I think, however, that you will find the task well within your capabilities and the risk within reason."

John stood and walked to the liquor cabinet. "I think I'll have that brandy now." He turned to Franz after he had poured a snifter half full. "Look, you know enough about me from what Rettler said, to know that I've never even laid eyes on that kind of cash, so I wouldn't even know how to negotiate in seven figures. Second, since you know what this operation entails and I don't, if you say I can handle it, I'll have to take your word; that is, at least until you read me into it. Third, anything that would rate that kind of a payoff couldn't be anything short of ... what ... a 'Goldfinger' style looting of Fort Knox?"

Heitzman waved his hand for John to stop. "No, no, Colonel. Nothing so exotic as Mr. Bond's escapades. We'll get into all of that tomorrow, but be assured that I wouldn't have selected you unless I were certain that you could carry out the mission. You see, success is what counts with me. I will go to any lengths to ensure that I achieve it."

LeCourt returned to the couch and sat back, sipping his drink. Heitzman continued, "I will be honest with you; you are the one man who can lead the team I have assembled. This is why I am willing to go to these lengths to secure your services."

John was listening without completely hearing him. The concept of a million dollars was clouding his consciousness, combining with his recent visions of wealth and the life it would bring him. Alec had hinted at some figure over $400,000, which had sounded unbelievable to John, but this was three times what he'd expected and it was real. God, anything he wanted, he could get; travel anywhere he chose to go; he could go into International Motors in the city and put down cash for a Mercedes and never even feel the dent in his bank account.

"It is quite a sum for a short period of work, is it not?" Heitzman asked, guessing correctly at the source of John's distraction.

LeCourt was annoyed at himself for being so obvious, but had to agree. "You're right. It's a hell of a pay raise for a man who was making twenty-seven thousand dollars a year not long ago."

"The only difference is that you'll be changing employers, Colonel LeCourt. To me, you're worth what I offered you."

"Do you want an answer now?" LeCourt asked. "I mean about my taking the job?"

Franz smiled again, this time with a glimmer of light in his eyes. "No decisions are required tonight. Take time to think it over and listen to my outline of the operation tomorrow before you commit yourself." He stood and finished his brandy. "I assure you that what you will hear will only reinforce your evaluation of our potential for success and yours. And now, I'll leave you to get some rest. I'm sure the trip tired you, and I want you refreshed for tomorrow's meeting."

LeCourt placed his glass on the table and stood. "You're calling the shots. What time should I be ready?"

"Say, noon? We'll have brunch together and then spend a few hours on the plan." Franz picked up his hat.

"Sounds good." The two men walked to the door and John bid Heitzman goodnight, watching the white suit disappear into the elevator before closing his door.

Franz had his driver take him directly to the villa, where Vargas was waiting on the terrace listening to soft Salsa rhythms over his elaborate stereo system. "We have him!" Heitzman announced, slamming a fist into the other open palm. "Even the idea of breaking into a nuclear power plant won't throw him off."

"Then my little exposure-to-wealth ploy was successful?" Vargas asked.

"Completely! By the time I arrived, I could see he had settled into the comforts that your money provides. Add our willingness to put out over a million for his skills and the final defenses vanished."

"Then congratulations on solving the last problem on your agenda." Vargas indicated a decanter and glass on the portable bar. "Try some of this. It is an Ambassador port from the Gonzales Byass stock; quite fitting for a toast."

Heitzman poured a glass for himself and raised it toward his friend. "To Prometheus."

"To Prometheus and our von Clausewitz who planned it."

"Not without your guidance and invaluable assistance."

Franz sat on one of the wicker lounge chairs, enjoying the heavy, rich flavor of the wine and the satisfaction of fitting the last piece of his puzzle in place.

"What name did you use with LeCourt?" Vargas asked.

"Franz Heitzman. I saw no reason to develop another

nom de guerre for use with these men. You are the only member of the board who knows my real name."

At the hotel, LeCourt closed the door and leaned against it for a moment. He was both elated and drained. Thoughts tumbled over in his mind as he began to regain control of the emotions that Heitzman's visit had aroused. Passed over for colonel... not good enough to stay with the program... your OER's do not support a recommendation from this board for promotion to the rank of colonel; sorry, John, there was nothing we could do... sorry, John, we're going to miss you around here. Well, damn you all, John LeCourt is back! No more excuses for not having been able to cut it; no more bitterness about getting screwed by the system. John LeCourt is as good as he damned well knew he was and these people recognized it.

He walked erectly across the room, feeling a new strength flowing through him. Team leader! Just like old times. Not a battalion, but that was immaterial. He'd be leading a group of specially selected men and if they were all in his league, they'd be better than a battalion of legs.

He poured another drink and glanced around until he saw the humidor. He selected a Havana and sniffed it before biting the tip and spitting it onto the rug. He picked up the heavy quartz lighter and flicked it, puffing contentedly until the cigar was glowing red at the end. Seated once again on the couch, he leaned back and put his feet up on the low coffee table. A cloud of white smoke curled slowly up from his mouth as he rested his head on the back of the couch and surveyed the paintings on the far wall. You lucky son of a bitch, LeCourt. Not only do you get to prove that you can lead men, but you're going to have enough money afterward that all of this won't be just a wild dream. You'll have all the fine homes, the cars, maybe even a plane or a boat; yeah, a yacht, and travel; see places you'd always wanted to go; come back here and get this sort of treatment, not because Franz Heitzman had arranged it, but because John LeCourt could pay for it.

But in the midst of his wandering thoughts, the old

caution crept in. What in the hell could be worth that kind of money? What good would the money do him if he were dead or in prison afterward? Both Alec and Heitzman sounded confident that there would be no problems, but so did McDowell before the first battle of Bull Run. But if they had been so thorough in their selection of a team and had the kind of power that Heitzman represented, they must have put together a solid operation. What the hell, he'd been shot at for $250 a month when he was a lieutenant in Korea and this couldn't be any more of a risk than that was.

He finished his drink and walked into the bedroom. Time to get some sack. It was going to be a big day tomorrow. Much later, he found that sleep wouldn't come. There had to be a curve ball somewhere in the midst of all the floaters Heitzman tossed up to him.

By two o'clock the next afternoon he had his answer. "Take over a nuclear power plant! You must've been out in the sun too long, Mr. Heitzman." John's normally calm manner broke when Franz disclosed the target of the operation.

Franz stopped the outburst with a laugh. "Colonel LeCourt, you are so predictable. I knew the first mention of the plant would cause you to react in this way, but I also know that once you hear the rest of the plan, you will agree with me that it is quite feasible."

John shook his head. "Well, I came here to listen, so fire away, but it had better be one hell of a plan."

During the next forty-five minutes Franz laid out the details of the operation, noting that LeCourt was impressed. John was astounded at the degree of proficiency evident in Heitzman's concept and execution phases. The amount of material that the man had available to him was staggering and indicated a great deal of inside information. There wasn't a point that hadn't been covered when Heitzman completed his explanation, leaving LeCourt scrambling to find some contingency that might trip them up.

"What do you think now, Colonel? Is it not a splendid approach to the problem?"

"I take back what I said about the sun, Mr. Heitzman. I can't pick any holes in it right now, but I'll be thinking about it."

Franz chuckled. "Please do, Colonel; please do. I invite your criticism and comments since you will be the cutting edge of my blade."

John looked up. "You seem certain that I'm going to say yes."

Franz returned the gaze. "Let me say that I would not have selected you had I not felt that you would ultimately agree."

"What if I said no and went back and blew your operation all over Washington. Haven't you taken a hell of a risk getting me all of this before I signed on?"

Franz's eyes reflected disappointment. "Colonel, you are a more intelligent man than that. Don't disillusion me." There was a coldness in his voice as he continued, "You know that I wouldn't allow any such disclosure; particularly with the stakes so high. I assure you that before you reached anyone who would listen to you and your wild story, you would be the victim of an unfortunate...and fatal...accident." He smiled again, his voice regaining its cordial tone. "But we don't talk of those things, among friends, that is, and I do consider you a friend now."

This was a side of the man that John hadn't expected. There was no doubt that he was serious, but John wasn't even going to test him. "You make your point, Mr. Heitzman. My question is withdrawn."

"Good. I'm pleased that you are questioning, no matter what the substance. I detest a person who merely absorbs like a sponge without a murmur, even though it might be acid in which he is being immersed."

"Well, now that I've seen the plan and I'm impressed, what next?" LeCourt asked.

"Very simple. Agree to lead it."

"Have I got an alternative?" John asked, feeling trapped for the first time.

"You could decline," Franz said simply. "But that would be of no value to either of us."

John thought for a few moments. It's a good plan; the team is sound; there's enough G-2 on the thing to cover contingencies, even to biodata on the guards who'll be in the plant; there's a good escape phase with an open end for all of us afterward and, God knows, the money's right. He nodded, "Okay, Mr. Heitzman. You've got yourself a team leader."

Franz extended his hand. "We are agreed, then."

John shook the hand. "Agreed."

"May I call you John from now on?" Heitzman asked. "My name is Franz and since we'll be working closely together, last names become burdensome."

"Fine with me, Franz." John felt the beginning of comradeship, as superficial as it might be. He was on the way to belonging again.

The next three days went quickly for John. Franz provided him with the team roster and background information on each man as well as the folders on the night shift guards at the plant.

He waited until Franz had left and spent the remainder of Wednesday reading through the files on the men he would be working with and against. Franz hadn't understated the capabilities of the team members; John was well satisfied. The files also explained why Franz had chosen him to lead this group of men; they had the potential of being a disciplined and effective machine or an ineffective group of skilled individualists. They were tough, highly trained, and disciplined to follow leaders who reflected the same degree of experience and knowledge. If he had brought in anyone who couldn't match backgrounds with these men, someone who hadn't led their special kind of soldier before, he would have loosed a team of mavericks. As it was, this team and its leader would mesh like the gears in a fine transmission.

The plant guards, on the other hand, were a typical bunch of past-their-prime retirees, filling in their budgets with an extra job. Well intentioned, but useless, John surmised as he read the security company files on each of the men. No problems in the shift, except for the ex-marine; what was his name? Marascoli. John looked at the photograph on the folder, good-looking kid. Might be tough if he remembers what they taught him. We'll keep an eye on him.

Thursday morning, Franz appeared for breakfast and spent the day with John, explaining the technical details of the plan and actions to be taken by each man after entry to the plant had been effected. There were floor plans, blueprints, and diagrams to illustrate each phase. John learned that, for the training period, Franz was having drawings and mock-ups prepared in order to give the men a better appreciation of the plant and its equipment. The final rehearsals would be run on a larger mock-up.

Franz included the intelligence gained from the terrain study his assistants had recently completed. This was a familiar format for LeCourt and he rapidly read through the data on roads, airfields, towns, topography, observation, avenues of approach, key terrain features, and the multitude of information describing the Bartonsville area. He made additional inquiries about state police and National Guard capabilities that set Franz to writing notes for further investigation. John added a police and military band shortwave radio to their equipment list to enable the team to monitor transmissions while they were anticipating reaction from the authorities.

When they took a break for supper, John was satisfied with the preparations. Franz had immediately agreed to the additions and suggestions John had made for the equipment and intelligence lists; it was much easier than LeCourt had anticipated. Their sources had even obtained the card-key openers for entrance to secure areas.

The last day, he went over the location and master schedule for their training. The schedule and subjects were well structured to bring the team to the peak of physical and psychological readiness for the operation. John was pleased that Franz had planned for the team to conduct its own training, except for the technical briefings that Franz would present. Everything looked as good as Franz had promised.

The overall schedule called for the team members to

arrive in Rio on June sixteenth for transportation to the training site on the seventeenth. Today was Friday, May thirteenth, a superstition John chose to ignore, as he calculated the actions that would have to be taken to meet the departure. The team would have until June third to clear up their immediate debts, give notice, leave their jobs, and prepare a cover story for their departures. Franz had advanced each of them enough cash to pay two months ahead on their bills. After that, it wouldn't matter.

They would proceed from their locations to either New York City, Washington, D.C., Dallas, or Miami for departures to specific intermediate cities in Mexico and South America. Alec was handling the ticketing arrangements through Bernie's people, although none of the team knew of that coordination.

John checked the critical dates: June seventh, depart location, arrive NYC, Washington, Dallas, or Miami. Hotel reservations for two nights. Passports and identity papers picked up at the hotels for travel as tourists to Mexico and South America. June ninth, depart for Mexico City, Quito, Lima, Caracas, and La Paz. Hotel reservations as necessary to allow flights on common carriers to reach Rio on June sixteenth. Passage through immigration and customs would be prearranged. Unknown to John, Vargas had put his contacts to work to ensure that the men on a list he provided would be given inconspicuous priority in entering and leaving each country.

In Rio, each arriving team member would be met and taken to a small private airfield outside of the city where helicopters would transfer them to the training site. It was all there, John thought; planned to the last detail. They would return via the same routes after the training period and regroup in Pittsburgh just before they hit.

John was curious about the passports. "Franz, these passports and visas we'll need. Are they valid or can we get tripped up with them?"

"No problem at all, John. All we need are your photographs to attach and they'll take you through the trip safely. It's tourist season, remember, and the volume of travelers adds to your disguise." Franz recalled the problem he had encountered in his early research. Following the outbreak of terrorism in the early '70s, the American State Department and Customs Bureau had been extremely cautious in granting visas to foreigners traveling to the United States. Anyone who came from an Arab nation, Latin America, or Japan who might have some affiliation with the terrorist groups based in those countries was denied a visa. The clampdown had been effective in halting terrorist penetration of the United States, but who would suspect a seemingly unrelated group of Americans, leaving from different cities in the U.S. bound for vacations in various Latin countries? When they reentered, it would be equally innocent.

After a night enjoying the many clubs in Rio, LeCourt departed on his flight to Trinidad on Saturday morning. In his baggage was a second passport, marked with entrance to and departure from Trinidad only. Should the need for confirmation arise, Franz had seen that John was a visitor to Trinidad; not to Rio.

The next time John saw Franz was on July ninth, when a single Alouette brought the coordinator into camp to begin the technical briefings. In the three weeks since the team had arrived, they had completed the preliminary physical toughening on the obstacle course and in the twice daily PT drills. In addition, they had undergone a basic weapons and demolition review and begun their specialized training for the skills each would employ in the operation. Now Franz would tie all of this together with the application of what they'd reviewed to an actual target.

John introduced the tiger-suit clad executive to the team, thinking that it was clever of Franz to wear their training uniform while working with them. No urban office-dweller image for this man.

"Gentlemen, this is Franz Heitzman. He will be with us for the next three weeks to present briefings on our target and supervise our training on the mock-ups." Franz had specified that his relationship with the planning of the operation and selection of the team not be revealed to the men. John merely added, "Mr. Heitzman has done the intelligence work for this phase of our training and is qualified to answer any questions you may have during it."

The men sat quietly in their folding chairs, accepting LeCourt's introduction but each forming his own opinion of the man on the platform in front of them. His stocky but trim frame and his crew cut gave the appearance of an aging mercenary that was immediately acceptable to the team. He was one of their own and they'd listen with more than normal classroom attention.

Franz took the center of the low platform after LeCourt had seated himself in the front row. Looking at the intent faces before him, he was immediately satisfied with his selections. They were hard and cool with the alertness in their eyes that came from years of facing down death, of living through months of combat where each instant was a ticket to eternity and a man's instincts became sharpened to a special keenness that ensured survival. He recognized them from the photos he'd studied; leaner now, but the same faces. Zimmerman, DeAngelo, Sanchez, Jones. He paused; Jones, the black. He had rejected him at first, purely on racial grounds, but Ernesto had argued for the man's obvious qualifications. It had been one of their rare disagreements. Franz had conceded even though he attributed Vargas's persistence to the unusual mixing of Indian, black, and white blood in Brazil's history. It was different in Franz's Germany.

"I will be brief in my remarks today," Franz began. "You will hear enough from me in the days to come." Franz outlined the topics he would cover and the practical application phase that would follow. After fifteen minutes, he asked for questions. There were no hands, so he turned the meeting back to LeCourt after indicating that he would like to meet each of the men individually after they were dismissed.

John closed the session with a quick run-down on the next day's schedule, which included PT, a class in expedient demolitions, a review of the guard personnel they would encounter, and a half-day with Franz on plant layout and equipment. Once dismissed, the men formed a line along the wall of the long classroom building, waiting to meet Heitzman. Vince stepped up. "Mr. Heitzman, I'm Sergeant Major DeAngelo." Franz's handshake was firm. "Good to meet you, DeAngelo. Jerry Francisco sends you his regards." There was surprise on DeAngelo's face. Francisco was a friend of his from the early days in Laos. Last word on him was that he'd signed on for Angola and gotten greased over there. Vince looked at the somber Heitzman with new respect. "Thanks for the word. If you see him, tell him Vince says 'keep his ass down.'"

That evening a special meal was prepared in honor of Heitzman's arrival. Pete Alexander and Cleave Jones had used some of their jungle survival training and snared two monkeys, which were quickly dispatched and served in the curried main course. Fresh meat was abundant in the forest and the men took turns providing wild game for the suppers. This was the first time they'd prepared the spicy hot curry that was one of their favorites, a dish borrowed from their days in training with the British Special Air Service. It was devoured with great gusto and numerous bottles of the light Brazilian beer that had been thoughtfully included in their rations. Franz almost gave away his urban background when he discovered that what he had assumed to be beef, or at worst, venison, was, in fact, monkey meat. Only his disciplined acting got him through the meal gracefully.

Later, while LeCourt and Franz met in the latter's quarters, arranged in the classroom alcove, the team gathered in twos and threes to study the guards' biographies once again. Pete Alexander and Bobby Jack Tomlinson were testing one another as they sat on the edge of Alexander's bunk. "Zuno," Alexander asked, looking up from his notebook.

Bobby Jack closed his eyes and recited in a monotone, "Zuno, Joe; age forty-nine, retired NCO; height, five-feet eleven-inches; weight two hundred fifteen pounds;

paunchy, out of shape. He's got a wife and four kids; two of them in college."

"Military background," Pete asked.

"Sergeant E-six when he retired; mainly supply sergeant duty; carried an eleven Bravo MOS, but never served in combat." Tomlinson paused, tapping his forehead with his knuckles, then continued, "Yeah, I got it now. He made E-seven, but was busted for drinking and tearing up an NCO Club bar in Frankfurt. Served with training and support units; no tours in 'Nam, one tour in Korea after the truce, first tour in Europe on occupation duty after World War Two. Never fired better than marksman on the range except sharpshooter with the forty-five pistol. Awards and decorations: Good Conduct Medal with a couple of clusters, Meritorious Service Medal. Bronze Star for meritorious service; no combat, no valor." He paused again. "Evaluation, no threat. Will comply with orders."

"Okay, champ. Now toss me one." Pete put his notebook on the bunk beside him.

Tomlinson thought briefly. "Marascoli."

"Oh yeah. The troublemaker," Pete murmured softly. "Marascoli, Albert; age twenty-eight, ex-marine, height five-feet nine-inches, weight one hundred fifty; works out, in good condition. Married, wife with one in the hangar. Left the corps as a buck sergeant; fire team leader, squad leader, and acting platoon sergeant. That last one was at Khe Sanh. He had two tours in 'Nam. No prior service. Fired expert in all light infantry weapons and at least sharpshooter on crew served weapons. He got three Bronze Stars for valor, Soldiers Medal, and Purple Heart with clusters." Pete stopped for a moment. "You know, BJ, this son of a bitch ought to be with us."

Tomlinson nodded. "It'd be easier on us."

"Yeah, well anyway, evaluation: prime target. Could react instantaneously or in calculated manner. To be treated with extra caution."

"Hope he doesn't do anything dumb," BJ said quietly.

"Shit, me too," Pete agreed. "He went the route at Khe

Sanh. That's enough for anybody."

"Aw well, we'll handle it when we get to it. Who's next?"

"How about old Arthur K. Potter?" Both men chuckled at the mental picture of the haggard-faced ex-cop. "You know who he reminds me of?" Pete was laughing now.

"No. Who?"

"Fish, the old cop on *Barney Miller*, the TV series."

"Oh shit!" BJ roared with laughter, drawing glances from Sanchez and Cooper across the aisle. "Him and Wojo, or whatever his name is. The pride of the Twelfth Precinct."

"You guys cool it." DeAngelo's voice came from the end of the aisle. "There'll be enough time for bullshit when this thing is over with. Taps in twenty-five minutes, so get your studying done."

The laughter subsided and only the muted sounds of recited heights, weights, and qualifications came from the barracks.

Before daylight, the team was awakened by Miller and Moran as they lit gasoline lanterns and shook the sleeping men. Grumbling and yawning, they climbed out of bed, wiping sleep from their eyes.

"Ten minutes till PT," Moran said loudly. "T-shirts, fatigue trousers, and boots. Carry your jackets."

"Goddamn, I hate PT," Joe Houser, the former Seal Team member grumbled. "I got out of the service to get away from this crap and it's still following me." His wide shoulders and narrow hips, coupled with a nose that had been smashed in his career as a lightweight boxer and out-thrust jaw, gave him a belligerently athletic appearance. He had been first in his class in the physically demanding Underwater Demolitions Course and during his three tours in Vietnam, had volunteered for the most hazardous and prolonged missions into NVA territory. Joe didn't mind doing something for real, but the practice tore him up.

"Hey, Ed!" Mike Baker called from his alcove.

"Hey, yourself. What'ya want Baker?"

"I hate to ask, but do we have to run the obstacle course this morning?"

Groans and hisses greeted the question. "Shut up, man. They might have forgotten it." "If he wants to run it, Ed, let him."

Moran walked back up the aisle. "Do we run the obstacle course, gentlemen? I ask you, does a hobbyhorse have a wooden dick?"

The men filed out of the barracks into the chill of the morning air. Dawn was barely streaking the eastern sky with bands of orange and gold as they began their "daily dozen." After thoroughly warming up with the familiar exercises, they trotted, single file, to the obstacle course. In the forest cover, it would be another full hour before the sun provided more than a dim light. They knew the path by memory and most felt they could run it with their eyes closed.

Miller acted as starter for the men as they lined up to negotiate the still difficult course. "Okay, Lee," he motioned Zimmerman to the starting line. "Best time was BJ's six minutes, thirty-four seconds, day before yesterday. Somebody's got to break it today."

Zimmerman shook his head. "Not me. Man, if I finish this thing, it's a record."

"Try it in less than six, thirty-four, flash." He checked his watch. "Okay. Get read-dy . . . go!" Zimmerman's legs drove in a low start and he disappeared quickly over the first wall.

"Rey, you're next. Up to the line." One by one, the running figures vanished over the log wall until Tony stood alone. He checked his start time and pushed off, his muscular legs carrying him forward in a short sprint, then forcing him upward to grasp the top of the logs.

Cleave Jones broke BJ's record by seven seconds. As Ed Moran announced his time, the others tossed good-natured jibes at him. "Showboat." "Damn!" "Super-Spook strikes again." "Hey, Cleave. Next time you run it on your knees and give us a chance . . . huh, man?"

The tall NCO walked in a tight circle, easing a cramp out of his right thigh. He flashed a broad grin through the pain of burning lungs and the cramp. "The man said beat the time," he managed between breaths, "an' I figured...you honkie muthas...weren't even...awake yet...too much easy life."

"Listen to that man talk," Simmonds gasped. He stood hunched over, hands on hips, sucking air into his lungs. "I can't even spell easy life."

LeCourt, between toe-touches, called over, "Hey, Cleave, good show. You're making me feel like an old man."

Jones looked up, pleased but still joking, "Hell, Colonel...when you start out...second best...you get used...to trying harder."

It was late in his military career before Jefferson Lincoln Jones had shaken the bitterness and suspicion that a childhood in Selma, Alabama, had instilled. He joked now about being second best, but his introduction to the military, serving under white, Southern NCO's who were unhesitating in letting him know they considered integration of the army a mistake, only reinforced what early discrimination and bigotry had begun.

Harassment, extra hours on KP, weekend duty when his squad-mates were on pass, and the lonely, beer drinking hours he spent with his black friends failed to discourage him. There was a determination that bordered on fanatacism driving him to excel. He was a good soldier and that proficiency brought the promotions he wanted so desperately.

From 1956 to 1962, it was slow going, but he had his Spec-4 rank and was in line for sergeant's stripes when he first tried to transfer into Special Forces. He failed the battery of tests and was turned down, but knew he'd get there someday.

He was on leave in 1963, when the Birmingham riots were brutally suppressed. Cleave and two friends were on the edge of the crowds when the snarling German shepherds were turned on the demonstrators. He watched in a rage as the dogs and fire hoses broke the people into smaller groups to be dealt with by club-wielding police.

He went back to Selma, to the often-patched three-room frame shack where he and his four brothers and sisters had grown up, sickened and angry at the inequality of the system he served. His father prevented him from going AWOL and joining the rioting. The soft-spoken old man, who had lived through the worst of Alabama's Klan days, pulled him away from the violence of injustice. Cleave had never stopped to realize that as a mere corporal he had achieved more in the world of the whites than any other male member of his family, that he had a future—they all had a future—if young men like Cleave continued to prove that as men, and over the disadvantages of being black, they were as good as anyone else.

He went back and fought the battle in his own way, picking up his nickname among his friends for his near worship of Eldridge Cleaver. He kept his hatred within him, turning the drive it created to fierce competitiveness against every other man in his unit. It paid off and by 1966, he was wearing staff sergeant's stripes and had a tour in Vietnam behind him; thirteen months in the field that earned a platoon sergeant's job and a Bronze Star for valor. That year, he made the transfer to Smoke Bomb Hill at Fort Bragg and joined the Seventh Special Forces Group as a light weapons specialist.

It took Cleave less than a week to learn that as good as he was, the men around him were equal or better. Competition was fierce and it wasn't a matter of being expert in one's own specialty; Cleave found himself being cross-trained in demolitions and communications as well. His first assignment to an operational twelve man detachment was another shock. He was confused and suspicious when the commander and executive officer, a captain and lieutenant, joined the NCOs in cleaning weapons after a demonstration for visiting VIPs. There was a nonchalant acceptance of rank with each man being aware of his superiors, but without the structured formality to which he was accustomed. It was the first time that he felt the mutual respect that each man had for the others; a respect stemming from the professionalism that was demanded. Each man had a job to do and everyone else depended on him to do it without making a mistake.

One of the other detachment commanders, Captain Jim Marley, a black, set him straight. Hall had two missions behind him, an old timer who had served with the Seventh when it had been designated the Seventy-seventh, one of only a trio of Special Forces Groups in the world. Marley had watched Cleave's development after the young sergeant entered the military mini-United Nations on Smoke Bomb Hill. He was cutting it with technical proficiency, but when it came to the critical teamwork that spelled survival and success for the twelve men once they were in combat, Cleave just couldn't open up. His armor of resentment and protective suspicion made him a mechanical doll in the midst of live performers.

Marley normally would have let attrition take its course; let only the strong stay on, but Cleave had touched a nerve deep in the captain's past. He saw himself struggling up from the bottom, fighting the same battles young Jones could overcome if he took the opportunity this unit offered him.

"Jones. Come here a minute." He called him over after their two detachments had finished a physical fitness test one muggy, overcast North Carolina afternoon. Jones walked over and stood in front of him.

"Jones, you think you're pretty good, don't you? Pretty hot shit, huh?"

Cleave looked at the wiry officer in surprise. "Yes, sir. I suppose I do."

Marley tapped him on the chest with a knuckle. "Don't suppose. You *are* good, but remember one thing and hear me loud and clear; you wouldn't be here unless you were damn good; none of us would. It's our job to be better at what we do than anyone else and it takes every second of every swingin' day, concentrating on being better, to reach that level of proficiency that gets the job done. Got me?"

"Yes, sir." Cleave wondered what he was driving at.

"Right on. Now with all the weight you're carrying to do your job, you don't have any space for that chip you're toting around on your shoulder, so get rid of it."

Cleave's eyes narrowed. "What are you trying to tell me, Captain?"

"I'm not trying anything, Jones, I'm telling you flat out that this is one place where nobody gives a good goddamn that you're black. You could be purple with little pink polkadots and as long as you did your job, you'd be in."

"I hear you, Captain."

"You take a look around. This place is like an international refugee camp for G.I.s. Man, there's Czechs, Hungarians, Poles, Chicanos, Puerto Ricans, Blacks, Italians, Hawaiians, Indians. . . . if you think you stand out because you're black, you're wrong. You stand out either because you're very damn good or you're not so good. If it's the latter, you won't be around long."

Marley paused, studying Cleave's sensitive face for a reaction. The sergeant's eyes held his for a moment, then dropped. "I guess I've been looking for the shit . . . expecting it to come like it always did."

"The only time it comes around here is if you let somebody down and then it comes no matter who you are. You've got to work together on that team like nothing you've ever done before and you can do it. Give them a chance to show you, Jones. Don't shut them out and get yourself bounced off the team for inability to work and live together." Hall tapped him on the chest again. "If it happens, my man, it won't be because you're black. It'll be because you can't forget that you're black."

Cleave left Special Forces in 1971 for an assignment with a basic training unit. The transition was difficult for him and he found himself intolerant of the unprofessional attitudes he encountered among incoming draftees. He was now one of the breed of "old soldiers" who valued discipline and performance above right of congressional appeal exercised by several of his trainees when they felt they were being harassed. Cleave was relieved of his duties and reduced one grade when a congressional inquiry brought pressure on his commanding officer.

Three years short of retirement, Cleave left the military, bitter and confused by the new army that suddenly gave privates the power to destroy an NCO's career. He failed to comprehend the massive changes in attitude that shook the fabric of the military he had known. This unexpected opportunity to once again be part of a group of men that he understood and respected had regenerated his drive and spirit that 1972 had seen destroyed.

When all of the men were assembled, Ed Moran formed them into a single file for the run back along the path to camp. "Okay, okay, let's get our asses in gear. We're gonna have to hustle to get showers before chow. First class is at oh-8-fifteen hours."

The morning went quickly. Men handled the clay-like C-4 explosive with practiced ease as they molded it into various shapes for the different charges. Lee Zimmerman checked each of the diamond charges that had been prepared for the last exercise, making minor comments as he went. Sheets of aluminum foil had been wrapped smoothly around the elongated diamond of yellowish explosive that looked like an oversized mass of rolled-out cookie dough. Two blasting caps were inserted, one in each end of the short axis. "You used high carbon steel in figuring your dimensions, Dieter," he said, pointing to the thickness of the man's explosive charge. "Should be a half-inch thick for mild steel. You've got three-quarters or a little more." He spoke louder for all to hear. "You people remember, we're using these expedient devices to get by with the least amount of C-four necessary to do the job. In this problem, I gave you a mild steel shaft which takes a half-inch thickness. Long axis is equal to the circumference of the shaft and short axis equal to half the circumference. You know all of that, so don't make careless errors in your calculations."

The remainder of the charges were correct and Lee finished with a brief summary of rules of thumb that could be used to calculate the amounts of explosive necessary for a variety of targets. The men cleared the C-4 off the long tables that were staggered around the classroom, replacing it in the wooden storage boxes for their next demolitions class. A quick lunch was followed by their class with Franz.

The windows along the bare walls of the classroom had been covered with black cloth and a projection screen set up to the left of the platform. Franz stood behind the slender lectern on the other side, watching as the team filed in and took their seats. The folding chairs had been moved to the front of the room and arranged in two rows of eight chairs each. A battery-powered slide projector had been placed on a small table just to the rear of the seats. Three overhead lanterns hissed as their brilliantly glowing mantles cast odd-shaped shadows on the rough wood floor.

The men became silent as soon as they were seated, waiting for Heitzman to begin. He flipped through the papers before him and looked up. "You are quite punctual. I shall be also as I have a great deal to cover with you in the next few days. What I will be presenting is extremely technical in parts and will require the utmost in cooperation between us for a complete understanding of the subjects. By this I mean that no one should be hesitant to question when he doesn't understand something. I will answer your questions or find the answers in my material. The goal is for each of you to understand perfectly and without the slightest doubt what function he will perform and how it affects the operation. Do I make myself clear?" There were immediate nods of assent from the group.

"Good. In your schedules, which Colonel LeCourt has distributed, you will note the breakdown of subjects. Today is a general orientation on the site itself, designed to give you an overview on which you will build your knowledge in later lectures." Franz lifted a paperclipped sheaf of papers from the lectern and studied it for a moment. He glanced up and motioned for Simmonds to dim the lanterns. As the room darkened, Franz pushed the button on his remote device and the screen flashed with a map of Pennsylvania.

"Our target is located in the western portion of the state of Pennsylvania, a small community, here." A red arrow pointed to the lettering, which had been under-lined, designating Bartonsville. He pushed the button again and a larger map appeared, showing only the Bartonsville area. This was immediately followed by a sketch of the town with key facilities drawn in red.

"Of interest to us are the road networks, key terrain features, avenues of approach to the plant, the local capabilities for police action and communication, and the plant itself. I will concentrate on the plant, as the other items will be thoroughly covered in the terrain study." The next slide was a photograph of the plant, clearly showing the parking lot, storm-fence-enclosed perimeter, domed reactor building, the rectangular shape of the control building and a number of associated sheds, warehouses, and maintenance buildings within the barbed-wire-topped fence.

"Good aerial photography," Miller commented to LeCourt.

"This plant is one of the few pilot commercial fast breeder reactors in the United States. As you may know, France, Great Britain, and the Soviet Union have had similar reactors in operation for some years now; but because of cost problems and environmentalist opposi-tion as well as a strong antinuclear faction, the United States lagged behind. Several project reactors of this type were begun and this one was completed at a cost of over 1.8 billion dollars." Franz tapped the podium with a small, chrome-plated pointer. "Remember that figure, one-point-eight billion dollars invested to date in this facility."

The screen flashed with a diagram of the buildings inside the chain-link enclosure. Franz pointed to each building on the screen as he described it. "The plant consists of several distinct elements. First the administra-tive and control building. In this building are located the guard room, offices, and, most important, the computer and control center for the entire plant. From the computer room, all functions of the reactor and associated systems are monitored, adjusted, and shut down, if necessary. This is the brain of the plant and, based on prior programming, establishes and controls the fission process within the reactor." He pointed to the reactor containment building.

"Next, the domed tower. This structure houses the reactor core, cooling system, and associated safety features which we will cover later. The wall consists of five-foot-thick reinforced concrete. Inside is a special containment vessel fabricated of eight-inch-thick carbon steel. It protects the reactor core, control rods, and coolant lines. An additional chamber encloses the containment vessel as another protective measure, thus providing three separate shielding layers between the core and the atmosphere. Specific dimensions will be covered in your classes on special sabotage techniques."

Franz completed his discussion of the main buildings and pointed to a warehouse near the Reactor Service Building. "This building includes a storage site for special nuclear material at the plant. It is one of several such locations around the United States. Inside are portable containers of Plutonium. You will learn of its importance to our operation tomorrow."

He turned several pages and selected one, placing it on top of the others. "Now for a brief look at the security measures we will encounter." His next slide depicted an overhead view of the buildings with their roofs removed and of the perimeter, including the gate house. In the main building, the first room beyond the door had figures placed at various locations.

"There are three eight-hour shifts of guards provided on a contract basis by A&T Security Service of Pittsburgh. Each shift consists of five guards, and you have already received the necessary material relating to the men who will be on duty when we strike."

BJ noted the positions of the guards. One in the gate house next to the main gate; one inside the building next to the main door; one at what looked like a console of some type, and two marked as roving patrols. The only problem would be catching the ones on patrol. Those in fixed locations could be zapped with no sweat. If they could catch the other two either before or after they made their rounds, it'd be a turkey shoot. He made a memo on his pad to ask about patrol routes and time schedules.

"As you know, members of the guard force are primarily retired personnel: police, military, store security, and public service work. On our shift, there are only two who pose any reasonable threat. One is the former marine, Marascoli, and the other, the back-up guard for the five, Hendricks, a former state highway patrolman. Both are young, smart, and skilled. The others should present no problems."

The slide changed and a diagram of electronic alarm devices and infrared barriers appeared. "The alarm and detection devices are inadequate to prevent penetration of the plant. They consist of pressure mats, door and window switches and electric eye beams. There are alarm wires at the base and top of the fence, which do not interest us since we will not be breaching it. Inside, there is conspicuous absence of sonic scanners, which will make our entry much easier." Franz pointed to the diagram. "As you see here, there are a limited number of closed circuit TV monitors which present their display on one of the six screens over the control console. Neutralization of the desk guard will nullify their effectiveness."

Franz pointed out the locations of the various devices in the plant, commenting on the effectiveness of each. He concluded, "We are now in the process of determining the location of the master control for the entire system. When our intelligence on this subject is complete, we may deal with the electronics very easily."

John LeCourt raised his hand. "Franz, question."

"Yes, John."

"It appears that this plant is rather poorly secured against an operation like ours. Am I to assume that there is still no great emphasis placed on prevention of a break-in even after all the publicity and inquiries?"

Heitzman stepped to the right of the podium, tapping the pointer against his leg. "John, you were in the military," he chided gently. "Security in a situation like this is merely a facade which contains a number of flaws, never discovered by their designer until tested and exploited. Unfortunately for them, the only true test will come when we seize the plant."

"But don't the security people run checks on their own system?" Miller asked.

"Indeed they do," Franz responded, "but they are unimaginative and unprofessional in their approach. They test the system to prove to their superiors that it does work, not that it can be penetrated. Wouldn't they appear foolish to design and install an ineffective security system?"

There was low laughter in the room. Franz continued, "We tend to prepare for such an eventuality while telling ourselves that it will never happen. When it does, we usually find, to our dismay, that the enemy, knowing of our preparation, sought out and exploited the weaknesses. When one is subjectively involved, he fails to see the most glaring errors."

Ed Moran pointed with his pencil toward the screen. "I think they could have done a better job if they'd spent a little more money on the electronic system. There's gaps in it they have to know about, but according to this they haven't done anything to plug them. Maybe they think the chances of someone picking a weak point are slim."

Franz nodded. "You're correct, Moran. Budgetary restrictions are a definite cause of inadequate security. They do what they can with what they have, though not always the best employment. Remember, the facade of security, gentlemen. Create the impression of security, but stay within the budget."

LeCourt had been scribbling on his pad as he listened. His forehead was creased with a frown as he spoke up. "I can't believe that they have a plant worth over a billion dollars and they won't spend whatever is necessary to protect it."

Franz answered, his tone almost condescending, "John, you must remember that any potential threat is viewed according to one's particular perception of that threat. Those individuals responsible for the security of this plant have no conception of a threat such as we present. They think in terms of vandalism or protest groups or, perhaps, the fanatical attempts of political extremists; however, I assure you, they have not considered the magnitude of the threat we present. They're prepared to stop the amateurs with their system, but not the professionals. Even at that, if the Nuclear Regulatory Commission doesn't put out an alert, they won't expect us." Franz paused, looking around the room, and asked, as if of everyone, "Does that answer your question?"

The weeks went quickly as the men began applying the techniques they had refreshed to the actual tasks they would be carrying out. Practicing first on scale models of each separate part of the complex, they became thoroughly familiar with their roles. Between rehearsals, they continued with PT, demolitions training and weapons familiarization. They would be carrying Soviet AK-47s and a variety of Communist-bloc side arms. Other weapons and equipment were all of foreign origin, thus adding to the impression of an international terrorist venture. In their fifth week, they began practicing on a larger mock-up of the plant, which had been laid out under heavy tree cover near their obstacle course. Blueprints and floor plans were distributed, as were photographs of the plant interior, to give them visual familiarity with the surroundings. Franz was completely satisfied with the team's proficiency, but there was something indefinable about their attitude that disturbed him. He had noticed a solemness on occasions when he expected levity and expressions of pride.

One evening after supper at the beginning of their last week, he confronted LeCourt with his perplexing problem. The two men sat on the rear stoop of the mess hall, listening to the wild sounds of the forest as dusk settled around them.

"John, I have an odd feeling that you people are going through the motions of preparing for the operation ... superbly and without flaw ... but there seems to be no spirit in it. Is there something wrong?"

LeCourt sat silently, staring into the forest.

"Could it be that the reward is enticing, but now that

the time approaches, the means of obtaining it has become frightening or distressing?" Franz added.

John knew Franz was touching a nerve. It had been nothing more than a twitch of conscience, so he had dismissed it earlier, but the euphoria of attaining sudden wealth, the chance to lead his kind of men again had made it inconsequential. Now there was a growing dissatisfaction, a feeling that the immensity of his, of the team's, contemplated crime would plague them, no matter how much they were paid. His years in the military had been consumed with an unquestioning allegiance to the country, to the government. He served, defending the country "against all enemies, foreign and domestic," without serious question; it was accepted and done, no matter what the cost, no matter how much you might disagree with the senselessness of some of it. All those years and now he'd be a criminal, going against that government. Hell, he used to worry when he got a traffic ticket and now he was going to be involved in a terrorist operation that would bring all the weight of the government against him and his men.

He began slowly, his voice barely perceptible, "Not frightened, Franz. We learned to control our fears a long time ago." His voice grew stronger, "Distressed... bothered... uncertain... yes." He dropped his cigarette and ground it under his combat boot.

"Franz, I served my country for twenty-two years, never struck out at it... took my orders and carried them out as best I knew how, no matter how much some of them hurt. You know what I'm saying?"

Franz nodded silently.

"I rarely even bitched, except when I was with a group of friends. It hurt me when I left the service, hurt more than anyone will ever know, but even then, I never thought of striking out. Now, my God, Franz, we're taking a hell of a shot at my country. Doing what I spent twenty-two years serving to prevent." He picked up a small pointed branch and drew absently in the dirt by his foot. "The others are probably feeling the same thing, now that the training and fun are over and we're getting down to the real thing. It's hard to consider myself a traitor...no amount of money, no new identity, no new country to go to can erase what I feel inside."

Franz felt an unaccustomed pang of uneasiness. Everything had been going so well and this sudden ethical weakness could ruin the entire operation. He searched with an uncommon inability to find something with which to reply, but there was no simple argument that would counter LeCourt's emotional contention. He could worsen the situation by responding unwisely.

The silence hung like an admission of defeat. Franz decided that there was only one avenue he could pursue, and it would require that he reveal to LeCourt more about himself than he had intended. He inwardly cursed himself for allowing this crisis to reach into his past, but it was a means of turning away a potential disaster. Better to trust to LeCourt's basic naiveté than to answer to Vargas for a failure.

"I think I understand what you feel, John," he began. "You see, there is a common thread that links our outlooks, although it might not be apparent." He paused, contemplated his phrasing, and continued, "You might be interested to know that I, even though not in the military, was faced with a similar decision some years ago. My country was Germany; my government, the Third Reich; my leader, Adolph Hitler." John's head jerked erect, his eyes staring into Franz's.

"I served as best I could; not in the front lines, but in the production of the munitions that enabled us to fight."

"Wait a minute, Franz," John interrupted. "There's no comparison between my feeling for my country and anything to do with that madman and Nazi Germany. Come off it."

The only indication that John's remark had stung came in the slight twitching of taut cheek muscles. Thirty-three years before, Franz wouldn't have wasted his time with a mere field officer...wouldn't have dreamed that he would be sitting in a rotten, abandoned camp in this abysmally uncomfortable forest attempting to alter this erstwhile patriot's foolish perspective.

In those days, the young man of only twenty-three sat at the head of the massive Gothic conference table in the portrait-lined board room of his family's firm. His father had suffered a mild stroke two years earlier, in 1942, and the two sons had stepped into leadership roles. Their sprawling factories had turned out thousands of tons of ammunition and untold rifles, machine guns, and artillery pieces since Hitler had begun rearmament in 1937. Franz was young, but his grooming had been strict, his dedication unwavering. There was no slackening of production under the leadership of his older brother and himself. It was through his initiative that their factories maintained output during the labor crisis that threatened to cripple Nazi industry in 1942.

Hitler's National Socialism was committed to the elimination of every living Jew. Goering, on July 31, 1941, wrote to Reinhard Heydrich, "I hereby charge you with making all necessary preparations for bringing about a complete solution of the Jewish question in the German sphere of influence in Europe." From that directive grew the specters of Auschwitz, Dachau, and the other terminal camps in which millions of Jews were murdered. Other prisoners were used as slave labor, but the Jews were deemed "unfit."

Franz was a practical man and argued successfully, against SS opposition, that every prisoner capable of work should be used to maintain production. "If the Jew must die anyway, let him die serving the Fatherland," he argued. Other powerful industrialists agreed, and Hitler allowed them to proceed.

Thousands of prisoners were brought into hastily constructed barbed-wire compounds near the factories where conditions proved as harsh as in the prison camps. There was inadequate food and few shelters for the number of people; many of them spent their last nights on earth huddled against the sides of the buildings, their pitifully shrunken bodies wrapped in ragged blankets. Franz was accurate when he boasted, "We can get a year's work out of one of these Jews in four months, even if we kill him doing it." The prisoners died by the hundreds in

Franz's camps, but he produced the steel that was so necessary for Hitler's armies.

In late 1944, however, Franz knew that the war was lost. The Allied bombing had severely damaged Germany's factories. Morale was down and mutiny was brewing in the officer corps of the military. Stalingrad had marked the turning point of the war on the Eastern front and the Ardennes Campaign was straining all industry to fuel the tanks and keep ammunition flowing to the front. The Allied invasion was crushing forward from France and there was little in the way to stop it.

Young as he was, Franz was too much of a scholar to have missed the lessons of the Treaty of Versailles at the end of World War I and too much of a realist to allow political allegiance to inscribe his epitaph along with the Reich's. He had been secreting gold bullion in anticipation of his departure. There would be no loss for him, no humiliation, no war crimes trial. The others could cling to their beloved Führer. Franz knew there were new bases of power to be built after the war, but he had to survive to be a part of them.

"John, please understand. I'm not drawing a comparison between countries or government, but between men's reactions to a similar situation. You have the advantage of a historical perspective and I, the disadvantage of serving a losing side; nevertheless, my decision to desert the government that had sponsored and nourished me was as difficult as yours must be to perform this act." Franz searched for the proper approach to convey his meaning. He couldn't allow LeCourt to question his Nazi background, but it was necessary to make the case.

"I deserted my government, not my country; a government that had ceased to lead us to anything but oblivion. It isn't your country that you offend; it's the government and the industrial giants who dominate it."

John fought an urge to accept any basis for rationalization Franz might offer. He hadn't known Franz was a former Nazi. But he said he deserted—not the country—the government. What a goddamned mess. Franz was a likable guy, a man who seemed to be straight with people he chose to work with. Now this. What can he tell me about my country, my government?

"Think of what I'm saying, John," Franz urged. "You served the government loyally and well. The government responded not to your needs but to those of the large industries that support its leaders. I ask you, what portion of your countrymen approved of what you did in Vietnam . . . on the orders of your government?"

"For an ex-Nazi, Franz, you sure as hell sound like a damn Communist," John blurted. "Who knows anymore about what they're doing in Washington or what the people want? I sure don't."

"I could hardly be a Communist, John. I'm a lifelong Fascist and enemy of the same forces you fought against in Korea and Vietnam. What I am trying to do will combat them more effectively than your military could ever hope to do. That is why this operation is so essential."

"I don't follow you."

"First, my point on your unreciprocated loyalty. The government paid you for your services and nourished your commitment to it. It also used you in any way it saw fit no matter what the cost to you."

"That's what I volunteered for."

"So you served, lost your family as a consequence, and when the military decided it could no longer use you—not because you weren't qualified but because the government required a drastic reduction in the number of officers—they spat you out."

John winced at the words. He had lost just about everything and who gave a damn besides him?

"Second, I and my associates are attempting to break the ideological conflict into so many tiny nationalistic struggles that there will be no major war between nuclear superpowers."

John looked incredulously at the man. "What in the hell do you mean by that? How can nuclear proliferation solve the problem of a future nuclear war? My God, all that means is that there will be more countries capable of starting it."

"Consider this, John. Sale of Plutonium, nuclear

reactors, or nuclear weapons merely extends the limits of existing weapons sales in the world. America, the Soviet Union, Communist China, most other industrial nations all sell the weapons they produce. We are different only because we sell to anyone, not just governments and factions we consider of use to us."

"That doesn't justify giving a bunch of third world nations and rebels the power to blow themselves and a hell of a lot of other people off the globe." John retorted sharply.

Franz smiled mirthlessly. "You talk just like a superpower bureaucrat. What if you were a citizen of one of the developing nations. Wouldn't you want self-determination? Or is self-determination acceptable only when it conforms ideologically to your own?"

John started to reply, "I don't ..."

"Don't answer now," Franz interrupted, "listen a bit longer."

John eased himself back on the stoop until he was leaning against the building, one knee drawn up, the other leg stretched out in front of him. He slapped absently at a bug near his ear.

Franz continued, "You see, while the small nation is trying to carve out an identity for itself, it is being played as a piece in the superpower chess game. When they offer military aid, it isn't a business deal, but a geopolitical maneuver. It doesn't favor the independent development of the nation, but merely cultures another colony of their particular ideological virus." He paused. "Do you follow my meaning?" John nodded, lighting a cigarette.

"With the Communists, it is a standard process, weapons sales at a good price or on credit, followed by military training missions to instruct in the use of the weapons. Next come technicians to build bases and open trade operations. Soon thereafter, Communist front organizations appear on the labor and political scene and the country is on the road to control. The U. S. is more subtle, but the end result is an inability for the small nation to be neutral. It must become involved in the ideological struggle on one side or the other."

Franz shrugged. "Is it any wonder that these countries would rather deal with us? Our nonaligned political stance makes us the purists. We sell no ideology, only the weapons that the government in power wants. And if a faction seeks to overthrow that government, we will just as willingly sell to them. The strongest of the species will survive, without the ideological domination of the superpowers."

"So you're going to break these little countries out of the grip of the superpowers, huh? Isn't that a pretty big undertaking considering the amount of trade that goes on?"

Franz agreed. "In the past that was true, but nuclear weapons are the great equalizer. It takes only one to make leaders seriously consider the consequences of a war; whereas it takes more artillery and tanks than one nation could supply."

John stared into the darkness around him, half listening to the muted sounds of insects and stirring creatures. What a fucking mess. The whole damn world is screwed up. One time they thought gunpowder was the thing that would be the ultimate factor in warfare. Now we've got nukes. Somebody is going to use them sometime just because they've got 'em. Who knows what's right? Who decides? The government? Not anymore. Not after Watergate, ITT in Chile, all the corporate bribery in Japan, Korea, Europe. Franz might just be right; the government can take care of itself, make all the screw-ups it wants. It sure doesn't give a damn about me. Why should it? I'm just a social security number to a big computer unless I write a letter to my congressman or senator. Then I'm a file card in his correspondence file. Only time they'd really get to know me is if I missed paying my income tax.

John felt a sudden surge of unaccustomed depression, a brief stinging in his eyes that he quickly wiped away. I haven't got a goddamned thing back there, he realized. I haven't got a family. Karen had insisted that it would be better for the kids if they grew up knowing only their stepfather. Didn't even have them. I haven't got the military anymore; I haven't really got a home; there's no real feeling for the government that runs the country. I'm not proud like I used to be. Maybe that's where the idealism went. Without something to be proud of, there was no way to keep the idealism alive. All there was in the world now was John LeCourt and this bunch of misfits who were depending on him.

He sat down beside Franz. "I guess it's time to put my tarnished ideals away and start looking at the real world, Franz."

"John, some twenty centuries ago, Dionysius said something which is a truism: 'It is a law of nature common to all mankind, which times shall neither annul nor destroy, that those who have greater strength and power shall bear rule over those who have less.' I have lived by that, but the power I use is in the form of money. This is the ultimate power that shapes governments, makes wars, builds empires, and destroys that which opposes it. What you and the men are doing will be of little consequence to your government. It will go on afterward as if nothing had happened. The corporation that owns the plant can afford to lose a little of its wealth and it will go on. You and the men will profit beyond your wildest dreams. You'll have wealth, a new identity, plastic surgery by one of the finest surgeons if you wish, and a new country from which to travel and truly begin to live. You've paid your allegiance to your government; now you owe allegiance to yourself."

John put a hand on Franz's shoulder. "Okay, Franz, you've made your case. I'm in and the rest will be too after I talk with them in the morning. No sweat on the government or the corporation. We'll happily rip them off. I only want one stipulation understood . . . my own."

Franz was fighting to suppress a smile of triumph. "Sure, John. What is it?"

"I will not have my people kill anyone without extreme provocation. I don't intend to have some innocent slob die unnecessarily, so count out any instant gunning down of the guards or bystanders. Furthermore, I won't allow execution of the hostages even though we threaten it."

"As you wish, John. I hadn't intended any unnecessary killing in the first place," Franz lied. There would have to be a few changes made in the plan, but the condition could be met. It was hardly a bad bargain for LeCourt's agreement. "Now it is time for us to consider only what is good for us. There are many other times to worry about the world." They stood and walked together into the building for a quick beer and a toast to the success of Prometheus. After John left the building en route to his barracks, Franz stood for a minute or two staring after him, then turned and closed the door behind him.

The next morning dawned bright and hot, without a cloud overhead to block the sun. It was one of the days when the forest and its coolness were a blessing. Vince DeAngelo stopped by Franz's quarters before the first class. The craggy-faced team sergeant was filled with renewed enthusiasm as he informed Heitzman that the team had held a meeting earlier and were all in agreement about the operation. "The colonel laid it all out for us, Franz; mainly how we could blow it if we didn't get our shit together. I suppose we were getting pushed out of shape by something that nobody will remember in five years. I just wanted you to know that as far as we're concerned, if the colonel buys it, we all buy it; so don't worry about us getting the job done."

Franz thanked him, sincerely relieved that LeCourt had been true to his word. He had accepted the explanation, and now the men were following his lead. Franz found himself grinning in satisfaction; that was the man he had selected to lead this operation. His judgment had been accurate . . . and the team had jelled around him.

It was none too soon, because the next two days were consumed with long hours on the transportation phase. Franz and the team reviewed methods of handling and moving the special containers of Plutonium. Military type dosimeters, looking like olive-drab pen lights, were demonstrated as a means of detecting the deadly gamma radiation emitted by the core element and certain waste products stored at the plant. These lethal, invisible rays, similar in wave-length to X-rays, pass through the body, causing damage to blood-forming cells and tissue. Depending on the amount absorbed, gamma radiation produces radiation sickness with effects from nausea and vomiting to incapacitation and death. Franz was careful to stress that Plutonium, which had not been subjected to neutron bombardment in the fission process, emitted only alpha particles of little significance. The team was briefed on the various types of containers they might find and proper handling techniques for each. It was one phase in which no dummy containers were available for practice, but Franz felt assured that the men were capable of adapting the lessons to whatever they found at the plant.

Larry Simmonds and Dieter Kreutz made their final communications checks, reviewing phone numbers for the offices to be called after the takeover, frequencies for police radios, and the sequence of communications linkup in the first hours after they entered the plant. Lee Zimmerman and his section of men went over demolitions emplacement to ensure the use of minimum time on target when they would be responsible for making the threat a reality. Exact amounts of C-4 had been precalculated and the required blasting caps, det cord, time fuse, crimpers, and friction tape already requisitioned.

John had the team talk him through the operation one final time with each man reciting his part in relation to the overall time schedule. Franz listened and observed as the team honed the final edge to their preparation. Franz was elated; it was better than he had hoped, and with the information he had received on the status of the new administration in Washington, the chances for success were higher than before. Imagine the good fortune of catching the new President in the midst of personnel changes throughout the administration.

At noon on July thirtieth, they buried all their remaining supplies in a pit dug between trees and clumps of brush in an inaccessible area away from the camp. The men threw fatigue uniforms, boots, and training material into the deep hole. It had taken most of Friday afternoon to dig it as they cut through thick roots and hauled rocks out of the pit. It was filling much quicker. John LeCourt stood at the edge of the rectangular hole as the men shoveled dirt onto the stack of equipment, watching it disappear under the rich black earth. He waited for a moment, gripping something behind his back, then quickly tossed a worn, wooden name plaque in with the rest of the discards.

Late that afternoon, the helicopters picked them up for the flight to Rio. At the same remote airfield from which they had departed long weeks before, sixteen leaner and harder civilians climbed off the Alouettes. The few curious Cariocas lounging in the shade of the two hangars saw only what appeared to be another oil or mining exploration crew coming back from their shift on some remote site.

Franz had arranged a pleasant surprise for them by alloting four days of relaxation on the beach to take some of the sting out of the training phase. John imagined that one of the side effects was to whet the team's appetite for the reward that awaited them at the completion of their mission. It was a carefully controlled four days with the noticeable inclusion of volleyball and beach athletics to maintain conditioning, while women and alcohol were conspicuous by their absence. They could come later.

On August fourth, they began their flights back to the United States, arriving in their original departure cities by Sunday, August seventh. There was one week to Prometheus.

They rested for two days in the widely separated cities and on Wednesday, August tenth, they flew to Pittsburgh, where they met with two of Albritton's men. Weapons, ammunition, equipment, and special supplies had been smuggled into the city. Two days passed as they checked out their equipment and made cautious reconnaisance drives through the area. Everything was exactly as it had been presented to them in training.

On Saturday night, the equipment was loaded into two cars. The third, a white Chevrolet Impala, had A&T Security Service emblems on its doors. A Ford Econoline van was parked nearby, its motor running. Black

jumpsuits were folded on the seats of the first two cars
weapons carefully concealed on the floorboards. Three o
the men in the Impala wore distinctive tan A&T Securit
Service uniforms. It was 1:30 A.M.

"You know, man," Mike Baker said as he fingered th
top button of his sport shirt, "we're really goin' to sti
things up when we pull this off. I wonder if th
government will cave in like Franz said or will they com
down on us like a ton of shit?"

"My man," Cleave Jones said in a laughing voice
"they're the same kind of dick heads who gave us welfare
the post office, and Vietnam. If they can fuck all that up a
bad as they did with what they had goin' for then
then . . . they sure won't be able to handle dudes like us
You dig, brother?"

Sam Waylor looked at his watch again, irritated that it was only fifteen minutes since he had last checked the time. He had relieved Joe Zuno at 3:45 and that was almost an hour ago. Time went too damn slowly out here. He wished they'd come out and take over for him.

The broad asphalt parking lot lay in a purplish neon glow from the overhead lights. The sharper arc of light around the main gate cut into the dimness beyond but revealed only the swarms of moths whirling about the faces of the spotlights and crawling aimlessly on the ground beneath. Sam didn't like the gate house. It was too quiet and lonely out here. He much preferred to be inside, in the reassuring security of the building. Another look at his watch showed that he had eleven more minutes before Joe would be coming out again to relieve him.

Inside the building, the guards were sitting in bored silence, scanning worn magazines or listening to the transistor radio pouring out a muted Stevie Wonder singing, "You Are the Sunshine of My Life." On the IBM clock over the main doors, the minute hand clicked upward a notch, pointing across the middle of the nine. Cal Bennett sat at the receptionist's desk, filling out the watch report he would have to submit. Another eight hours of occupying space, he thought as he wrote "negative report" under the significant incident heading.

Al Marascoli had finished his walking tour and made his report a half hour ago. Now he was sitting hunched over his textbook, struggling through a chapter on Social Interaction. Al was memorizing phrases he didn't understand in the hope he could bluff his way through class tomorrow. This psychology was heavy stuff. He didn't even hear Stevie Wonder fade and Led Zeppelin take over.

Sam Waylor's head snapped up suddenly as the twin shafts of headlights swept across the front of the guard hut. A car sped across the parking lot and pulled up sharply in front of the main gate. Sam barely had time to recognize the A&T Security Service emblem on the door before two men jumped out and walked rapidly to the window facing him.

The taller of the two men thrust forward a leather folder with the familiar A&T badge on one side and a security pass on the other. "A&T Security Inspection Team," he snapped. "I want this gate open. Now!" Sam was stunned and didn't have time to get a good look at the pass before it was pulled back and the man stepped up to the gate, awaiting admittance. In confusion, he obeyed automatically, fumbling for his key as he hurried to unlock the gate.

As soon as the lock was removed, the first man pushed through impatiently, heading for the building. The short, dark-complexioned one flipped open a leather folder identical to the first. "The name's Thompson, I'll relieve you here at the gate while you accompany Mr. Nelson into the plant," he said crisply. Sam responded with a mute nod. He had heard of the sneak security checks, but there had never been one on the swing shift. These guys weren't supposed to work these hours. I ought to tell the guys inside, he thought frantically, but how can I? Shit, we're goin' to get clobbered on this.

Tony Miller walked briskly toward the main doors while Vince DeAngelo took care of the gate. "So far, so good," he thought as he glanced back, checking to see that the A&T emblem was clearly visible from the building. Waylor ran to catch the security officer before he reached the door. "I gotta give them some sort of alert," he thought frantically.

Inside, Joe Zuno jumped in his chair, shocked out of a doze by the buzzing admittance signal. He sat forward, looking through the narrow window into the face of a stranger. Then he saw the A&T badge and security pass. His sleep-dulled eyes caught fragments of the scene. A&T company car; security pass; and Sam Waylor appearing foolish standing behind the man shading his eyes like an old Indian scout and pantomiming a search. The man's sharp command was unnecessary. "Nelson, from Inspection Division. This is a security check. Open this door immediately."

Zuno turned and spat out, "Security check. Get ready quick." He delayed several seconds before he pushed the disarm lever on the control panel. The room went into instantaneous high gear. Bennett grabbed his reports and scrambled toward the unmanned master console. Marascoli slammed his book and shoved it under a couch cushion. Art Potter came at a quick shamble from the snack bar, buckling his pistol belt. Cal Bennett looked quickly around the room and at each of the guards. "Uniforms look like they've been slept in," he thought immediately. "Too late to change anything now though." They were all standing at their positions when the door opened and Tony Miller strode in.

As soon as the main door opened, DeAngelo opened the vehicular gate and Lee Zimmerman drove the car through, turning along the asphalt toward the rear of the building. In the parking lot, two cars and the van materialized out of the darkness as the rest of the team headed toward the plant.

Inside, Tony faced Cal Bennett and demanded the watch report. Cal handed it to him with a feeling of impending doom. They had been caught cold. Art was already recorded as having completed his five o'clock inspection and it wasn't five yet. This could really hurt if the company wanted to be chicken shit about it. Only Al Marascoli saw DeAngelo slip the automatic pistol from his coat as he stepped through the door. "Freeze!"

The command coincided with Tony Miller's slipping his pistol free as both men confronted the stunned guards. Before anyone could react, Lee Zimmerman walked through the door and moved quickly behind the guards, stripping pistols from their holsters.

"What the hell is going on?" Cal asked in an indignant voice. Sam looked bewilderedly from Miller to DeAngelo to the automatics in their hands. What is this? His mind refused to accept what he was seeing as more men came trotting through the main door, moving past the helpless guards toward the interior of the plant. It can't be. Sam's mouth was dry and he could feel his heart pounding.

John LeCourt walked in, followed by Ed Moran. They watched as Zimmerman finished searching the guards and pushed them, in turn, onto the deep couch where they sat, immobilized and staring. Al Marascoli wasn't overwhelmed by the suddenness of the action. As soon as he saw the pistol appear from DeAngelo's coat, he knew this wasn't a drill. Instinct made him surrender his weapon with the other guards even though he thought he could take the one who was pulling pistols. The other two looked too hard to screw around with. They'd blow him away before he could move. As he was being searched, he determined these weren't amateurs. Zimmerman hit every spot where you could hide a second weapon.

Once the guards were seated, LeCourt stepped in front of them. He studied their faces for a moment. Waylor, sweating across the forehead, lower lip trembling; Bennett, still shocked and unbelieving; Potter, the old man, looking very tired; Marascoli, you cool bastard, we could have used you with us; and Zuno—his eyes are shifting around so fast they're going to slide out of their sockets.

LeCourt stood, hands clasped loosely behind his back. "This plant is now under our control. What happens from here on is beyond your influence and will concern you only if you attempt to interfere with us. That would be foolish and I'm making these comments in order to spare you the grief that misplaced heroism would cause." He waited several seconds, studying their eyes for a reaction, and then continued, "We mean you no harm as individuals. It's unfortunate that you were here at this particular time, and we intend only to hold you until our work is complete and then release you." There was a noticeable relaxation among the guards.

He continued, "We have a number of tasks to accomplish and I'll be required to secure you while we're here. In order to conserve my men for more important matters, I have an alternate method for keeping you out of trouble." He turned and motioned to Cooper, near the door.

The guards' eyes widened as four snarling Doberman pinschers lunged into the room, pulling their two handlers behind them. The lean, black and tan attack dogs bared ugly fangs as they snarled and bit huge chunks of air. Sam Waylor recoiled deeper into the cushion as if to escape the violence of the animals. "Caesar! Turk! Duke! Attila! Down." The dogs dropped obediently at their handlers' sides while continuing to stare menacingly at the seated guards.

"These dogs have been trained specifically to contain you five men and I warn you now that if you are attacked, it'll be your own poor judgment in violating one of the simple rules which will be set down for you. These dogs will kill. I encourage you to follow our instructions implicitly. Do I make myself clear, gentlemen?"

LeCourt was pleased as he watched the rapid nods of acquiescence. Even Marascoli was shaken up by the Dobies. John knew the ex-marine had seen these dogs at work in 'Nam and there was no doubt now that they'd keep the kid from doing something stupid.

The control room was sterile; like the inside of a pressure cooker. It was a panorama of aluminum facings, gray steel cabinets, and banks of glass-faced dials. Across

the top of the computer bank, a long panel of condition
lights glowed a dull green or amber as they portrayed the
status of the various reactor systems. Bluish white neon
bulbs produced a cool, shadowless luminosity from
overhead. The neutral, off-white tile floor was polished to
a gleaming luster that reflected the impersonal, futuristic
atmosphere in the command center.

The shift engineer and the unit operator sat in swivel
chairs behind a curving, gray metal desk in the center of
the room. Idly the unit operator studied the dial readings
that indicated coolant temperature in the intermediate
heat exchanger and consulted a manual on the desk to
check allowable tolerance. Neither man heard the door
open as three team members slipped in behind them. Only
when the coldness of gun muzzles touched the backs of
their necks did they realize something was wrong.
Tomlinson's flat midwestern voice commanded, "Stand
up slowly, put your hands behind your heads and walk
away from that desk."

They complied immediately, silent and frightened.
Once away from the controls, they were hustled out of the
room and down the long corridor to the employees'
lounge. From the other end of the building, Zimmerman
and the dog handlers were herding the guards toward the
same room. It had taken less than five minutes to gain
control of the plant.

Back in the reception area, Vince DeAngelo, watching
the TV monitors, announced, "We have the control
room." It was twelve minutes past five A.M. LeCourt,
Tony Miller, and Ed Moran gathered by the receptionist's
desk as the team leader checked items off his master
schedule. "We're three minutes ahead and all elements
have reported their areas secure. Have demolitions place
the charges and tell Simmonds to go ahead with the phone
links. We'll transmit the demand at 0630 hours as
planned."

Miller acknowledged and reached for the intercom.
LeCourt faced Moran, "Ed, you check perimeter security
to ensure that we're buttoned up in case they try to crash
in on us. The booby traps and claymores should be

emplaced by now, and I want the whole thing completed before the local police finally realize that the oh-five-hundred check-in is not coming this morning. I'd hate to have to kill one of them to prove a point if they try to hard-nose it, rather than taking a warning." Moran nodded and walked quickly away toward the main door.

Outside the plant, the demolition team had been concealing and planting booby traps. The last group was shaped like oversized, olive-drab golf tees and had been pushed into the ground at selected locations around the perimeter of the fencing. These "toe-poppers," when stepped on, exploded upward with little effect to the sides, but blew a substantial hole in the foot of their victim. At fifty-yard intervals, claymore mines had been placed with their fragmentation arcs interlocking to create a barrier of steel in front of the main access routes. Several of the claymores had been intentionally aimed upward to be detonated as a warning. Ed Moran noted the progress and passed LeCourt's sense of urgency for speedy completion of the task on to the men.

Inside, the guards and technicians were pushed into the employees' lounge. It was half the size of a tennis court and seemed even larger with all the furniture removed. The chrome and vinyl couches and chairs were stacked in the corridor. The Currier and Ives prints and even the drapes that had covered one wall to simulate windows in this totally enclosed room had been taken down. The starkness was interrupted only by seven mattresses laid at careful intervals across the floor. Light green walls stared across the vacant room at one another.

"Strip to your skivvies." The grim-faced raider pointed with the muzzle of his German Schmeisser submachine gun to a spot inside the doorway. "Pile your clothing here with any valuables you have in a buttoned pocket. They'll be returned to you when you're released."

Sam sat on the edge of one of the mattresses and began to untie his shoes. His coat, tie, and shirt were lying beside him. He was conscious of the holes in his undershirt. Martha had nagged him about his underwear, but he never bothered to get new ones. Now they were showing

in front of everybody. These guys don't talk like they're
gonna hurt us, he thought as he listened to the men
standing in the door. They look mean as shit. I hope no
one does anything to piss them off. They said they weren't
gonna hurt us unless we did something wrong. Man, I'm
gonna sit right here for as long as they want me to if that's
what it takes. He glanced into the corridor where the
Dobermans sat poised beside their handlers, ears
forward, eyes watching every move in the room. Sam felt
the trembling start. Oh God, dear God, please don't let
anything happen to me. He couldn't concentrate on
undressing. He fumbled with his shoelace, cursing at his
clumsiness. Oh God, I've got to hurry. They'll kill me if I
don't get my clothes off. He tugged hard at the tightly
knotted lace, breaking it and jerking his shoe off with a
grunt of relief.

Marascoli had finished undressing and was piling his
clothes carefully where the raider had indicated. Al was
cautious to make no suspicious moves. It was obvious
that they were paying more attention to him than the
others. Every time he looked up, one of them was looking
back at him. When he moved, even though someone else
might be moving at the same time, one of them would
follow him with the muzzle of his submachine gun. I
wonder what they know about me? he pondered. They
look like they're just waitin' for me to make my play so
they can go ahead and waste me. Al stared at the two men
in the doorway and noted the ease and assurance with
which they handled their weapons and gave commands.
There were hard calluses along the knife edge of their
hands, karate calluses from pounding boards and soaking
the hand in salt water. He walked slowly back to his
mattress and sat down, facing the door. These guys are
pros; probably ex-military from the way they handle
themselves, and those Dobies are K-9 for sure. No odds in
trying to brace these dudes, he decided. Don't worry
about me, motherfucker. I'm not goin' to make a stupid
play and become a statistic for this fuckin' plant. No
way.

Tomlinson and Pete Alexander stood cooly alert in the
doorway, their eyes following the guards' movements in

the room beyond. Everything was going like a charm so far, but they remained suspicious. There was no nervous, amateur fingering of the triggers. If they had to fire, they knew exactly how long a burst it would take from each weapon to trace a gut to shoulder stitch of bullets in every one of their hostages. They also knew that John LeCourt had ordered no rounds fired unless the situation went totally beyond control by other means. Either one of them could wade into this bunch and kill them with bare hands, if necessary. Marascoli might put up a fight, but the others wouldn't even raise a sweat. But with the Dobermans there, the hostages weren't going to make any trouble at all.

The guards and technicians had finished piling their clothes in untidy stacks near the door and, attired only in their underwear, either stood or sat uncomfortably in the center of the room. Alexander scooped up the clothing and carried it out of the room. Tomlinson kept the men covered as two of the Dobermans were led into the room. The handler unsnapped his leash from the choke collars. One dog immediately walked to a position ten feet to the left of the door and sat down. The second dog sat in the doorway. Each Doberman continued its impassive vigil over the men in the room. The hostages who were standing sat down slowly and tried to get close to another man.

Bobby Jack Tomlinson lowered the muzzle of his weapon as he noted the paralyzing effect of the dogs on the hostages. "All right, give me your attention," he snapped. "You're settled now. Stay that way. This lounge will be home for you until we leave. Food will be brought to you at mealtime and you are free to use the latrine one at a time. There will be no talking among you while you are in this room. Finally, don't try to leave this lounge for any reason, or move your mattresses beyond the white line painted on the floor." The hostages realized for the first time that a painted white line divided the room, leaving the front third nearest the door a no-man's-land occupied by the dogs.

"These dogs won't bother you unless you make a threatening gesture toward them or move into the area this side of the line." Tomlinson swept his finger in an arc, pointing at each man in turn. "Get that clear. Don't make a threatening gesture and don't cross into this area. These animals will attack without hesitation if you do either of those things and there will be two other Dobies in the hall backing them up. I can't guarantee that my handler will get to you in time to save you. Do I make myself clear?" There were violent nods of understanding.

At Bartonsville's red brick police station, the desk sergeant paused in reading a paperback copy of *The New Centurions* and checked the clock. It was after five A.M. and there had been no call from the reactor plant. He jotted down a note to himself on the legal pad at the edge of the desk. There would have to be an entry in the phone log if he called them and there was no sense in getting one of the guards in trouble. Benny could just as easily drop by on his regular rounds.

At his Harrisburg mansion, Governor Archibald Reaves snored softly in his sleep, unaware of the chaos about to break around him. In the Pentagon, Major General Craig Alexander had pulled the duty in the Intelligence Center, down in the bowels of the huge building. He eased his softening six-foot frame out of the cushioned leather chair as he handed the latest intelligence summaries to the White House courier. More general reading for the President after breakfast. Craig was fighting a migraine headache and his normal, imperturbable nature was disintegrating rapidly. It didn't take long on a staff assignment to wreck a man's physical and mental condition. Even with the officers' gym, jogging, and golf, Craig could feel that his fine edge was worn down and a lassitude was developing. His heavy eyebrows knitted together and creases wrinkled his forehead as another pounding pain slammed through his head. "Double damn this weekend duty," he cursed under his breath. After he finished his tour at 1200 hours, he was going home to sleep off the headache and try to get in a round of golf at the Army-Navy Country Club later in the afternoon. Only another six-and-a-half hours.

*   *   *

Meanwhile in the Bartonsville plant, Larry Simmonds walked to the receptionist's desk where LeCourt was conferring with Tony Miller. "Beg your pardon, sir," he interrupted them, "but communications are set. I have the switchboard arranged to provide a master phone for conference call transmissions and four separate phones for individual communications. The radios are tuned for broadcast and reception on both commercial and official frequencies and we're monitoring local and state police right now. So far there's no radio traffic relating to us." Simmonds read down the list of items on his clipboard. "That's it, sir. We're wired for sound and ready to go."

LeCourt was inwardly pleased at how well the initial phases were progressing. The hostages were secure and quiet. The demolitions were placed and the parking lot had been covered with crowsfeet, the small iron balls with four hollow steel projections, so arranged that one would always be upright. Any vehicles attempting to drive into the lot would have their tires punctured immediately and be easy targets for the three Soviet RPG-7 antitank rocket launchers that had been manned around the perimeter. If the National Guard brought armored vehicles in, the five pound projectile would penetrate up to twelve inches of armor, which was more than enough to stop them. It was good that they had both high explosive and armor-piercing rounds. Early detection radar sets had been placed on the roof and Cleave Jones had two men with him equipped with sniper rifles and scopes. For night work they had infrared and starlight scopes. Nothing would get past them.

Vince DeAngelo walked over with a cup of steaming coffee and a napkin-wrapped doughnut. Setting them down in front of the colonel he grinned. "Our hosts were good enough to keep the pot on for us, sir. I'll put up a new brew in a couple of minutes 'cause this one's sort of weak."

"Thanks, Vince. How are we doing with the reactor charges?"

"Zimmerman checked in a couple of minutes ago and

said that the diamond charges were set on the primary
sodium lines from the pumps and they were working on
the emergency core-cooling lines. He said it was really
something to see everything exactly like it was on the
plans we studied . . . no sweat finding the access doors and
correct compartments. I'll bet you could really get your
ass lost down there if you didn't know where you were
going."

"Probably so," John agreed. "There are eight stories'
worth of chambers, tunnels, cells, and compartments
under the floor of the reactor building, along with all that
equipment and piping."

"This place is something else. Anyway, Lee's people
are already on the ECCS."

LeCourt nodded, "Okay, Vince. That's good news.
We're still running a couple of minutes ahead of schedule,
which doesn't hurt us a bit." The greatest problem for the
team lay in premature reaction by either local or state
police in attempting to investigate the missed report. It
was a calculated risk that their undisturbed routine over
the past years would lull them into a false assumption of
guard oversight rather than a takeover. Once the threat
was transmitted to the authorities and the implications
understood, no one would be willing to risk destruction of
the plant. If only some local cop didn't try to play hero
and get himself killed.

Lee Zimmerman, wearing his bulky protective suit,
had just emerged from the hatch leading down to the
reactor cavity cooling unit cell and stood on the rough
steel plating, looking around the towering interior of the
building. The Reactor Containment Building arched
upward another 135 feet to the top of its center dome,
almost as tall as a fourteen-story building. It was wider
than half a football field and seemed larger, even with the
bulk of giant cooling and exhaust fans, metal staircases,
and a monsterous overhead polar crane that extended the
width of the building. To his left, a 40-foot-high
equipment hatch led to the Reactor Service Building,
allowing transfer of fuel rods via the overhead crane to
and from the reactor core. Beside it was an airlock for

personnel and smaller pieces of equipment. Both of these were designed to remain airtight in the event of a core disruptive accident, thus preventing escape of radioactive aerosol and particles to the outside.

Beneath him in the labyrinth of concrete and steel-walled rooms, surrounding the heavy reactor vessel, were vast arrangements of pipes, valves, heat exchangers, and a variety of pumps and cooling units. Zimmerman had walked to the very bottom of the structure to locate the access door leading to the reactor cavity, directly below the core. In it was the ex-vessel core catcher, a dish-shaped raised platform of Aluminum Oxide bricks, surrounded by insulating firebrick and cooling coils. The designers had placed this device under the core to perform the function that had given it its name—catch the molten core as it melted through after an accident and contain it until it cooled. Lee had calculated the size shaped-charge that would be required to rupture the center of the bricks prior to the arrival of the lava flow of radioactive core materials. There would be no attenuation of flow after that.

He shivered involuntarily as he looked about him, thinking of the hellish force they could loose were they to carry out their threat. Blowing the primary coolant line from the pump would spray highly radioactive Sodium throughout the subchamber, transforming it into a flaming ball of gases that would burst through open hatches and exhaust vents to the chamber in which he stood. The reactor core, thus deprived of its essential coolant would instantaneously begin to overheat and, with control rods withdrawn and shutdown aborted, would melt the fuel pins. They would have already opened the reactor head access area and used the gantry crane to pull the access plugs to the core. There would be nothing to stop the escape of the superheated vapors and fission products into the chamber. As the core melted through the bottom of its carbon steel containment vessel, the core catcher would not serve to stop it. God only knew what would happen after that. Lee was thankful that they had to do no more than threaten. What would occur should they carry it out was beyond his comprehension. It took twelve pounds of Plutonium to destroy Nagasaki. There was over fifty times that much in this reactor.

Benny Slocum pulled up in front of the station house and picked his tan and black uniform hat from the seat as he opened the door and slid out. The '75 Dodge was about due for an overhaul soon, primarily because it had been driven only within the limits of Bartonsville and the plugs were fouled all to hell. Benny treated the patrol car as if it were his own vehicle, insisting on maintenance whether the car needed it or not. He settled the cap over his curly blond hair and tucked his shirt in neatly around his trousers. He was thirty-nine years old and probably would stay a patrolman until he retired, which didn't really give him much incentive, but he did strive to make a good appearance when there was someone to see it. He was conscious of the still muscular body under his uniform. Almost as solid as he had been when he played football and baseball for Bartonsville High. Made All-Conference his junior and senior years in both sports; the only one to have done it. He still had his letter jackets at home and would wear them over to the Lions Club softball games where he pitched for the local club. He hadn't been able to get to college and had lived here all his life, but it was a good town and he was comfortable in it.

As he pushed through the twin-glassed doors, the sergeant glanced up. "How's it goin', Ben?" he asked perfunctorily.

"Pretty quiet, Charlie," Benny responded, walking over to get a cup of coffee. He selected one of the cups that looked somewhat cleaner than the rest and poured a cup of the boiling brew. "Caught me a lost New Yorker comin' from Charleston tryin' to make it to Pittsburgh." He placed the cup on the table and stirred in a teaspoon of sugar. "Fella told me he didn't see the twenty-five mile per hour sign." Ben chuckled. "I told him he sure must have seen the fifty-five and forty-five mile per hour signs outside of town and he was doin' sixty-two when he came through the radar. Unless he figured we set higher speed limits in town than outside, he was in trouble." He took a sip of the coffee and blew on it before taking a second. "Damn, Charlie, you sure keep this stuff hot."

The sergeant looked up from his book. "Can't taste it when it's real hot. You figure which is worse, tasting it or gettin' a little singe on the lips." He leaned forward, placing the paperback on the desk. "Oh yeah, I didn't get a five o'clock call from the plant. How about swinging by there and tellin' the gate guard to have Cal give me a ring so I can enter it on my report."

Benny sat down in one of the wooden swivel chairs to the left of the door and pulled it up to the railing that ran the width of the sparsely furnished room. A wooden bench and coat rack were against the wall on the other side of the room and behind the railing were the sergeant's desk, chair, a flat top wooden table, and several metal filing cabinets. The small table with the coffee pot and a brass spittoon by the wooden bench filled out the furniture.

"I'll get them on my way out to the shoppin' center. They probably got into a hot pinochle game and forgot about it. They're just waitin' for eight o'clock so they can go home." He continued to sip the coffee, holding the cup between his palms and blowing on the liquid. "That the same book you were readin' last night?"

"Yeah. I skipped around and read the good parts last night. Now I'm going back and reading the rest of the book."

Several minutes later, Benny finished his coffee. He stood up and stretched, covering his mouth as he yawned. "Well, I guess I'll get on my way and finish up the run. See you later, Charlie."

"Okay, Benny. Don't forget to have them call me now."

Ben straightened his cap after he replaced the coffee cup. He walked to the door and looked out to the east. "Light's breakin'. Gonna be a good day today. Maybe take Sally and the kids out to the park for a picnic this afternoon." He was talking to himself as Charlie sat intent on his book.

*   *   *

Oh-six-hundred hours. Larry Simmonds placed a phone call, instructing the operator to set up a conference call between his number, the executive office of the governor, corporate headquarters of Continental Nuclear Corporation in Chicago, and the newsrooms of TV stations KPPA, WTIP, and WEPA in Pittsburgh. The latter would reach the CBS, NBC, and ABC affiliates. As she was instructed, the young operator alerted each of the numbers she was given that a priority call would be received at exactly 0630 hours and a responsible party was to be at each number to accept it. Once he had completed his assignment, Simmonds reread the telegrams that would be sent to each of the offices later that morning.

A sleepy aide took the call in the governor's office. At the glass-walled executive suite of CONUCOR's sky-scraper offices, a security officer accepted the call and immediately phoned his supervisor. In the newsrooms of the network stations, morning programs were being assembled when the calls came in. Desk editors made a note to handle the 6:30 message and returned to their work.

Benny turned off of High Street onto the narrower access road that led to the plant. There was a turn to the left about twenty yards ahead and then straight into the parking lot. As he drove, Benny was weighing whether or not to spend the afternoon watching the Pirates and Giants game instead of driving out to Danz Park for a picnic. It'd be a good game.

He wasn't aware that his car had blown all four tires until the steering wheel went slithery in his hands and the car began flopping along on the shredding, flattened rubber. "What the . . . ?" he blurted aloud as he fought the car to a halt. He reached down and switched off the ignition, opening the door with his left hand. "Oh Jeezus." Pain lanced through the arch of his left foot as he stepped down. One of the razor sharp spikes pierced through the sole of his shoe and into his foot. Benny clung to the steering wheel and pulled himself back onto the front seat.

As he gingerly lifted his foot to examine the bottom of the shoe, blood dribbled over the back edge of the shoe, soaking his white sock. He saw the crowsfoot still protruding from the bottom of his shoe. Benny felt himself going lightheaded and his fingers trembled as he tried to pull the spiked device from his foot. "I'm not goin' to pass out." He was shivering. Tiny beads of sweat covered his forehead. He gripped the three protruding spikes firmly, closed his eyes and jerked it from his foot. Immediate burning pain preceded a throbbing that marked time with his rapidly pounding heart. He bit his lower lip as he fumbled in his hip pocket for a handkerchief to use as a bandage. There was a full first aid kit under the glove compartment, but it didn't occur to him to use it. After pulling off his shoe, he wrapped the handkerchief tightly around his instep to staunch the flow of blood and pushed the bottom of his foot up against the dash to get pressure on the wound. His headlights revealed what he hadn't noticed as he drove into the lot. Across the dark asphalt were scattered hundreds, even thousands of the spiked objects.

A bud of fear began to blossom in Benny's mind as he stared across the vacant parking lot toward the familiar concrete structures. As he fought down a feeling of nausea, he began to sense that the missed five o'clock report might have been more than oversight. The guards' cars were in their regular spaces, but these things, he looked at the spikes with revulsion, these things sure shouldn't be here. I'm still bleeding and I think I'm gonna barf, he thought miserably. Better just sit a second and get this under control.

In the gate house, Mike Baker saw the headlights turn into the parking lot and then slew off to one side as the vehicle slid to a halt. He picked up the phone and pushed the intercom button. "Control, this is gate one over." Miller's voice came over the phone, "This is control, go ahead."

There was a tinge of excitement in Baker's voice, "Vehicle stopped at far end of parking lot, sir. He hit the crowsfeet. It's the local police cruiser with one man in it."

Miller paused, passing the information to LeCourt, and then came back on the line. "Roger, gate house. Use the bull horn and advise the officer to abandon his vehicle and depart the area on foot. Once he's clear of the car, have one of the positions put an H.E. round into it. Make certain that officer gets clear first."

"Roger, control," the NCO responded as he reached under the cabinet top for the portable loudspeaker. He replaced the phone with his other hand and steadied the bull horn in the direction of the stalled patrol car. The sound rasped loudly across the lot. "Attention, patrolman! Attention, patrolman! Abandon your vehicle. I say again. Abandon your vehicle, walk out the way you entered until you reach High Street. Do not hesitate. This is an order." The sound echoed strangely in the quiet morning. People were just getting up in their comfortable homes in the surrounding neighborhoods, unaware that Benny Slocum was in trouble.

The voice crackled again, "You will have five minutes to leave your vehicle and clear the area." The sweep second hand on a Rolex moved past the twelve. "I am beginning my count now. You have five minutes to clear the area."

When the voice had first shocked Benny into awareness, he had listened incredulously. Then as the instructions became clear, Benny found himself jamming his shoe back on over the handkerchief. When the voice stopped, Benny kicked the spikes away from the pavement below the door. He stepped out onto the newly cleared space and braced himself against the inside of the open door, pushing against the armrest with his hip. He cupped his hands around his mouth and shouted as loudly as he could, "You there. This is the police. What are you doing in there?"

"You have four minutes, twenty-five seconds to clear the area," the disjointed voice boomed back.

Benny steadied himself, unfastening the holster flap and withdrawing his Smith and Wesson .357 Magnum. He crouched slightly and rested his gun arm on the open window, aiming in the direction of the gate house. The range was too long for a shot, but it gave him confidence to have the pistol out. "This is Officer Slocum," he shouted. "Step out where I can see you and identify yourself."

"You have three minutes, fifty-five seconds to clear the area." The NCO placed the bull horn on the counter top and reached for the phone. "Control, this is gate one."

"This is control, go ahead."

"He isn't leaving the car, sir. I have three minutes, forty seconds left."

"Hold on. We'll jog him a bit." Miller punched another button on his phone at the control console. "Roof, this is control."

There was a short delay and Cleave Jones's voice came over the line. "This is roof, go ahead, sir."

"Fire four rounds into the car on my command. I want windshield hits on the passenger side."

"Roger, control. We've been monitoring and have the patrolman in sight. We'll miss him, but he'll get the message."

"Good. That's what I want." He repunched the gate button. "Gate, give him a last warning."

Benny heard the voice again, "Move away from your car and depart the area. This is your last warning." The nausea and coldness was from more than his wound now. Fear was beginning to immobilize him and he fought to regain control of himself. "This is all wrong and I'm supposed to handle it. I gotta stay and find out what's goin' on," he thought determinedly. "Maybe I can get Charlie to get some help if I get him on the radio." He started to duck his head and slide back into the car when Miller gave the command to fire.

Snap! Bang! The first round was the only one he heard as the sound of smashing glass and three subsequent rounds blended together with the "thunk" of bullets punching through metal. Benny froze, halfway into the driver's seat as the windshield dissolved in front of his startled face.

"Oh God." Benny's voice was only a squeak. His knees gave way and he slumped to the seat. "Oh God, they're

shooting at me. They're gonna kill me." He was trembling
violently. "I got to get out of here." He slid out of the car
and crouched behind the open door, his pistol forgotten
on the front seat. "Hey! Hey you in there!" He shouted as
loudly as he could. His voice jumped to a high-pitched,
pleading note, "I'm going. For God's sake, don't shoot
anymore." He searched the front of the building wildly,
waiting for the next rounds to come crashing into him.

"You have two minutes, fifty seconds to clear the
area."

Benny turned and slowly picked his way through the
spikes, crouching low as he worked back toward the road.
Unconsciously he noticed that the tires on his car looked
like some sort of porcupine with all the spikes protruding
from them.

He was limping up the hill toward High Street when
the antitank rocket hit his car. The explosion of the shell
and gas tank threw him to his knees. He sank to the
ground, digging his fingernails into the rocky soil, his
body shaking as confusion and fear overrode his self-
control.

Inside the plant, John LeCourt nodded with satisfaction as Miller reported that the officer was safe and the car
burning. "Well, Tony, we're about to draw a crowd for
our little performance and that was about as effective an
attention getter as could have been devised. Wait until the
patrolman is debriefed."

"If nothing else makes the point, that RPG round
will," Miller replied. "I always wondered what one of
those would do to a soft-skinned target."

"That cop should be damned thankful he took our
advice and bugged out," DeAngelo remarked.

"Roger that. I would have hated to start this off by
greasing a local. It'd be like putting a Golden Gloves
lightweight against Joe Frazier," Miller said.

LeCourt agreed. "It's different when you're up against
someone who can fight back, but that poor guy is just
doing the best he can, trying to make a living. There's no
reason for him to die over something he can't stop." He
dismissed the topic. "We'd better get the calls made and

make certain that the governor stops any other local reaction that could get these people hurt."

At precisely 0630 hours, Larry Simmonds placed the call to the Bartonsville operator, instructing her to complete the prearranged conference call. Within seconds, phones rang in widely separated offices.

Steven Murtaugh, taciturn assistant to the governor, sat sipping a cup of hot chocolate while reading through a pile of correspondence that would go to the governor for his signature on Monday morning. He had been mildly irritated when the young aide had called him about an unusual phone message that had come in. It was early Sunday morning, but Steve was accustomed to working odd hours and it could be important. He had assured his drowsy wife that he'd be back in time to make the eleven o'clock church service with her and their two children. That had been almost an hour ago and now the aide sat across the large, walnut-paneled room from Murtaugh, nervously waiting.

The gentle, dual-tone chime of the governor's phone startled them both, even though they had anticipated it. The aide reached for the phone as Murtaugh replaced the papers in the governor's in-basket. "Governor Reaves's office, may I help you?" His eyes searched Murtaugh's as he acknowledged that an executive was present. "Yes, Mr. Murtaugh, assistant to the governor, is here. One moment, please."

Murtaugh picked up his extension, motioning for the aide to remain on the line. "This is Mr. Murtaugh speaking. May I help you?"

In Chicago, the chief of security had finally awakened Taylor Atkins. The thirty-six-year-old assistant director of CONUCOR's public relations was the executive-on-call for the weekend, designated to handle any decisions that came up or to forestall them until Monday. After determining that the call warranted his attention, Taylor drove the six blocks from his midtown apartment to the office. Two Alka Seltzers and a quick Bloody Mary hadn't even dented the racking hangover that was sending pulses of pain up the back of his head. He wasn't accustomed to getting smashed at parties, but the vodka martinis last night had slipped up on him. He sat miserably at his desk trying to ignore the incessant conversation from the guard and wishing that the call would come so he could go back to bed.

The ringing of the phone was uncommonly loud. He cringed slightly as he picked it up, identified himself and waited for the message.

In the Pittsburgh newsrooms, the desk editors cursed as they read copy, red inking news items, while cradling the phones against their shoulders.

At the plant, Dieter Kreutz reread the ransom demand to himself for the seventh time. He had almost memorized it. There could be no mistake when he read it on the phone so he kept going over the curtly worded paper. His heavily accented voice would be a vital factor in creating the impression of terrorist action when it came over the line to the listeners. A foreign voice, the details of the demand, the magnitude and audacity of the threat, and the imaginations of the recipients would suffice.

John LeCourt listened intently on an extension as the operator completed the call and each of the recipients answered. Once all had identified themselves, he pointed to Kreutz and nodded.

"This is a representative of the Popular Liberation Army." His coarse, Platt Deutsch pronunciation of the English words was ominous. "We have seized control of the Bartonsville Nuclear Power Plant and hold seven hostages. We have secured the control room and completely dominate the operation of this plant."

All inattentiveness and unconcern vanished at the other ends of the lines. The initial shock was followed by comprehension of what was happening.

"We have prepared for the destruction of this plant. To confirm this, I will relate part of our measures. Demolition charges have been placed on the liquid sodium cooling lines serving the reactor, and we are prepared to destroy the emergency core-cooling system. We have access to the computer and are prepared to abort all system control tapes."

Taylor Atkins sat immobilized, his hangover forgotten as he realized why the corporation had been contacted. Bartonsville was their pilot fast breeder reactor and there was over a billion dollars tied up in it already. He put his hand over the mouthpiece and yelled for the guard to get his supervisor. He went back to his scribbled notes as he tried to copy the message.

The desk editors had dropped everything else and were typing rapidly to keep up with the message as it came over their phones. Alan Hardy, WTIP, was shouting for one of the radio staff to get on the other line.

Kreutz continued in his harsh tone, "We are prepared to destroy the reactor and create a nuclear accident of such proportions that it will make a wasteland out of the metropolitan Pittsburgh area. I assure you we are completely versed in the operation and possible destruction of this plant and do not make an idle threat. I call to your memory the incidents at the Fermi Plant near Detroit and the Brown's Ferry Plant fire in Atlanta in which accidents precipitated near disasters. This will be no accident."

Steve Murtaugh sat rigidly in his high-backed leather chair. He appeared outwardly calm, but his mind was in turmoil. The impact of the situation was staggering . . . if it were true. He motioned for the aide to come over to his desk. Covering the mouthpiece, he said, "Pete, get on the other line. Call Bartonsville and get the police to check this out. Let me know as soon as you get an answer. Is this thing really happening?"

"I will now present our demand and conditions. Any act of noncompliance will result in the death of selected hostages, and a serious violation of our terms will force us to destroy the plant." He paused, counting to four to himself. A break for emphasis.

"First, a ransom of fifty million dollars will be delivered to this location in seventy-eight hours. That is, by twelve-thirty P.M., on Wednesday, August seventeenth. Second, a means for our safe departure, which we will specify later, will be provided. Third, the media will provide coverage as we dictate and will present statements prepared by us. Fourth, no action will be taken against us during our period of control. No one will attempt to force entry of the area of the plant and there will be no ground or aerial surveillance of our activities."

Atkins stared incredulously at the figure he had just written. Fifty million dollars! Lord almighty, where could they come up with that kind of cash in seventy-eight hours? The son of a bitch sounded like he knew what he was talking about and if they managed to destroy even parts of the reactor, it'd cost a lot more than fifty million to put them back together.

He wasn't certain exactly what would result if the threat were carried out, but the Fermi and Brown's Ferry accidents were near melt-downs. That was about as bad as an accident could be.

As he continued to listen, he was listing the calls he'd have to make. The plant manager at Bartonsville to check out this story; key executives who would be able to activate the corporate disaster plan should the plant supervisor be unable to handle it.

Kreutz was completing the conditions. "Finally, we will maintain communications by telephone and telegraph. You will receive written transcripts of this demand in a short while. There will also be separate instructions given each of you in the next hour. I warn you once again that any act of noncompliance will cause the death of selected hostages and a serious breach will force us to destroy the plant . . . and now I terminate this call." There was a click followed by the buzzing of an open line.

Dieter pushed the disconnect switch and looked inquiringly at LeCourt, who gave him a circled thumb and forefinger for a good job. "Perfect, Dieter. Now give the governor's office five minutes to digest it and then hit that turkey with the instructions about noninterference."

Murtaugh sat immobile, the buzzing phone still against his ear as he stared at the pages of notes in front of him. Slowly he returned the phone to its cradle. This is wild . . . one whopper of a bad dream. A takeover of the Bartonsville Nuclear Plant . . . Bartonsville? That was a little town out west of Pittsburgh. Never paid much attention to it. Better get a quick run-down on the damn place before calling the governor.

"Mr. Murtaugh, you'd better get on the line," Pete Nowak said excitedly, "I've got Sergeant Charles Perkins on the line from Bartonsville. It sounds bad."

Steve snatched the phone and punched line seven. "This is the governor's assistant, Perkins. What's happening there?"

"We've got a big problem at the plant, sir." Perkins's voice was even, but carried a strong note of concern. "They almost killed my patrolman. Shot up his car and, best as I can get it from him, blew the damn thing up with some sort of rocket."

"Blew it up with a rocket? Who are 'they'?"

"Don't know yet, sir. I heard the explosion at six-fourteen. Thought I heard rifle shots before that, but wasn't sure. Then all Hades broke loose with people from the neighborhood over by the plant calling in. They said a car was burning in the plant parking lot and a couple said they thought it looked like the gas tank exploded. I tried to get Benny, he's the patrolman, on the radio. I sent him over to check the plant out 'cause I hadn't gotten a five o'clock check-in call from the guard. Well, I couldn't get him to answer and then one of the people who lives out that way came in the front door with Benny."

"Go on," Murtaugh said impatiently.

"Well, sir, Benny was in pretty bad shape. Not shot up, but really shook. I got him to drink some coffee and start tellin' me what happened."

"What did?"

"Seems he drove into the parking lot and there were some sort of spikes spread all over it. Blew all the tires on his cruiser. Somebody in the plant had a loud hailer and told him to leave his car and get out of the area. Benny tried to brace 'em and find out what was goin' on and they fired a burst at him. Nearly killed him. He got away from the car since he couldn't do anything with just a service revolver and no sooner cleared the parking lot when he heard a sound like a loud pop, then a whoosh and then the explosion. He said it knocked him flat."

"You said you missed the five o'clock check-in from the guards at the plant. Do they check in with you at regular intervals?"

"Yes, sir. We get hourly calls from them, but on slow shifts, they forget once in a while and make it up when they remember. Don't usually miss two hours like they did today though."

"Have you checked it out yet?"

"No, sir. I just finished getting Benny squared away and called the chief to alert him. I was gettin' ready to go over when your man called."

Murtaugh had heard enough to know that odds were heavy in favor of the terrorists' threat being authentic. "Perkins, you alert your chief and use whatever men you have available to seal the area around that plant off from traffic. I don't want anyone going into the area. You got that?"

"Yes, sir. Should I . . . uh . . . say this is on orders of the governor? That is, in case anyone asks. I'm just the desk sergeant."

"You tell them that. My name is Murtaugh. M-U-R-T-A-U-G-H. I'm the governor's assistant. Have the chief by the phone as soon as you can get him there. We'll be calling back with further instructions and until then, you keep everyone . . . I mean every single spectating soul . . . away from that plant. Got it?"

"Yes, sir. I'll do it right now."

Murtaugh hung up, his face tense. "Pete, we've got a live disaster on our hands. Get me all you can on Bartonsville and the power plant there. Who operates it, how big it is, the exact distance from Pittsburgh."

His mind was forming an orderly sequence now. What he had to know, who he had to contact, the bases he had to touch immediately. "Okay for now. Get on it and let me know as soon as you get each piece of information."

The swiftly moving aide was at the door when Murtaugh called out to him, "Pete, call Helen and tell her we need secretarial help in here fast. I want at least two girls here before nine o'clock and get Allen on the phone. The governor will need his press staff standing by for a release. There'll be reporters all over us as soon as this breaks."

He was dialing the State Police Headquarters when the governor's phone chimed. He punched the blinking button and the same alien voice came over the line. "Is this Murtaugh?"

"Yes it is."

"This is the PLA. I have instructions for you. You will take them down and carry them out completely. Do you understand?"

Steve acknowledged as he reached for a clean legal pad. Got to start keeping a log of events and messages, he thought as he prepared to write.

"You will have Governor Reaves in his office by ten A.M. for an important communication. In the meantime, you will ensure that no force is used against us. Do not involve the National Guard, state police, or any other body against us. They are not equipped to hinder us and will only cause unnecessary death and destruction. Do you understand?"

Steve could only acknowledge and hang up when the line went dead. The aide reentered the room as Steve was dialing the number for the governor's mansion. He took the red-lined synopsis of geopolitical notes Pete handed him. It was an excerpt from their 1974 campaign manual for Beaver County.

Meanwhile the newsrooms were pulsing with uncommon activity for a Sunday morning. News flashes were written for morning radio news broadcasts and TV bulletins prepared for insertion on scheduled morning programming. Calls went to the Bartonsville Police Department, providing later listeners with the story of Benny's encounter with the terrorists. Groggy news directors were rousted out of bed by urgent calls from their weekend desk men. Only Hal Bloomfield of Station KPPA slept undisturbed.

Jerry Lampton, the station's aggressive young news editor sensed a national level story breaking in front of him. The PLA, whoever the hell they were, had already started punctuating their demands with bullets and it looked like they were set to carry out their threats, if necessary. Jerry realized immediately that this could be for him like Hurricane Betsy was for Dan Rather back in '65. Chances for something big rarely came to a newsman and he was going to make the most of it. If you made the networks, it was by breaking something big, just like this.

He called the standby electronic news-gathering crew and dispatched them to Bartonsville. Next he'd call CBS News Headquarters in New York and alert them. Finally, he would call WLK in Harrisburg to cover the state response. When he had done all that, he'd call his news director.

The morning shift for the Bartonsville plant had begun arriving at 7:25, only to find the access road barricaded with a line of fifty-five gallon drums and a determined Charlie Perkins. The police sergeant had parked his '73 Nova at the turnoff with a portable rotating red light affixed to the roof, and stood on the roadway, motioning the cars to stop as they approached him.

"What's up, Charlie?" asked one of the drivers.

"Got a problem at the plant and there won't be any shifts workin' today. You can just head on home and relax. You'll get a phone call later to explain."

"What kind of problem?" the man asked suspiciously, looking over the steering wheel toward the tree-obscured plant.

"Don't know yet, but the call will clear it up for you. Okay, move on. Traffic's stackin' up." He stepped back waving the car on and motioning for the next one to move up.

It had been a hell of a job to get this thing organized after that call from the governor's office. The chief had to deputize most of the volunteer fire department to get enough men to handle traffic control and seal off the plant. He really got a case of the ass when he found out Benny lost the only cruiser. Couldn't act too pissed off though, what with Benny almost gettin' killed. Does look sorta funny, he thought, that gumball machine on top of a yellow Nova.

*   *   *

Tony Miller walked across the gleaming tile floor to the receptionist's desk where LeCourt sat with Kreutz and Simmonds. "John, report on demo preparation."

LeCourt looked up. "Right, Tony. How's it going?"

"We found the cable-spreading room and put four thermite grenades on the main cable trays. They'll burn the room out and what they don't get, the polyurethane foam sealant in the wall and the cable covering will finish. That stuff's so flammable we could have done the job just by igniting it. I guess they don't ever learn."

"Just like Brown's Ferry?"

"Exactly, John. One cable-spreading room with all control cables for the plant and highly inflammable coverings and sealant."

"Jesus Christ."

"We found the valve that controls flow of the chemical foam for the extinguisher system in the room and can cut it out anytime you give the word. Zimmerman's people have placed diamond charges on the primary coolant line pumps in all reactor chambers and rigged the time fuse and 'det cord' so they'll go simultaneously. The RAPS surge tank is set with a four foot linear charge that'll split it wide open."

"Any problems with it?"

"Not a one. This is a walk-through after the briefings down at 'T camp.' Man, everything is exactly as Franz described it."

"The man's been right on everything, so far. Let's hope the rest goes as well."

"Sir," Simmonds interrupted. "I'm getting something on the state police frequency. You'd better listen in." He switched the shortwave set from earphones to the small loudspeaker on the table beside it as LeCourt and Miller moved closer.

"... vicinity Bartonsville. All units vicinity Bartonsville. Proceed to back up local authorities in cordoning off the Bartonsville Nuclear Power Plant. Armed terrorists have seized control of the plant. Shots have been fired. Report to Bartonsville police station for initial instructions. Do not take individual action. Handle Code

Two. That is all. Car eighteen. Car eighteen."

A burst of static was followed by another voice. "This is car eighteen. Go ahead."

"Car eighteen, proceed to Bartonsville police station and establish field supervision for all state units on scene. Instructions follow. Proceed Code Two.

"Car eighteen. Ten-four."

LeCourt tapped Simmonds on the shoulder as he stood. "Good, Larry. Keep on top of them and let me know if anyone deviates from our instructions. You can handle the phone schedule and monitoring both, can't you?"

"No sweat, sir. I'm set to operate nonstop."

"All right. Good show." He turned to Miller. "Let's go see how Ed is doing in the control room. I want to check that and then take a look at the excitement outside."

6

"Governor, this is Steve Murtaugh," he said, after he had finally convinced the maid to awaken the sleeping executive for the phone call. Archie Reaves's normally resonant voice came over the receiver in a croak. "What in the Sam Hill do you want at this hour, Murtaugh? It's not even seven-thirty yet."

"We've got a big problem at the Bartonsville Nuclear Plant, Governor. Terrorists broke in early this morning and seized the plant. They've got seven hostages and we've got a ransom demand for fifty million dollars by Wednesday at noon." Steve's sense of urgency was evident as his words spilled out, "They're threatening to destroy the plant if we don't follow their demands."

There was a long pause at the other end of the line before the voice came back stronger and alert. "This is a real one, Steve? No drill, no hoax?"

"Governor, I wish to hell it was, but this is the real thing. I've got staff coming into the office; Allen will be here any minute and I'll brief him. I talked with the Bartonsville and state police to insure that the plant is cordoned off until you decide what to do."

"What about the Emergency Operations Plan, Steve? Have you begun contacting the key personnel?"

"I've got Pete looking for it, sir. We don't know where Helen filed it but should have it before you arrive. In the phone call I received from the terrorists, they said they wanted you in the office for an important call at ten o'clock. I assumed you'd be in as soon as possible."

Reaves was fully awake now and assimilating the information as his assistant reiterated the steps he'd taken. On a Sunday, no less. It was going to be murder trying to find people today unless Steve could catch them at home. Good thing Allen was going to be there; the press would want some sort of statement and the wrong one could start a panic. They'd better come up with that plan, damn fast. "Steve, get my phone list out of my top drawer and look up Walczak, the state Civil Defense director. Get him to activate the Emergency Operating Center and contact the local CD director in Bartonsville. I want us tied in with them within the hour so I can have a full evaluation of the situation before that ten o'clock call."

He glanced at his bedside clock radio. It was set for 9:30 and the large digital numbers read 7:24. He could be dressed and out by 7:50; ten minutes to the capitol with no traffic, that would make it. "Steve, I should be in by eight-ten at the latest, so hold all inquiries until we get ourselves sorted out. Let's keep it low key until we find out how serious it really is."

"I don't believe we're going to be able to low key this one," Steve responded. "When they placed that first call at six-thirty, they had the networks on the line."

The governor grunted. Steve heard the sound of the radio over the phone as Reaves switched it on. "What stations had it?" he asked.

"Both WLK and WOV should be carrying the story. I'm looking for their camera crews to come in anytime now. Maybe you should use the lower entrance instead of your ramp."

Marianne Reaves, matronly attractive even in newly awakened déshabille, was sitting up in the canopied four poster, listening to his side of the terse conversation with Murtaugh. He cupped his hand over the receiver. "Get my suit ready, hon. I've got to get into the office in a hurry." He hesitated a moment, "Get one of the pin-stripes with a gray shirt and solid tie." There would be TV coverage and he'd need correct colors to look good on camera.

"Sorry, Steve, I'll catch the report. Meanwhile get on the calls and be certain we have that plan when I get there. I'll call you from the car as I leave the house."

As soon as Steve hung up, he swiveled around in his chair and turned on the small Sony TV set behind the governor's desk. A Spanish lesson was on the first channel. He flipped to the next. A medical missionary described the conditions among Indian tribes in the Amazon. "Pete!" he called. "Get that radio on and listen for the news bulletins while you find that E.O.P. Give a yell when you hear something."

In Pittsburgh, Jerry Lampton had finally gotten the lonely desk editor at WLK in Harrisburg on the phone. It was one of the junior men on the station staff who had drawn the normally dull Sunday morning routine and Jerry spent precious time explaining the importance of the story to his indecisive listener. "What stringers do you have on call this morning?" he asked impatiently. He realized he would be better off talking directly with the reporter than risking a translation through this fellow.

After a long pause, the man came back with the name of a reporter who was on call for Sunday news stories. "Okay," Jerry said, "call your news director. Wake his ass up, and clear this with him; then have the stringer give me a call before he goes out. Next, have a minicam ready to go with him to get the governor's comments. Keep them hot on his office 'cause this baby is going to balloon fast and the first word will be coming from there. If your director wants confirmation or details, have him call me. You got all of that?"

With the affirmative response, he hung up and immediately called his own news director at home. He had already taken the initiative by alerting his ENG crew to cover Bartonsville and by calling into CBS Headquar-

ters in New York. By now, the KPPA news team with one
of the new Ikegami cameras was en route to the plant and
the CBS desk editor had Lampton's name as the news
source on the story. Once he reached Bloomfield and got
him awake, he could report that all necessary steps had
been taken and ask for follow-up suggestions.

The three stations ran the story as a lead on their early
radio news although few listeners were up to catch it.
Nevertheless, AP and UPI picked it off the broadcasts
and called in for details. They got what data was available
and immediately shot it out over the wires. Within an
hour, events at Bartonsville, Pennsylvania, were being
followed by news bureaus nationwide.

In Washington, the CBS Bureau received a warning
message from CBS Headquarters alerting the desk editor
there to scramble a correspondent and camera crew for a
trip to Bartonsville. Once the story was verified, they
would charter directly into the town's airport to begin
network coverage. Anticipating the magnitude of the
events unfolding, the bureau put one of their mobile van
units on standby. It would give them complete programming capabilities on location.

Archie Reaves reached his office ahead of the newsmen
and spent his first twenty minutes listening to a
comprehensive briefing on the situation. He was
immaculately groomed and would remain so no matter
how hectic his activities became. Fourteen years in
politics had taught him, if nothing else, the importance of
appearing unflappable even if the walls were caving in
around him.

Murtaugh handed him the thick, red-covered Emergency Operations Plan that provided the necessary
guidance for bringing all of the state's resources into play
to control a crisis. He took the call list from the front of
the volume and passed it to the waiting assistant. "Get on
those calls, Steve. I want all key personnel on board by ten
o'clock. Is the E.O.C. operating yet?"

"Yes, sir. I caught Mr. Walczak just as he was going
out the door for a golf game. He has us tied in with the
E.O.C. in Bartonsville and is waiting for word from you."

Reaves was reading rapidly through the pages of instructions as he listened. "Okay, get him on the line. This damn thing covers what to do after an accident occurs, but doesn't say much about what to do before-hand."

Murtaugh punched out four numbers on the red phone and waited. He handed the phone to Reaves. "Joe, this is Governor Reaves. What's the status at the plant?" He listened attentively as the Civil Defense director briefed him on activation of the operations centers in Bartonsville and Pittsburgh. Personnel were already on duty and communications established. "What about the plant's emergency plan? Has the Emergency Coordinator there taken any action?" His face took on a look of disbelief. "You're not serious are you?" he asked. "No wonder there hasn't been any contact with him. Get him over to the local E.O.C. and hook in with our communications. I'll contact corporate headquarters and insure that we're all together on this. Now, I want a complete rundown on the seriousness of the threat and potential consequences before ten o'clock. That bunch of thugs is calling me then and I want some ammunition to work with. Can you do it?"

Satisfied, he hung up. "Steve. Do you know why we didn't hear from the plant supervisor when this broke?" Murtaugh, with a phone to his ear, shook his head. "Their Corporate Disaster Plan, all the call-up lists and procedural charts; the whole thing is locked up in the filing cabinet in his plant office ... and he's locked outside along with his Emergency Coordinator." He patted the manual on his desk affectionately. "At least we could get into our office to look for this thing." Murtaugh smiled grimly and then spoke into the phone, alerting another of the key personnel.

Taylor Atkins, working feverishly in the CONUCOR Headquarters, had activated the emergency plan. Calls had gone out to the directors of the Power Security Section, Public Service Branch and Legal Division, setting in motion a second sequence of calls that aroused sleeping executives across Chicago's residential areas.

This was the big one that all of them had been dreading.

Atkins's first call to the plant supervisor had confirmed his worst fears with the report that the penetration had occurred before any countermeasures could be employed. The plant was like an armed fort, and the lives of the plant personnel held hostage inside were forfeit if any action was taken. Taylor slumped in his chair, drained of energy and at a loss about anything further he could do until the division heads arrived.

Lawrence Flary, the phlegmatic head of CONUCOR's Public Service Branch, sat behind the Scandinavian modern desk in his lake front condominium in fashionable Highland Park. He wasn't fully awake yet, but automatically went down the list of names on his call sheet, rousting subordinates out of bed for the crucial 8:30 meeting. As awareness crept into his sleep-drugged mind, he tried to picture the Bartonsville plant. Western Pennsylvania . . . little town . . . when did they last audit the plant's physical security plan? How in the hell could someone just walk in and take over? What were the security guards doing? There had better be some pretty substantial answers or we're all in very deep trouble. If anything happens to the plant we're set to lose a bundle, and some heads.

Just then, the private line to his home office rang and Flary picked it up. It was Atkins informing him that Governor Reaves was calling from Harrisburg. He told Atkins to put him through and waited for the switch-over.

"Mr. Flary, this is Governor Reaves speaking." The voice was calm and resonant. "I understand from Mr. Atkins that you're aware of the Bartonsville incident and have already activated your response process."

"That's correct, Governor. Our essential personnel are on the way in now for a meeting to assess the situation." He was fully awake now and wishing he had more information on what was happening. This was no time to get caught without answers.

"Good. I'm depending on you to give me an early evaluation of the severity of the threat and extent of the consequences. If possible, I would like to have something prior to ten o'clock this morning."

Flary swallowed hard. It was 7:35 in Chicago, and he was going to have to hurry just to make the meeting. To get anything solid by ten Harrisburg time would be a miracle. "Governor, I don't know if we'll have a substantive report by then, but you'll hear from us as soon as we get all the facts in and have a chance to look them over."

There was a pause. "Get me what you have no later than ten. It's extremely urgent."

"All right, Governor. We'll have a preliminary assessment to you."

Archie Reaves hung up and returned to reading the emergency plan. One hour and twenty-two minutes until he would talk with the terrorists. There was a lot to be done in that time.

At nine o'clock, Dieter Kreutz placed a call to CONUCOR Headquarters. Taylor Atkins received it as the PLA representative outlined the specific damage they were prepared to do to the plant. Atkins wrote quickly as Dieter's heavily accented voice dictated details. Core disruptive accident ... control rod withdrawal ... prevention of SCRAM ... coolant loss ... ex-vessel storage tank sodium cooling system destroyed by demolitions ... back-up lines cut ... RAPS surge tank rupture by demolitions ... PHTS pumps for CAPS destroyed ... all external doors and air locks jammed open ... computer systems control tapes aborted. The voice continued, reciting structural damage to the outer containment building, demolition of stored radioactive waste containers and destruction of the core catcher assembly, but Taylor's hand was beginning to shake so badly that his script became almost illegible. Any one of these could be disastrous, could spill radioactive aerosols into the atmosphere with God knows what damage; but all of them ...

Kreutz ordered him to read back the message, and

Atkins struggled to keep his voice under control. The terminology was so familiar; these people even had the correct acronyms for the Radioactive Argon Processing System and Cell Atmosphere Processing Subsystem. RAPS processed the radioactive cover gases from the primary sodium system, the whole spectrum of radioactive gases. If they were released into the atmosphere . . . oh, God. He managed to complete the read-back and sat stunned after Kreutz disconnected. There was a bubble of warm liquid in his throat that he couldn't swallow. He glanced at the clock over the door. It was 8:07. He should have been having breakfast before taking a leisurely drive over to the Evanston Country Club for tennis with Angie. He tried to concentrate on her for a moment to settle down: her shoulder-length blond hair, done in a pony tail for tennis; the little upturned nose; a melt-down that couldn't be stopped; back-up cooling destroyed. It was no use. There would be some sick division chiefs when they got this word.

He flipped through his roto-file phone directory, selecting assistants from his own division. He'd get them started before he called his boss. Public Relations would have its own problems handling the media when word of this takeover got out. How in the hell do you explain security that didn't work and safeguards that were inactivated? How do you waffle the fact that those terrorists probably can create one hell of a nuclear disaster?

Seated in front of the television set in one of the comfortable suites in Washington's Madison Hotel, Franz Heitzman felt elated as Channel 9 interrupted its scheduled program to issue a brief bulletin. "A terrorist group calling themselves the Popular Liberation Army seized control of a nuclear power plant in Bartonsville, Pennsylvania, early this morning. They hold seven hostages and threaten to destroy the plant if their demand for a fifty-million-dollar ransom is not met. There has been no official reply."

They were inside the plant and had succeeded in communicating their demand! Excellent, excellent; the media response had been quicker than he had anticipated. Now the brief lull while the authorities gather themselves together on this cloudless Sunday morning and attempt to find a way around the checkmate. He turned off the set and strolled back into the bedroom, shrugging out of his robe. He could sleep now; nothing further would be happening until late afternoon when there would be full TV coverage.

In the plant, Larry Simmonds watched the bulletins break into morning programs on the TV set he'd pushed next to his desk in the reception area. It was the big Zenith set they'd had in the lounge and had moved into the hall prior to herding the hostages into that room. Between phone calls with his various messages, Dieter was listening to news reports on the radio. There would be no suppression of news on this operation. It was already a major story. Simmonds jotted down the substance of the reports in order to relate them to the colonel when he returned. Dieter checked his watch. Nine minutes until he made the call to the governor's office.

At that moment, Archie Reaves was listening silently to the alarming verdict from the head of CONUCOR's emergency operations board. If the terrorists carried out the actions specified in their last phone message, there would be a major discharge of radioactive aerosol and high activity fission products into the atmosphere. It was impossible to estimate the area that would be contaminated until further studies were made, but with current meteorological data, it would certainly affect the metropolitan population of Pittsburgh and intermediate points. The Nuclear Regulatory Commission in Washington had been notified and federal aid requested, since this was beyond the capabilities of corporate resources.

The governor stared at a patch of sunlight reflecting off the polished surface of his desk as he listened. There it is, he thought, the incident that was never supposed to happen. Pittsburgh; my God, even if the plant stays intact, we've got a hell of a problem preparing for the worst. Murtaugh had contacted the FBI field division in Pittsburgh to alert them; and Walczak, on Reaves's instructions, had reported the situation to the Defense Civil Preparedness Agency in Washington. There was no way that he could handle this at state level. He thanked the CONUCOR executive and gave his approval of their decision to bring maximum assistance into play. After replacing the phone on its cradle, he leaned back against the contours of his chair and continued to stare at the rectangular splash of light on his desk. He would wait until after the ten o'clock message, then call the President.

By 9:48 A.M., it was obvious that the terrorists had a clear advantage. The preponderance of emergency planning had gone into circumventing or containing an accidental malfunction. The concept of "defense in depth" produced reactor protection systems designed with redundancy and multiformity, each incorporated under strict criteria and regulations to assure that radiation-release accidents could be quickly arrested and any radioactive spill contained. There was little value in all of this, however, once the terrorists penetrated the plant and took control of all of its systems.

Steve Murtaugh's call to the FBI field office in Pittsburgh threw the first federal machinery into gear. Special agents from the office were dispatched to the Bartonsville site while contact was established with the Justice Department and FBI Headquarters in Washington. Immediate computer runs were made to determine the origin of the terrorist group and Special Action Teams were called in to prepare to enter the plant by force, if necessary.

At the suburban Bethesda, Maryland, headquarters of the Nuclear Regulatory Commission, the weekend duty operator took the call from CONUCOR and immediately placed calls to the director for Operations and the director of the Safeguards Division. There was no answer at either man's home and she moved down the list of calls until she reached the assistant director of Operations. In minutes he was on his way to the office. The operator's reiteration of the CONUCOR evaluation warned him that major accident sequences had already been established and the men now controlling the plant were confident enough to announce their intention. He'd have to get Energy Research and Development Agency on an assessment of the threat as soon as possible. This one was going to be nasty.

At precisely ten o'clock, Dieter Kreutz placed the call to Governor Reaves. Dieter carefully identified their group once again as the Popular Liberation Army and proceeded to outline the constraints that would apply to any actions taken to alleviate the situation. There would be no National Guard or federal troops used against the plant nor any force employed in an attempt to enter the plant. There would be no aircraft overflights and no surveillance devices set up within one mile of the plant. State and local police could be employed to control the population around the plant, but were not to venture within five hundred yards of the plant perimeter.

As Kreutz went on, Archie Reaves was listening carefully to the accented voice, trying to decide what European nationality the man represented. He wasn't familiar with international terrorist groups, but at least he could help the FBI by identifying this nationality. Steve was copying the message on the other phone, so Archie was free to concentrate. When he was certain it was German, he began mentally listing the questions he would ask to clarify the limits within which he would be able to respond to the threat. Walczak, earlier, had given him the estimates on possible evacuation of Pittsburgh and had stressed the need for an immediate call-up of the National Guard. There were nearly two thousand police in Pittsburgh and half that many in the surrounding communities, but the problems of traffic control for a mass evacuation would be beyond their capabilities. There were only two options: evacuate the area or protect the population in place, using the fallout shelters and basements.

Archie was careful not to let the hostility he felt come through over the phone. Who in the hell did these creeps think they were, threatening the lives of hundreds of thousands of innocent people? The audacity, the gall. Here in Pennsylvania. They should be taken out and shot.

Damn the harshness of capital punishment. This crime affected him and the heaviest penalty was too light.

"Now that you've finished, I have a number of questions for you that require answers," Archie said firmly. "First, I will require National Guard troops for use in traffic control and to maintain order. If they are not used in the vicinity of Bartonsville, will their presence elsewhere be considered a violation of your terms?" Archie almost choked on the question. Imagine, the governor having to ask permission from a ragged-assed terrorist to use the Guard.

There was silence on the other end of the phone as Dieter quickly had Larry Simmonds relay the query to John LeCourt in the control room. "I have made note of your question," Dieter responded. "Do you have others?"

"I would like an answer to my first one." Archie fought to control his temper.

"We will decide when to answer you. Do you have further questions?"

Archie's knuckles whitened as he gripped the chair arm and bit back a caustic response. "Yes, I do. Will you negotiate for the safe release of the hostages prior to discussion of your principal demands?"

"Your question is received. Do you have others?" Dieter's calm arrogance was more irritating to Archie than his refusal to answer immediately.

"Look, whoever you are," Archie snapped, "I need to know certain things right now. If you can't answer me, then get someone on the phone who can!" Steve gave the governor a warning glance, motioning for him to calm down. Archie's frustration and anger were beyond restraint at this point, however, and he continued, "You better realize right now that you can't get away with this and you had better begin thinking about how you can best get out of it."

"Governor," Dieter's voice was insolent, "you are in no position to dictate demands or advice to us, and I warn you to watch your tongue. It might cost one of the hostages his life.

"Meanwhile," Dieter continued, "we will deal through

you in completing arrangements for fulfilling our demands. When your federal government becomes involved, they will communicate with us through you. Is that understood?"

"I understand," Archie replied in a subdued tone. "When can I expect answers to my questions? I have to ensure proper control over the affected population areas and it requires a great deal of coordination. Will I have the freedom to act accordingly?"

Dieter was smirking at Simmonds as he played his role over the phone, verbally mauling this governor who probably wouldn't even glance at him if they should pass on the street. "We will call you when we have reached a decision on your requests. You will be available."

There was a click and Archie was alone on the line. He hung up and slumped back in his chair, running a hand over his eyes. "Dear God, I almost made a mistake on that one." He looked up. "Steve, do you think they would execute a hostage just to make a point?"

"Governor, right now I wouldn't put anything beyond them. You're going to be on a very hot seat until this incident is resolved, particularly since they want to communicate only through this office."

"Not just this office, Steve. They want to communicate through me. I can see a long four days ahead." He shook his head slowly. "Well, there's only one thing to do now. Get the White House on the line and have them reach the President. This should certainly wreck any plans he might have had for a quiet Sunday."

The air quality index had been above 120 for two straight days in Washington and William Barrington was conscious of the brief stinging in his eyes as he and his wife entered the presidential limousine for the ride up Massachusetts Avenue to the Washington Cathedral. Seven months into his first term and he still couldn't adjust to the uncomfortable humidity and frequent pollution alerts that plague the capital during the summer. Once inside the spacious, air-conditioned interior of the car, he wiped his eyes with a linen handkerchief and leaned across, gripping his wife's hand gently.

There had been scant moments of relaxation for the boyishly handsome chief executive since his inauguration in January. It seemed more like seven years than seven months since he had moved his personal items into the Oval Office and began unraveling six months of stalled domestic and foreign affairs. The campaign had been a strenuous one for him, but even more so for his predecessor. The strong challenge for his party's nomination that finally was decided at the national convention left the incumbent weakened in political power and an odds-on loser in the general election. For the President, in the interim between convention and Barrington's inauguration, it had been nothing more than a discreet period of job hunting by his aides and appointees. Congress chose to ignore him and rammed through a number of its pet bills, foreign governments put all talks and agreements into a diplomatic limbo, and the machinery of government slowed to mere housekeeping, awaiting the inevitable change of administrations.

Barrington entered upon his duties with the same vigor and determination that had marked his two gubernatorial terms prior to winning the Democratic nomination. There was, however, a vast difference between running the state and attempting to harness the burgeoning mechanism of the presidency.

The limousine, with its Secret Service escort vehicle, had just passed Thirty-fourth Street, opposite the domed buildings of the Naval Observatory when the President's phone began buzzing. He leaned forward and picked it up from the recessed communications module facing him. "This is Barrington speaking."

He listened as the White House operator relayed the source of the call. "All right, put him through on this line." He waited until Archie Reaves's voice came over the phone. "Good morning, Archie. What have you got?" He and Archie were old friends from their days as governors of their respective states. There was a growing look of concern on his face as he listened to the governor's concise summation of the events. "You say Justice Department, NRC, and Civil Defense have been brought into this already? Okay, it'll take them a couple of hours to get organized and start procedures rolling. I'll be back in the office by then and will get back with you as soon as I get an evaluation. You can count on full cooperation from this end, Archie."

He ended the conversation and sank back against the cushioned seat. Pamela Barrington knew from the expression on her husband's face that it was something serious. She had been through enough with him to recognize the deep concentration that foreshadowed decisions of importance. Barrington was a man who became quieter and calmer with increasing stress, acting decisively when he had reasoned through the problem, but never giving way to snap decisions or violent reaction. She respected his silence and waited for him to tell her what had happened.

As the vehicle parked in front of the majestic Gothic cathedral he turned to her, placing his hand over hers. "Say a special prayer for guidance this morning, love. I'm going to need it very soon."

Across town in the new J. Edgar Hoover Building, initial reports were coming in from the Special Agents who had arrived in Bartonsville and completed their interviews with local officials and the plant manager. Their observations of the plant and the still smoking wreckage of the police car reinforced the earlier assessments of the terrorists' capabilities. Scanning the plant perimeter through binoculars, they had detected two of the emplaced claymore mines and surmised that more were scattered throughout the area. The police car had been hit by some type of antivehicular rocket of unknown make, which created an additional problem in determining the exact amount of firepower available to the group. The only terrorist visible was partially hidden by the gate house and was wearing a ski mask.

The FBI computers had turned up a "Popular Liberation Army" in the COINTEL files. That program, instituted under Hoover's direction, had been aimed at disrupting militant political groups in the United States during the Vietnam conflict. Much of the material gathered had been destroyed as a result of subsequent disclosure of civil liberties violations; however, the files still carried references to the existence of this group along with other ad hoc organizations. The Popular Liberation Army was listed in the same category as the Purple Sunshine Clan, which had claimed responsibility for the bombing of an Oakland police station; The Revolutionary Action Party; and the Northwest Liberation Front, which had been charged with the bombings of several military recruiting stations in 1973. None of these groups had the capability to carry out an operation of this magnitude.

Immediate queries went out to the CIA, the intelligence services in Great Britain, France, Latin America, and Israel, seeking information on the group. In the United States, only the Weather Underground had the potential to undertake such an act; however, the initial feeling was strong that the PLA was a trained, international group having resources beyond those of any indigenous organization.

By noon, Federal agencies were operating according to their emergency plan procedures. Executives and staffs had been called into their respective offices and lines of communication opened between responsible departments. The Nuclear Regulatory Commission and Energy Research and Development Agency working groups were in the midst of evaluating the consequences of the radiological accident if the terrorists were to carry out the threat as stated in their demand and subsequent call to CONUCOR.

In the labyrinth of offices of the mammoth Government Services Administration Building in the center of Washington, the Federal Preparedness Agency began functioning as a coordination center for government response. The Controlled Conflict Preparedness Division offices were designated the operations center and within two hours, the agency's communications network was linking key departments into a semblance of organized effort. Phone lines, call numbers, teletypes, and interagency TWX circuits were activated and tested while harried supervisors walked amid the confusion, operating procedure manuals in one hand, directing the staff members.

Layton Edwards, former business executive and current division chief, sat in his comfortably furnished office studying the situation report handed him by his deputy. It was one of the early sitreps and contained only items from the first broadcast demand. Layton saw little to be alarmed about. Break-in and threat with an exorbitant ransom demand—probably one of the radical groups trying to bluff their way through using hostages as the bargaining mechanism. If it couldn't be handled at state level, he'd have the government resources tied in and ready to go. Coordination would be established between this center, NRC, ERDA, Environmental Protection Agency, Defense Civil Preparedness Agency, FBI, and the White House. He already had issued instructions for his plans section to review possible options for the President should they be required. As additional information became available, they could refine the options to fit the situation. Right now, everything was well in hand.

In Pittsburgh, the Sunday afternoon doubleheader at Three Rivers Stadium was jammed with exuberant Pirates fans. It had been six years since the Pirates had taken the pennant in 1971, and they were three games out in front of the National League with a fourteen game streak on the line against Cincinnati in this series. On this warm, sunny day, the crisp emerald-green stadium grass and kaleidoscopic hues of sport shirts and dresses in the stands gave the game a carnival atmosphere. No one was worried about events beyond the score at the end of the ninth inning.

At that moment, high above Bartonsville on the walkway circling the town's watertower, Carl Zellerman was doing a stand-up report on the developing situation for KPPA news. His cameraman had managed the long climb up the tower's ladder only because his miniaturized

Ikegami equipment was easily carried. He stood on the narrow perforated steel planking, leaning against the rail, taping Carl against a background of the town and, in the distance, the ominous bulk of the Bartonsville plant.

"Early this morning, an unknown number of terrorists broke into and seized control of the Bartonsville Nuclear Power Plant. The terrorists have barricaded themselves inside the plant holding five plant security guards and two plant technicians hostage. They have demanded a fifty-million-dollar ransom. If this ransom is not paid by noon Wednesday, the terrorists threaten to destroy the plant and presumably themselves and the hostages along with it. What this threat means to the city of Pittsburgh and suburban areas around it is a potential radiological disaster. There are no estimates available at this time, but release to the atmosphere of the radioactive materials contained in that plant as a result of explosive destruction could spread the highly dangerous particles and vapors over metropolitan Pittsburgh.

"Civil Defense personnel here are hesitant to comment on the magnitude of this incident, but this reporter has learned that plans are already prepared for the evacuation of Bartonsville and the surrounding area. State police are on the scene, aiding in the isolation of the plant and controlling traffic. As more news is available, I will be bringing it to you direct from the scene. This is Carl Zellerman, reporting for KPPA news, Bartonsville."

As he finished the report, his cameraman unshouldered the Ikegami and turned off the power pack. "I hope you don't plan to stay around for the Wednesday noon story in case someone doesn't pay the ransom Carl," he said. "In case you do, you may have to do it yourself because I'm going to be a long way from here."

Carl brushed the strands of blowing hair out of his eyes and placed the microphone in the equipment case. "Don't worry about that, Frank. If the station wants coverage of the plant exploding, they'll have to get someone else besides me. This job doesn't pay enough to make me heroic."

"Or stupid," Frank added. "I wonder where the others

are taping from?" he asked, looking down at the buildings below. "I saw the WEPA crew at the police station when we went by. They were standing outside with what's his name from the UPI Bureau in the city."

Chief Burns had spent the last half hour talking with reporters outside the police station. It was an unusual experience for him, one he found enjoyable. All these city reporters asking him about the plant and Benny's shoot-out with the terrorists. Nothing like this had happened in Bartonsville before, and it gave a man a feeling of importance. He had to break it off when the state policeman drove up to take him to the operations center, but the chief remarked to the reporters as he climbed into the patrol car that he'd be available for their questions after the meeting.

Benny Slocum, the most sought-after personality, had escaped to his grandmother's house along with his wife and kids. Reporters had overwhelmed him with rapid-fire questioning about his encounter with the terrorists and reactions to it. Benny had begun by answering as best he could, but the reporters refused to let him go and kept digging for additional comments. "What did he think about the threat to blow up the plant?" He didn't know about the threat. "Would he take his family away from Bartonsville?" He didn't know. "Did he think the terrorists meant to kill him in the parking lot?" If they wanted to, they sure had their chance. "How did he think the terrorists gained entry to the plant?" He didn't know.

Finally, his wife had pulled him into the house and shut the door. Benny desperately wanted to lie down and try to rest. He was still shaken by the events of the morning, feeling nauseated and weak. The reporters had persisted, knocking on the door and peering in windows until his wife had loosed their German shepherd and run all of the trespassers back into their cars. After that, the phone began ringing as reporters called in their questions. As a last resort, he had piled the family into their car and driven out the back way to the only refuge he could think of.

In the KPPA news library, Jerry Lampton was rapidly

pulling items relating to nuclear power and nuclear-connected accidents. He had already contacted a nuclear physicist and a former employee of Nucleonics, Incorporated, a research facility that had developed a number of the safeguards used in plants like Bartonsville. They would appear this evening as part of the special report he was putting together. With one more panelist and the clips he had lined up, this would be a bombshell special. None of the other stations would have this kind of coverage until tomorrow, and he was producing it. Look out network, he thought with anticipation, here comes your new star, Jerry Lampton.

The network news correspondents and their crews were arriving in Bartonsville to begin coverage of the story. Preparation for a field producer and mobile unit to support a correspondent were completed at CBS in Washington. The networks had alerted their White House correspondents to probe this story and be prepared to feed directly into the anchor station. There had been several special news reports out over the network programming by early afternoon and the evening news was set to carry a major story.

President Barrington listened to several of the early reports over the radio in his office Sunday afternoon. He had called in his Domestic Affairs advisor to brief him on the agencies available to him for meeting this crisis and was waiting impatiently for an answer. Outside the Oval Office, Travis Chambers, appointed to this position from Barrington's gubernatorial staff, frantically sought a response. He was still unfamiliar with government organization and finally resorted to the U.S. Government phone directory.

"Travis, you looking through the organization manual?" his assistant asked from across the room.

"No. I'm trying the phone book. Maybe someone will be listed under 'Disaster.' If they aren't, that's exactly what's going to happen to me when I walk back in to see the man with no answer."

"There has to be some kind of chart or plan that lists who we call in different situations," the assistant offered.

"Should be, but I have no idea where it is. I wish to hell it was a weekday with the secretaries here. They'd know where the damn thing is."

"What about the Standard Operating Procedures, those black-covered folders left over from the last administration? They should have all the information."

Chambers rapped the desk top with his knuckles and groaned, "Damn it all, you're right. It's all in the SOP's and I've got them at the apartment. Started to read them and never finished. Who can I call? There isn't enough time to get them."

The assistant shook his head. "It's Sunday, Travis. None of our people have been around long enough to know the answers and I doubt any of the holdovers are working today."

"Well, it has to be the NRC for sure, since this a nuclear power plant, and I'd bet on the Department of Justice since the FBI handles violations of the Atomic Energy Act. This certainly qualifies in that category." He flipped through the Federal Directory until he found the numbers. "Here, you call them and verify that they're working on the thing. I'll tell the Gov—I mean President—that you're checking with them."

The call reached NRC Headquarters just after the working group had reached an initial evaluation of the threat. In their conservatively furnished conference room, the six staff scientists were utilizing the office terminal to run computer codes in which accident models had been mathematically constructed and programmed. Dr. Ruben Whitaker, head of the group, reviewed their findings.

"Howard, we're looking at basically four major system failures. Any one of them is serious even if we could be assured of safeguard response to counter it. With the terrorists in control of the plant and obviously versed in its operation, it's difficult to predict Reactor Protection System response. Frankly, we don't know which safeguards have been neutralized."

Howard M. O'Brien, tall and slightly overweight in his middle age, sat attentively forward in his chair. His heavy black eyebrows arched like thunderclouds over constantly moving azure blue eyes. The tenseness he felt was expressed in the tight line of his mouth. He had worked long hours and driven his subordinates to correct many of the weaknesses he had found when he assumed leadership of this commission to succeed the old Atomic Energy Commission. Now all of that work was being tested.

Whitaker continued, "The threatened sabotage would produce both a Transient Overpower core disruptive accident and Loss of Flow core disruptive accident. In the first case, withdrawal of control rods and prevention of SCRAM would produce the largest reactivity insertion. We must assume that the threat to circumvent reactor shutdown is valid in the light of knowledge of the system demonstrated by the terrorists."

"Even with the diversity we've had built into the system?" O'Brien asked.

"If they have had access to design plans, which it seems they have, then it becomes a matter of systematically disengaging the safeguard responses. I'll give you more on this as I reach the other threat targets."

"What makes you assume they've had access to design plans?"

"The accident sequences, Howard," Whitaker answered. "No amateurs could have hit upon these sequences. It required a great deal of expertise to seek out the specific systems they are attacking."

"All right. Go on."

"In the loss of flow, they've threatened to produce what we considered theoretically impossible in coolant reduction. As you know, our codes dealt with flow coast-down as a result of loss of power to all sodium coolant pumps. In accident consideration, it was felt that sodium leaks large enough to cause loss of core coolant flow at a greater rate than pump failure were highly unlikely. As a result, they were not included in calculations of failure of the Reactor Protection System. They have threatened to use explosives to cut the primary sodium loop lines serving all pumps."

"Jesus Christ," O'Brien said softly.

"That's right, Howard. They know enough about the

system to go a step beyond the failure we deemed to be worst case."

"That means there will be sodium from the primary coolant loop, coming directly from the core at a thousand degrees Fahrenheit, spewing into one of the chambers and igniting as soon as it hits the atmosphere."

"Correct. With access doors and hatches opened, the resultant sodium oxide aerosol will vent directly to the Reactor Containment Building and with it, the thirty-seven isotopes, including Krypton and Xenon."

"What about the Reactor Containment Building? We've had sufficient safety factors designed into it to reduce further dispersion," the chairman suggested.

"If they functioned, Howard, I'd agree; but the threat involves opening the maintenance hatch and airlock as well as aborting the exhaust fan close down. Everything venting to the Reactor Building will spread through the exhaust system and into the Reactor Service Building. The Service Building will have all external doors and hatches opened, providing immediate expulsion due to overpressures. It's a virtual straight line to atmospheric escape."

O'Brien sat back in the chair, his face looking older than when he had entered the room. "That's just the sodium line failure. We've still got a core melt-down going."

Whitaker nodded somberly. "We're running SAS, VENUS II, PAD, REXCO, SOFIRE, and HAA computer codes to the limit that they're able to predict the dynamics of such a core disruptive accident. Beyond the codes, we have to rely on our best understanding of the controlling physical phenomena."

"So we're dealing with an assured melt-down?"

"Without a doubt. Core geometry would be impossible to maintain under the circumstances. Our problem centers about the ultimate core reaction before it melts through the vessel. We have both increased reactivity and loss of coolant. We're not prepared to comment at this time on the potential for energetic recriticality. Certainly there will be voiding to the atmosphere of the entire

spectrum of core related isotopes. There will be no
sodium pool or cover gas to absorb or attenuate the
reaction. There's also a threat to open the reactor port
plug prior to initiation of the accident sequence."

"How can they do that? There are sequencing actions
and electrical interlocks involved."

"They can be circumvented with proper actions and
the polar crane used to remove the plug. It leaves little
protection," Whitaker responded.

"What about the rest of you?" O'Brien asked, looking
toward the representatives from the Energy Research and
Development Agency. "Is this as bad as it sounds?"

Gordon J. Pollock, research scientist from ERDA,
answered for his group. "Mr. O'Brien, it's as complex an
accident sequence as we've ever faced; almost as if the
people inside the plant had taken critical accidents and
worst-cased them. Not a single serious failure, but a series
of simultaneous system failures, each contributing to the
other. The situation is extremely serious, but we have the
entire safeguard defense system operating to protect the
reactor."

Whitaker broke in before O'Brien could speak.
"Howard, we still have explosive rupture of the ex-vessel
sodium storage tank and RAPS surge tank, the failure of
the PHTS pumps, and threatened demolition of on-site
stored radioactive waste containers. It's a tough one."

O'Brien acknowledged in silence. All the work that had
gone into making the system function safely; the
protection systems, backup systems; the man-hours of
research and testing; the millions of dollars in system
refinement, the assurances that this would never
happen...and now everything was hinging around the
safeguards. He pushed his chair back from the table.
"Thank you, gentlemen, for this briefing. Whit, please
have the written report to me as soon as you have it
completed. I'll need to have it ready for the President's
briefing and provide copies for the other agencies." He
paused, looking out the tinted glass window at the tree-
lined street. "The backup systems are sound and well
designed. They'll do the job." He thought for a moment

and turned once again to the men who stood as he did. "Whit, be certain that no copies of that report leak out. I don't want any layman interpreting your findings for public consumption."

It was 6:30 in the evening before the President received his first overall assessment of the situation. He had been in contact with Layton Edwards after Travis Chambers had located the Federal Response Operations Center and put a call through to Edwards. All that was available at that time was the fact that the center was functioning, and coordination was being effected between involved agencies. Barrington spent his afternoon reviewing the Government Response Plan that Chambers had obtained from the F.P.A. It was an involved document that left him more confused than informed.

When the call came that an initial report was ready, he interrupted his supper and instructed the Task Force representatives to come directly to his private briefing room in the White House. Layton Edwards, junior in grade to his associates in the room, took charge of the briefing. The President was seated in a leather armchair at one end of the highly polished table. Flanking him were Travis Chambers and Dr. Francis Stratton, a Harvard Ph.D. who served as his national security advisor. At the other end of the table in this compact, map-lined room were the representatives of the agencies.

Layton Edwards began by familiarizing the President with the organs of government that would be involved in formulating and carrying out the response he dictated. A series of charts and graphs on large poster boards were displayed to his left. The first was an organizational chart. Layton indicated block diagrams with a slender, chromium pointer. "The coordinating agency is the Federal Preparedness Agency. Supporting and action agencies include NRC, ERDA, the Federal Disaster Administration, the Department of Justice; specifically, the FBI; the Defense Civil Preparedness Agency, Environmental Protection Agency, and your Cabinet Committee to Combat Terrorism which provides policy options. There will be inputs from a number of other agencies, but this group is the working body." He then gave a summary of events, including the stated threats and the ransom demand. "The FBI, ERDA, and NRC have evaluated the threat and their findings are stated in this report." He handed Barrington a copy of the twenty-page document. "To summarize, Mr. President, the terrorists are suspected to be of foreign origin, highly trained, and well armed. The group calls itself the 'Popular Liberation Army,' a designation which has not yet been identified with any of the known international terrorist organizations; however, there is no indication that they belong to any indigenous militant group. From the initial profiles, we must assume that they are politically motivated and would be willing to sacrifice themselves in carrying out the threat. They hold seven hostages and have threatened to kill them if their conditions and constraints are not complied with. Considering their reaction to the local policeman this morning, their use of what appeared to be a Soviet RPG-seven antitank rocket, we must assume that they are serious."

Layton turned to the second section of the report, tabbed with the circling atoms of the nuclear energy symbol. He was more relaxed now that he'd gotten into the presentation. Barrington seemed like a pretty straight fellow...quiet, but he obviously knew what to listen for...and for an outsider to Washington politics, he handles himself well.

"From ERDA and NRC, Mr. President, initial indications are that the threatened sabotage sequence, if carried out, would pose a credible threat to the integrity of the plant containment system. There is a potential for release of radioactive aerosols to the atmosphere; however, safeguards incorporated in the Reactor Protec-tion System are deemed adequate to control certain of the accident sequences. However, the report states that it is difficult to fully evaluate the efficiency of the safeguards with the terrorists controlling the plant."

Layton braced himself and continued. "Aside from the

potential venting of aerosols and fission products to the atmosphere, there is a more critical problem under consideration."

"It gets worse?" the President asked.

"I'm afraid so, sir. If they cause loss of coolant, simultaneously extract control rods, and are able to prevent the SCRAM shutdown of the reactor, there is the potential for an accelerated fission reaction and super-heating of the core."

"Go ahead."

"In the absence of a temperature moderating fluid, there will be a loss of core geometry in what is termed a 'melt-down.' We can't state conclusively, at this time, that there won't be a rapid compaction of the core debris. If it should occur, there is the chance that the mass would go supercritical."

Barrington sat forward intently. "You mean that when the melting core material begins to puddle, the fuel elements could be in such a state that they'd be uncontrollable?"

Edwards nodded grimly. "Energetic recriticality, which might possibly occur in this situation, would produce a violent energy release...either an extreme pressurization or an energetic explosion. There's no..."

"What you're trying to tell me," Barrington interrupted, "is that we might be dealing with a nuclear explosion. Right?"

"Our people are considering every possibility, Mr. President, no matter how remote. I assure you that there's a total effort to evaluate the consequences of this reaction. The people aren't just working on melt-down phenomena, sir. They're running every tape available on containment margins necessary for core disruptive accidents."

"You didn't answer me, Edwards."

Layton looked to the NRC representative for support. Markham was staring at his hands. "I would have to say, sir," he hesitated, "it is a possibility."

"When will they have answers for me on that?" Barrington asked.

"They will be working around the clock, sir. I can't give you an exact time, but it should be by tomorrow at the latest."

The President nodded and then gestured toward the charts. "All right, let's get on with this."

Edwards was relieved as he switched to the Civil Defense portion of the presentation.

Barrington studied the graph showing time periods required for evacuation of the various areas around Bartonsville. There wouldn't be sufficient time to evacuate Pittsburgh if they had to sweat a decision past Monday night. My God, the problems of evacuating over 700,000 people . . . routing them out of the city . . . food and shelter in hosting areas . . . some hosting areas would have to be changed based on meteorological data . . . if there was going to be fallout, you couldn't move them from one threatened area to another. There would be crossed state lines, adding to the problem of coordination. It would require a maximum effort from state authorities and the National Guard to keep it under control.

Layton continued with the briefing, covering actions taken so far in response, proposed expansion of the effort to be accomplished on Monday and a schedule of reports that would be coming to the President. Finally, he covered the decisions the President would have to make in the next eighteen hours. The negotiation phase would begin as soon as Barrington met with his advisors to discuss options open to him.

The President's eyes narrowed as a sudden thought struck him. He turned quickly to Chambers. "Travis, I want you to put calls through to the corporate heads of the networks in New York. Their coverage of this thing could start a panic and we'll have to head them off. After you put those calls through, I want to see the Security Council. It's what . . . ?"

"Seven-twenty-five, sir," Edwards offered.

"Yes, seven-twenty-five. All right, Travis, have them in the cabinet room by nine-thirty for an emergency meeting." He turned back to the seated group at the end of the table. "Thank you, gentlemen. That will be all for now. Please be available should I need you." He rose and turned to leave the room. The men were on their feet with him. "Edwards," he faced his briefer, "has anything of this magnitude been war gamed before? What I mean is . . . has this response plan been more than a paper drill before now?"

Edwards hesitated momentarily. "Mr. President, this is the shakedown cruise for all of us."

Barrington stood quietly, staring at the presidential seal over the movie screen at the far end of the room. "Well," he said slowly, "if there's a weakness in the plan, we've certainly got a situation that will bring it out."

By 9:50, the President had talked with the last of the network chief executives and gained agreement from them to cooperate fully with him in preventing sensational or irresponsible coverage that might bring about an adverse public reaction. They were obviously miffed that he would suggest that such reporting would be allowed, but realized the delicate balance he was striving to reach in structuring an atmosphere of restraint in which to attempt negotiations with the terrorists. He went back to the meeting with his council members, relieved and more assured than he had been earlier.

Unfortunately, the word did not reach station KPPA in Pittsburgh in time. In the station's control booth, Jerry Lampton nervously flipped the ashes from his cigarette as he watched the camera monitors on the display to his front. The director was seated at the console, talking over his headset to the cameramen in the studio as they shot test angles on the panelists. There were three chairs side by side and across the low coffee table, sat Ted Conners, popular anchorman for KPPA's "On the Spot News" show. On the coffee table was a scale model of the Bartonsville plant that Jerry had managed to have completed only minutes before the special was scheduled to go on the air.

Seated with Conners were Dr. Charles Bernstein, Dr. Elliot C. Van Dusen, and Daniel Thorn. Bernstein had flown in from Washington, Van Dusen from his home in

Hartford; and Jerry had found Thorn in Pittsburgh doing research for a story on the Calter Atomic Power Laboratory. The clock above the monitors showed 9:57. They were wrapping up the network sitcom and would break for a two minute commercial before the special went on at ten.

The director and his assistant were intent on three of the five camera monitors on the console. "One, give me a wide shot. That's good . . . ease it back a bit . . . okay, hold. Two, tight on Ted for the intro. Three, wide on the guests . . . good." To the director's left, an attractive brunet sat before a keyboard panel, ready to switch camera shots on the director's command. Further to her left, the audio man sat at his console, adjusting voice levels as the participants gave him a test count.

Jerry ground his cigarette out in the ashtray and found himself counting down with the second hand on the clock. He had so damn much riding on this—taking the chance on scripting it before he'd gotten clearance to run it, selling the chief on paying for the guests' flights out of the contingency fund, digging out the film clips and references he wanted. He was taking a chance, but it was worth it if this thing went big. The station brass still weren't completely sold on the idea. Blanking thirty minutes of news for one special report didn't go over too big, but this was red hot and they'd have the jump on the other channels. It had to be a winner.

The commercial was on. "Ted, thirty seconds," the director warned his moderator. "One, we're coming out on you." In the studio, Ted Conners made a last minute check of the notes on a small pad placed inconspicuously on the arm of his chair. Thorn adjusted his coat and squinted into the brilliance of the arc lights overhead.

"Everyone ready?" The director took a last look around at his crew. His assistant began the countdown. "Fifteen seconds." At the five second mark, the center cameraman would begin the five-four-three-two-one finger count for Ted. "Roll tape . . . ready on one." The director was intent on the timer his assistant held. Jerry Lampton took a deep breath. "Audio, background and...ready one...now!" He snapped his fingers and the brunet keyed up camera one.

The opening was a back-lit silhouette of the four men with an announcer's strident voice on audio. "This is a KPPA special report. Tonight's guests are Dr. Charles Bernstein, formerly a research scientist with Nucleonics, International; Dr. Elliot C. Van Dusen, professor of nuclear physics and applied reactor theory at the Connecticut Technological Institute; and Mr. Daniel Thorn, noted author on the subject of nuclear power. Your moderator, Ted Conners. Tonight's special subject, the terrorist takeover of the Bartonsville Nuclear Power Plant."

The camera switched to a close-up of Ted Conners's serious face. "Good evening. I'm Ted Conners and for the next thirty minutes I'll be talking with these gentlemen as we discuss the implications and possible consequences of a threatened nuclear accident at the Bartonsville Power Plant." He turned from the camera and faced the three men. "First, let me thank you for taking time from your weekend to be with us tonight and to provide valuable insight on this situation for our viewers."

Across Pittsburgh and its suburbs, people were gathering around their sets, turning the volume up and phoning friends to tune in to Channel 9. Forgotten suddenly was the Pirates' decisive sweep of the double-header. Other news was disregarded. The special was hitting just as Jerry Lampton had predicted.

In the studio, Ted Conners introduced the subject with the two minute video-taped report Carl Zellerman had done earlier. The reporter provided overview coverage, leaving the details to be handled during the special. He finished his report with a long shot of the burned-out hulk of the patrol car and the plant in the background. Chief Burns's voice was saying, "That's a damn mean bunch in that plant. Nearly killed my man and blew up his cruiser with one of them Russian antitank rockets."

"Do you think they are serious about destroying the plant, Chief Burns?" Zellerman asked in closing.

"You're askin' me if I think those terrorists are serious?

You bet I do, young man. They're dead serious."

Conners turned to Dr. Van Dusen. "Let me ask you first, Dr. Van Dusen. Considering the fact the terrorists are in control of the entire facility, is it possible that they could effectively damage parts of the plant's mechanisms to such an extent that there would be a radiation hazzard?"

Van Dusen's pinched face was lengthened by a carefully trimmed Vandyke beard and his watery blue eyes encircled by large horn rimmed glasses. It was unexpected when a resonant bass voice answered, "Within the various systems inside the facility are elements containing amounts of irradiated liquids, vapors, and solids. Should any of these be damaged accidentally or intentionally, there would certainly be a radiation hazard. Let me add, however, that redundant safeguards have been included in the plant design to reduce the possibility that such a hazard would extend beyond the inner limits of the plant."

"The terrorists in their first announcement this morning, specified that they had placed demolition charges on the liquid sodium cooling lines and had prepared similar demolitions on the Emergency Core Cooling System," Conners stated. "What effect would that have?"

There was a quick arching of Van Dusen's eyebrows. "H-m-m. That is an interesting gambit." He paused. "I would have to say that should they succeed in disrupting flow of the coolant to the reactor core and simultaneously preventing ECCS response, the most serious of radiological accidents would occur."

"Dr. Bernstein, do you have a comment?" Ted asked the slender, crew-cut researcher. Bernstein was in his mid-forties, but gave the appearance of a much older man. He spoke rapidly, almost in a jerky, machine gun pattern. "Let me preface my remarks by stating that I resigned my position with Nucleonics, International at the end of last year because of my dissatisfaction with the safety standards and guidelines in my work."

"What was that work, Dr. Bernstein?" Ted probed.

"I worked on safeguard evaluation and systems improvement for the Liquid Metal Fast Breeder Reactor program in our organization."

"And what about this work disturbed you to the point that you resigned from the firm?"

Bernstein was full face and close up in the screen as he answered. "The safeguards we were designing were based on mathematical models, computerized to provide test vehicles upon which the systems could be imposed. Major safeguards, like the ECCS, were never tested in a live situation; never in a crisis such as this. The core catcher assembly which is designed to contain a molten core as it passes through the reactor vessel and allow subsequent cooling in a subcritical configuration was never tested. These systems are presumed to be effective, but we really don't know until they're tried live."

Ted stopped him. "You mean that even without intentional destruction these systems that are supposed to prevent a major disaster might not function correctly?"

Bernstein nodded vigorously. "Exactly. There is no way to duplicate the entire spectrum of potential effects of a core disruptive accident. I felt then, as I do now, that far more research was necessary before we let the designs be included as viable components of a safeguard system."

In the control booth, the director was orchestrating the cameras. "One, stick with Ted . . . get tight on his face for this. Two, see if you can get Bernstein's hands. Three, cover me on Thorn." Jerry Lampton felt a surge of supreme satisfaction. Goddamn this is great! Sock it to 'em, Ted; you've got the touch now.

Ted Conners, as professional as he was, allowed the genuine concern he was beginning to feel to penetrate his normally composed expression. The change was evident to his viewers. "What you gentlemen are saying, then, is that the terrorists do have the capability, even under the best of conditions, of causing a major accident that would result in the release of radioactivity . . . gas, particles, whatever . . . should they carry out their threat."

Van Dusen answered, "Whether or not the internal release of radioactive isotopes in various forms would reach the atmosphere is open to conjecture, but I would have to say that, yes, they do have that capability."

Dan Thorn leaned forward in his seat. His close-set eyes, prominent nose, and tight, straight lips gave him an aggressive air that was reinforced when he spoke. "Ted, I've covered every reported accident that has occurred at a nuclear power facility and a couple that weren't reported. There's no doubt in my mind that once those people got inside that plant with the information they obviously have on how it operates, they could do anything they damn well pleased." He jabbed a finger at the plant model on the table. "This baby may very well be the nuclear disaster that the industry has barely avoided in the past.

"What will that mean to those of us here in the Pittsburgh area?" Conners asked.

"Let me go back a step before I answer that, Ted," Thorn answered. "I began following reports on this incident after the first bulletins came out this morning. One report that you may not have gotten covered a call that the terrorists made to Continental Nuclear Corporation in Chicago. They're the ones who own and built the plant, you know. Anyway, someone leaked that the terrorists have set a whole series of explosive charges that will break the inside of that plant up like the Fourth of July. To top it off, they threatened to jam the airlocks and access doors open, to open the exhaust vents and flush the whole gawddamned mess into the atmosphere."

Bernstein's hands began to twitch nervously as he tried to hold them steady in his lap. "Two, now . . . tight on his hands . . . beautiful! Three, crunch down on three . . . ready, three, ready three . . . now."

Dan Thorn sat back in his chair as he continued. "Now, with that bit of background, we have to consider the meteorology in this area. Winds are from the west and generally steady at this time of year. I hate to say it, but it looks to me like whatever comes boiling out of that plant is going to cover the thirty odd miles between here and there in a matter of hours."

In homes across the city, families weren't waiting to listen to the end of the program. Calls were made to

relatives outside the area, motel reservations called ahead
and belongings packed as the specter of nuclear
devastation spread panic through the viewers. Even
before the program ended, Jerry Lampton was guaranteed of having produced the bombshell of a special that he
wanted.

At midnight, Archie Reaves received a call from the
Civil Defense director in Pittsburgh. There was an
unusually heavy amount of traffic on roadways leading
out of the city. No evacuation plan had been called for,
but the city's inhabitants were leaving and all possible
state police that could be spared would be needed to
control the flow of vehicles.

Archie, the lieutenant governor, and the emergency
council had spent the entire evening reviewing the state's
response options and had drafted their proposed plan.
The negotiations with the terrorists would begin in the
morning while simultaneous preparations for evacuation
of the population within a ten mile radius of the plant
were carried out. The notification of the exodus from
Pittsburgh caught them by surprise.

In the plant, the team had been divided into two
sections of eight men each. Half had already been asleep
for several hours while the others maintained security. At
four A.M., the men on duty would be relieved and allowed
to sleep until ten. John LeCourt was depending on
Franz's evaluation of the government's lack of immediate
response to give his men necessary periods of rest. On
Wednesday, they would begin taking dextroamphetimine
tablets, if necessary, to keep them going. Tony Miller and
Matt Overmeyer, who would be piloting and navigating
the escape aircraft, would be the only team members
allowed full rest periods until departure.

Moran reported that the hostages were sleeping and
Cleave Jones had given an "all quiet" on the plant
perimeter. LeCourt was beginning to feel more confident
now that the first day had passed. There were three days
to go, but the situation was under control and their
position in the plant was obviously being accepted by the

authorities as too dangerous to challenge without federal support. Tomorrow would give him a better idea of what to expect.

Vince DeAngelo, breaking into a slow smile, leaned back and stretched languorously. "Sir, I'll bet we've got those bastards climbing through their own apexes trying to figure out some way to slickie us out of here. Don't you think?"

LeCourt agreed, realizing the turmoil that must exist after the involved agencies got word about the second set of accidents that had been prepared. The element of doubt, it'll get them every time. No one is going to put his name on a piece of paper that states definitively that there is absolutely no danger of the reactor core producing a hundred-story-high mushroom cloud. There's always that one chance in a million that he could be wrong. Who gives a shit about all the other chances that he could be right.

"No one has the balls to tell the President that we might be bluffing and they should do a job on us, Vince; you know that. They'll drag out their plans, contingency plans, backup plans, and God knows how many tons of view graphs, slides, charts, and all that good eyewash."

LeCourt laughed mirthlessly. "Wait till they find out that we had this place G-two'd well enough to really do it in, if we wanted to. That's when the cheese'll get a little binding. You'll see a bunch of high-powered civilians running around with both hands covering as much of their asses as possible. God, I'd love to be there watching that."

"You really think they'll give us the money and the aircraft?" DeAngelo asked.

"If I didn't, Vince, I wouldn't be sitting here right now. I may be a lot of things, but I'm sure not a kamikaze. They're going to try to get around paying the ransom, but they want us out of here and they want this plant intact. We're giving them the only way to accomplish it."

"What the shit is going on?" Vince exclaimed as the snarling and barking of dogs suddenly broke the calm.

Both men were on their feet and running toward the lounge.

As they pushed through the doors into the long corridor leading past the lounge, Tom Cooper was struggling to pull two frothing, snapping Dobermans off Art Potter. The older man was lying, half wrapped in his shredded sleeping pallet, moaning and covering the back of his neck with his arms. Blood was streaming from a multitude of punctures and lacerations on his arms and shoulders. Joe Houser stood braced in the doorway, covering the remaining hostages with his AK-47. From the other end of the hall, Pete Alexander and Mike Baker came running, their weapons at the ready.

"What happened?" LeCourt asked sharply.

"Dumb son of a bitch tried to rush us, sir," Houser answered without taking his eyes off of the men in the lounge. "Wrapped himself in the mattress and tried to bust through the doorway. Probably figured the Dobies couldn't bite through the cotton padding."

"What the hell was he going to do in the hall?" DeAngelo asked.

"Beats me," Cooper answered as he finally pulled the agitated dogs to the side and restrained them. "Maybe he figured he could get a gun."

Baker was squatting beside the guard, examining the wounds. Potter continued to moan. His legs thrashed as if he were still trying to run.

"How's he look, Mike?" LeCourt asked quietly.

"Not too bad, sir. Mostly flesh wounds; no arteries; possible shock. He's lucky."

"Okay, Tom, get the dogs settled down and put them back on guard. The ones inside get anybody else?"

Cooper looked up from soothing the two dogs. "No, sir. No one else moved to help Potter. He caught it all."

There was an instant of compassion in LeCourt's eyes as he looked down at the crumpled form. Potter's lined face was ashen, but without the stamp of fear. John stepped through the doorway. Houser moved inside, never taking the muzzle of his weapon from the hostages.

The technicians sat huddled on their mattresses, visibly shaken by the dogs' attack. Sam Waylor had moved back against the wall, farthest from the door. Cal Bennett was on his feet, ready to say something to LeCourt. Marascoli sat sullenly, staring at the floor.

"He could have been killed..." Bennett began.

"You shut up!" LeCourt snapped with unaccustomed harshness. "Sit down and don't let me hear another goddamned word out of you." In the hall Vince looked questioningly at Pete Alexander. It was the first time they'd heard the colonel really pissed.

LeCourt swept the group with his gaze. "I told you people what would happen if you tried anything stupid. Well, now you've had a live demonstration. There better not be a next time, because if there is, no one's going to pull the dogs off. It's a hell of a painful way to die... and just in case the dogs don't get you, my people have orders to cut you down." He stared at the cowering men, but no one met his eyes. "You want to try us... go ahead. It's your life. If you're smart, you'll learn from this and do as you're told." He turned and strode out of the room. Cooper led the two Dobermans back to their positions and removed their choke collars.

Outside, LeCourt paused by Mike Baker and tapped him on the shoulder. Baker rose and stepped over to LeCourt. "Mike, take good care of the old bastard," he said quietly, "he's a good man... the only one in the whole bunch."

DeAngelo had reestablished the security detail and joined LeCourt as he walked back to the guard room. "We sorta misjudged Potter. Who would have thought he'd be the one to make a move?"

LeCourt thought for a moment as they walked. "The old cop, Vince. Not much sense, but a lot of guts. He must have sat there and psyched himself up to the point that he had to do something, even if it got him killed."

"Pretty smart, though, using the mattress to try to get past the dogs."

"Yeah, I never figured on that," LeCourt acknowledged. "Wonder what he thought he could do once he got out of the room?"

"Not much that one man could do. Might have been different if someone had backed him up. Someone like Marascoli. Fuckin' cowards let him take on the dogs by himself." DeAngelo's last words were filled with scorn.

They sat down at the desk and refilled their coffee cups. "Well, that ought to guarantee a quiet ride for the next three days," John said. "Marascoli knows he's a dead man if he tries anything now and the others knew it before this."

A spot broadcast came over the state police frequency, and the two men listened as the dispatcher ordered extra cruisers to Pittsburgh to help control traffic that was building on routes leaving the city.

Vince looked at LeCourt with a puzzled expression. "No one ordered an evacuation yet, did they?"

"Not that we heard, Vince. From the sound of it, it's the first that the state police knew of it."

"We sure are getting things stirred up out there."

LeCourt was smiling, his eyes fixed on a spot overhead. "You know, Vince, I'm beginning to feel like one of Macbeth's witches."

"You're what?"

"You know, the scene where the witches are gathered around their cauldron, brewing up a charm. They're tossing all sorts of garbage into this boiling pot . . . poisoned entrails, lizard's leg, a hemlock root, a finger of a birth-strangled babe . . . anyway, the chorus of their chant is 'Double, double toil and trouble; Fire burn and cauldron bubble.' That's what we're causing with our little bubbling reactor in here."

DeAngelo looked somewhat confused. "You really go in for that stuff don't you."

"Yeah, I guess so. I spent a lot of hours reading Shakespeare. You learn so damn much if you read what went on before our time. Not that it helps us avoid making the same mistakes they write about, but at least you know you weren't the first to screw up."

"You had a bunch of those books with you down at 'T camp' didn't you?" Vince asked.

"Uh-huh. They were the ones I carried with me while I was in 'Nam. Used to read them when I had the time. It was a good way to forget where I was for a while." John thought back to the nights he'd spent in his sand-bagged command post, reading by flickering lantern light after the generators had been shut down. You couldn't run the noisy generators after dark when you were expecting an attack. Even muffled down, the sound would cover any noise made by Charlie as he crawled up on the positions.

John spent hours reading, and writing letters to Karen. He winced as he thought of the letter she'd left for him when he came home from the last tour. They used to trade Shakespeare's sonnets or a piece of prose or something they'd composed themselves to close their letters, a sort of intimate touch between them over the long miles. When he came back, she was already gone and all he had was the sonnet. It said everything for her. He could still remember the lines. His eyes focused beyond the far window as he softly repeated,

Let those who are in favour with their stars
Of public honour and proud titles boast,
Whilst I, whom fortune of such triumph bars,
Unlook'd for joy in that I honour most.
Great Princes' favourites their fair leaves spread
But as the Marygold at the sun's eye,
And in themselves their pride lies buried,
For at a frown they in their glory die.
The painful warrior famoused for fight,
After a thousand victories once foil'd,
Is from the book of honour razed quite,
And all the rest forgot for which he toil'd;
Then happy I, that love and am beloved
Where I may not remove or be removed."

He felt the loneliness creep back into the tight-locked recesses of his mind. It still hurt him after all these years.

"You want to get some sacktime, sir?" Vince's voice

broke into his thoughts. "Tomorrow's going to be a big day and I can handle things here."

LeCourt shook his head. "Thanks no, Vince. I don't need much sleep and it's just a couple of hours until we wake the second shift up. I'll have plenty of rest." He'd get four or five hours sleep before anything happened and that would be enough.

John drained his cup and pushed back from the desk. "I think I'll take a walk down to the infirmary and see if Potter's okay. We'll have to keep him separated from the others until we leave and I'd hate to have to do any more than lock him in one of the storage rooms. If he's weak enough, he won't try anything more and we can just keep him in sick bay."

"The old bastard get to you, sir?" Vince asked grinning.

"I guess I like to see somebody willing to try to stop us, even if it means a hassle. Never did like sheep." His voice dropped off as he walked out of the room. "Old Potter, can you beat that."

The remainder of the morning hours were uneventful for the men in the plant. It was not so calm in Washington and Harrisburg. William Barrington had worked out the negotiating posture he would assume in dealing with the terrorists. Once decided upon, he called Governor Reaves and outlined the specific points that would be relayed to the plant. It was 5:30 A.M. when Archie Reaves had the complete statement in front of him. One of the President's staff members had flown in from Washington to aid in coordination between the two men and was on hand when Archie placed the 9 A.M. call to the plant.

Dieter Kreutz took the call and had Simmonds wake John LeCourt. John signaled Dieter to proceed. "You have an answer to our demands, Governor Reaves?" he asked.

Archie steadied himself and began reading the statement, trying to sound as if he were speaking instead of reading. "I'm authorized to speak for the U.S. government and this state in rejecting your demand for a fifty-million-dollar ransom."

Dieter's eyes widened as he looked toward LeCourt. John gave him a sign to go on. "You have more to say?"

"I am to inform you that the policy of this government precludes the payment of any ransom to terrorists and that your threatened act of violence against innocent civilians stands condemned in the eyes of the world." Archie was gaining confidence as he continued to read. "The government is willing, however, to provide you with safe passage from the plant and out of the country to a destination of your choosing, provided you release the hostages, unharmed, prior to your departure."

John listened calmly. Just like Franz had said; the hard-nosed approach first. Try to bluff us out and see if we'll show our cards. He motioned to Dieter to cut the conversation.

"I have received your statement and we will respond to you after considering it."

"But I'm not finished," Archie sputtered. The line went dead as Dieter hung up. The governor looked up helplessly. "He didn't let me finish."

"They have the gist of it, Governor," the presidential aide said. "Now we wait for them."

At the plant, John LeCourt replaced the phone and turned to Moran. "Ed, it looks as if we'll have to shake them up a little. Start getting things ready for tomorrow morning." He faced Kreutz. "Dieter, I'll write out a response for you. Let them sweat until this afternoon and then call the governor back. Make it around sixteen-hundred hours."

Vince DeAngelo walked up beside LeCourt. "What's the word, sir?"

"They're playing it tough on the first exchange, Vince. We'll slap it to them in the morning. I want full security after sixteen-hundred. If they're going to try to hit us with anything, it'll come either right after the call or tonight, so get the men ready."

The hours passed slowly for Archie Reaves as he waited for the return call. It was a damned strain waiting and wondering what that would do. Maybe the statement shouldn't have been worded so harshly; give them more of an out; not hit them head on with a refusal. Then again, if they accepted the terms, it would all be over in another day.

The governor jumped when the phone rang. It was 4 P.M. and that same voice was there. "Governor Reaves, your terms are unacceptable. Apparently you do not believe we are serious in our threats and choose to ignore them." The men in the governor's office looked at one another in apprehension as the voice went on. "You bear full responsibility for the consequences that will follow. I assure you that we do not fear our own deaths. We consider ourselves dead already. It is up to you to determine how many more people must die."

Archie felt queasy. His hurried lunch was beginning to churn in his stomach. They weren't just bluffing in that plant. He knew it now.

"To demonstrate the truth of what we say, there will be an execution of one hostage tomorrow morning at precisely seven A.M."

Archie closed his eyes. The PLA had said he'd better watch his mouth or he'd get a hostage killed, and he didn't believe them. The presidential aide was wiping his face with a handkerchief. Only Steve Murtaugh spoke. "Who? Ask him who."

"The burden of guilt for this act of violence lies on you and your government," Dieter's voice continued, "and further bloodshed will follow if you persist in your obstinate refusal to meet our demands."

"Who is the hostage?" Archie managed to ask.

There was a pause. "The hostage to be executed is Arthur K. Potter."

Monday afternoon was muggy and hot. The continuing temperature inversion over Washington held the pollution from the thousands of vehicles in the city like a misty shroud. High humidity made the walk from air-conditioned offices to air-conditioned cars seem like a trip across the bottom of a heated swimming pool.

William Barrington glanced at his watch. It was 3:58. He was tired. It was more than just a physical need for rest; the psychological strain of the last months had reached a peak with the addition of Bartonsville to his list of major concerns, and he was disturbed by his reaction. In the past, he had thrived on pressure; actually bloomed in his potential to lead his state under crisis conditions, but never had there been the constant pounding of daily decisions that came with the presidency.

He was seated at the long table in his conference room adjacent to the Oval Office. With him at the table were the secretary of state and representatives from the department who had briefed him on foreign policy hot spots. The soft wall colors and gracious Colonial furniture established a calming atmosphere to offset the tense overtones of the discussion in which he was involved. For nearly two hours, he and the secretary had been reviewing the multitude of decisions facing him. Stalled SALT talks with the Soviets and the arguments over the cruise missile carrier as a counter to the Russians' Backfire Bomber; the continuing threat of guerrilla actions in the Canal Zone in response to Congress' deadlock over a new treaty; the intricate balance in the Mideast as the United States sought to find a formula for peace in that region; the crucial question of diplomatic relations with the People's Republic of China that had to be decided in the face of political upheaval since Mao's death. To establish that relationship would give us leverage in preventing subsequent Sino-Soviet reconciliation, but would require abandoning Taiwan.

Barrington found his analytical approach to problems virtually useless in the face of conflicting political considerations. He caught himself bargaining away portions of one position to gain support for those of another, leaving him with partial satisfaction on both. The frustrations of necessary compromise were beginning to drain his abundance of determination and self-confidence. There was so much he didn't know; he had to depend on the counsel of his advisors, even to the abandonment of his personal beliefs.

Now, in the midst of a normally crowded daily schedule, blocked solidly with briefings and conferences on backed-up domestic and international issues, he was receiving reports on the status of the Bartonsville situation. Matters had been complicated by last night's surge of people fleeing the Pittsburgh area. Archie had responded immediately, but the panic was spreading and it now required the full attention of his state police and a number of National Guard units to try to keep the mass of vehicles under control.

The Defense Civil Preparedness Agency had put its emergency broadcast station on the air to keep the citizens informed and counter the flood of rumors that were circulating about an imminent disaster. Barrington had decided to use regular troops and impose martial law in the area immediately around the plant after Archie had called requesting aid. The situation had to be contained before it deteriorated further.

Update reports from the Nuclear Regulatory Commission hadn't been encouraging. There was an unquestionable potential for a major radiological dispersal from the plant if the terrorists carried out their threat. Calculations were being made to determine the total dosage of radiation that could be expected along the path of predicted fallout, a path that included all of metropolitan Pittsburgh.

At 4:18, an agitated Travis Chambers entered the room and strode directly to the President's side. "The answer from the terrorists to your statement, sir. Governor Reaves just called in."

Barrington unfolded the paper and read slowly, his face expressionless until he reached the impending execution. His jaw muscles tightened perceptibly. "Those scum. Those murdering scum." He looked up at the State Department personnel. "They've scheduled the execution of one of the hostages for tomorrow morning at seven A.M. and went so far as to command the television crews to cover it, to put it out live over the networks." There was silence in the room.

He placed the paper carefully on the table and leaned back in his chair, folding his hands in front of his chest. He said nothing for several moments and then softly to himself, "Arthur K. Potter. I wonder if he has a family?" There were long seconds of silence before he sat forward again; this time his voice was firm. "Get Edwards on the phone, Trav. I want to know if there is any way we can head this thing off. After that, tie me in with the secretary of defense. It looks like they're playing for the whole pot."

Dieter Kreutz had phoned the Pittsburgh stations immediately after he concluded the call to Governor Reaves. His instructions to them were brief; there would be an execution of one hostage at 7 A.M. as a direct result of the government's refusal to deal seriously with the PLA demand. There would be TV coverage of the execution that would be presented to the viewers as it took place. He provided them with technical details of the distance from which the cameras would have to tape, the windows in the plant through which the execution could be viewed and finally, the name of the victim. He reiterated that full blame for the execution rested with the governor and the federal authorities, assuring that more would follow unless the demands were met.

By the time his notification reached the stations, the networks had already established mobile van units at Bartonsville with additional cameras and veteran field producer-directors to handle the coordinated news effort. CBS Washington became the anchor station as their correspondents covered the plant, governor's office, White House, and the building free-for-all on the roads around Pittsburgh. There would be a minimum of eighteen cameras covering the execution along with news photographers and free lancers. That evening, Bartonsville began to fill with sightseers who braved the dangers of threatened radiation poisoning to witness the morning's event. Police were less than gentle in their efforts to clear the area and keep the morbidly curious away from the plant.

The President was on the phone with Archie Reaves as soon as he received a response from Layton Edwards. Bill Barrington had grabbed a hurried supper with his wife as he waited for the Task Force analysis of the situation and options for dealing with it. He had begun to realize how inflexible the system was when it came up against a totally unscrupulous enemy and Edwards's declaration of a single option, "wait and see" inactivity, reinforced his deduction.

"Archie, this is Bill." He still used the familiar first name that had characterized their communications before Barrington's election last November. "I wanted to get back and touch base with you as soon as I heard from my advisors. They finished meeting a couple of minutes ago and we're going to have to sit this one out as far as any intervention is concerned."

"You mean we can't do a thing to help Potter?" Archie asked.

"I'm afraid that's the size of it. There's too much at

stake for us to show any sign of weakening or overreaction with the first execution." Barrington read the last from the notes he'd taken during his brief conversation with Edwards, knowing that it sounded unlike himself.

"You expect more executions, Mr. President?" the governor asked quietly.

Barrington leaned his forehead against his left palm and closed his eyes. It wasn't Bill Barrington talking. He wouldn't let even one life go without some sort of challenge. It was the President and he had to look at the bigger picture. One life wasn't that important when so many others were at stake.

"Archie, I have to be ready to accept the execution of every last one of those men without giving in to the demand. You know I went as far as my options would allow me in offering to transport those murderers out of the country safely." Damn the options, he thought bitterly. No one asked him what he would do. They merely handed him a list of options from which to choose. A, B, C, D or E . . . there was no line that said "none of the above." Even then, he needed those options because he wasn't quite certain what he would do without them. He needed the crutch that his advisors and the planning groups provided. He didn't even know the man who had written the option he chose.

"I understand, Bill. It's a rough one for you . . . tougher than my position here." Reaves voice was understanding. Barrington failed to notice the undertone of relief in it. The President had made the big decision, and Archie had to do no more than go along with it.

"How's the traffic control around Pittsburgh? Have you got it in hand yet?"

"I've got every available man on that one and it's getting worse. I'm getting pressure now from the corporations. Plants are having to shut down because there's no one to run them. They've had skeleton crews on today, but can't keep them open much longer. It's a son of a bitch."

There was a new consideration. U.S. Steel, Westinghouse, Alcoa, Rockwell International, and a lot of others had big plants in Pittsburgh that would be affected by the unannounced evacuation. It would be as bad as a general strike.

"I understand. Keep me informed on any developments. That thing might be as bad as the plant going up."

"Bill, there's another thing I need to ask you."

"Fire away."

"What's going to happen when the networks carry the execution? The reaction around the country and particularly here in the state could damage the dickens out of our bargaining position."

"I've already talked with the networks. They agreed to hold the coverage...tape it as ordered, but not show it until we give them the word. I've got people working on that tonight."

"Do you think they'll let us get away with that?" Reaves asked.

"We'll try it. That's all we can do," Barrington answered.

"Okay, if you say so."

"What about this Potter, Archie? Does he have a family...wife, kids?"

"Potter has a wife, Dolly, two grown children, and four grandchildren. They all live in Pittsburgh except for his son and two grandchildren who live in Scranton. They know about the execution. I took a call from his wife about an hour ago and tried to reassure her, but there wasn't much I could say."

"Dear God, I'd hoped against that," Barrington said. "Have someone with the family tomorrow, Archie. Give them as much support as you can."

"You know I will. I only wish there was something I could do to stop it."

"Both of us do, but we're fighting something bigger than a single life," Barrington responded. "Pray that we save all the others. We've got thousands of people depending on our judgment."

"We'll be doing our best here, Bill, and all of us have full faith in you."

"Thanks, Archie. I'll be back to you in the morning or later tonight if anything comes up," Barrington said, as he closed the conversation. There wasn't much to count on between now and 7 A.M. It was the terrorists' move.

At the moment the President was hanging up, the NRC's working group on Hypothetical Core Disruptive Accidents with top level scientists from both ERDA and NRC had just completed a final rerun of all their available computer codes that defined the scope and sequence of events for a core disruptive accident. They were in a somber mood as it became evident that the full range of events exceeded the models they had programmed.

Ruben Whitaker, his face showing the strain of long hours of intensive work, slumped in his chair. "That's it. We've run every code, calculated every known factor and the terminal phenomena is still undefined."

"With all of this work, one thing still bugs me," Henry Frankinson said. The technician from ERDA had been called in shortly after the crisis began and had slept for less than four hours in the last thirty-eight. "How did this group of terrorists, assumed to be novices in terms of reactor theory, gain the knowledge to structure this nightmare? It's almost as if they took our own system failure sequences and restructured them with an elimination of safeguard protection."

Gordon Pollock shook his head. "To do that, Henry, they would have had to have access to both plant design plans and the entire accident and safeguard interrelationship. For a layman to interpret that material, even if he had it in hand, would be extremely unlikely."

"But, Gordon," Frankinson responded, "the accomplished fact is before us. It's an even more remote possibility that they could have stumbled on all of this by trial and error."

Whitaker broke in, "They may not be novices. From what I understand, the FBI hasn't been able to identify them as belonging to any known terrorist organization. We don't know their level of expertise."

"That remains the problem of the FBI, gentlemen," Isaac Kaminsky stated. "Our problem remains and I suggest we proceed with the critical analysis of containment margins. We must be able to predict whether or not the reactor will withstand the potential pressure forces. If sufficient margins exist, we will have taken a substantial stride toward solution of the problem."

"True, Isaac," Pollock said, "but we've searched our codes and none of them met the requirement. The data bank is exhausted."

Kaminsky acknowledged with a shrug, "So we look further. Rerun what we have, examine possible international sources. France and England have substantial data banks."

"Any suggestions about international codes?" Pollock asked.

Whitaker slammed the table with his palm as he sat forward suddenly, "Apricot!"

Kaminsky echoed, "Computer Code Apricot."

"What in the world is Apricot?" Pollock asked.

"The year before last we were members of an international panel," Whitaker said. "On it, we combined and compared research and models used by the various nations in analyzing responses of breeder reactors to Hypothetical Core Disruptive Accidents, on the scale of what we face here. Apricot is the acronym we assigned to our computer model of this input."

"What this means," Kaminsky continued, "is that we have at our disposal the combined technologies of all the breeder reactor nations, except the Soviet Union. There are no finer analytical methods in existence for predicting the containment margins of a reactor under melt-down conditions."

Whitaker was on his feet. "I'll arrange for access to the tapes. The rest of you get some sleep. There will be a great deal to accomplish in a short period of time when we go back to work, and you'll need to be ready. This could give us the answers we're looking for." The men rose and left the room, unaware of the drama scheduled to break at sunrise.

In the plant infirmary, Art Potter slept quietly, turning slightly on the metal bunk as his dreams of a comfortable

Florida home, small flower garden, and the laughter of his grandchildren transported him far from the approaching dawn. John LeCourt reviewed the procedures with DeAngelo and Moran. Everything was ready. All that was left was the waiting.

The sun rose shortly after five A.M. on the sixteenth of August and broke over the mountains onto Bartonsville an hour later. A light mist clung to the ground, dissipating slowly in the warming air. There was a strange silence in the town, even with the gathering crowds at the edge of the perimeter established by state policemen. People spoke in low, hushed tones, not realizing that they were doing so. The plant squatted dark and forboding against the backdrop of leafy trees and green mountainside, the only light glaring in contrast came from the broad windowed second floor hall where the execution would take place.

Cameramen adjusted their cameras, ranging the telescopic lenses to focus clearly through the window. Photographers found locations that would offer them vantage points from which to record the event. The police kept a stern vigilance over the gathering crowd, their barely suppressed anger and frustration threatening to vent itself on some unruly spectator.

Carl Zellerman did a quick introduction for his story, standing in the specified press section at the edge of the parking lot, his back to the plant. Frank adjusted his camera to catch the lighted window in the background as Carl finished. Only a little longer, he thought, as he rechecked his lens for the sixth time. He'd filmed a lot of things for the station, but this was the first time for an execution. He was cold even with the windbreaker he was wearing. It was an inside cold, somewhere near the base of his spine and spreading.

From the slight rise at the entrance to the lot, Frank had a level camera shot into the hallway. His four hundred millimeter telephoto lens would pull the action right up to the viewers' faces; put them eyeball to eyeball with a man as he died. Goddamn bunch of vultures. We should have a good audience, if anyone is left in Pittsburgh. He had called his wife Sunday night and calmed her down. She had watched Jerry's big special on the plant and had come unglued like everyone else. Frank reassured her that he would be out of Bartonsville long before the place blew up. She finally quieted down, making him promise to be sure to leave well before anything threatened to happen. She had everything packed, the kids were ready to go and Jake and Miriam were expecting them in Baltimore.

At 6:55, the crowd suddenly gave an excited surge as people pointed toward the building and jabbed their friends. Even from the road, they could see figures moving in the hallway. In the parking lot, Frank stood behind his camera and focused on the two men who had entered the brightly lit hall. He shivered as he looked at the close-up of the scene through his viewer.

The men were wearing dark ski masks, covering their faces, and black uniform coveralls. They placed a straight chair at the left end of the hall, facing it slightly toward the window so Frank had a half shot on the front of it. When they had adjusted the chair, they stood, one on either side of it, waiting. The other cameramen and photographers were focusing in on the hall. Reporters and radio correspondents spoke into microphones as the drama began.

From the right edge of the window, two more black uniformed men walked slowly into view. Between them sagged a third man, barely able to walk as they half led, half carried him to the chair. Arthur Potter, the old retired Pittsburgh cop, his gray hair in disarray, his uniform shirt rumpled, was placed in the chair and his arms tied at his sides by the first two men. They worked efficiently, and in seconds, stepped away.

Potter's head raised slightly as he seemed to look around and then dropped back on his chest, moving slowly from side to side. It was a gesture of resignation or weak protest at the unjustness of what was about to happen. The two men who had led him in made minor adjustments around the chair before stepping out of sight. The victim was spending his last moments alone; not even his killers were near him.

At 6:59, the plant loudspeaker boomed out Dieter's

announcement of the execution. The government bore full responsibility for the death of Arthur K. Potter and would bear guilt for the deaths of the other hostages by their refusal to meet the PLA demands. By order of the people's court, Arthur Potter was condemned to die.

As he spoke, a single, masked rifleman, carrying a Soviet AK-47, stepped into view only ten feet from the seated figure. He tapped the base of the curved magazine, took careful aim and as the second hand reached the hour, pulled the trigger.

The staccato burst of automatic fire sounded clearly from the plant. Five tufts of cloth exploded across Potter's chest. His head jerked back as his body and chair were flung over backward by the force of the impacting bullets. There were screams from the crowd, policemen turned their heads away, cursing softly, cameramen were locked to their eyepieces in stunned fascination.

The rifleman calmly removed the weapon from his shoulder and pulled back the cocking lever, ejecting a live round. Two other raiders reappeared and stepped to the fallen body, out of sight below the window ledge. They crouched there for almost a minute and then straightened up. Between them was the limp body of Arthur Potter. Holding him under the arms, they dragged the body until it was fully visible against the window. His head was thrown back, mouth open in a frozen scream. Across his chest were five bloody splotches, running from armpit to armpit, the crimson stains spreading down the front of his shirt.

Frank felt as though he was going to faint as he struggled to keep his camera steady. Jesus Christ, oh, Jesus, this is bad. Put the guy down, you fucking animals. He's dead . . . isn't that enough?

After what seemed like hours, the terrorists dragged the body away from the window and out of sight down the hall. The executioner started to walk after them, then turned to the crowd outside and thrust his arm overhead, brandishing the weapon in defiance. At that, he spun and swaggered out of sight.

Dieter's voice again came over the loudspeaker.

"Arthur Potter has been executed as ordered by the PLA. Let this be a warning to your government that we do not tolerate its attitude."

The lights in the hall went off and the shocked anger of the crowd was transformed into an unspoken fear. Frank focused on the window for his closing shot. There was a visible smear of blood on the window where Potter's body had pressed against it.

LeCourt, DeAngelo, and Miller had been watching the crowd and newsmen during the execution. Their position in the plant supervisor's office just at the end of the hall was a perfect location in which to remain unseen. The portable TV set on the series of bookshelves by the desk was tuned to a Pittsburgh station. DeAngelo had chosen it at random since they all would be covering the incident. The 7 A.M. news was giving primary coverage to the growing traffic problem and related municipal and industrial labor shortages.

"When are they going to show it?" Miller asked impatiently. "It ought to be on by now, shouldn't it?"

LeCourt checked his watch. "It's oh-seven-twelve. They might be waiting for the oh-seven-fifteen break to show it. We'll give them till then."

At the White House, William Barrington was sitting in front of a large TV monitor that had been moved into the Fish Room, next to the Oval Office. The room was so named because President Franklin Roosevelt, during his terms in office, had elected to keep his collection of tropical fish in that particular room. This morning, however, Barrington's full attention was on the TV screen as the tape of the execution was previewed for him. No sound was dubbed on the preliminary tape . . . none was necessary for him to recoil at the stark scenes of premeditated murder. The jolt of bullets hitting flesh and hurling the old man's helpless body to the floor. Barrington sat in horrified fascination as the bloody figure was presented to the cameras. Those masks and black uniforms, a scene from a terror movie, mindless killers, without a shred of compassion—look how they're holding him up, like some grisly trophy.

As the tape ended, he had two clear pictures in his mind. Arthur Potter's lifeless body pressed against the window, the blood drooling from his wounds, and the rifleman—Barrington could feel the fanatical hatred pouring from the man as he shook the murder weapon over his head. There would be no bargaining with them. No matter what he wanted to do, what the procedures and politics called for, those killers wouldn't give in.

"Should we run it, Mr. President?" his press secretary asked. "The networks are waiting for you to decide."

Barrington took a deep breath before answering. "No, Clay. There's nothing to be accomplished by advertising their willingness to kill. Nothing. I . . . I don't think his family needs to be subjected to the torture of watching it. They've lost too much already."

At 7:23, the announcers on the TV news programs issued a brief bulletin that one of the hostages at the Bartonsville Nuclear Plant had been executed by the terrorists. John LeCourt quickly reached Dieter on the intercom. "Put a call through to the governor. Tell him they have thirty minutes to put the execution over the networks, exactly as we specified, or they can keep their cameramen in place for another one at oh-nine-hundred hours. Tell him we'll kill hostages one after another until the government finally realizes we're not bluffing." He turned away from the intercom panel toward Tony Miller. "Damn drill is getting a little sticky. I hope it doesn't take more than a couple of these to break them down so we can get the rest of the show on the road."

At 7:45, the nationwide audience watched over morning coffee as programs in progress were interrupted. Shocked and disbelieving, they saw the brutal slaying of a hostage fill their screens—the ultimate exclamation point at the end of a terrorist demand—calculated, dramatic, and cruelly effective. Barrington had reversed his decision. He wanted no one else to die.

There was an immediate reaction to the execution. Additional operators had to be placed on the White House switchboard to handle incoming calls. The mail room began to receive the first of the deluge of telegrams and letters. Travis Chambers and Clay Tabor, his modishly dressed news secretary, scanned the incoming messages. There were the predictable protests of outrage and indignation that such a thing would be allowed to happen in the United States; the messages of support for the President in dealing with the situation; the few calls from radicals, praising the terrorists for striking a blow against U.S. imperialism and the capitalist exploiters of the working class. They called Potter a "retired pig"—a "senior pig"—just another cop. Many of the messages expressed concern and fear about the outcome if the terrorists were driven to carry out their threat of destroying the plant. The picture of a radioactive cloud and winds carrying fallout over an indeterminate area was in the minds of the people. Clay saw quickly that the latter sentiment was growing as more messages arrived. The PLA had gotten the threat across to the people and from here on, public opinion was in the ball game. Unfortunately, fear was going to be working on the side of the PLA.

By 2:30, the President was meeting in the White House Cabinet Room with his Emergency Task Force. Barrington sat midway down the long, octagonal table. To his rear were the American and presidential flags and, flanking them, the French windows opening over the tree-shaded lawn. The first breeze in days was stirring leaves and scattering spray from the spouting fountain.

Around the table were key members of his cabinet and department heads involved in threat reaction. To his right was the undersecretary of state, sitting in for the secretary, who was out of the country; to his left, the secretary of defense and deputy secretary. Across from him sat Howard O'Brien from the Nuclear Regulatory Commission. In armchairs around the walls of the room were other executives, aides, and briefing teams.

The growing feeling of impotence among Task Force staff members had communicated itself to the executives. The involved plans and procedures that had been drafted during the past three years were bogging down. The terrorists had short-circuited the system when they gained access to the plant and demonstrated an unexpected comprehension of its functioning in their threatened destruction. The new Government Emergency Reaction Plan, which was revised to include this type of situation, was still lost somewhere in the bureaucratic labyrinth having comments and annexes attached. It would be another six months before it could go to final draft.

After this morning's execution, not even the new plan would help. There was little doubt that the PLA was committed beyond any compromise solution, and with no basis for negotiation, the drafting of options became a mechanical process. Even the most imaginative staffers were running short of ideas.

Meanwhile, in the meeting, the impending political embarrassment of capitulation to the terrorists' demands provoked a neatly phrased round of bureaucratic back-stabbing. No one wanted his agency to be saddled with the burden of responsibility for the debacle.

"Mr. President," one NRC representative addressed Barrington, "in retrospect, my working group has found nothing to indicate a single substantive violation of published safeguard or operating regulations by the plant. As you know, the NRC inspects all nuclear power facilities to ensure compliance with federal regulations and to promote safe operation within the entire industry. We are reviewing all standing regulations to determine if they can be tightened in order to preclude a recurrence of this act. However, I feel that there is a certain laxity in other areas which offsets any positive effect we may have."

"And what is that?" Barrington asked.

"The terrorists obtained a clear advantage in their bargaining position immediately after they were able to penetrate and secure the plant. I would respectfully suggest that the State Department failed to adequately screen visa applicants or our Immigration Department failed to apply federal guidelines in passing individuals through our borders."

The undersecretary of state barely restrained his indignation. "Mr. President! I must object to this unwarranted insinuation that State is responsible for this incident."

"If the terrorists had not been able to pass, undetected, into this country," the NRC representative continued, "they would not be in control of the plant at this time."

"What about the FBI?" the State Department member asked, looking across the table.

The head of the FBI's Internal Security Division shifted uncomfortably in his high-backed chair. "Mr. President, the Bureau has made a maximum effort in this case to determine the origin of the terrorist group. We had no advanced warning, no information that would have led us to believe that the operation was impending. I'm afraid that even with the assistance of our colleagues abroad, we have been unable to pin down where they came from. Let me add, at this juncture, that our efforts have been somewhat hampered by the dismantling of much of our internal security apparatus, that is, our sources which would identify indigenous radical groups capable of this act."

Barrington sat in disbelieving silence as the discussion went on. Implications of corporate negligence in providing adequate security were countered by the citing of government regulations that stated that a five man guard shift would be maintained on a twenty-four hour basis. A&T Security Service was challenged for not providing suitable men for the job; ERDA was provoked by questions concerning safeguard margins insufficient to withstand a combined series of disruptive accidents.

The President's voice cracked sharply over the degenerating discussion, "That is quite enough, gentlemen!" There was an immediate silence. All heads were turned toward the new chief executive, whom they had disregarded in their heated exchange.

Barrington was frowning as he stared around the table. His advisors, heads of departments, key men in this effort to deal with the threat, and here they were tossing the time bomb from one agency to the other, not wanting to be caught holding it when it went off. He was conscious of his fingertips drumming on the chair arm and halted the gesture of irritation. His voice was restrained when he finally spoke. "We're shifting a long way from the purpose of this meeting and it's time you got one thing completely clear in your minds." All eyes were focused on him now. "*I'm* the one who will shoulder whatever blame is forthcoming in the wake of the government's actions. That I expect to do." His voice dropped a tone as it always did when he was angered. "But I'll be damned if I'll sit back and be cursed for what the government *failed* to do! Now I want options from you that will stop these people, not a bunch of useless recriminations and excuses. Do I make myself understood?"

Without waiting for a response, he turned to Lewis Cartwright, the highly vocal NRC representative who sat diagonally across from him. "Cartwright, one of the early options I received involved powering down the entire plant by cutting primary and secondary electrical lines. Can we do it and what effect will it have?"

The man's heavy jowled face lost some of the aggressiveness it had shown during his volley against State Department. He flipped rapidly through a folder and selected a memo. "Sir, I'm afraid that option has been determined to be inoperative." There was no bluster now.

"Inoperative? Why?"

"There's a diesel generator...uh...on site that ...uh...provides emergency power in the event of main power loss. We must assume, Mr. President, that they're aware of it and...uh...would cut it in immediately."

"What about fuel?" Barrington asked. "Can't we cut the fuel supply?"

"No, sir." Cartwright's voice was almost apologetic. "There's a forty-five-thousand-gallon emergency fuel storage tank...buried next to the generator building."

Barrington stared at the man in disbelief. "You mean to say they've got emergency power right there and we can't cut it?" Cartwright nodded silently.

"Well, now, that's just beautiful for an opener. An option that fails even before we try it." He wadded up the paper and tossed it toward the classified waste container.

"This is hardly an encouraging beginning, gentlemen. I trust the other options will prove to be less in favor of the terrorists. What about military options, General Young?"

Michael Young wore his four stars with ease and competence. Six rows of multicolored ribbons over his left uniform pocket topped with master pilot's wings attested to his military capabilities. His extension of tenure as chairman of the Joint Chiefs of Staff, despite a barely concealed dislike for bureaucrats, established his ability to survive in the Washington sociopolitical jungle. He sat two seats to the left of Wilson Marks, the recently appointed secretary of defense, and looked to him for approval before speaking. Marks, understanding the President's awareness of his unfamiliarity with the situation, motioned for Young to proceed. Marks was still settling into his new job at the Pentagon and could hardly add anything to the discussion.

"Mr. President, the Joint Staff estimates of this situation were begun immediately after our notification Monday morning. Although the intelligence estimate is incomplete at this time, several possible plans were staffed for comment. Of three possible options, one was considered suitable for presentation. Colonel Johnson, from my office, will outline it for you."

At that, a tall officer in a sharply pressed green uniform stood from the row of chairs behind Young and stepped to the podium at the head of the room. A captain and master sergeant walked from the rear of the room with an easel and stack of charts, which they placed next to the podium.

"Mr. President, I am Colonel Johnson, briefing officer from JCS, Operations."

Further down the room, a State Department aide shifted restlessly in his chair and checked his watch. "Goddamn it," he muttered to himself, "another DoD horse and pony show."

"The operation I am about to outline has been code named 'Eagle Claw,'" Johnson continued in a clipped, precise voice. "The situation involves a terrorist element of indeterminate numbers and unknown origin holding seven hostages in the Bartonsville Nuclear Power Plant. There is..."

"Six hostages, Colonel Johnson," Barrington corrected him. "After this morning."

Johnson caught himself quickly, "My mistake, sir. Six hostages. They have threatened the destruction of the plant..."

"I know all of that, Johnson. Get on with something new."

"Friendly elements involved will be Charlie Company of the Fourth Ranger Battalion, located at Fort Moultrie, South Carolina," the colonel managed, referring to the elite six-hundred-man unit whose distinctive black berets and camouflaged fatigues marked them as a special battalion.

"Those are the commandos. Right?" Barrington asked.

"Yes, sir. They're a highly skilled infantry battalion, trained for ranger and commando operations worldwide. On the order of the Israeli raid at Entebbe last year."

"Um, yes. Well, what can they do for us here?"

"Sir, their mission is to secure the plant, kill or capture the terrorists, disarm all demolitions and allow normal operation of the plant to resume. In accomplishing the mission, we have made special efforts to assure the safety and rescue of all remaining hostages."

Barrington took a briefing paper handed to him by a second NCO who passed similar documents to the other members of the Task Force. Across the top and bottom of the page were stamped in glaring red ink, "TOP SECRET/Restricted Access." The master sergeant uncovered the first chart and stepped sharply back, standing at attention as the captain used a pointer to indicate squad and company capabilities depicted.

"We estimate that one company will be sufficient to accomplish the mission. As shown on the chart," Johnson said, "three squads of the first platoon will act as an assault element. The remainder of the company will form the main body. I call your attention to the various qualifications of the men in each element. Snipers, weapons experts, and chemical warfare specialits in the assault squads. The same plus demolitions experts, medics, and a radiation monitoring team in the second element. There will be a decontamination unit on call."

The sergeant replaced the first chart with a large scale drawing of the plant area.

"The operation will be conducted in two phases. First, vertical envelopment by the assault squads using free-fall parachute techniques. They will exit a C-one-thirty aircraft at fifteen thousand feet, fall to approximately two thousand feet and deploy their canopies. Their landing will be in the clear space behind the Reactor Containment Building and adjacent to the cooling tower and pump house. As you see on the diagram, there is an area one hundred sixty yards by two hundred fifty yards which is blocked from view of the main building by the mass of the containment building. There is additional clear space to the southwest, still within the security barrier, in the event that winds change on us."

Barrington halted him. "What makes you assume the terrorists won't spot the parachutes merely because the drop zone . . . that is what you call it?"

"Yes, sir, drop zone."

"Merely because the drop zone is obscured from view of the main building? I'd think they'd be pretty obvious hanging up there at fourteen hundred feet."

"This will be a night drop, sir," Johnson answered. "If the weather holds and with the moon phase, estimated time of drop is oh-three-thirty hours."

"Wel-l-l," Barrington exclaimed, "that makes it pretty risky, doesn't it?"

"Negative, sir. These squads are specially picked. Each man has over two hundred free-falls to his credit, including a minimum of forty night jumps of this type. In addition, the terrorists have continued to use the plant's perimeter security lighting system at night. This gives us a perfect outline of the area."

The President swiveled his chair to look more closely at the plant diagram. The briefing was beginning to catch his interest. It just might work.

"Two men will clear the area of canopies and set up pathfinder beacons for the second element landing. The remainder of the team will proceed immediately to exterior access doors and force entry. Once inside, they will infiltrate the plant, maneuvering to seal off corridors leading away from the control building. They will engage the terrorists with automatic weapons fire wherever they locate them and will be under orders to kill on sight. Our first priority is to prevent any of them from reaching the demolitions."

"What if your people encounter outside security?" Barrington asked.

"We have two snipers with silencer equipped rifles to handle long kills and each man is prepared to deal with close-in work."

"All right. It sounds good so far," Barrington responded. "What about the hostages?"

"A four-man snatch team is responsible for locating and protecting them, sir."

"What if there are more terrorists than you've counted on?" the President asked. He picked up the briefing paper and read the first paragraphs before looking up again. "You show in your estimate, a figure of six to eight terrorists total."

"If I may, Mr. President," General Young spoke up. "I mentioned that we have varying estimates on the enemy situation; however, as in many of our training exercises, we deal with unknown factors on the ground. Contingency planning is done ahead of time, but the men react to what they find."

"And this is your best estimate?"

"This type of terrorist activity has, in the past, involved no more than six to eight men. J-two estimates they will have to keep fifty percent alert while allowing the others to rest. That gives us three to four of them manning the plant. Should we launch this raid after the government has agreed to meet their demands, we can plan on their security being looser. They'll be looking toward their escape, not the prospect of defending in place." Young finished smoothly, "We'll already have the advantage of surprise, Mr. President. With numerical superiority and one other item I've approved for this operation, I believe we can take the plant. Johnson," he motioned for the briefer to continue.

Johnson acknowledged and went on, "As an additional precaution, the assault teams will go in wearing M-seventeen-A-one protective masks to allow the use of a cannister DM agent, Adamsite gas, which will be dispersed throughout the buildings to incapacitate the terrorists."

There were startled looks exchanged around the table at the mention of gas. "What is this Adamsite?" Barrington asked. "Is it a tear gas, or what?" Without waiting for an answer, he turned to Young. "Is it necessary to use a gas in gaining control of the plant?"

Mike Young sensed the sudden disapproval. Well I'll be goddamned, he thought. They're worried about what some media mouth is going to say about our gassing the bastards. He leaned forward, hands tightly clasped on the table in front of him, and addressed the President. If he could make Barrington understand, that was all he needed. The rest of them could go to hell.

"Mr. President, my men will be going into that plant to kill or capture, in that order, a band of terrorists who have already demonstrated *their* willingness to kill. By our actions, we'll prevent these animals from spreading even greater destruction and death."

His eyes drilled into Barrington's as he strove to make the man understand, in this one instant, what war, no matter how big or small, was all about. "This isn't some sort of athletic contest where both sides are supposed to have an equal advantage. There are no Marquis of Queensbury rules. We're going in there to kill those men, and I'll give my people whatever advantages I can to make certain they do their job . . . and come out alive. Hell, sir, if I thought using a nerve gas would have done the job better, I would have tried that; but in this case, Adamsite physically incapacitates, causes mental depression, and extreme confusion. If there are more of them in that plant than we counted on, then this will be our equalizer."

Barrington ignored the hum of conversation around the table. "I'll buy your explanation, General Young, but tell me what the Adamsite actually does."

"It's a nonpersistant aerosol, sir. Once inhaled, it causes coughing, nausea, cramps, and vomiting as well as a king-sized headache. The effects are short-lived and we can get to the hostages before they take in too much of it."

"The latter was my major concern. Thank you, General." He turned back to Johnson who had been standing patiently by. "Go ahead, Colonel."

"After the assault squads are on the ground, they'll radio the second element to begin phase two. The main body will be aboard CH-forty-seven Chinook helicopters, orbiting over Mechanicsburg." The captain pointed to a small town on the blowup map of the Bartonsville area. It was southeast of the plant.

"They'll cover the distance in three to five minutes and we'll have them on the ground in under twelve minutes. While the assault squads are engaging the terrorists, the main element will move in, seal off the critical buildings from the inside and disarm known demolitions. There will be plant technicians landed with the special demolitions teams to aid in seeking out all devices. Radiation monitoring teams will scan the plant for leakage and the decontamination teams will be standing by. As soon as the plant is under our control, we'll open access to its regular staff for a return to normal operation."

The President allowed himself a brief smile. "You really give me the feeling that your people can do the job, Young."

The general relaxed in his chair and answered cooly, "Sir, with the personnel in this unit, the training they've undergone, and the motivation they have, I'd hate to be one of those terrorists." Young's normally tight mouth arched in a broad grin. "It's like the old Texas Rangers, Mr. President. They used to say, 'One riot; one Ranger.' Here we're not going to take any chances, so we're using over a hundred of them."

Barrington chuckled and slapped at the chair arm. "One riot; one Ranger. That's the way it should be. Do any of you gentlemen have questions or comments?" he asked abruptly, looking around the table.

There were several hands. Latham, the dour-faced FBI representative, spoke first. "I have to disagree with the basis for estimating the number of terrorists, Mr. President. There is no past case of a terrorist attack on a nuclear power plant and our estimates are far from reliable at this point. In addition, they've employed a sophisticated antitank rocket, and we've identified the weapon used in this morning's execution as a Soviet Kalashnikov AKM assault rifle. There is also strong indication they've emplaced early warning devices and some type of antipersonnel mines."

There was agreement from the CIA representative. "General Young was accurate when he said there were no hard estimates on numbers of terrorists involved. It will be risky to base an operation of this magnitude on Defense Intelligence and J-two figures since none of our agencies agree."

Howard O'Brien answered for NRC. "Mr. President, I would add that it takes only one of those men with his hand on a detonator to initiate the disaster we're trying to avoid. If, God forbid, that should happen when this raid is launched, then we truly will have lost."

There was no comment from the director of the Defense Intelligence Agency. Bill Barrington watched Young's face as the comments poked holes in the plan. There was carefully masked disgust in the general's expression. He really believes in his men and their chances of pulling this off, Barrington thought. I like that—someone who's got solutions instead of more problems. Still, the objections are well founded. The whole plan hinges on containing the terrorists and keeping them from reaching the demolitions. There are a lot of "if's" involved, but this is the best option on the board.

"General Young," Barrington asked, "would you care to respond?"

Young thought for a moment. "Sir, if I may borrow from General George Patton. He said something to the effect that 'a good plan, violently executed now, is better than a perfect plan next week.' I'll stand on that."

"What about tomorrow night?" the President asked quickly. "Tomorrow at noon is the deadline for ransom delivery. We don't know when they'll make their departure after that nor what means they'll employ. If we're going to get them, tomorrow night looks like the time."

Young hesitated, wishing he could retract his comment. Tomorrow night. God almighty, less than forty-eight hours from projected drop time. He glanced at Johnson standing stiffly by the chart. The barely perceptible negative shake of the colonel's head was what he expected. It took months to put the Son Tay Operation together; took the Israelis part of a week to come up with the Entebbe raid. He'd have to override nonconcurrences all down the line to have this staffed in time to give the Rangers at least eight hours for preparation and rehearsals.

"It'll be close, sir," he finally answered. "This plan is only an outline and we have to fill in some gaps in our intelligence picture, as indicated by the comments from the other agencies. If you could talk the terrorists into buying a one-day delay..."

"Can you or can you not do it by tomorrow night?" Barrington asked. "It might just be too late after that."

"If you'll excuse Colonel Johnson, sir, he'll begin work immediately. We'll do our damnedest."

Barrington nodded and as the colonel and his briefing team left the room, he returned his attention to the men at the table. "Well, gentlemen, now we wait for two answers." He looked at O'Brien. "First, the conclusions on potential damage and radiological effects if the threat were carried out. These we'll have by early evening. Correct, Howard?"

"My staff is running the Apricot tapes now, Mr. President," O'Brien answered. "We should have the estimate by six P.M."

"Good. Second, General Young, you'll tell us whether or not you can get our military response off the ground in time to stop these people."

"I should be able to give you an answer by tomorrow morning."

Barrington felt the tenseness in his neck muscles. It was going to be too late at that point. He had to make his decision by ten o'clock tonight in order to have time to respond to the ransom demand. If the Apricot code gave any hope for containment of the radioactivity, he could stall and give Young time to work the plan out. Agree to the demand, but ask for time to get the money together...take the chance that they wouldn't kill another hostage. It might work.

"What are the odds that you can do it, Young?" Barrington asked.

"Sixty to forty, against, right now Mr. President. The unit must have time to rehearse once they receive the order. They have to execute the operation perfectly the first time. No second chances here."

Mike knew the President wanted him to give an indication, any indication that Eagle Claw could be launched. Of all the options that had been presented, this was the big, bright hope and Barrington had latched onto it. The man was caught with a bunch of new faces in his administration, most of them still learning who worked for them in their departments and none of them able to help him with this decision. We'll go all out for you, Barrington, Mike thought, not just because it's our job. I want to see us teach those bastards a lesson. "The odds should be much better by morning, sir," he added.

The President seemed to relax momentarily and then he was back in motion, gathering up his personal notes and shifting his chair away from the table. "I think that will be all for now, gentlemen. I want all involved agencies to provide maximum assistance to General Young's people in this intelligence estimate business and...that's it. Let's get back to work. Time is short." He stood and walked out quickly.

Once in the vaulted corridor, Barrington turned to Travis Chambers, instructing him to have the appointment secretary cancel everything for the next two hours. "I'll be upstairs, Trav, and I don't want anything short of a red phone to interrupt me."

From his briefing folder he withdrew a handwritten list of congressmen and passed it to Chambers. "I was thinking about the support we'll need and jotted these down. While you're holding the fort, touch base with all of them and give them an update on the situation."

Chambers took the list and read it. "You'll call the speaker and floor leaders yourself?" he asked.

"Right after the O'Brien meeting. Have numbers where I can reach them." Barrington answered.

"I've already contacted our Senate keys," Travis said. "They've been briefed and are waiting for your decision. The only flak came from conservationists and the Pennsylvania contingent. Lehman and Bradley wanted to see you, but I stalled them off."

"I'll have to talk with them. I need them too. Set up a meeting tomorrow morning before the press conference." As they reached the main staircase, Barrington paused. "One other thing, Trav. I want the chairman and vice-chairman of the Joint Atomic Energy Committee to sit in with O'Brien tonight. They should be up to speed on what we're looking at in terms of legislation after the smoke clears from this." He gave a short grunt, "Humpf! Maybe I shouldn't say, 'after the smoke clears.' There better not be any smoke."

"There was some already . . . at the press briefing after the execution. Clay had to field a dozen or so real scorchers on our negotiating posture. Now that the terrorists have drawn first blood, the crowd in the Colosseum is screaming for us to do more than talk."

The President took a deep breath. He had expected to come under fire no matter what he did, but he was determined that the criticism would not be for indecisiveness or inactivity. Fortunately, General Young had provided the answer to the problem. Now it was a matter of giving him the best possible odds of success.

"We'll give them action, Trav. I want you to change the press conference location from the East Room to the State Auditorium so we'll have maximum coverage." He was thinking about Young's proposition to throw the terrorists off guard by seeming to capitulate. They might suspect a trick if he informed them of his decision by a private phone call through Archie Reaves, but a public announcement to the press would be different.

Trav anticipated his intentions. "You're taking a big chance. If anything goes wrong, you'll get deception hung around your neck like a milestone, along with caving in to the demand. On top of that, you're really pushing them to go ahead and blow the plant." He shook his head slowly. "You've done some gambling before, Governor, but this pot is the biggest one I've ever seen on the table."

Barrington placed his free hand on Chambers's shoulder, patting it reassuringly. "That's why I'm going upstairs now, Trav. I've got a lot of thinking to do . . . and a lot of praying."

Another decision was being implemented as Barrington walked up the broad staircase to his second floor living quarters. The Defense Civil Preparedness Agency had relayed the President's approval for the evacuation of the Bartonsville area. National Guard and regular units aided Civil Defense personnel in the movement of families from Beaver, Midland, Monaca, Coraopolis, and all the small communities in the immediate vicinity of the plant. The Ohio National Guard and State Police cooperated in providing traffic control over already jammed roadways. Civil Defense teams and Red Cross volunteers staffed the reception centers in scattered Ohio towns, upwind from the plant, where gymnasiums and churches were opened to receive the flood of refugees. Food and medical supplies were flown in from government depots. Amid the chaos of the mass evacuation, teamwork began to evolve and the families found themselves welcomed and made comfortable in their temporary quarters.

In Bartonsville, only the security force of state policemen allowed by the terrorists were maintaining the perimeter of the plant. Two black and white cruisers prowled through deserted streets, on the lookout for potential looters, although there was little likelihood that anyone would risk being caught in the area. The military had taken responsibility for the surrounding area after martial law was imposed. There had been no other method of keeping order since state police and National Guard units were overcommitted in handling the Pittsburgh panic and evacuation. Weary troopers grabbed a few hours sleep between shifts as they worked around the clock to contain the traffic and crime that followed in the wake of the exodus from Pittsburgh and its suburbs. The fire departments around Pittsburgh found themselves fighting suburban house fires on an increasing scale as blazes were set and unreported, progressing beyond control before the departments could respond. It seemed that only the street gangs remained in the city and were preying on undefended stores and homes.

Cleave Jones, sipping a Coke after finishing his lunch, sat in the main building snack bar watching NBC coverage of the traffic jams around Pittsburgh. He had taken the portable TV set from the plant supervisor's office and plugged it in where the team could watch it during breaks. He was absorbed as he viewed the spectacle of thousands of cars packed along the freeways leading from the city. "Oo-wee, man. Seems like no one wants to be around for the day-nou-ment...and it's the best part of the play."

"Looks like Labor Day weekend on the L.A. Freeway," Alex Mendoza said. "Bet the fuzz hates our guts."

"We were on their shit list before this," Rey Sanchez added.

"Come on, Rey, you been on their shit list since you were old enough to steal hub caps," Mendoza quipped.

They were sitting around the red Formica-topped tables waiting to go on duty. Food and drink dispensers lined the walls and two overflowing plastic garbage cans flanked the door. The early tension that had gripped all of them after LeCourt's decision to stage the execution was gone. They had pulled a full alert, with all weapons manned until noon. After that, it was a cinch that there wasn't going to be any retaliation.

Sanchez nudged Cleave Jones who was still staring intently at the set.

"Hey, cuñado, your turn to take chow to the guards."

"Wait, my man, wait. This thing isn't over yet." The narrator was describing the scenes of violence in Pittsburgh as police clashed with looters. "Man, they don't have time for us. There's too much goin' on out there. Look at those dudes scatter when the law comes at 'em." Street scenes, filmed from a vehicle showed figures running from the front of a hardware store, arms filled with merchandise, as police cars screeched to a halt and officers piled out. "Bargain days at your friendly downtown stores. Run, brothers, you can lose those honky bastards." He was grinning broadly. "Shee-it, man, I'd have my whole house furnished if I was there."

Jones eased his lanky frame out of the chrome and plastic chair, draining the cup and setting it on the table. "What're we giving them today?"

"Crack one of the new cases of 'Cs' and take out the good stuff," Mendoza suggested. "They can make it on chicken and noodles again."

"They had that last night," BJ countered.

"Fuck 'em. It's the one thing that none of us like." Mendoza answered. "Give 'em some of the cans of fruit and some of the pound cake. That'll make up for it."

"Hold on the pound cake, man. The colonel likes that."

Jones held up a huge hand. "Let the ol' Cleaver make up the menu. I got the duty; I get to make the decisions. How's that grab you?"

"Jeez, man," Sanchez said, "you give a minority one taste of responsibility and he turns into a dictator."

"Keep that up, man, an' I'll cut your supply of peppers." Cleave smirked.

He was laughing to himself as he walked out of the room and down the hall to the storage room where they had cached the cases of C rations that sustained them during their stay in the plant. The rations weren't too bad when you used one of the heat tabs to warm up the main ration. It was good enough for the short time they were going to be here.

After tearing the tape off a new case of rations, he pulled out several of the individual cardboard boxes and sifted through the cans and packets inside each, selecting rations for the hostages. To one side, he set a special ration, which he intended to heat and take to the infirmary. The men in the lounge would eat theirs cold. It wouldn't kill them.

In the Reactor Service Building, John LeCourt was studying the shielded storage pit where unused fuel rods waited to be lifted out and installed in the reactor core. He and Ed Moran had begun planning the procedures for removal of the rods and transfer of their Plutonium fuel pellets to transport containers. The Special Nuclear Material containers would be little problem since they were already packaged for movement.

When they were through, there would be nearly six tons of fissionable material. Counting the pure Plutonium from the SNM storage, that would give them over a ton of the pure stuff. Amount of Plutonium in the fuel rods should run around eighteen to thirty percent and the organization had access to labs that could chemically separate it from the Uranium. That was enough Plutonium to put together a lot of devices, figuring twelve pounds for Nagasaki.

"Hey, ol' buddy, wake up. Come on out of it now." Cleave was gently shaking Art Potter by the shoulder. He was stretched on the infirmary's folding bed, his torn and stained uniform covered with a light blanket. Potter's eyes fluttered open, then closed.

"Come on now, I got some good hot chow for you, but you've gotta be awake to eat it." Cleave pulled the heated cans of food over beside the bed and stirred the contents with a clear plastic spoon.

Potter's eyes opened and he tried to focus his vision. The room kept sliding into a fuzzy haze. Jones was an indistinct voice and a presence he couldn't identify.

He pulled Potter to a sitting position and sat beside

him on the bed, holding him up. "Okay now, you just take a sip of this coffee. It'll flat knock those cobwebs outta your head. Come on now, you've gotta help me." He held the cup to Potter's lips as the man tried to sip the brew.

"That's good now. Little more... swallow it now." He held his arm gently around the older man's shoulders, supporting him as he began to drink, his Adam's apple jerking as the hot liquid slipped down his throat.

Art's vision cleared and he recognized the room with its glass-faced cabinets of medications, gauze, Band-Aids, and cotton. He turned slightly and looked at Jones. "Who are you? Have they gone yet? What happened?"

Jones chuckled as he moved away, letting Potter sit upright on his own. "I *am* they, ol' man, but don't let that worry you." He picked up the can of meatloaf and gravy he had heated moments before. "Here, you eat this... or try the soup, if you want it first. We can talk after you eat." Potter took the can and began to eat ravenously. Cleave watched him with an amused solicitude. *He eats that dog food like some grunt just back from a patrol. Only time it tastes good is when you're hungrier than hell.*

Potter happened to glance down at his shirt as he ate. The spoon stopped midway to his mouth which remained open, not to accept the food, but in shocked puzzlement. He looked up at Cleave. "Wha... what happened?"

Cleave gestured casually toward the holes and bright red stains across the man's chest. "Nothin' much, man. We executed you this morning, but you're okay now."

"You what?" Potter had placed the can on the floor and was fingering the holes in his shirt, probing through to the skin on his chest. "What is all of this?" He was looking at Cleave in alarm.

"Be cool, my man. You're A-okay."

"I don't mean that. What happened this morning?" Art had shaken off the stupor that had kept him immobile since early morning.

"It was a real show," Cleave beamed. "You were a star on nationwide TV and now that everyone thinks you're dead, we decided you did a good enough job that you need to be around to pick up your Emmy or whatever they call it." He pointed to the C ration can. "You better eat that before it gets cold. Damn gravy thickens real fast and doesn't taste for shit."

Potter automatically picked up the can and began spooning chunks of meatloaf into his mouth. "Tell me what happened?" he asked between bites.

Cleave leaned back against the stainless steel examination table and folded his heavily muscled arms across his chest. "Well, when the people out there didn't come through, we figured an execution would make them think again, so we gave them one."

"But I'm still alive."

"You better honk you're still alive." Cleave laughed. "We wouldn't kill you, man. You're the meanest dude in the whole bunch. Anyone who'd take on those Dobies has either got to have shit for brains or be one tough mutha."

Potter shook his head. "You're confusing me. What's this?" He indicated the holes and red stains with his spoon.

"Oh that. We hit you with some pentathol...enough to put you under and strapped a metal plate to your chest. Then we put five of those Hollywood stuntman exploding caps across there." Cleave pointed to the series of holes. "Right above each one, we put some blood bags...you know, like they use in the movies. Anyway, when you were tied in the chair out there where all the cameras could see you clear, ol' Tom..." he caught himself before he gave Tomlinson's name, "stepped out with an AK and blew off a burst of five. He shot off to your right, but from the outside, it looked just like he greased you good."

Art was again fingering the torn shirt as he listened.

"When he fired, we shot off the caps electrically and everyone saw the holes blow through your shirt. We jerked you and the chair over backwards...you were out by then...had thin wires attached to the back of the chair. Man, it looked real enough. They thought for sure you bought the farm."

"You mean it was all on TV?" Potter asked.

"Every swingin' camera they could cram into the lot."

Potter's head drooped. "Oh my God. Oh my God." The sound was a strangled plea.

"Hey, what's the matter?" Cleave was surprised at the reaction. "You're alive, man. Nothin' happened."

"My wife...Dolly...she thinks I'm dead. Oh God, she'll go to pieces."

Cleave was genuinely touched by the man's concern for his wife. He reached over and put a hand gently on Potter's shoulder. "Hey, now, don't get all upset. You're goin' to be out of here in a couple of days and she'll be happy as hell when she finds out you're alive."

Potter shook his head. "She always worried about me on this job. Said I'd done my time on the force...took my chances when I was young enough to take care of myself, and now...and now this. God help her."

Cleave picked up the can of soup and extended it to the man. "Here, you finish your meal. Won't do any good starving yourself. We want you in good shape for that reunion, man. Think of how happy she'll be when she sees you again."

Potter looked up slowly as if seeing Cleave for the first time. "Why didn't you go ahead and kill me? Why're you doing this for me after I tried to break out of the room...tried to get to your man?"

Cleave thought for a moment. "I suppose it's because you've got guts. We never figured you for a hard case, but you jocked us. Took a lot for one man to take on the dogs and then try to brace one of us. Like I said, either you got guts or nothing upstairs. Either way, somebody's gotta take care of you." Cleave motioned toward the can of soup. "Now quit your talkin' and eat. That's why I brought it for you."

Potter nodded and went back to eating. He was totally confused by this group of men. They had every reason to kill him.

"Here." Cleave tossed a small packet of cigarettes from the C ration accessory kit. "You can smoke if you want. I'll lock the door when I leave, so don't try to set anything on fire with the matches. The room is concrete and the only thing that gets fried will be you." He straightened up and turned to walk out of the room.

"Hey," Potter said. "Thank you."

"Don't mind it," Cleave answered as he walked out, "my pleasure."

The President sat quietly beside his wife on the Truman Balcony, overlooking the tree-lined South Lawn. This curving, second floor gallery, which opened out from the Yellow Oval Room, had become a presidential retreat. While busy traffic flowed around the Ellipse and on Seventeenth Street, he had the feeling of separation from the crush and impatience, of relief from the pressures inside the building. Over the trees there was a splendid vista of the Washington Monument and Jefferson Memorial in clear outline against a light blue sky. Here, he didn't even know that the first protest marchers were parading along the Pennsylvania Avenue sidewalk north of the White House. From their vantage point in Lafayette Park across the street, mute statutes of Lafayette, Jackson, and Rochambeau witnessed the line of marchers carrying printed placards protesting nuclear power. A smaller group of marchers, their hand-drawn posters calling for dissolution of CIA support for foreign intelligence services, found themselves being pushed away from their chosen route as the nuclear protestors grew in number.

The Barringtons shared a white wicker love seat that Pamela had brought from the governor's mansion. He was relaxed, puffing on one of his infrequent cigars, his stockinged feet propped on an ottoman. On the wicker coffee table were the estimates, briefing papers, and assessments he'd reread several times and the options that had been submitted in a *pro forma* rush to meet deadlines. How patently ridiculous they were after Potter's execution.

Pam Barrington's high-cheekboned face mirrored her husband's concentration. Petite, delicately beautiful, she was his closest and strongest confidante—the one person he trusted implicitly. She had shared all his crisis decisions with him, relieving some of the overwhelming sense of responsibility, and allowed him to open his thoughts rather than make guarded commentary that was symptomatic of official discussions.

He replaced a stack of estimates on the table and sat rubbing his eyes. "That's the last one, Pam," he sighed. "A lot of paper, a lot of words... and what a waste of time." He picked up one of the acetate-covered folders. "Look at this. An assessment of the 'impenetrable security' of the Bartonsville Plant." He tossed it back with the others, shaking his head. "It must have been reasonable to the man who drafted it a year ago. The PLA didn't read it."

"You've been through all of them?" she asked.

"Hon, I've read and I've listened." The cigar went into the ashtray. "I'm lucky to get a straight answer from anyone. Seems the vocabularies up here don't have a simple 'yes' or 'no' in them."

"How soon do you have to decide?"

"Decide? Oh, this evening. Final meeting with the councils at 6:30, then I've got the ball." His voice trailed off, "Then it's all mine."

"That soon?"

Bill Barrington was silent as he gazed over the skyline, his eyes briefly following a 707 on its final approach to National Airport. It was all so quick. So short a time since it began—so short a time until he'd choose the response that would end it. But how long to live with the decision if it went wrong? Young gave the only solid option, the violent one. Apricot was the one chance it wouldn't be necessary. So little time—so much at stake. It wasn't just Bartonsville. If the PLA succeeded, there would be others. They have to be stopped. It's odd, with all the resources in government, the brilliant minds, the sophisticated techniques and equipment, computer banks of information—all of this—to try to stop a few men with some explosives and a willingness to die, taking innocent people with them. We've made ourselves vulnerable. The barbarians are at the gates...

"Bill?" Pam's voice broke through.

"I'm sorry, love. You know, I think—I think I know

what Rabin must have gone through before Entebbe.
PLA, PLO, Black September—it doesn't matter what
they call themselves. The senselessness, brutality—it's the
same." A shy, fleeting smile changed the serious contours
of his face. "I got a telegram from him—I forgot to tell
you. It's almost as if he knew me—really knew me. At the
last, he said, 'Be strong. Trust your God, your conscience
and your judgement. They are your strengths in the lonely
seat of leadership. Trust them.'"

She gripped his arm, sensing the emotions that ran
through him as he spoke. "There's nothing more to say,
Bill," she murmured. "He knows what you're facing,
better than anyone. You have those strengths. Trust
them."

They sat quietly for long minutes before he broke the
silence, letting his thoughts play out for her to hear.
"Maybe this industry is too complex, too dangerous for
us to regulate; too dangerous for us to try to protect the
people against it. There has to be perfection . . . and our
agencies could never guarantee it. Lord, look at welfare
and social security. We can't even manage the programs
we initiate ourselves."

He gestured down toward the papers covering the table
top. "This happened when we had ideal conditions. Even
without the PLA, we've got operational hazards, waste
disposal, malfunctions, the 'normal problems.' What
about a war? Natural disasters? Civil disturbances? Is it
worth it?"

"Bill, don't tie yourself to today," Pam urged. "This is
going to pass. Think of tomorrow, all the tomorrows.
There have to be answers, and men who can find them. If
it's good and it's needed, then you have to make it work."

He leaned over and kissed her gently on the lips,
holding the moment, the tenderness, to last him through
the hours ahead. When they finally parted, she smoothed
strands of hair from his forehead and then stood. "The
country is your responsibility, Mr. President, but you're
mine. It's almost time and you need something to eat. I'll
have the kitchen send something up."

"My super-efficient wife," he chuckled. "I could use a

bowl of split pea soup and a roast beef sandwich. This could go on for hours tonight."

At 6:20, Travis Chambers, clean shaven and with a fresh shirt, but looking somewhat haggard, met the President in the Treaty Room on the second floor. As they stood beside the door, Travis handed Barrington the latest estimate of casualty potential and a list of phone calls that had come in.

The President was disturbed by the Environmental Protection Agency's estimate. It was in opposition to the NRC estimate and raised the level of immediate and delayed deaths by as much as ten percent. The EPA report evaluated delayed cancer deaths at a far greater number than had been projected and added a note of further concern when it questioned the limitations that had been established for dispersal of the radioactive cloud. There was danger that upper level winds could carry the radioactive particles and vapors far outside the Pittsburgh area, contaminating more of Pennsylvania and even New Jersey. People caught in their cars would be in greater danger than those who had remained indoors, and the panic had caused thousands to flee. They'd all be caught in the open.

He was still reading as they left the room and walked down to the conference room. At precisely 6:29, Barrington entered the room and took his seat. The others around the table and room then resumed their places.

The President had selected members of both the National Security Council and Domestic Council with him in the Cabinet conference room for this decision conference. When the door was closed, he leaned back and glanced at the men seated around the table until he found O'Brien.

"Well, Howard?"

O'Brien colored slightly and plunged ahead. "I'm sorry, Mr. President, we've done everything possible. I reviewed all the data personally and it is as accurate as we can be."

"Get on with the bottom line, Howard. I don't doubt your efforts."

"Apricot is inconclusive in this case. There are too many variables for our codes to deal with and we don't have time to program a new model."

He had expected it. Nothing had come out of the agencies yet that would give him a leg to stand on. That left it all up to Young and the Rangers. He thanked O'Brien and decided to allow discussion before announcing his decision. not much anyone could add, but he'd give them a chance to get their thoughts out in open forum. "Comments, gentlemen."

There were several hands immediately. He indicated the member of his Cabinet Committee to Combat Terrorism. "Mr. President, although my committee has been only peripherally involved in this incident, having dealt primarily with skyjackings and protection of our diplomats abroad, we feel that a clear precedent must be set, no matter what the act involves. We cannot give in to this demand. There is a clear policy established by our government which is based on the premise that compliance with one demand will lead to a repetition of the same. We've held the line with skyjackings and embassy attacks, with kidnappings and threats of sabotage. This is no time to change."

Barrington acknowledged a hand at the end of the table. "Mr. President, there is a difference between an aircraft with fifty to a hundred people aboard and a metropolitan area with over seven hundred and fifty thousand people involved. You can hardly equate the two. The policy will have to bend."

"Mr. President..." the discussion began to flow around the table. "Mr. President, if we give in to this group, there is no telling how many others will try the same thing. My God, we'll have a potential disaster each week until they run out of plants."

"Then someone will think up variations and we'll be off and running again."

"And at fifty million a throw, we'll run the national debt up faster than an uncontrolled defense budget."

"It's a tough one. They've got the plant sewed up and from all reports..."

"What reports? No one really knows anything except what those terrorists decide to tell us."

"From the reports which we just heard, they do have the capacity to cause, at the very least, a large-scale melt-down which would place radioactive material over Pittsburgh. They're not playing small stakes poker."

Barrington interrupted. "Rogers, what are the current estimates on total casualties?"

"At present worst-cased estimates, Mr. President, a minimum twenty-five percent of exposed personnel in the immediate unevacuated zones will receive a lethal dosage. That is, they'll be incapacitated within twelve hours and die within a week. Fifty-five percent of exposed personnel will receive a moderate dosage and will require hospitalization. Up to fifty percent of this group could die. The extent of delayed cancer deaths is virtually impossible to estimate since the primary entry will be by inhalation. Until we determine the fallout radius, we can only guess. Protected persons will not be in immediate danger, but the decontamination process would have to be implemented immediately to protect them. Water supplies and exposed foods would be contaminated, thus posing major problems. The only favorable factor is the effect of the mountain ranges in deflecting a portion of the cloud."

"So what are the numbers?" Barrington asked.

"With the traffic situation around the city, sir, we can expect upwards of two hundred and twenty-five thousand casualties at the outset. Delayed cancer deaths resulting from the incident could approach another three hundred thousand."

Barrington had been lost in thought during the discussion, but caught the last statement. He held up his hand for silence. "Gentlemen, I've reached my decision. The incident was actually beyond our control after the terrorists gained access to the plant equipped with sufficient knowledge and equipment to prepare for its ultimate destruction. I had my staff check possible sources they could have used and discovered something which will interest all of you. . . . Trav." He pointed to Travis Chambers who was seated near the wall.

Travis stood and spoke to the men at the table. "On investigating possible sources of information which might have aided the terrorists, our staff found that the blueprints, systems diagrams, plant layout, safeguard technical information, and all potential accident sequences are available either through the NRC library here in Washington or from Oak Ridge, Tennessee. In addition, all research and test records and technical data are available for a nominal fee from the National Technical Information Service in Springfield, Virginia. It seems that whenever a plant seeks licensing from the NRC, it must submit all design and safeguard plans to the commission. All of this is available to the general public. All you need is the patience to go through the microfiche and enough dimes to Xerox them."

Barrington nodded. "Thank you, Trav." He faced the table again. "All these people had to do was walk into Seventeen-seventeen H Street to acquire the information to learn the inside of that plant as well as the men who built it. I would expect that they took the accident sequences and duplicated the steps required to initiate them while eliminating the corresponding safeguards. They knew about the defenses because they read the plans used to install them."

"Goddamn Freedom of Information Act," came a voice from the table.

"Do you believe this is the way they did it, Mr. President?"

Barrington smiled grimly. "It's about the easiest way I could imagine. No espionage necessary. Just pay your dimes."

"Good Lord."

"Now then, I have decided that we will publicly agree to pay the ransom." There was boiling conversation up and down the table as the hardliners voiced opposition to the surrender.

"Quiet!" Barrington's voice chopped them off. "I'm not through. Tomorrow morning, at a press conference, I will announce that the demand will be met in order to save the plant from possible internal damage and, more important, to save the lives of the hostages. As naive as this may sound, it should serve to put them off guard, and a perfect target for our Ranger company that will attack the plant in the early hours, Thursday morning." There was immediate and sustained applause from the group. Even the executives who favored a nonviolent solution found themselves carried by the emotion of the majority.

Barrington waited until there was quiet, then concluded, "This is going to be a fifty-million-dollar lesson for all of us. It will not happen again. Starting today, we are going to reverse this cost cutting on security, this 'it can't happen to us' syndrome. We're going to put together a set of coordinated reaction plans that will go beyond mere paper drills and provide us with the ability to respond quickly and effectively, no matter what the situation." He looked down the line of faces. "If we can't do these things and more within a very short period of time, then we had better revise our thinking on the entire question of nuclear power. The cost and dangers of this industry might well outweigh the advantages to be gained if it cannot be controlled and protected. We have Armored Personnel Carriers and M-sixteen rifles at thirteen nuclear plants as an increased security measure. The PLA hit a plant where there were none. This will not happen again. We've seen the potential for disaster and haven't yet avoided it, but we have a chance, a slim one."

He was resolute in his decision and prepared to take whatever came after it was carried out. "There is a great deal to accomplish in a short space of time, gentlemen. I want a quick response on everything from here on. The faster we conclude this episode, the better for all of us. What are your comments?"

"Federal Reserve will prepare for disbursal of funds on your orders."

"I have the staff writing sufficient briefs to cover you on the legal aspects, should it come to that," the attorney general commented.

"We've got a breakfast meeting arranged for you with House and Senate leaders tomorrow morning at 8:30 so you can brief them. Enough members are on board already to guarantee support for your move."

"The press has been interviewing the families of the hostages and along with the radiation scare, the climate is good for your decision. People want those hostages alive and free. More than that, they want that plant intact."

"Department of Defense is prepared to support state and local agencies in post-incident recovery. Radiological monitoring and decontamination teams are standing by."

Barrington accepted the reports. Everything shifted into high gear now that he had made the move and there was only one visible candidate for crucifixion if it went wrong.

"Thank you. I'll contact Governor Reaves and inform him of the decision. All of you may expect a great deal of activity in the next few hours. I'll be in touch as I need you. That's all."

Twelve minutes later, John LeCourt barely suppressed a cheer as Dieter, speaking with the governor, gave him the thumbs-up sign for government cave-in. He felt like hugging the beaming, stubble-faced Kreutz. There it was, just about as Franz had calculated. They couldn't wait any longer and still meet the deadline. There would be a public announcement in the morning. That almost guaranteed the deal.

"Acknowledge and tell him we'll contact him in ten minutes with our shopping list for the departure phase." LeCourt felt a swelling pride. They were on the downhill slide now; the only problems lay in possible ambush or sabotage of the aircraft. He had a couple of tricks left to cover those contingencies.

The team was immediately set to work preparing the nuclear material for transportation. Pallets had already been fabricated in the plant workshop. The containers of nuclear material would be wrapped in rubberized canvas and strapped to the lightweight platforms for ease in loading and transport. Each of the men working around the fuel rods and Special Nuclear Material containers wore the bulky protective clothing with individual dosimeters, there were as well two radiacmeters in the room.

Miller and Overmeyer closeted themselves in one of the offices and began reviewing flight maps and the instrument manuals for a 727 jet liner. It would be their show after the team was airborne.

Dieter contacted the governor on schedule and ordered him to provide three two-and-a-half-ton cargo trucks from the motor pool of the Seventy-third Transportation Battalion motor pool in nearby Aliquippa. They would be driven to the parking lot no later than 11:30 that night and their single drivers permitted to clear the crows feet from a lane wide enough to allow passage to the main gate. At that point, the drivers would dismount and leave the vehicles by the same path. On Wednesday, a single CH-47 helicopter would be permitted to make one pass over the plant, hovering at an altitude of a hundred feet above ground level to drop bags containing the fifty million dollars onto the grassy area immediately to the rear of the Reactor Service Building. The pass would be made so that the drop was completed by twelve o'clock noon. There would be a total of 5,000 packets, each containing one hundred $100 bills. Finally, a 727-200D would be landed at the old air force base that served as Bartonsville's airport. It would be on the ground and refueled by Wednesday at 4:00 P.M.

Dieter proceeded to the security precautions in their plan. The state police would provide a safe corridor from the plant to the airport on Thursday morning in order for team members to inspect the plane and to prepare for departure. On command from the plant, this corridor would permit safe passage for the three trucks from the plant to the aircraft. There would be no interference either with the departure or the in-flight path of the aircraft as it left the continental United States. Radio detonators were being installed in the plant that would allow remote destruction of the facility if the departure were interrupted. The location of the hostages would be revealed after the terrorists were safe. There was a possibility that they would accompany the terrorists on departure. Their safety was guaranteed if there was no interference or entry into the plant for twelve hours after the plane's departure from Bartonsville.

Archie Reaves received the message and relayed it to
the President. He then contacted the National Guard and
ordered the trucks to be delivered to the plant. The FAA
contacted United Airlines to provide the specified
aircraft. Barrington talked with Mike Young and got
nothing more than a reassurance that the plan was
progressing in spite of bitter opposition over Defense
intelligence and FBI intelligence pictures. Barrington felt
a twinge of apprehension when he finished speaking with
the general. That plan had to be finished on schedule. He
was giving the PLA everything they asked for and if they
weren't stopped . . . he didn't even want to consider the
implications.

Federal Reserve officials were pulled out of bed when
the ransom was announced and the collection of $100 bills
begun. The major Federal Reserve vault complex, deep in
the mountains of western Virginia, was tapped for a large
portion of the amount. Special helicopters, flying with
armed AH-1 Cobra escorts, picked up the funds and
transferred them to Fort Meade, Maryland. The ransom
drop would be carried out by a CH-47 taking off from
there in the morning.

Meanwhile, Travis Chambers was in touch with
Archie Reaves, explaining the necessity for a twenty-four-
hour delay in the schedule. Archie would have to convince
the terrorists that the money would take longer to
assemble because of the requirement for a specific
denomination. They would have to accept a partial drop
on Wednesday and a final drop on Thursday. If they
agreed, Young would have his extra time.

That night TV cameras were at the plant to record the
delivery of the three olive-drab cargo trucks with their
white-star door markings. The three fatigue-uniformed
drivers, parking at the edge of the lot, dismounted and
carefully swept away the spiked obstacles to their front
before remounting and driving them to the main gate.
They left the deuce-and-a-halves and walked rapidly away
from the plant. The canvas tarps that covered the ribbed

truck beds had been rolled toward the cab, indicating that no troops were hidden in the rear.

Several minutes passed before five of the masked terrorists appeared from the main building and walked to the gate. Three proceeded to the trucks while the other two manned the gate. After the trucks were driven into the enclosure, the gate was again locked and the men disappeared inside. The trucks went out of sight to the right, turning the corner of the Plant Service Building.

TV crews were covering the action closely now. There would be some opportunity to tape portions of the departure, and anything on the terrorists was drawing great interest from viewers. It was one of the quirks of human nature where the strange and terrifying has a magnetic effect. There was satellite coverage of the incident with EBU, the European Broadcasting Union, buying the time and marketing it to BBC in England, ZDF in West Germany, ORT in France and RAI in Italy. CBC in Canada and the Tokyo Broadcasting Corporation had also obtained coverage. The impact of this successful raid was hitting every nation that had operating nuclear power plants. Their biggest question was, when and where would it happen next? Only the Soviet Union remained aloof.

Inside the plant, the team had popped enough amphetamines to keep them going for another forty-eight hours. They were busy inside the Reactor Service Building, loading pallets aboard the parked trucks. The massive doors that would admit a rail car had been opened for their entry and closed behind them. All activity was hidden from view. Tony Miller and Matt Overmeyer were already asleep, resting for their major roles in the escape phase.

In Washington and Harrisburg, lights were burning in government offices until the early hours of the morning. Pittsburgh was still the scene of confusion and violence. Bartonsville was quiet. LeCourt had refused to allow the delay. Execution of hostages would begin again at one P.M. Wednesday if the complete ransom were not delivered. LeCourt had Dieter list the East Coast Federal Reserve banks and resources. There were sufficient deposits available.

Wednesday was catastrophic for Bill Barrington. His press conference drew immediate international censure and a spectrum of editorial comments in this country. The United States was giving in to nuclear blackmail and opening the door to terrorists around the world in similar actions. He bore up well as he waited for the word from Joint Chiefs of Staff. His neck was on the line, but just like Entebbe, he would be okay after everything was over. The lack of a twenty-four-hour delay failed to daunt him as he built a picture in his mind of the successful raid and subsequent ceremonies on the South Lawn, awarding medals to the participants.

Thirty minutes after the conclusion of the press conference, General Mike Young was seated beside him in the briefing room. "Mr. President, the delivery of the trucks changed a number of estimates. Five men came out to get them . . . more than we expected. We had to go along with CIA's higher estimate of the total number inside the plant. Even with that, the final draft will be ready by tomorrow morning."

Barrington sat stunned and disbelieving. "Tomorrow morning?" he managed. His voice grew louder, "Tomorrow morning, Young? How much time do you think we have? You know they rejected the delay."

Mike Young's tanned face paled. "Rejected it? Rejected the delay? My God, I didn't get the word."

"Never got the word!" Barrington exploded. "You told me you could get this operation off in time to stop these people and you . . . you didn't even know how little time we had to work with. What was that staff of yours doing?"

This time, Young flared. "Sir those men have been working around the clock to put this plan together. We've done more in a shorter period of time than any department in this entire government. I don't . . ."

"You still don't have an operation ready to go," Barrington snapped, "and that's what counts."

"Sir, let me remind you that it took the Israelis a week to put together the Entebbe raid, it took us six months to stage Son Tay and we've had less than seventy-two hours to work on this."

Barrington slumped back in his chair. "That's enough, Young. Shouting isn't getting us anywhere. What's the earliest you can hit the plant?"

Young sat silently. The schedules, marshaling plans, flight times, the rehearsal times were too tight as it was. Now they'd have to be pushed up even more. He'd already steam rollered over nonconcurrences to the point of endangering the operation and now this. Christ, Barrington had really gone the route to set it up for us, agreed to the demands, put his ass on the line. Bastards wouldn't buy a delay. What in hell happened to that damned notification? Caught flat by the man who was betting on me to come through.

"Sir, we can try to put our people in during daylight hours tomorrow. It'll be a higher risk. I need at least six hours for my commanders to prepare after the plan is in their hands. One thing in our favor, I've already had the company flown into Fort Meade and married them up with the aircraft and equipment they'll be using."

"Then there's no chance of making it tonight?"

"Negative, sir. We're just not equipped for this fast a response. I've crammed this through faster than anything before, but we have to maintain the degree of accuracy and completeness that will give us good odds of success. Without those odds, we're going to lose our men and you're going to lose Pittsburgh."

"What's your optimum time for execution?"

"Tomorrow night. We can hit them after E.E.N.T., end of evening nautical twilight, which would be approximately nineteen-hundred hours."

Barrington's fist slamming against the table shocked Young. "Damn it all! After all of this, we're reduced to hoping that they'll wait long enough for us to get to them."

At the plant, the team was in high spirits after the

ransom drop was made exactly on schedule. Cooper, Rey Sanchez, and Joe Houser retrieved the heavy nylon sacks, wheeling them into the huge service building on equipment carts. Once inside, the men not on security gathered around as LeCourt cut through the metal bands fastening each sack. He reached into the first one and pulled out a neat packet of new and used $100 bills.

"Would you look at that," he said as he held the bills at one end and riffled through them. "Ten thousand dollars in beautiful green."

"Can I check it out, Colonel?" Rey asked. "I never seen a hundred dollar bill before."

LeCourt tossed him a packet. "Here, enjoy it. You've got this and ninety-nine more like it that belong to you."

The others grabbed at the sack, pulling out ten-thousand-dollar packets and caressing them, flipping the bills and joking among themselves.

John let them carry on for a few minutes and then called a halt. "Okay, that's enough for now. We've got some work ahead of us inspecting each of these packets to see that they didn't pull any tricks on us. By the time each of you finishes going through hundreds of these bills, you'll feel just like a big-time banker."

"Shit, Colonel," Houser said, "I think I'll go through my pile twice just to be sure I've got the feel of it."

John smiled at the men. "You may have to, just to be sure there aren't any funny bills in the bunch. Take those cards that Franz gave us on counterfeits and use them to check each bill. Let me know if you find anything wrong."

Later that day, as the team was busily inspecting the ransom money, a sleek jetliner landed at the Bartonsville field.

Dieter made a final call to the governor's office at 9:30 that night to review procedures for the next day's departure. Everything was in readiness and it was only a matter of hours now.

Thursday morning began as one of those soft, cool days that seemed out of place in the earlier procession of summer heat records. Haze hung on the mountains and the sun seemed to take pleasure in a lazy climb to its zenith. The early morning quiet was disturbed by the piercing whine of jet engines coming from the airport as Miller checked the aircraft. Matt Overmeyer sat behind the copilot's seat in the instrument-crammed cockpit, itemizing the navigation equipment he would use. They had arrived at the plane at 6:45 A.M. after an uneventful drive from the plant. Their predesignated route had been thoroughly cleared and protected by the state police. It was 10:20 and the trucks were just arriving. Miller watched Lee Zimmerman in the first deuce-and-a-half, as he pulled past the wing, heading to the tailgate where they'd load the pallets. Miller was conscious of the nylon mask he was wearing. It would be good to be out of here and to take the damn thing off. Wearing it was the worst part of the whole operation.

Once the team had gotten off the trucks, the loading took only forty-five minutes. Canvas had been draped over the opening made by the lowered rear ramp to shield the transfer of pallets from truck to aircraft from curious eyes. Tony sensed the presence of riflemen up in the thickly wooded slopes bordering the field. At times he thought he caught the glint of sunlight on binoculars. Look all you want, fellows, he thought. Maybe you'll see me wave good-bye when we leave.

At exactly 11:48, the rear ramp was raised and John LeCourt gave Miller the signal to start the engines. The fuel had been topped off after Tony had completely checked the aircraft and Matt rechecked their course, verifying the fuel load and weight calculations. Everything was go.

"Looks like we're ready, Ed," LeCourt said to Moran. "Cargo is secured and trucks are clear. Time to roll."

In the first class compartment where the team was sitting, Matt Overmeyer stood facing the rear of the plane. He held an oxygen mask daintily in one hand and an emergency procedure card in the other. "Good afternoon, gentlemen, and welcome aboard Titanic Airlines Millionaire Flight 69 from beautiful downtown Bartonsville, P.A., to Shangri-La. I am your crew and steward, Mr. Overmeyer, Esq., and here's the word on what we're gonna do..."

Tony taxied onto the main runway and, at 12:00 noon, released the brakes with all engines at full power. Prometheus was rolling and the black face-masks came off.

8

The United Airlines 727 cruised above a patchwork of clouds as it passed over Chesapeake Bay. There had been no interference with their departure from Bartonsville and now the gently curving expanse of the Atlantic Coast lay before them. Inside the cabin there was a relaxed, triumphant atmosphere.

Carts of soft drinks and hors-d'oeuvres occupied the aisle as the men lounged in their seats, joking among themselves as they sampled the food. Taped music played softly over the intercom in the forward compartment where the team ignored the lethal object of their mission. In the rear of the tourist cabin, where seats had been removed, the cargo of Plutonium-filled containers was stacked and secured.

"A cool million bucks, man. I wonder what it's gonna be like spendin' all that loot?" Lee Zimmerman leaned back in his seat, fingers laced behind his head, as he talked jubilantly with a smiling Pete Alexander.

"Good buddy, you won't be able to spend it all," Alexander chuckled. "Even at a dollar a bottle you

241

couldn't drink that much beer. Besides, by the time you've spent any of it, the rest of it, the rest that they invest for us will have earned enough to make up for it. It's going to be like drinking from a bottomless bottle."

"Whata y'mean, 'couldn't drink that much brew'? I'm gonna get me a car, man. Maybe a Continental. And a boat and a camper and, shit, I'll have me a set of threads that'll take a semi-trailer just to carry from one place to another." He closed his eyes and continued in a soft voice. "I'm gonna have the best of everything I ever wanted, and it's gonna be so-o-o nice."

In the front row of the First Class compartment, big Cleave Jones sprawled lazily across both seats. He raised a Coke-filled wine glass in a toast to the United Airlines emblem on the bulkhead. "Here's to the friendly skies of United Airlines for makin' this trip possible an' gettin' me a First Class seat." His grin broadened. There was no trace of the hardened, professional soldier in his jocular manner. He could have been a professional athlete returning from a victorious play-off game.

Laughter and scattered horseplay filled the cabin, the obvious release of tensions built up over four long days. There was still the remainder of the flight and danger of interception by fighter aircraft if anyone called their bluff and crashed the plant before the team was safely over their rendezvous. They were betting that no one would risk causing the destruction that $50,000,000 had been paid to avoid.

In the pilot's compartment, Matt Overmeyer leaned above the navigator's desk, checking instruments and his computations. Tony Miller sat at the controls. "We're still riding the Baltimore-Washington beacon outbound, Tony; so hold on a hundred twenty-four degrees for another six minutes. We'll come to a hundred forty-five after that and ride it north of Puerto Rico. Okay?"

"Roger that. One-two-four for six minutes and then one-four-five."

The two men had guided the aircraft southeast from the point of departure, avoiding crowded airspace near metropolitan areas and laying a course out over the

Atlantic. In six minutes they would make the first direction change that would ultimately take them safely over international waters northeast of Brazil.

One man not celebrating with the others was John LeCourt. He walked between the Plutonium containers, tugging at the nylon webbing and checking the parachute packs attached to each. They had been rigged for airdrop by the men immediately after takeoff. The cargo chutes were equipped with both a barometric opening device and a timer to insure against a malfunction. When dropped, the bundle would fall to the preset altitude and a small detonator would be triggered to deploy the canopy. There could be no error in this drop, so LeCourt double-checked the equipment even though his men were experts at the job of rigging.

Getting the bundles out of the plane was another thing entirely. When the plane reached the drop zone, the rear ramp would be lowered slightly and the piston arms on each side released. At the same time, carefully placed explosives would be detonated to cut the ramp hinge from the body of the plane while limiting airframe damage to a minimum. The ramp would fall away and the containers could then be pushed out the rear just as if it were a tailgate drop from a military aircraft.

Lee Zimmerman had already molded the clay-like C-4 plastic explosive into the crack in the floor that marked the joining of ramp to airframe. When they were ready to blow it, he would insert an electric blasting cap, place sandbags in line atop the charge, and use a hand generator to detonate the charge. One twist of the crank and the hinge would be cleanly cut.

Ed Moran turned in his seat and glanced back toward LeCourt. The containers of Plutonium gave him an uncomfortable feeling. He recalled the briefing on the effects of radiation poisoning and trembled involuntarily. Nausea, vomiting, bone marrow decaying from gamma ray damage, hair falling out, teeth going bad. You just sort of rotted away and then died. That Plutonium emitted an alpha particle less dangerous than beta and gamma; but they were all bad news. He felt relief as he watched LeCourt. As long as John is back there, it can't be bad. He'll keep things straight.

LeCourt wasn't as confident as Moran at the moment. He had completed his inspection of the parachute rigging, and although each was satisfactory, there was something disturbing him. Subconsciously he knew it, but nothing obvious revealed itself. Maybe I'm just jumpy, he told himself. The pressure these last few days has been tough even for me to take. Then again, his instinct rarely betrayed him. How many times had those instincts saved his life and the lives of his men?

God, he remembered that first time in Korea when his platoon had been overrun by Chinese. It was freezing cold and darker than three midnights. All you wanted to do was curl up in a sleeping bag and get away from the icy wind that came sweeping over the ridgeline. It had been quiet for a long time even though the Chinks were dug in no more than a thousand meters away. Then, without any warning, the trip flares in their barbed wire burst into that wierd, magnesium torch brilliance and grenades began exploding all over the place. Right in front of his position hundreds of Chinese in their padded uniforms swarmed through the wire. Then came the bugles and loudspeakers blaring above the sound of burp guns and answering American carbines and BARs.

It didn't last long as waves of Chinese broke over the top of his foxhole and rampaged through the area. Battalion gave the order to withdraw. John, then a young lieutenant, immediately reacted to follow the order and break out of the encirclement. His instinct stopped him. He chose not to leave the positions, but to stay and fight it out.

When dawn finally came and the American counterattack threw the enemy back off the ridge, LeCourt's men were still fighting and alive. The three platoons that withdrew toward safety had walked into a bloody ambush, caught on open ground, and only 7 out of 126 survived.

Time and again after that John had depended on that instinct to bring him through the worst of combat, keeping him and his men alive. Now that instinct was flashing warning lights inside his head.

Tony Miller made his last course adjustment and trimmed the aircraft out at 25,000 feet. In four hours, thirty-seven minutes they'd be over the drop zone. Matt had calculated the course and airspeed right on the button. It would be about six minutes from sunset when they reached the periphery of the drop area. There would be enough light for a visual pass, yet dark enough that they wouldn't be detected should there be ships in the area. He punched the course, airspeed, and altitude into the auto pilot and leaned back in his seat, stretching. "It's all over but the shouting, Matt. How about joining the celebration for a while?"

"Sounds good, Tony, but one of us ought to keep an eye on things up here while the other goes back, don't you think?" Matt had swiveled to face the pilot.

"Yeah, I guess you're right. Go ahead and take the first break. I'll sit with the beast while you're gone."

Overmeyer stood and rubbed the small of his back before switching off the small lamp above his desk. "Lot of work in a short time, Tony. I didn't realize how stiff I was. You want anything special from the gallery or just a little of each?"

Tony passed his coffee cup back. "More of the same and a double order of whatever we're having for supper. A plate of appetizers would be good, too. I can smell them up here. By the way, if there are steaks for supper, see if you can get the chef to make mine medium rare. Okay?"

Unnoticed on the blue table of an ocean below, the destroyer USS *John Paul Jones* knifed through the water on a course parallel with the 727. The gray steel grid of the ship's radar fan tilted sharply upward as it tracked the aircraft. In the dim red light of the ship's Combat Control Center, the radar operator droned continuous altitude and distance figures to the officer in charge. These were immediately encoded and transmitted to the Pentagon's National Military Intelligence Center where they were translated into coordinates. A plot of the jet's progress was being maintained on a huge Plexiglas map that was suspended from the ceiling. Communications consoles and computer terminals were arranged in orderly rows facing the map. Above the "bull pen" a glass-fronted command center overlooked the activity.

An exhausted General Craig Alexander ran his fingers through a wiry, graying crew cut as he watched the latest position go up on the board. Stress lines were deeply etched on his face after almost seventy-two hours on duty. The brief naps hadn't helped. His eyes burned, and rubbing only made them worse. His tongue felt like a piece of charred liver after the countless cigarettes he'd half smoked and ground into the ashtray. When he had last talked with her, Margaret had tried to mask her concern about his working under the stress; but she was close to the limit herself. It had been over three months since they last heard from Pete, and it was getting to her. Vietnam had done something to their boy. He'd been a good soldier, a Green Beret, then everything broke up and he left the service, drifting around. That idiot trip with those friends of his for that mercenary operation in Angola. Almost got his ass burned. Damned lucky he made it into Zaire before the roof fell in. Even with that, he'd always called or written. God, I hope he's okay; for all our sakes. He shifted his attention back to the map. The 727 was still making its steady, unimpeded progress away from the nuclear plant and everyone here was still just watching.

It was on a general southeasterly course now, staying over international waters and giving no indication of its destination. No radio transmissions, no major heading changes, nothing for a clue. He studied the range arcs that had been drawn across the projection of its current course. They indicated the distance the 727 could reasonably be expected to cover with the fuel it had on board. Much depended on the airspeed and altitude, but the arcs at least gave a basis for estimate.

Craig forced his mind into a sluggish computation of distance the plane could travel before it would have to turn toward land. Those people knew what they were doing when they specified the type of jet they required for the departure. Not just a 727, but a 727-200 and a D model on top of that. They had increased fuel capacity and range, as well as a luxury interior. If you're going to go, go in class. "They can't fly the damned thing over water forever, even with the extra range," he muttered to himself. "They'll have to set down, at least to refuel, and there's nothing near them but Puerto Rico, the islands, and then South America, unless they've got pontoons."

He turned to his deputy, a florid-faced senior colonel who had spent too many tours in the Pentagon. Twenty-eight years of commendable mediocrity had brought Colonel Bolzer to his present rank. A process of elimination thinned the ranks of his contemporaries as those less commendable in their performance had either retired or had been retired in the various manpower cuts. Some made their star, but not Bolzer. His last two consecutive tours of duty on the staff of the Joint Chiefs made him realize that the closest he'd get to that brigadier's star was sitting next to one at a Fort McNair Officer's Club happy hour. He was older than Craig, but Craig was a major general.

"Jack, get the latest plot over to White House Liaison and the Disaster Operations Center. Tell both that chief of Naval Operations has diverted four more vessels to intersect with the projected line of flight. They'll be out of range of the *John Paul* in another eight or nine minutes and, let's see," he picked up a teletype message from the clutter atop his desk, "looks like the *Walker* C-G-N-seventeen, a missile cruiser, will pick them up east of Puerto Rico."

Bolzer stood with the briefcase containing the classified documents resting on the desk. "Right. I'll also check with State to see about the diplomatic messages going out to alert the Latins on the presence of unscheduled warships."

The general nodded assent. "That's right. Somebody over there got their bowels in an uproar when they found out we were diverting some missile ships to do the job. The 'man' said 'track them' and that's what we're doing. Shouldn't be too much of a flap if the countries understand the overall situation and realize we're not intruding as a threat to them."

"I wonder if State knows what the overall situation is?" Bolzer asked. "Your recommendation to go ahead and enter the plant would certainly give us more answers than we have right now."

"My recommendations, hah!" The general snorted. "Can't get anyone to get off his head ass and do anything. It's the rule of the bureaucrat, Jack. Rather than take the chance of doing anything wrong, don't do anything at all. Hell, we don't even know if they took anything from the plant. My God, the technology that went into setting that thing up. If they didn't have them already, they could have walked out with everything from design blueprints and tech manuals to the blasted Plutonium itself. We still don't know what their mission was aside from the money. We don't even know what terrorist group they belong to or what country they came from."

He leaned forward, elbows on the desk top, and pointed a finger at his deputy. "The only way we're going to know is to get into that plant, check it out and debrief the hostages, if they're still alive. I'll bet you ten to one there's no more danger of that plant going up than of the Redskins making it to the Super Bowl this year. Unless they have stay-behinds who are willing to vaporize themselves and push the plunger on the spot, we should be able to walk in there right now."

He leaned back in his chair, lifting his hands in resignation. "What the hell. It doesn't matter what I think. Doesn't matter what any of us think. We get paid to sit here and do our jobs while the young men in pin-striped suits across the river do the thinking." He paused, his eyes dropping momentarily. "I'm a little tired and loose of tongue. Go on and feed what we have to the lions before they come to get us. Can't afford a bad efficiency report for failing to relay a set of coordinates." He shook his head slowly. "God, what a difference from command-ing troops."

In the FBI Special Operations Center, Sam Varella stood behind his desk glaring at the two agents who had just reported to him. "What do you mean we don't have a make on any of the suspects? No ID on any of them when they left the plant? No one even got a look at them? No faces showing in the photographs?" He slammed his fist down, knocking over an American flag paperweight. "Shit! Three days and we still don't even know how many of the bastards were in there. What a hell of a note."

He turned his back on the men and took a swallow from a glass of milk on the desk. "All right, get back on it and let me know when the hostages are freed. Maybe they can let the FBI in on the secret," he snarled. It had been a frustrating period of time for Sam. From that first warning phone call that jerked him out of bed in the early morning hours, to his present impotence. He hadn't been able to respond to a single major query from the White House concerning the terrorists other than the obvious fact that at least one of them was of German extraction. He winced as his ulcer shot a burning pain through his stomach. "All I needed was three days of this to really fix me up," he thought miserably. "Much more of this goddamned milk and I'm gonna grow a goddamned udder."

Why couldn't I have been on another assignment when this thing broke? he wondered. The director was already getting cut by the press for the Bureau's inactivity and the crap will flow all the way down to old Sambo. Problem was, Sam thought, no one realized just how good these guys were. They didn't make a single mistake and didn't give anyone a chance to force them into one. It was like they sat in there fiddling and watching all of us dance. They sure knew the right tunes because we never caught our breath. Sam sat down and began to fill in the last page of the report. No way out, he thought as he wrote another "No further information."

Several blocks away, the Government Services Administration Building was the scene of continuing activity. The Disaster Operations Center had been collecting and compiling all data available on the crisis since the takeover had begun. Layton Edwards had just made his report to Vance Austin, director of the agency, and was preparing to brief the President on the latest events. It was going to be a tough session because there had been no way to cloak the fact that the terrorists had accomplished their mission with what seemed to be absolute success.

Layton walked through the operations center, immune to the clatter of teletypes, ringing of telephones and babbling voices. Coordination of governmental efforts in natural disasters had never assumed the proportions of this four-day period. A potential nuclear disaster broke all rules of limited implications. Why couldn't it have been something like a flood or an earthquake— something they'd handled before.

Once in his office, he called for his deputy, who had been meeting with the division chiefs. His assistant was already preparing the most recent updates that had come in from the Pentagon, State Department, Defense Electric Power Administration, and the Bureau of Radiological Health. Frank Collins entered the office in shirt sleeves, having shed his coat and tie early in the day. He marveled at the calm exterior of his boss as Edwards read through the updated material.

"Get Bonders on the phone," Edwards said to the assistant. "Find out if he has any update on the traffic problem that isn't incorporated in my report." He tapped the sheaf of papers against the palm of his hand. "Frank, I think we're going to have more casualties from that evacuation than from any threatened nuclear explosion, and it was totally unnecessary."

His deputy acknowledged, "I agree with you on that. If the network had given any warning that they were coming out with that special program we could have anticipated it and set up traffic control measures. As it is, the situation has degenerated almost beyond control and all we can hope for is that no one resorts to physical violence."

Edwards knew that no amount of reassurance, ordering, cajoling, or pleading was going to head off the stampede. Governor Reaves must surely realize that by now. His radio and TV appeal to those people didn't even slow them down. "My fellow Pennsylvanians, I want to reassure you . . ." and his credibility went down the tube. There he was, speaking from the safety of the mansion in Harrisburg; they were packed on the highways, threatened with a nuclear disaster.

There was no solace in the report Edwards would give, except the plant was still intact, although it could be destroyed anytime if there were, in fact, remote devices installed. The risk level was too high to accept in early penetration of the plant. The only chance was to track the aircraft and to attempt to pick them up on the ground after the plant was safe. His recommendation to the President would remain the same: avoid any possibility of initiating a disaster and put maximum diplomatic effort on apprehending the terrorists after the twelve-hour period. State Department was working on that, but wasn't getting too much response from some of the Latin countries. He took the briefcase his aide extended to him and slipped the report inside. "Time to go, Frank. The 'man' is waiting."

Governor Reaves was freshening up in the private lavatory of his office. He spoke through the open door to his assistant. "This press conference is going to be a bastard since they got away clean and that plant is still closed to us. Get Allen in here and have him come up with a palatable explanation why we aren't doing anything to free the hostages. Something like, uh, our major concern is for the lives of our citizens and since we know the hostages are in good shape, there isn't any reason to barge in and take the chance of blowing the plant up. Something to let them know that we're on top of the situation. Got it?"

"As you wish, Governor."

"All I want to do is survive the press conference. By the way, we do know the hostages are still in the plant and unharmed, don't we?"

Murtaugh gave a slight shrug. "At last report yesterday, they were okay, except for Potter. There was no word when the terrorists took off. For all we know they may have taken the hostages with them."

Reaves walked from the bathroom, buttoning a fresh

shirt and looking relaxed after his nap. "What's the latest from the President?" he asked, disregarding the hostages.

Murtaugh picked up a memo pad from the seat of the chair next to his and flipped through the pages. "He commented on your broadcast, suggesting that you coordinate any further appearances of that nature with Mr. Edwards at Federal Preparedness Agency." Reaves flushed.

The assistant continued, "A phone call came in at twelve-fourteen from General Meyers, President's staff, to confirm the President's agreement with our recommendation that there be no forced entry of the plant during the twelve-hour period."

The governor finished knotting his tie in front of a large antique mirror. "Steve, could we word a statement to make it sound clear that the President's directives were responsible for my lack of action at the plant? I hate to come across as less than forceful in this situation and yet all I've done is sit on my hands and respond to outrageous demands. It's weak stuff and the press is going to eat me alive unless I can change that image."

Murtaugh shifted uneasily in his chair. "Sir, if I may, I think we played this thing wrong from the beginning by hitting these people as a rag-tag band of terrorists. As it now stands, we've been buffaloed by what we called punks. You know what that makes us."

Reaves's unruffled manner cracked. He pulled his tie into place with a jerk as he swung to face Murtaugh. "Steve, don't you even say that in private." His voice snapped across the room. "This is a federal foul-up, not one that we could do anything about. They establish and enforce the security and safety standards that were so lax that this group could walk in and create a potential Hiroshima right next to Pittsburgh."

"Nagasaki, sir," Murtaugh corrected. "That's where the bomb had a Plutonium core."

"Whatever. It doesn't matter. Don't interrupt. There was nothing we could do about it. The plant belongs to Continental Nuclear and we don't do any more than tax them and use the power they produce. The only thing we could do was to protect our people, which we did." He relaxed slightly, smiled and put a hand on the younger man's shoulder. "Look, Steve, think positive. We did all we could. Right? How do I look?"

The massive traffic jams in all directions around metropolitan Pittsburgh had kept state and local police and the National Guard totally involved as they sought to prevent vehicular mayhem. Thousands of cars, vans, and trucks were packed bumper to bumper along the William Penn Highway. West Liberty Avenue had been turned into a one way route going south. The Monroeville entry ramps onto the Pennsylvania Turnpike were clogged and vehicles made detours across fields and embankments to reach Highway 48 south. Frightened people were fleeing the threatened area and, in the confusion, created the most colossal traffic snarl in the nation's history.

Accidents, breakdowns, and cars out of gas were scattered along the roadways and shoulders making the congestion impossible to clear. Wreckers and emergency vehicles had given up trying to reach those in distress. Helicopters whirled overhead, the chop-chop of their rotors almost drowned out by the blare of horns. A state police cruiser was perched half in a culvert, one front wheel turning lazily in the air. Farther up the highway, another cruiser was radioing for one of the helicopters to land and pick up a young pregnant woman about to miscarry. Tommy Elder stood helplessly by, cursing the empty gas tank in their stalled Trans Am and pleading over and over, "Hey, man, don't take her back to Pittsburgh."

In the plant meanwhile, computer reels clicked in their cabinets as they spun off instructions to the plant's mechanisms. Whirring, clicking, humming, and a myriad of softer, less distinct machine sounds filtered through the vacant corridors. In their containment area, the hostages lay inert on their mattresses. The Dobermans sat alert and impassive near the doorway, maintaining their vigil. The heavy sedative had taken effect and all the men were deep in a drugged slumber. It would be another six to eight hours before they began to regain consciousness. From the outside, the plant was a lethal weapon, ready at any moment to explode. Inside, there was calm.

Seventeen-hundred hours. The 727 began its descent to 2,000 feet. The men checked their main parachutes, reserves, and Mae West life preservers. They had already changed into wetsuits. Flotation collars had been attached to the bundles along with small beacons for ease in sighting. As the men stood checking their gear, LeCourt walked past for a casual inspection to ensure that all were ready to jump. The frivolity of the past hours had faded into a nervous humor. No matter how many times a man jumped from a plane, each new time was a little like the first.

"Just like steppin' off a bus," Lee Zimmerman quipped. "Bet there aren't too many people who get to unass a seven-twenty-seven at two thousand feet." DeAngelo glanced at Zimmerman and muttered, "Most people pay their fuckin' fare and don't have to get off in midflight." There were grunts and brief laughter from the other men. Ed Moran made the final adjustments on his parachute harness and hit the quick-release box on his chest with the heel of his hand. The four metal harness fasteners popped free and he shrugged out of the rig. "This is a little different from fifty-five dollars a month jump pay, isn't it, Vince?" he asked as he laid his parachute carefully on a seat. "Captain, I worked more, enjoyed myself more, and made more money in the last couple of months than anybody has a right to, but I'm not about to feel sorry for all the years it took to get me here."

LeCourt stepped to the center of the aisleway and held up his hand for quiet. The chatter dropped off and he began, "Okay, men, here's the procedure for the drop. At seventeen-fifty-four hours, Ed Moran will lead the stick out over the drop zone. We will be flying at an altitude of two thousand feet actual and a speed of a hundred twenty-two miles per hour. Tony says he can lower flaps and drop to that airspeed without stalling, so it should be an easy jump. You have the twelve-foot extended static line which will allow you to drop beneath most of the turbulence before opening. It's pretty close to tailgating a C-one-forty-one. All right now, DeAngelo will be pushing the stick and Vince," he looked toward DeAngelo, "I don't want more than two seconds between jumpers. Got it?" DeAngelo gave a thumbs-up in acknowledgement.

John continued, "Figuring a little over thirty seconds to clear the aircraft, you should shave an initial spread of about a mile. Now, you're jumping the MPC-two with a double-L cut." John was referring to the standard T-10 canopy that had been modified with two L-shaped cuts in the rear sections to provide forward speed and a turning capacity. "It doesn't have enough running speed for complete grouping, but I want you to work in toward the center man while remaining on the general line of flight. You should have enough time under canopy to cut that spread to a half mile or less. Any questions?" He paused and glanced around.

"No questions. All right, next. After Vince clears the ramp, Larry and I will start pushing bundles. There are fifty bundles, ten bundles to a pallet. It should take no more than twenty seconds per pallet and a total minute forty-five seconds to clear the cargo. Larry, Tony, and I will jump after the last bundle. We'll be approximately three miles from you and bracketing the bundles between us. They'll be at four hundred feet to prevent drifting all over the area and we'll slip in less than a half mile on the other side of them." He paused again while he sat back on the seat arm.

"For reasons of security that all of you understand, the retrieval phase was withheld from you until we were ready to implement it. Had anything gone wrong and some of us been captured, we couldn't risk compromise. We're approaching a rendezvous with a third-country submarine. As we begin our personnel exit, the sub will surface and begin pickup. Their general course will be the same heading as our flight path. This is why I emphasized your staying on the flight line. Should you be off the line, your flashlight will guide them to you. They have a roster and photographs of the team and will identify each of you upon pickup. Personnel will be brought in on the foredeck, bundles aft. There should be nothing for us to do then but lie back and count our money." LeCourt motioned with his hand for Cleave Jones, who was standing near the pilot's compartment, to join him. The broad-shouldered NCO picked up what looked like a large, olive-drab body armor vest worn in Vietnam and wedged his way through the other men until he stood beside LeCourt.

LeCourt took the vest and opened the front zipper to display the inside lining. In the front, just below the center curve of the neck, was a narrow pocket with what looked like the top of a penlight. Down lower, beneath the heart area, was a triangular shaped pocket the size of a small folded handkerchief. He lifted out the penlight object and held it up. "This should be familiar to most of you from survival kits. This flare pen contains one emergency red flare." He handed the vest to the man in front of him. "Hold this for a second," he said as he unsnapped the waterproof flap and pulled an automatic pistol from the triangular pocket.

"This is a Walther PPK nine millimeter. It's coated with Vaseline, has a tape strip over the muzzle, and there are eight rounds of ammunition in the magazine. These are two clauses in the life insurance policy I took the liberty of writing for us. You shouldn't need them, but they're available should the situation arise. The flare is to be fired if you see or experience any harm while being picked up. It will alert the others beyond you as well as the aircraft, should we still be aboard. The pistol's use is obvious; self-protection. Not enough ammo for a war, but collectively, enough to get a Mexican standoff should the need arise. I don't anticipate any problems with this phase, nor do I doubt the reliability of our sponsors, but I would hate to be proven fatally wrong. Questions?

"None, from anybody?" he asked, looking around. "That's a change. Okay, these aren't just a way to carry a flare and pistol and they aren't flak vests unless money will stop bullets. This is a third clause to that insurance policy because each of them contains one hundred packets of hundred dollar bills. At ten thousand per packet, each of you will be wearing a million dollars."

There was appreciative murmuring from the men as they looked more closely at the vests that Jones was now passing out.

"These will be worn over your wetsuits, so take them now and slip them on." LeCourt reached to his left and picked up a container that looked like a canvas one-suiter. Two heavy snaps were attached to the top and a nylon drop cord to the middle.

"Okay, zip up." He waited until the men had zippered their vests. "Ten of you will jump these undersized G.P. bags. Cleave will pass them out. Hook the snaps to your reserve D rings and belt the end of the line to your waist. When you cut your reserve away, drop this with it. Be sure you've got it attached securely to your waist because there's over three million dollars in each container. They'll float, but we don't want to have to go fishing for them."

Jones handed the containers to the designated men and helped them as they slipped into their parachute harnesses. The others were pulling on their rigs and adjusting the web straps. LeCourt watched them with satisfaction. "I think that should give us enough reassurance that the sub won't botch the pickup," he said softly.

LeCourt continued, "All right, standard procedure applies for the jump. Keep a tight body position when you exit. I don't want arms and legs flopping around in that slipstream, getting broken. You'll have enough light to see all the way down and, at fifty feet, remember to release your reserve chute, hit your quick-release box and prepare to make a water landing. Be sure you don't drop free until your feet touch water. Once you enter the water, your Mae West will inflate automatically and keep you afloat." He paused and quickly reviewed the points in his mind, confirming that everything had been covered. The men waited quietly for him to complete his briefing.

"That is about it for the jump unless you have any questions on what I've covered or something I haven't covered." Again, no questions came from the men. LeCourt surprised them with an unaccustomed smile.

"You people are like an OCS class at the first orientation briefing. Either you trust me or I've overwhelmed you with details." He glanced down at his feet, then back up at the men. "You people did a hell of a fine job. I can't remember having led a better group of soldiers and my biggest regret is that there isn't more action for us. You know, I actually enjoyed this operation. It's a good feeling to do something well, no matter what it is. This time, though, there won't be any medals, no promotions, no one saying, 'it'll look good on your record.' All we get is a million dollars apiece!" His smile broadened. "Good jumping, you bunch of super crooks. Let's get the show on the road!"

The men grinned in return, several began to clap, DeAngelo found himself pounded on the back; Cooper gripped Simmonds's arm, his voice choked. "Son of a bitch. He's somethin' else. Anywhere that man goes, I'll follow him."

Radar track aboard the missile cruiser *Walker* had indicated that the 727 had descended from 25,000 feet through 17,500 feet and altered course slightly. The information was confirmed by the air force tracking station near St. John's, Antigua, and relayed to the USS *Perry*, a destroyer cruising five hundred miles northeast of French Guyana. At 1748 hours, the *Perry* reported that the jet was at an altitude of 2,000 feet, holding steady course.

In the console room of the Intelligence Center, General Alexander read the message and sat rubbing his forehead as he watched the plot marked on the board.

"Tom, I wonder what they're up to now?" The young major sitting at the next desk looked up at the data written in grease pencil beside the plot.

"They're using up fuel for one thing, sir. That baby is gulping it down at that altitude, so I wouldn't think they were planning to go much farther. There's no place out there to refuel."

"Could they be getting ready to ditch it?" Alexander queried.

"Yes, sir, but I doubt it. Latest report on sea conditions

indicates it would be extremely risky to try to belly that aircraft in. They've had things figured down to a gnat's ass so far and I wouldn't bet on them screwing up this late in the operation. There's got to be another reason."

"Well, if they're not going to crash it in, then we'd better find out what they are doing out there. Tom, have CNO's office direct vessels in the vicinity to close on that track. Instruct them not to make contact, but to observe and report."

Seventeen-forty-four hours. Depressurization of the cabin was complete. Lee Zimmerman finished placing the sandbags above the long strip of plastic explosive and reeled the thin wires from the blasting cap back to the latrine. He attached them carefully to the two posts on the hand generator and turned to LeCourt. "Ready, sir."

John checked his watch and motioned for the ramp to be lowered. As soon as the lock disengaged, Simmonds and DeAngelo released the side arms and dove back, away from the ramp. Simultaneously, LeCourt snapped, "Now!" and Zimmerman vigorously twisted the handle. The muffled "whump" of the explosion was accompanied by a screaming cacophony of wind and jet exhausts as the ramp dropped free, turning slowly as it fell to the ocean below.

Tony Miller stabled the plane out after several seconds of bucking and prepared to trim it for cargo drop. In the rear compartment, the men lined up along the aisle and snapped their static line hooks securely onto the length of quarter-inch steel cable that had been anchored from front to rear of the cabin over their hands.

Ed Moran gripped the snap fastener tightly as he slid it along the cable toward the gaping ramp opening. Seventeen-fifty-three, LeCourt and Simmonds crouched by the first pallet of containers. Simmonds would hit the timers just as LeCourt released the drogue chute into the slipstream. The pallet would be jerked along the floor rollers and out the opening, allowing the containers to fall free. First in line, Ed watched the whitecaps now visible on the dark blue of the ocean. "Almost time. Just step out and take a tight body position. I'll get a five or six count before the chute opens with this long static line." He felt the handle of his reserve pack and checked the safety clip that prevented premature opening of the quick release box.

Seventeen-fifty-four! Tom Cooper slapped him on the butt and he stepped out into the turbulence. Cooper stepped out and Pete Alexander was shuffling into the opening.

LeCourt was conscious of the click, click, click of snap fasteners as they slapped against one another, their human cargo pulled away from them. John could see the canopies blossoming in a rough line behind the plane. "Go, go, go," he ordered subconsciously as each man stepped out and was snatched away. Larry was making a final quick inspection of the canvas tie-downs that fastened each bundle to the pallet. Each was slipknotted around a ring on the pallet and run to the drogue chute. When the pallet pulled free of the aircraft floor and turned to the vertical, the knots would open and the bundles separate from the base. The timers were all attached to a common cord that he would pull to activate them simultaneously. Larry worked automatically, the procedure drilled to habit.

Vince DeAngelo flashed a "V" with his fingers to LeCourt before he jumped. As soon as the sergeant disappeared, LeCourt braced himself and kicked the first deployment bag out of the plane. It dropped and was caught immediately in the slipstream. The bag shot straight behind the opening, its flap separating and flying clear of the small ribbon chute inside. The chute popped open and dragged the first pallet rapidly off the edge. John watched it sail out and down, noting the bundles tumbling crazily away. He was already turning to the next pallet that Simmonds had pushed down the rollers toward him.

Tony Miller fought the yoke as the 727 tried to climb away. Its burden was growing lighter and the jet heaved itself upward with new freedom. The auto pilot was set to take the craft back toward 15,000 feet after everyone was out. The timer on the explosives packed in the cabin was set for twenty minutes, giving the plane enough delay to be almost two hundred miles from the drop zone when it exploded. There would be no trace of the team or the aircraft after all of this was over. He took a quick glance back along the length of the cabin and saw the two men working on the final two sections of bundles. It wouldn't be long now. Tony returned his attention to the controls.

LeCourt turned for the next to last pallet and felt a stab of annoyance as he saw Simmonds crouched over it. He could see Larry groping along the side of one of the containers, frantically feeling the rubberized fabric. LeCourt stepped over to him, ready to pull the pallet toward the opening. He started to shout at Simmonds, but the man's wide, frightened eyes stopped him. He reached out to feel the edge of the container where Simmonds's fingers were gripping. The young NCO's mouth was working, without a sound coming out.

The edge was even and regular under the heavy fabric until he came to the bottom corner. He froze, not comprehending immediately. Underneath the covering was the unmistakable double ridge of a long fracture in the container.

He grabbed for his jump knife and slashed at the covering as Simmonds stood dumbly by, unable to help. The fabric tore away and he tasted bile in his mouth. There was a rupture in the shielding. A stress crack split the seam of the container.

"Oh good God, no." LeCourt felt a coldness shoot up his spine as the impact hit him. A radioactive leak. He saw crimson markings on the container and pulled the cover down, tearing it away. The trefoil symbol for radioactive material was supplemented by a crimson stencil. In bold lettering he read, "Danger. Fission Product Waste. High Activity." Waste container! How?

He sank to his knees. All of them had been confined in the closed space of the cabin with a radioactive leak. All that time.

9

LeCourt then moved automatically, acting swiftly, as his mind calculated the possible options. He slashed the heavy rubber flotation collar on the bundle with his jump knife, then quickly sawed through the battery wires attached to the parachute-opening detonator. Dropping the knife, he grabbed the deployment bag with both hands and pulled it toward the tailgate. A violent kick sent it hurtling into space. There would be no opening parachute, no flotation. The bundle would hit and sink. He kicked the last deployment bag into the slipstream.

"Go, Larry!" He shouted over the roar, pushing the sergeant toward the opening. "It's okay now!" He gave him the thumbs-up sign and a forced grin as Simmonds stepped out. Tony Miller was beside him before he could turn. John pointed out the opening and Miller stepped to the edge, waved, and jumped.

One quick look around and LeCourt followed the others. He stepped off the deck into nothingness, feeling that quick vacuum in his stomach as he tucked into a tight, coiled body position before the giant hand of hurricane wind snatched him away.

"Hut thousand, two thousand, three thousand, four thousand, five thou!" His head snapped even farther down on his chest as the canopy fully deployed. Leg straps of the harness jerked into his thighs. Then he was swinging gently under the familiar olive-drab mushroom of a canopy.

He reached high on the risers, spreading them and arching his back as he looked up to check the canopy for holes other than the modification cuts. It was okay. He looked around him for the other canopies. Tony was open slightly below him and about fifty yards away. Larry was a good two hundred feet below and another seventy to eighty yards beyond Tony. John could see the conning tower of the submarine breaking water and along its path, some of the orange dots of inflated Mae Wests. The last of the bundles were splashing into the ocean on line between him and the sub. It had been a good drop.

John allowed himself a brief moment to relax in the gentle calm that always followed a good opening. The water below had a few white flecks, but nothing too bad. Certainly no big whitecapped waves to worry about. Looking over his right shoulder, he could see the 727 climbing out toward the horizon. "Climb, baby. Get that altitude so you'll be really visible for our viewing audience."

The mass of low-hanging clouds that blended into the line where ocean and sky met was tinged in shades of orange and red. The sun had dropped beyond the curve and its last rays were reaching into the blue velvet curtains across the sky above him. Right on time. John felt a quick surge of satisfaction at the precision they'd achieved. These people wanted a professional job and his team had delivered. Delivered, shit! He had momentarily blanked out that bundle.

There was no option but to deep-six the damn thing. If they had pulled it aboard the sub, it would have contaminated everything. So what the hell if it did, he asked himself, my people got dosed in the plane. Rey Sanchez, he remembered, had been leaning against that section of containers during the briefing. Poor son of a bitch is going to feel it before he even sees land again. All of us must have had four hundred to five hundred rads' worth of exposure. That gives us something like six hours from the time we reached dosage. No one knows it except me . . . and Simmonds! Maybe we won't get it. Dear God, maybe.

He turned in his harness, looking for the lower canopy that carried Larry Simmonds. Got to get to him before he gets aboard the sub; all I need now is for him to panic them with this. Good God, with weapons there's no telling what they'd do. There he is. Good, we're closer. He's holding into the wind.

Larry had turned his canopy to face the wind and was using the thrust of the air escaping through the open gores in his chute to counter some of the wind's velocity. The "double-L" modification would manage an eight-mile-per-hour forward speed and, faced into the wind, would cancel about that much of the wind speed. John pulled down on his left toggle to turn his canopy toward Larry. He'd be running with the wind and could cut the distance quickly. He felt the acceleration as his chute pitched forward, oscillating him beneath it.

Come on, baby, grab sky, he encouraged the canopy silently. Gotta get close enough to be able to shout to him and get him to shut up. It's bad enough aboard a sub without a panic. Some of them might have a chance if I can keep them cool until we get help. He threw his legs out till he had his body in an "L." Shifting the center of gravity would cause the canopy to tip forward and spill more air from under the trailing edge and give him a little more forward speed.

He was abreast of Tony Miller who waved happily and pointed at the now fully visible submarine. John waved back, acknowledging him, then reached high on both front risers, pulling them sharply into his chest.

Gotta lose altitude! This should do it. The front lip of his canopy sucked under as the suspension lines took the full weight of John's body. He hung there, chinning himself on the risers, anxiously watching the front half of the mushroom begin to fold inside itself. He was dropping!

Watch it! Don't let it suck through the modification... little more... come on, baby, just a little more. He suddenly released the risers, dropping with a jerk as the nylon popped fully open once again. He was level with Simmonds and close enough to shout to him when they went into the water. First thing, cool Larry down. Then figure out what to do next.

The combat commander's reflex controlled John's thinking. Never think of yourself. First the mission, then your men. His mind refused to dwell on the fact that he too had been exposed to the radiation. The mission was accomplished and now he had to do what he could for the team.

Water's coming up fast. Face into the wind... can't turn too low or the chute'll drop out on me. Larry was ready to land as John's canopy turned him away. Water's not choppy at all... some swells, but it should be easy.

John unsnapped his reserve pack, chopping it away, and pulled the safety fork from the quick-release box on his chest. He turned the flat aluminum disc to the unlock position while glancing down to estimate his height above the water. Close... he slapped at the disc with the palm of his hand and threw his arms over his head as the harness snaps popped free. There was an immediate drop as the leg straps and seat flew out from under him, releasing him from the buoyancy of the chute. The brief fall and then water.

He gulped lungs-full of air before he went under and remembered to keep his legs tightly together as he splashed in. This was no time to get your nuts smashed. The wet coldness was immediate on his face and hands as he kicked vigoroulsy toward the surface. His life preserver hissed to full inflation and John popped to the surface.

After wiping his eyes, John searched for the sergeant's orange Mae West. There was a momentary chill as he couldn't locate it, then he discovered he had faced away from the line while underwater. Larry was only ten or

fifteen yards away from him and swimming toward him.
John rolled on his back and began kicking to close the
distance.

"How was that for a Hollywood jump?" He yelled in
greeting. Simmonds didn't reply until he was beside
LeCourt. "What was wrong with that container? It was
leaking wasn't it?" His face was blanched white. "I saw the
markings. I saw the stencil. It wasn't like the others."

He's panicking, LeCourt realized as the man continued, almost babbling. "Hold it, Simmonds. Don't get all
wound up over the damn thing."

"It was waste, sir. We got dosed by that shit, didn't we?
Didn't we?"

"Shut up, Simmonds, and let me answer." The man
quieted momentarily trying to gain control of himself.
LeCourt glanced toward the submarine, which was
picking up the last of the team members before coming
after him and Simmonds. Not much time.

"It was a waste container and the outer casing was
fractured. I . . ."

"Gawddamn, I knew it. I knew we were fucked when I
felt the thing."

"Will you shut up and act like a soldier." This is a hell
of a place to be arguing, LeCourt thought, as he kicked
against the swells to stay next to Simmonds. "Grab my
hand so we can stay together." Simmonds grasped his
extended hand and pulled himself beside the other man.

"Now get this straight, Simmonds. I don't want you
getting on that sub and spreading a stupid-assed story
that could get a lot of people hurt."

"Get people hurt? Isn't an overdose hurting bad
enough?"

"Nobody got an overdose."

"The casing was fractured. You said so yourself."

"The outer casing was fractured, but there's an inner
casing that was still intact," he lied. "There wasn't any
leakage because that inner casing is shielded. Can you
understand that? There was still another layer of
protection between the waste and us."

Simmonds's eyes began to focus on LeCourt and his

voice dropped its tenor pitch. "You mean none of it got out?"

"That's right. I told you it was okay before you jumped, you dumb-ass. Didn't you believe me?" LeCourt brushed salt water out of his eyes. They were stinging because of the spray. Even with the brine he'd swallowed, his mouth felt as dry as a sun-baked roof. If Simmonds would just buy the story for a little while. A plan was developing in John's mind.

"I thought you were bullshitting me. Honest."

"I never did before, did I?"

"No, sir."

"No reason for me to start now. Remember, Simmonds, I picked you to help me on that detail because I could trust you to do a good job. Don't screw all of us up now."

"I wouldn't, Colonel. I just thought we were in big trouble. I was scared shitless. I guess you know that."

"I got a scare myself, babe. Don't think you were alone, but I checked it out and we're okay."

"Why'd you cut up the flotation gear and timer?"

"What'd you want to do, Larry, pick up a container of radioactive waste and take a chance on something else happening? That thing is on the bottom by now and can't hurt anything."

The sergeant began to smile and LeCourt felt the tight knot in his stomach dissolve. "Shit, that was quick thinking. I couldn't have done it."

"Forget it. We handled the problem between the two of us and let's keep it that way. I don't want any of the others to even know there was a problem. Got it?"

"Got it, sir. You . . . you won't tell anyone that I froze on you, will you?"

LeCourt gripped the other's hand firmly. "What d'you mean? I don't remember you freezing on me. We kicked bundles just like we planned. The only problem was that one of the damn things malfunctioned and clobbered in. Must have burst the flotation collar on impact. Nothing anyone could do about that."

Simmonds returned the grip. "Got you, sir. Shame to

lose it, but nothing we could do." There was still a tinge of doubt in his voice, but LeCourt felt certain he'd hold together long enough.

The shark prow of the submarine was only a hundred yards away and both men could see the crewmen on deck with ring buoys. The huge conning tower obscured their view of the afterdeck, but LeCourt could imagine the containers being lowered into the below-deck storage compartments. The rest of the team was already aboard and probably stripping off their wetsuits, headed for a hot shower. The captain would meet him when he came on board and he'd take care of Larry then. He glanced around to locate Tony. The pilot's Mae West was visible on a high swell about fifty yards away. John waved to him and got an immediate return wave.

It was only minutes before the sleek gray hull slid alongside them, waves from its bow buffeting them as it passed. Ring buoys sailed out over their heads and the manila cable dropped beside them. Grinning faces lined the deck. The crewmen, wearing shorts and T-shirts, laughed and shouted encouragement as LeCourt was hauled aboard. Strong hands grabbed him as he stepped over the flotation tanks and pulled him on deck. When he straightened, he found his hand grasped by a deeply tanned officer, wearing shorts and T-shirt like the crew, but topped by the regulation submariner captain's hat.

"Welcome aboard, Colonel LeCourt. Captain Antonio do Santos y Dias at your service. May I . . ." LeCourt took the startled sub capatin by the arms and led him away from the deck edge. "Excuse my abruptness, Captain, but I've got an emergency and I need your help."

"Certainly, Colonel. What can I do?" Dias answered, regaining his composure.

"The team member who came aboard with me was under an excessive strain during the final day of the operation and is in danger of a psychological breakdown. He needs almost total rest for a couple of days to allow him to stable out. I need your ship's doctor to sedate him heavily and keep him quiet and away from the other men. Can this be done?"

"Immediately, if you desire." Dias glanced toward Simmonds, who was on deck and approaching them. "Is he violent?"

"No, but he could become so. Let's do this." LeCourt walked toward the conning tower, the captain beside him as if in casual conversation. "We'll both go directly to sick bay with you for some sort of inoculation that you require when we come on board. Lead him to believe all of the men have gotten it. Have your doctor give me a shot of glucose or something like it... a vitamin injection. Hit him with phenobarbital, morphine sulphate, or anything like it that will put him under fast."

"I understand. I will have my physician prepare before we arrive."

"You go ahead. I'll wait for Simmonds and Miller. Better give Miller the glucose also. It'll look better... on second thought, no. Keep it just the two of us. I'll get rid of Miller."

"Comprendo, Colonel. I will meet you inside the control room and guide you to the dispensary." He strode toward the tower, leaving LeCourt to meet Simmonds and Miller, who was just coming on deck.

"What about this. A Portuguese submarine to pick us up." Simmonds was elated as he looked around him. "I took some Portuguese at language school and never used it, but these guys are sure speaking it now."

John hadn't even noticed the nationality of the crew, so intent was he on eliminating Simmonds. It wasn't obvious from the markings and there wasn't an ensign flying from the mast, but the crew had to be either Spanish speaking or Portuguese.

Tony Miller joined them, draping his muscular arms about both their shoulders and giving a quick squeeze. LeCourt forced a grin in response, shedding the mask of concentration.

"Damn, John, you look too serious, man," Miller blurted jovially, removing his arm and playfully punching LeCourt on the bicep. "This is a time for celebration, not worry. We have just pulled the smoothest goldarned operation in the history of organized rip-offs and I, for

one, am enjoying the new sensation of being a millionaire!" He gave Simmonds shoulder another squeeze.
"How 'bout it, Larry? You ready to do a little heavy
partying?"

"Soon as I can get this wetsuit off and find a bottle of
booze on this boat." He looked up at Miller. "They do
carry booze aboard, don't they?"

"They stocked it specially for us, knowing that we'd be
cold, tired, and in need of something to revive us."

"So why're we standin' here talkin'?" Simmonds asked.

They walked along the wooden planking that covered
the deck until they reached the ladder leading to the
conning tower. LeCourt clambered up first with Miller
behind him. As they reached the upper deck with its
surrounding metal bulwark, LeCourt motioned for Tony
to go ahead of him past the periscope and snorkel mast.
"Go on below and check the team out. I've got to stop off
and see the captain for a minute. Larry and I'll be with you
in a while."

Miller acknowledged and lowered himself through the
hatch. "I'll save you a drink," he yelled back as his head
disappeared.

John and Larry climbed down the narrow runged
ladder into the gray painted, tubular interior of the sub. It
was a compactly arranged mass of pipes, cables, and
valves on all sides and overhead, with a control panel
against the far bulkhead and unexpected clearance for
movement through the command center. Wire mesh
protected the light bulbs that produced a shadowless
illumination without glare. Captain Dias met them as
they stepped into the compartment.

"Colonel and Sergeant Simmonds, if you will follow
me I will take you to the dispensary for your inoculations.
It should only take a moment and then I will show you to
your showers and fresh clothes." He led them through a
hatchway and down a long corridor with wooden doors
on either side, obviously quarters of some type. Near the
end of the passage, he stopped and directed them into a
spotlessly scrubbed dispensary. Stainless steel, glass, and
gleaming white walls and floor surrounded them. The

familiar dispensary smell of alcohol and disinfectant seemed to relax Simmonds, who was obviously dubious about the inoculation, which hadn't been mentioned in any of the briefings.

"My ship's physician, Lieutenant Gomes." A slender, delicately featured young doctor in immaculate white uniform trousers and shirt shook hands with them and then indicated for them to peel off the upper half of their wetsuits. They had no sooner done so than he expertly hit each of them with an injection, withdrawing the needle almost before they realized he'd stuck them.

"God help him get the right syringe to the right man," LeCourt prayed silently as Gomes swabbed their arms with alcohol soaked cotton.

"Please sit on the edge of the table while the doctor takes your blood pressure and temperature," instructed the captain. He watched LeCourt and nodded imperceptibly when he caught his eye. Both men sat easily on the table and watched as the blood pressure sleeves were wrapped around their arms and thermometers inserted in their mouths.

Gomes pumped up the sleeve on Simmonds's arm and seemed to be casually watching the silvery column of mercury as it rose in the measuring tube. He paused for a moment and checked his watch, then reached for the thermometer in Simmond's mouth. Just as he removed it, Simmonds's head dropped forward and his body sagged. LeCourt helped the doctor catch the limp body and ease it into a supine position on the table.

John waited long enough to ensure that the sergeant was safely sedated and reaffirm his instructions that he was to be kept under for at least forty-eight hours. Gomes confirmed that he could give glucose intravenously to sustain the unconscious team member. With that, LeCourt asked Captain Dias to accompany him to his quarters.

In a concise and complete explanation, John LeCourt laid out the grim situation that faced his team and himself. Fortunately, Dias was familiar with the dangers of radioactive contamination and realized there was no danger to his ship or crew because of the team's contamination.

"We've got a maximum of about five hours and a minimum of two or so before any signs of radioactive poisoning begin to show. Major Miller is the only one who should be competely clean." John had remembered that Tony Miller had never left the pilot's compartment and should have escaped exposure. At least he wouldn't have to sweat it out.

Craig Alexander read the final message from the *Perry*. The aircraft had climbed back to 12,000 feet on course and, at 1817 hours, disappeared from the radar screen.

John showered after the captain had left and changed into the new trousers, shirt, and shoes that were laid out for him. In the medicine cabinet, he found a shaving kit with a bottle of Aramis after-shave and one of Aramis cologne, which he used regularly. An electric razor, a Norelco, also the kind he used. They had taken great pains to see that the welcome aboard was complete. The others must have enjoyed these little touches. The beginnings of being a millionaire when everyone catered to you.

It was difficult to build his spirits to the level he would require in order to join the celebration that was surely going on in the wardroom. So close . . . so damned close. He picked up the money-filled vest and carried it with him out of the room. Cleave would be collecting them for the team and would secure them until they reached their destination.

He was two hatches from the wardroom when he heard the laughter and inharmonious mixture of enthusiastic voices. As he ducked through the hatchway and stepped into the ship's wardroom, Lee Zimmerman, who was leading the impromptu chorus, spotted him and silenced his group with a sweeping wave of his hand. "Team, ah-htens—hut!"

The booming voice rocked the small room and brought an instinctive response from every man. Heels slammed together, arms locked at sides, backs ramrod straight, eyes forward. No one moved.

Zimmerman spun in an about-face and reported to Vince DeAngelo. "Sergeant Major, the team is formed."

"Carry on, Sergeant."

Zimmerman executed another smart about-face while LeCourt stood dumbfounded just inside the room. "Sir, we don't have any band to play 'Hail to the Chief,' but gawdamn it, sir, we're all thinking it!" He spun toward the team members once again. "Let's hear it for the best fuckin' C.O. any bunch of paddy-walkin' grunts ever had! Hip, hip—hurrah!" The cheer slammed across the room with a phsycal impact. "Hip, hip—hurrah! Hip, hip—hurrah!"

They came to him as a group, wanting to shake his hand all at once, to pat him on the back, to congratulate him for leading them through. John caught himself looking through blurring eyes as long-dried tears pushed through years of restraint and emotional control. God, how long had it been since he had cried. What difference does it make now. He gripped DeAngelo and hugged the burly NCO; Cleave Jones gripped his hand with the soul shake and nearly crushed it, so intense was the emotion that ran through all of them.

John regained control and motioned for the men to give him some space. They stepped back a few steps and stood waiting expectantly. He looked around at their faces, the men he'd come to know better in these months than men who had been in his units for a year. Look at them, like a bunch of fraternity kids after a football game, not a tough guy in the bunch. What a Jekyll and Hyde world this was. How can they transform themselves with such ease from trained killers to a bunch of sentimental clowns . . . but then, he wouldn't want it any other way. If they stayed either way very long, they'd be unbearable. Some of them weren't going to be in any condition in a while, not ever again.

He cleared his throat and managed a smile that broadened when it was reflected by the men. "You people manage to surprise me, no matter how much I try to anticipate. I, uh, thank you for, uh, the feelings you expressed..." He looked at his feet and then back across the faces. "They're mutual, you know... you almost got me to go choked-up, but, uh, I caught myself... can't have any of that at a celebration."

Pointing to the naval chronometer on the wall behind them he continued,"It's twenty-thirty-five hours right now and in about ten minutes the sub's crew is treating us to one of the finest banquets prepared at sea. If you'll move yourselves away from the tables and over to the far corner, the mess stewards will set the tables. I think this will be a fitting way to end Prometheus. There will be champagne and some of the good wine that we can all afford to buy now. So go easy for a couple of minutes and the wardroom will be ours for as long as we want."

Tony Miller came up to him as the others drifted to the corner, chatting excitedly while the white-uniformed mess stewards efficiently set a silver service for the meal. "Where's Simmonds?" he asked quietly.

"He had a problem that required a little medical treatment, but he'll be okay in a couple of days. Why, anyone worried?"

"Negative. They asked, but figured as long as he made it on board and he was with you, he was all right. Is it anything serious?"

"Just a little problem with nerves that a couple of days rest will clear up. The ship's doctor is pretty good and can handle it."

"Okay. I was just wondering. Hey, by the way, these jokers really think your shit is chocolate ice-cream. You know it?"

"I never thought of it that way, Tony, but I'm sold on them. Maybe they sense that."

"Whatever it is you've got, chief, I feel the same way they do." He held out a huge hand. "I only wish that every time I'd taken orders, it would have been from a John LeCourt." They shook solemnly.

"Tony, if every time I gave an order it had been carried

out like they were on this operation, I'd have been chief of staff of the damn army, but, there again, who would trade that for a million bucks?"

At exactly 2045 hours, gleaming silver trays, piled high with the first course of a seven course feast were carried into the room to the cheers of the seated men.

"Look at that spread of caviar and bread and butter... and lemons." Tom Cooper was calling out the menu like players on a baseball roster.

"Oh hey, look at the champagne flow," added Solis as he held his glass for the steward to fill. "You just wait here a second until I finish this first glass and you can give me a refill."

Rey Sanchez watched the oncoming food with a growing sense of uneasiness. He was cold and he felt trembly in his knees and shoulders and elbows. Maybe he got chilled in the water. Maybe the release from tension was getting him. The warm waves of nausea began to wash up from his stomach as he sat trying to fight off the unpleasant sensations.

Tony Miller stood at the captain's table and rapped on his water glass for silence. When he had the attention of all the men, he raised his glass of champagne. "I'd like to offer a simple, but sincere, toast. Will all of you join me?"

The men stood, holding their glasses or reaching quickly for a refill before he began. Rey stood and almost fell. He caught himself on the edge of the table and braced his legs against the bench behind him.

"To courage, to loyalty, to professionalism, to success. To all of these in a single toast, a toast to an operation that had them all..."

Rey felt bile rising in his throat and he was getting light-headed. God, he felt shitty. He couldn't wait. It was a reflex that got his legs free from between the table and bench and he found himself lurching toward the hatchway, leaning toward it for support.

Overmeyer saw him staggering away from the table and nudged Pete Alexander. "Poor Rey must have had a snoot full of that early booze; he's really loaded."

The glasses went up in toast. "To Prometheus."

Rey clutched the cold metal side of the hatchway feeling a vague sense of shame as warm vomit splattered on the deck and spewed over his new shirt.

The Best of Berkley's Nonfiction